I0573900

RAVEN'S DAUGHTER

✤

THE STORY KEEPER

✤

WENDY HALLEY

Three Worlds Press
threeworlds.media

The story, all names, characters, and incidents portrayed in this production are fictitious. No identification with actual persons (living or deceased), places, buildings, and products is intended or should be inferred.

Copyright © 2025 by Wendy Halley

All rights reserved.

No portion of this book may be reproduced in any form without written permission from the publisher or author, except as permitted by U.S. copyright law.

ISBN 979-8-9923164-0-7 (hardcover)

ISBN 979-8-9923164-1-4 (paperback)

ISBN 979-8-9923164-2-1 (audiobook)

Book Cover Art and Design by W. Halley

First edition 2025.

Published by Three Worlds Press

threeworlds.media

Praise for

❖

RAVEN'S DAUGHTER

❖

"*Raven's Daughter* is a beautifully written and deeply imaginative story that weaves myth, spirit, and nature into something truly memorable. The story feels realistic, like an ancient tale passed down. It speaks to our connection with the Earth, with each other, and with the stories we carry. The lyrical imagery creates a sense of calm, inviting stillness and reflection. At its heart, the book gently reminds us of our natural belonging and the healing that comes from remembering who we are. More than just a tale, it's a quiet journey back to wholeness."

Gail Lynn, *Inventor, Author, Filmmaker – harmonicegg.com*

"I feel like I just ate a star! *Raven's Daughter* speaks to the critical junction we face at this moment in our human evolution. It points us back home, to the necessity of human connection and the health of the whole living organism, where people and nature thrive together, where music is medicine, and laughter the currency of celebration. Charlie is a frustratingly human and wildly mythological heroine, who makes superpowers from both her weakness and her strength. *Raven's Daughter* is a story to help spark our remembering and save our world."

Meredith Heller, author of *Write a Poem, Save Your Life* and *Writing By Heart*

"Wendy Halley's book *Raven's Daughter* swept me away from the opening chapter. It's a time transcending story, wonderfully tailored for our present moment. What is real? What is truth? Are we living a dream or dreaming from a finite life? The answer to these questions are fluid and self-determined. We become what we see. The veil is as thin or thick as we make it.

What we see determines what we do and what we do determines what we get. Wendy imparts this wisdom and more as she takes us on a spellbinding adventure that is beyond yet within us all. This book is fun, edgy, quick cadenced, and colorful – just like the author herself. *Raven's Daughter* brings the depths of spirit to the palm of the reader's hand. It's a brilliant book – accessible to anyone willing to pause, look within, and see beyond."

Kevin Hancock, author of *Not For Sale: Finding Center in the Land of Crazy Horse*

"Wendy Halley is a gifted psychotherapist and guide to shamanism. Turns out she's a crackerjack storyteller, too. This page-turner, seasoned with sly humor, suspense, and moments of strange and startling beauty and terror, follows the literally mind-bending Hero's Journey of Charlie, a young woman struggling to escape her profound alienation from life. She's fun to spend time with: intelligent, perceptive, witty, tough, determined. Through her, we witness the enormous costs of our society's willful forgetfulness of the innate human ability to hear the world's voices, and we're given hope that recovery may yet be possible."

Seth Steinzor, author of *The View From The Other Side Of My Head*

Music plays an important role in the story you're about to read. If you're curious about the music referenced in *Raven's Daughter*, please visit the Three Worlds Media YouTube channel where you can listen to "Charlie's Playlist": @ThreeWorldsMedia

In loving memory of Hank and Jill.

And with heartfelt gratitude to Tony, The Name Retriever.

THE REALMS

THE PHYSICAL REALM

A version of the world we live in that exists in the not-too-distant future.

THE DREAMING REALM

A timeless place of possibility that dreams the Physical Realm, and all its inhabitants, into existence.

THE MENTAL REALM

The archive of human thought that exists between the Dreaming Realm and the Physical Realm.

There's nothing fundamentally wrong with people. Given a story to enact that puts them in accord with the world, they will live in accord with the world.

Daniel Quinn, *Ishmael*

BEFORE . . .

SHE SLEPT THE DEEP, unburdened sleep of innocence. Her petite frame, tangled in bedsheets, spooned a stuffed purple stegosaurus under a pretend sky of glowing stars. The serenity of the scene was disrupted when the air above her bed stirred like ripples on a pond and began to spin. The movement created a subtle whirring that could only be heard at the threshold between sleep and dreams. From the other side, a glassy black eye peered through the funnel-like opening and watched her sleep.

The sleeping girl's eyes stirred behind her lids. Charlie began to dream.

SHE'S ON THE BACK of a raven gliding through a cloudless indigo sky. Below, a symphony of exotic birdcalls echoes through the primal forest of the Dreaming Realm, the place that dreams the Physical World into existence. The forest shimmers silvery white as if starlight runs through the veins of its flora. Charlie smiles when she spots the deep burgundy canopy of the First Tree, which towers over the forest like an otherworldly skyscraper. It's familiar somehow. A vague memory of running her hand over the countless intertwining trees of its trunk, the bark of each having long worn away.

In the distance, though, something is off. A peculiar optical illusion of sorts. A portion of the sky and forest has a subtle gleaming metallic hue. Gaze long enough and it becomes evident that this region of the Dreaming Realm lacks depth and the shadows are all wrong; they're reversed and the silvery sparkle is dull. For the briefest moment, Charlie glimpses the convex mirror-like edge of the anomaly Dreaming Realm inhabitants refer to as the Mental Realm.

Her attention shifts when her raven escort suddenly descends and lands on the forest floor in front of an enormous abstract living canvas of swirling turquoise and blue. She slides off the raven's back and her eyes try to make sense of what or, rather, who she's seeing.

The First Mother sits, eyes closed, at the base of the First Tree; her proportions mirror its enormity, her full breasts and round belly bursting with life. Thick mahogany dreadlocks sprout from her head and cascade down her mottled turquoise and blue body, spreading over the surface of the Dreaming Realm like spiraling roots.

Charlie's eyes widen with wonder as they travel up the First Mother's towering body.

First Mother opens her sea-glass eyes to find Charlie looking up at her.

"There you are, Little Bird," she says, her deep, melodic voice a lullaby.

With a smile as warm as a spring day, First Mother reaches out to Charlie, her body reverting to human proportions the moment her hand touches Charlie's shoulder. She invites the little girl onto her ample lap.

"I have a story to tell you," she says.

Charlie's curious little hand reaches out and touches one of First Mother's dreadlocks. Her raven escort takes flight, distracting her, and settles on a low branch of the great tree.

"It was your story long before you were born, and now it's your destiny." With the softest touch, First Mother tilts Charlie's head up until they're looking into each other's eyes. "So, it's important to pay very close attention. Do you think you can do that?"

Charlie responds with an earnest nod.

First Mother pulls her closer until Charlie's head is gently resting on the pillow of her breast. As First Mother speaks, the words of the story float out of her mouth, taking the shape of black, luminescent feathers that hover in the air above them . . .

Long before you were born, Grandmother Spider taught my human children how to weave the first stories, and they became the Gamah-teh, the Story Tellers. Grandmother Spider, perched on her web, told them, "You are one thread in the web of life." She gestured with several of her thin, black legs to the forest around them. "The plant and tree and cloud beings," she said, "the land and water and sky creatures—they are the other threads. They're your kin." She plucked several silky strands of her web, so they hummed in unison. "When the web is strong, there's harmony," she told them.

The Gamah-teh wove tales from their hearts, celebrating all their kin. Their stories were like the most beautiful songs you've ever heard. They sang and danced their stories under the night sky in good times and in bad.

But as the years passed, the minds of some grew restless, eager to understand themselves and the world and the vast universe they lived in. Their stories began to change. My human children became the heroes of their new stories, where they battled and conquered and devoured. The new stories no longer included the plant and tree and cloud beings, nor was there any mention of the land and water and sky creatures.

It was easy for the Gamah-teh to fall in love with these stories and to want to believe they were true. But what they didn't understand was that stories coming from the mind alone were tricky. And these new stories were very tricky. The Gamah-teh could not sing or dance these stories. They had no melody. They had no heart. Over time, they forgot they were part of the web of life and they forgot about their kin.

They carried their empty stories across the land and the sea. It didn't take long for their stories to become the law of every land.

The Gamah-teh didn't know it, but they were starving themselves. They filled their minds with countless stories, ones that became more outrageous and boastful with each telling. These stories didn't nourish them and pulled them farther and farther away from themselves and each other.

They became so full of each other's twisty words that they could barely move.

The more stories they told, the emptier they became. The emptier they became, the more lost they felt. They became the Hakolah-khan, the Hollow People. My human children couldn't understand why they were so heartsick.

First Mother pauses and brushes a lock of Charlie's messy, bluish-black hair away from her face.

The little girl looks up, her large dark eyes heavy, and watches the luminous feathers of First Mother's story slowly swirl in the air above them, waiting for the rest of the story to join them.

"This is a sad story, isn't it?" First Mother says.

Charlie nods.

"A lot of stories start that way," she says. "But you know what I love about stories?" Her full indigo lips spread into a knowing smile. "They can change . . . sometimes in surprising ways." She glances at the floating feathers. "Let's see what happens to the Hakolah-khan."

ONE DAY, THEY HEARD a strange sound far in the distance. They heard the sound of two ravens laughing. But it had been so long since they'd heard laughter, they no longer knew what it was. Slowly, they moved toward the sound.

It took hundreds of Earth years, but they kept moving because they liked the way the mysterious sound made them feel.

They finally arrived at an ancient tree, much like the one behind me, but instead of leaves, this tree was filled with thousands of brilliant tiny white stars. Perched high on its twisting branches were the two laughing ravens. The Hollow People gathered around the tree, awestruck by its beauty, and many cried happy tears.

Grandmother Raven stretched her wings before addressing the crowd.

"We're glad you made it!" she told them. "We've been waiting for you."

"And we know how hungry you are," Grandfather Raven added.

The ravens flew to the top of the tree, each snatching a star in its thick black beak.

Grandmother Raven swooped down to the crowd below. She flew to the first Hollow Man, whose round face looked up with wonder, his mouth open like a baby bird's, and dropped the star in the Hollow Man's mouth. The star floated down, deep into his chest, and settled in his heart, where the rays reached out into every nook and cranny of his hollow body.

And then Grandfather Raven flew to the first Hollow Woman and gently placed a star in her mouth. She swallowed the star, and it filled her with the most beautiful light.

The crowd inched closer to see what would happen next.

The first Hollow Man and first Hollow Woman turned toward each other, retreating into the radiant depth of each other's eyes . . . and they fell in love. They moved toward one another until they were locked in the warmest embrace.

When their lips touched, the stars in their hearts began to spin and grow bigger and brighter until their bodies melded and they became one. Their new body exploded with color and was filled with trees and flowers and mountains and rivers.

Grandmother Raven took in the breathtaking new person and said, "I remember you!" And then she turned to the rest of the Hollow People and asked," Who else is hungry?"

THE FINAL WISPY WORDS of the story float out of the First Mother's mouth and join the others swirling above their heads like a murmuration of starlings. Charlie watches as the feathery words move in unison and finally take the shape of an ethereal raven, which spreads its wings and glides in graceful circles above them before setting its sights on Charlie. She clings tighter to First Mother when the bird-shaped story locks eyes with her. Keeping eye contact, the ghostly raven dives toward the little girl and merges with her body, as if entering a pool of water, and settles into her heart. Charlie gasps.

"Now, you're the Story Keeper," First Mother says with a melancholy smile.

In the periphery of Charlie's vision, a delicate amber twinkle gets her attention.

Perched within the massive branches of the First Tree are the fierce warriors of the Raven Clan, whom Charlie finds to be all at once familiar and strange. Their lithe bodies are wrapped in wide swaths of charcoal fabric, and their sleek, black hair is pulled tight against their heads, highlighting the elaborate facial tattoos adorning their dark, olive skin. Each member of the clan wears a simple glittery amber pendant reminiscent of the interior of a nautilus shell.

While caught in the gaze of hundreds of obsidian eyes, Charlie clings tighter to First Mother, who kisses the top of her head.

The clan members collectively spread their arms, which simultaneously transform into elegant black wings, and chant, "Rah-hīnah . . . Rah-hī-nah."

First Mother smiles and whispers in Charlie's ear, "Raven's Daughter."

All at once, the clan shapeshifts into raven form and takes flight. The breeze generated by their wings moves the leaves in the surrounding trees and ruffles Charlie's hair. They circle in the sky above the First Tree, making celebratory vocalizations. The blackness of their bodies fills the sky.

CHARLIE SIGHS IN HER sleep as her raven escort, having delivered her back from the Dreaming Realm, makes his exit through the spinning portal over her bed.

That is, until they meet again.

PART ONE

LITTLE BIRD

CHAPTER 1

CHARLIE'S FIANCÉ DIDN'T NOTICE when she stirred in her sleep. Not this time. Maybe because Dan had his back to her and was as far away as their queen-sized bed allowed.

Her body jerked as if someone had punched her square in the stomach, the air escaping her lungs in a forced exhale. Her eyes popped open, she gasped, and her body reflexively shot upright while she reached her fingers into her mouth to extract the object she was choking on. *Don't swallow, don't swallow, don't swallow.* With her other hand, she palpated her neck to see if she could feel the edges of the lodged object from the outside. She couldn't feel it, but she knew it was there. *Don't swallow, don't swallow.*

Dan woke but didn't move.

She pulled her wet fingers out of her mouth and realized that maybe she *was* able to breathe. Maybe. A tentative swallow, and relief flooded through her. There was no obvious obstruction in her throat. But that didn't mean anything. She may have already swallowed it and would have to go to the emergency room. A new wave of anxiety coursed through her at the thought of having to ask Dan to drive her to the hospital. Maybe she could drive herself.

"You're fine," Dan mumbled, his voice conveying an eye roll. "Go back to sleep."

Heart still pounding, eyes wild, she was having trouble pulling herself out of the dream. She always did. Charlie glanced at him and wanted to tell him that no, she actually wasn't fine; that a tiny metal ladder was lodged in her throat and she was suffocating. But she kept quiet because she was remembering how familiar this feeling was, and also—a tiny metal ladder? She's had this dream before. But maybe this time it was real. She could be choking.

She took a deep, shaky breath that would either reorient her to waking reality or prove that it wasn't a dream, that she was suffocating and likely dying. This usually worked, she was starting to remember, but it always took a while. Another deep breath. She was going to be okay. This time.

Charlie knew she wouldn't be able to get back to sleep, but she settled back and tried. She promised herself that first thing in the morning she'd call the therapist she'd been stalking on the internet. She needed to feel normal again.

Through all the commotion, she didn't notice the glassy, black eye that peeked through the small opening of the spinning portal over her side of the bed before it blinked out of sight. She never did.

CHAPTER 2

LET ME HAVE MISTER Malloy get back to you this afternoon," Charlie said into her wireless headset. "He's in a meeting right now."

She sat, ankles crossed under her chair, at the sleek front desk counter adorned with an expensive bouquet of fresh exotic flowers. She jotted the caller's name and number down on her old-school message pad before ending the call. Behind her, a brushed-gold sign read The Malloy Group. The scene was a corporate still life.

Charlie was out of place in the same way that a sexy black sports car looked out of place in a parking lot filled with boxy brown sedans. If asked, she would've likened herself not to a sexy sports car but to a sun-faded yellow moped. Her long, normally unruly dark hair was pulled back in a tight ponytail. It was too perfect. Her white button-down shirt, light pink cardigan, and brown pencil skirt were too uptight, and the makeup she wore hid her natural beauty. No matter the dress code, it was impossible to hide her latent sexual yet tomboyish allure. And she had no clue.

She was quite proficient at selling herself short. Charlie had decided not to attend college, despite encouragement from just about every one of her high school teachers, and instead applied to be a receptionist at The Malloy Group, where she'd been for almost ten years now. She told herself she was thankful because otherwise she never would've met and fallen in love with Dan, who at that moment was exiting the conference room across the lobby, accompanied by his friend and colleague, Milo.

Both were conservatively dressed in business casual. Dan's tidy blond hair never varied. He sported what he referred to as his signature "classic boy's haircut," while Milo's style was a little trendier. Standing there chatting, they reminded Charlie of JCPenney catalog models.

"Man, you're smooth," Milo said to Dan with the slick smile of a used car salesman. "Every time I see you in action, my mind—" His hands finished the sentence by miming the universal "explosion of one's head" gesture.

In the privacy of her thoughts, Charlie referred to Milo as "Lieutenant Lapdog," and Dan as "Captain Humble."

"How'd you get him to change his mind, bro?" Milo asked.

Right on cue, Dan delivered his trademark shrug of humility. "FOMO. No one likes to miss out on the deal of the century."

Charlie caught Dan's attention by waving the message.

"Maybe I can pry some of your secrets out of you at dinner tonight," Milo said. "Mason's at seven?"

"We'll be there," Dan said, walking toward Charlie.

Milo replied with two enthusiastic thumbs-up.

"That cleaning supply CEO you met with last week just called," Charlie said. "He seemed really anxious to talk to you."

Dan took the message. "Thanks," he said. He glanced at the flowers on the desk. "Wow! Who'd you get the flowers from?"

"My fiancé," she boasted.

"He must really love you," Dan said. He winked at her in a way that always made her think he was born fifty years too late.

"Hey, I'm leaving a bit early today," she said. "I have an appointment, and then I'm going directly to class."

"Appointment?"

She was afraid he'd ask. "Yeah, just some wedding stuff," she lied. "Brenda's gonna cover for me."

"Righty-O. I'll see you when you get home."

He concluded their exchange with a definitive double slap on the counter. "Don't forget to clock out," he said over his shoulder as he walked away.

Invisible poison darts shot from her eyes and slammed into the back of his head.

CHAPTER 3

SHE DIDN'T KNOW HOW to begin. Charlie stared at the plain, middle-aged woman sitting across from her, wondering if all therapists wore a drab uniform to exude a certain asexual blandness so as not to distract their patients or clients or whatever you called someone who was sitting in Charlie's chair.

"So, Charlotte," Marilyn said, looking up from Charlie's intake paperwork, "what brings you in? How can I help?"

"You can call me Charlie. I haven't gone by Charlotte since I was a kid." She paused. "Well, except my fiancé. He calls me Charlotte. I think he's afraid people will think he's gay." She cringed, thinking she'd already revealed too much.

"Charlie it is then. But why would people think your fiancé is gay if—" The therapist smiled as if she'd just figured out why the chicken crossed the road. "What's your fiancé's name?"

"Dan," Charlie said.

"Charlie and Dan."

"He's a bit homophobic."

"Does that bother you?"

Charlie eyed the therapist. "That he's homophobic?"

Marilyn nodded.

"I try not to think about it."

"But if you did think about it, would it bother you?"

"I don't know. That's just how he is. He's actually a really sweet guy. But he's not the reason I'm here."

Marilyn referenced the intake form. "Nightmares."

"I've never really talked to anyone about this before." She hesitated and forced a smile. "You may need to get your straightjacket out."

Marilyn's gaze softened. "I know it's hard to talk to a stranger about personal things. It's okay if you don't want to talk about it yet . . . or ever. You can talk about anything you like."

The thought of dragging this out any longer filled her with even more anxiety. *Time to rip the Band-Aid off.*

"No," Charlie said, shaking her head. "I need to figure this out." She took a deep breath. "I've been having these disturbing dreams . . . where I'm choking." She focused on the geometric pattern in the tan area rug. "They seem so real."

"How upsetting," Marilyn said, her voice warm with genuine concern. "Do you eat late? Before going to bed?"

Charlie shook her head.

"Do you have any stress in your life? Big transitions? Recent losses?"

"I'm getting married next month."

"Planning a wedding is certainly stressful."

"Yeah, I guess. You think my dreams are about planning the wedding?"

"It's possible. When did the dreams start?"

Charlie reached back into her memory banks. "It's been a long time. I was a teenager. Back then, they used to happen once or twice a month. Now they happen a few times a week."

"When did they start happening more frequently?"

"Probably in the fall. Around Halloween—" Charlie stopped. She smiled as realization seeped into her awareness "—when the wedding planning kicked into high gear."

"The subconscious mind has a way of getting our attention when we're really stressed," Marilyn said with an air of finality. Problem solved.

Charlie melted into the chair and sighed. *What a fucking relief! I'm not crazy!*

"Now that I think about it, the dreams started around the time my mom died. I never would've connected the two."

Marilyn's expression softened. "What a devastating loss. I'm so sorry."

Uh-oh. She'd said too much. She slipped back inside the rug's geometric pattern.

"It's okay," Charlie said, wanting to change the subject. "It was a long time ago. I was fourteen."

"It's not okay, Charlie. I can't imagine what that must have been like for you."

She avoided Marilyn's gaze.

"What was she like?" Marilyn asked.

The question caught Charlie off guard. A memory of her mom executing a perfect belly flop into their pool on a sweltering summer day popped into her head and made her smile. With a straight face, her mom had climbed out of the pool and offered the imaginary crowd in their backyard a triumphant and soggy bow. She remembered cheering for her mom.

"She was so fun and silly." Charlie shook her head at the memory. "I thought she was the coolest person on the planet."

"What made her cool?"

Backlogged memories of her mom spilled out in a rush. "She was smart and edgy and rebellious. She liked to flirt with old men and make them blush." She shook her head at sepia-tinged memories as they surfaced, unaware that she was smiling. "She loved to gossip and was a huge smartass. I think she made it her life's purpose to make my dad laugh whenever his mouth was full."

Marilyn laughed. "She sounds amazing."

"She really was."

"You must miss her terribly."

Her chest and throat tightened, and tears reached the corners of her eyes. She pushed the pain down with practiced ease and locked it away before it poured out and filled Marilyn's office.

"Was it an accident?" Marilyn pressed.

She shook her head. "Brain aneurysm," she said, as if reporting the news.

The memory replayed like a television show she couldn't turn off. She and her mom had just returned home from grocery shopping. Charlie was sliding a box of cereal into the kitchen cabinet when she heard a heavy thud and the crack of glass behind her.

"We were putting away groceries . . ."

Snippets of that horrible day were permanently stained on Charlie's psyche. The distorted grimace on her forty-four-year-old mother's beautiful, youthful face; the disturbing way her unfocused eyes stared right through Charlie; how her mom clutched the sides of her head as if she were trying to keep her skull from breaking apart. She could still hear the anguished sounds of her mother's unintelligible words trying to make their way through dense, wet cotton that suddenly seemed to fill her mouth. The helplessness Charlie felt in that moment rekindled.

When Charlie closed her eyes, she could still see the thick red splatters of ketchup and the shards of broken glass from the bottle that had slipped from her mom's hands and spread across the white linoleum floor. It was a gruesome tableau.

"No child should ever have to go through something like that," Marilyn said.

She took a shaky breath. "I think a part of me died that day too," Charlie whispered.

CHAPTER 4

CHARLIE STEPPED OVER THE threshold, bowed, and breathed in the pungent, sweat-stained air—the disgusting yet comforting smell of the only place where she felt at home. She glanced at the front desk where her ever-effusive instructor, Mark, a third-degree black belt, was chatting on the phone, and smiled hello. He waved at her, and his permanent grin grew a little bigger. She'd never seen Mark in a bad mood.

Practicing Shaolin kung fu was her escape. A temporary holiday from wedding plans, the tedium of her job, her disturbing dreams, and—as of today—her first therapy session. Her primary goal when she stepped into the studio was to train hard and try not to get her ass kicked too badly.

She sat on the wooden bench next to the entrance and took off her high heels. As she slipped them into her gym bag, she heard a voice carry from the equipment room in the back of the studio, and a seductive smile spread on her lips. Her training partner, Goatman, was here.

She looked up and saw his lean, muscular silhouette exit the equipment room. He was wearing a traditional all-black martial arts *gi*; a hard-earned black belt cinched his narrow waist. Goatman's coy smile greeted her as he approached. Anyone looking at her at that moment would have seen her eyes soften and pupils dilate.

"Hiya, Chuck," he said. "You're here early."

"I'm eager for my ass beating," she said.

"Atta girl." He pointed at her in a menacing, yet playful way. "Padded room. Five minutes." And then he gave her the death squint. "You're goin' down."

She smiled with a little too much enthusiasm and instantly regretted it. In his presence, she was an awkward thirteen-year-old.

Charlie imagined she wasn't the only girl captivated by him. Goatman had that just-rolled-out-of-bed, sexy, bad-boy thing going that bored, damaged women find irresistible. He earned his nickname years ago, the story goes, not for his scruffy goatee but after knocking his sparring partner out with a deftly placed head-butt. He's since been known as Grandmaster Goatman, creator of goat-style kung fu.

She changed into her bright white *gi* and tied the stiff new green belt around her waist. She'd reluctantly tested to green two weeks prior, figuring that, with the wedding fast approaching, it was better for her mental health if she got it over with. She hated being in the spotlight. All those eyes watching and judging her were torture. When she first started kung fu, it took her five months to drum up the courage to take her first test. All the new students passed her by. She joked with her instructor, Mark, that she was like the dude in high school who sported a full man-beard because he was held back so many times. That's when Mark asked Goatman to help her out.

She made her way to the "padded room," her favorite place to train not only because the soft floor mats made for less painful landings but because it was hidden away and rarely used. No scrutinizing eyes watched her awkward attempts to be a martial artist, and she looked forward to her time alone with Goatman. Case in point—when she stepped into the padded room, an unaware Goatman was bent over stretching, which gave her several unadulterated seconds to admire his assets from afar. Until he looked up.

"You weren't checking out my ass, were you?" he asked with a grin.

Charlie's face flushed. "Get over yourself." She rolled her eyes to hide her embarrassment and walked over to him like she owned the joint.

His expression suggested that he didn't believe her.

"Today," he said, getting into teacher mode, "the art of sweeping."

Charlie's face dropped. She hated sweeping drills.

"You still need to learn how to sweep," he insisted. "Because you suck at it."

"But I'm really good at being swept!" she said. "And you know how much I love being humiliated. It's my favorite thing."

"Shit, and all this time I thought you just liked being close to the earth."

"If I wanted to roll around on the ground all day, I'd learn jiujitsu," she joked. But her distress seeped through. "Plus, I'm too small to sweep anyone."

He looked at his imaginary watch. "Wow, it only took you thirty seconds to express doubt in yourself. That's a new record."

"I hate you," she whispered.

She took as deep a breath as the circling vultures in her stomach would allow. "We gonna do this or what?"

He nodded and got into a sparring stance. "Okay, make like you're gonna strike me in the face with your left."

In slow motion, Charlie extended her left fist toward Goatman's head. Like a freaking ninja, he stepped to her left side, blocked her punch with his left forearm, while he slid his bent right leg behind her and, in one fluid motion, his rigid right arm came across her chest, making her body pivot backward over his leg. She landed on the mat with a humiliating thud and no idea how she got there.

Not saying a word, he helped her up, but didn't let go of her hand. He looked at her longer than was comfortable, but she managed to hold his gaze. He slowly released her hand and moved several loose hairs out of her face.

"You have really sexy eyes," he told her, his voice quiet.

Charlie blushed and looked down. "I bet you say that to all the girls after you sweep them."

"Can't take a compliment either, I see."

She gave him a shy smile.

"It's customary to say, 'Thank you.'"

She glanced at him sideways and managed a wimpy "Thank you."

He shook his head.

"What'd I do now?" she asked.

He sighed. "You have no idea, do you?" He ran his hand through his dark James Dean hair and shook his head. "When are you getting married?"

Charlie's heart raced. *What's happening?* He actually seemed uncomfortable. "Next month. No idea what?"

"It's not important. I need to be a good boy." He collected himself. "Alright, let's see if you can even the score." He got into a sparring stance. "Try knocking me on *my* ass."

CHAPTER 5

CHARLIE PULLED INTO THE driveway but wasn't ready to go inside yet. Instead, she turned off the engine but left the music on, reclined her seat a bit, eyes closed, a goofy grin on her face. At that moment, everything was perfect. She wanted to flash freeze the awkward yet intoxicating exchange with Goatman in the vault of her mind for safekeeping, so she could access it at any time. She let the memory loop to the soundtrack of her favorite Team Sleep song, *Blvd Nights*. She was getting addicted to the way Goatman made her feel. If she had to describe the feeling, she'd probably say free.

Music was the place where Charlie let herself experience all the emotions and feelings she kept hidden. The place where she didn't have to be the good girl, the accommodating girl, the girl who was afraid. The sad girl. She was drawn to dark, edgy music. The music her mother loved, like Deftones, Tool, Queens of the Stone Age, Massive Attack, and Killing Joke. Was her mother just as repressed as she was?

Charlie had different playlists. Her favorites were currently the ones where she could, for minutes at a time, fold herself into minor chords, dissonance, and raw vocals, and vicariously—safely—feel pain, triumph, confidence, sensuality, sadness, and anger. So much anger. Shit she wasn't always even aware of, but in some magical way, the music she loved settled into her like a long-lost soulmate. It was her medicine, and for a few fleeting moments, made her feel almost as cool as her mother.

When the song ended, she grabbed her gym bag and headed inside.

Dan was in his recliner, watching the local news in their living room, his back to her.

The graphic on the large-screen TV read, "WATER CRISIS: ECONOMIC IMPACT."

She caught a snippet of the news anchor's staccato update. "... hit a new milestone. Thirty percent of Maricopa County residents are out of work as the ripple effects of this unprecedented water shortage continue to cause . . ."

She kissed him hello and quickly did her usual weeknight empty beer bottle tally. He was on his fifth beer. She unconsciously steeled herself.

He muted the TV and finally looked at her. His smile was tight.

"You know, honey," he said, trying to hide his annoyance, "I can hear your car stereo a half a block away. Our neighbors are going to think you're some kind of drug addict thug."

He cocked his head and raised his eyebrows in a paternal way. She knew that look. He wasn't done. *Charlotte Hanover, please report to the principal's office.*

"It's really pretty rude to assume that other people want to hear your kind of music." His lofty tone was like a giant foot stomping on her good mood. "Maybe you could turn the stereo down before pulling into our neighborhood." It was a directive, not a request.

Her ears flushed with white heat and her jaw clenched. "Will do," she replied. She walked past him and put her gear down on the kitchen table.

"That'd be great, honey. How was class?"

"Fine," she said. Her tone was clipped. *I wish I were still there.*

"Everything okay?"

"Yup," she forced a smile. "Everything's fine."

"Great. Get cleaned up. We're supposed to meet Milo and Ginger in an hour," he said as she disappeared down the hallway toward the bedroom. "And please don't wear jeans, okay?"

When he was out of view, she turned and gave him the finger.

As she got ready, all she could think about was how, at that moment, she wanted to wear jeans more than she ever had in her life. The vindictive part of her, though, wasn't strong enough to actually do it. It wasn't worth the grief she'd get from him. Especially when he'd had a few.

CHAPTER 6

DURING DINNER, CONVERSATION CONSISTED mostly of business and gossip about business. While Milo and Dan clucked like two wrinkled and freshly powdered ladies playing bridge, Charlie and Ginger made small talk. This was all Charlie could manage since most of her energy went into eyeballing their very attractive young waiter. She didn't question her frequent excursions into the red-light district of her mind (giving the concept of "mind fuck" a whole new meaning). She justified her habit of admiring beautiful men and women by telling herself it was nothing more than the byproduct of a healthy sex drive. It was hormonal and therefore normal.

"Have you gotten your dress?" Ginger asked.

"Yeah. It's being altered. I go for the final fitting in a couple weeks."

"That's so fucking exciting!" Ginger said. "Has Dan seen it?"

"Absolutely not," Dan interjected, overhearing his name. "I'm a man of tradition. I have no doubt that my Charlotte is going to be the most beautiful bride in the world."

Charlie melted and for a moment forgot about the waiter.

"Oh, you two! Makes my teeth hurt, you're so sweet," Ginger teased. "What's your first dance gonna be? Ever since I was little, I've fantasized about the first dance at my wedding." Ginger batted her eyes at Milo, who pretended to ignore her.

"It's corny to admit this," Dan said while staring into Charlie's eyes, "but me too." He grabbed her hand and softly kissed it. "I can't wait to have my first dance with my new wife."

Charlie's olive skin turned tomato red.

"I've never told anyone this before," Dan continued, "but when I first heard Elvis sing *Love Me Tender*, I saw myself dancing with my future wife. I must have been around nine years old."

Charlie's surprise was obvious. *No, no, no, no. Please, not Elvis.*

"I mean, is it not the perfect song to mark the beginning of a lifetime together?" Dan said, as if addressing the entire restaurant.

"God, Dan," Milo chimed in. "I had no idea you were such a romantic."

Charlie cleared her throat. "I—I didn't know we'd be—" She lowered her voice. "We never talked about this before."

"It's a no-brainer, Charlotte, honey," Dan said with a chuckle. "There should be a law requiring that every first dance should be to *Love Me Tender*. It makes perfect sense, doesn't it?"

I guess it's settled then. Charlie stared at him, not knowing how to respond.

"You're okay with it, honey, aren't you?"

Charlie forced a smile and nodded with a subtle shrug.

Noticing Charlie's discomfort, Ginger changed the subject. "Hey, let's move this party to the bar!"

Dan looked in the direction of the bar. "A nightcap sounds good."

CHAPTER 7

THE FOURSOME SAT IN a booth, sipping after-dinner cocktails. Dan and Milo were back to sharing office gossip and laughing.

When a classic Stevie Wonder song came on, Ginger grabbed Charlie by the hand and pulled her out onto the dance floor. Charlie loved to dance. It was one of those rare instances when she didn't feel self-conscious—a surprising paradox for someone who constantly felt like the whole world was scrutinizing her every move. For three to four minutes at a time, she could escape into her own little primitive, rhythmic world. A world where Elvis didn't exist. *Fucking Elvis.*

And this song was one of her favorites. It reminded her of her mom. Her mood lifted as she lost herself in the sweet memory of the two of them dancing unabashedly in their living room. Their faces radiated pure joy.

After exorcizing Elvis from her system, her thoughts wandered back to Goatman. She danced as if he were watching her. Just as she relaxed into her Goatman reverie, a flash of black caught her attention out of the corner of her eye. Something flying. But when she looked, it was gone.

She tapped Ginger on the shoulder. "Did you see that?" she yelled over the music.

Ginger looked perplexed. "See what?"

"Something flew by me," she shouted, and pointed to where she'd seen the black thing.

Ginger squinted at Charlie and shrugged.

"Never mind." *I must be more buzzed than I thought.*

Charlie saw the handsome waiter at the bar and turned her sexy up a notch, hoping he'd look her way. She pretended he was Goatman and bored a hole in the back of his head, willing him to turn around with her mind. When he finally did, he caught her eye and smiled. She smiled back. Almost instinctively, she turned her attention to Dan, who was watching her from their table. Dan winked at her, which she took as her cue to get off the dance floor. *Busted.*

CHAPTER 8

DAN WAS UNUSUALLY QUIET on the drive home. The tension between them pulled at her like rubber cement. He was also pretty intoxicated, which tripled her stress. She wasn't fond of Drunk Dan. At least he let her drive. She found herself stealing looks at him, trying to gauge his mood. He just stared out the passenger window like a mannequin.

She clambered for something neutral to say to ease her sense of dread and break the silence. "That was a great meal, wasn't it?" she finally said. It came out a little over the top, making her wince.

Dan took a frustrated breath. Charlie prepared herself for what was to come.

"Do you take me for some sort of chump?"

"No, of course not. What's wrong?"

"I saw the way that waiter smiled at you when you were dancing."

"He was probably just being nice. Maybe he appreciated the tip you gave him."

He banged a fist against the dashboard. "Damn it, Charlotte!"

Charlie recoiled and braced herself. Dan never cursed.

"Do you have to dance like a stripper? Don't you realize, when you dance like that everyone thinks you're a whore? I've never been so embarrassed."

A frenzied rush of conflicting feelings coursed through her. In an instant, she felt guilty, angry, trapped, but all she could say was, "I'm sorry."

"You should be sorry. I have to be honest, Charlotte. When you behave like you did out there tonight . . . you tell the whole world that you don't respect me."

"Of course I respect you, Dan. I didn't mean to embarrass you. I'm really sorry. I just like to dance. If it makes you feel better, I just won't dance anymore."

"What kind of solution is that?" Condescension dripped from every word. "You just need to dance like you weren't raised by perverts. Like a proper young woman."

Wow. You didn't just say that.

"Don't worry, Dan"—Charlie's tone dipped into the "you've crossed the line, pal" register—"I won't embarrass you at our wedding if that's what you're worried about." *And I'm going to fucking wear jeans.*

"I hope not."

Asshole.

CHAPTER 9

CHARLIE COULDN'T SLEEP THAT night. She imagined giving Dan the verbal smackdown of the century, where she delivered a flawless tirade of ego puncturing discourse. At that moment, she was angry enough to tell him not only how much his words hurt her, but also how wrong he was and how much of a dick he was. And how she was going to give both his father and mother a lap dance the next time she saw them. She decided she would have this talk with him in the morning. First thing.

But, as the hours passed and the morning light crept into the bedroom, her rage gave way to panic. She slipped out of bed and retreated to the living room. She couldn't sit still, so she paced from the couch to the kitchen and back again. Over and over. This was a well-worn path. For years now, she'd absorbed Dan's drunken and sober vitriol and condescension until the hurt became volcanic, and then would fantasize about confronting him. But the reality was that she'd never confront him.

Especially this time. She'd never seen Dan so angry before. She couldn't take a deep breath. Her worst fears consumed her, fueling an anxiety-spurred fantasy. She imagined Dan leaning against the kitchen sink, staring out the window while she sat at the small kitchen table. She envisioned him shaking his head and releasing a tense breath.

Not looking at her, he says, "I can't do this."

She holds her breath, eyes wide, and readies herself. "Can't do what?" She hears her voice crack.

He turns toward her and gestures to her and then to himself. "This."

"What are you saying?"

"It's over, Charlotte." He holds his hand out, palm up.

"You don't want to marry me?"

Dan responds by looking at her left hand.

Through tears, she removes her engagement ring and places it in his open hand. And then her life implodes.

Like a zombie, Charlie packs her belongings into a cardboard box at the front desk where she's worked her entire adult life.

She's asleep in the reclined passenger seat of her car, all of her belongings stuffed in the back. The sun hits her face, and she opens her eyes and stares at nothing.

Maybe he's right. Maybe my dancing is a bit much. If I hadn't tried to get that waiter's attention, everything would be fine right now. I'd be upset if I saw Dan flirting with another girl. Probably. Maybe. Unless she was cute. She tried to erase that thought. She knew she couldn't ease her growing sense of dread until she apologized to Dan. She needed to know that everything was back to normal. The truth that hovered right at the edge of her awareness, if she dared to look, was that she couldn't fathom life without Dan. Not out of love, but because a long time ago, she made an unconscious bargain with herself: in exchange for security and the illusion of love, she became someone who was valuable to Dan. Without him, she was no one.

Since sleep wasn't happening and it was almost dawn, she got to work making Dan a special I'm-sorry-for-dancing-like-a-whore-please-don't-call-off-the-wedding breakfast. When Dan came into the kitchen, he went right for the coffee machine. He didn't look at her. Charlie's stomach dropped. His typical routine was a good-morning peck on the cheek followed by coffee.

It's over.

After he poured his coffee, he sat at the kitchen table and got lost in his phone.

She took a deep breath. "I'm making pancakes," she said with as much enthusiasm as she could muster.

"So you are," Dan said without making eye contact.

"Dan," she whispered. "I couldn't sleep. Couldn't stop thinking about what happened last night."

He finally looked at her.

"I'm really sorry." Her eyes filled. Once the first tear fell, all of the emotions she'd been trying to contain burst out of her like a torrent.

Dan's stern expression softened. "Come here," he said.

She sat on his lap and buried her face in his neck.

"It's in the past. Everything's okay."

The tension released from her body, and now she cried because she was both relieved and exhausted.

"I think the pancakes are burning," he said. She laughed through her tears.

CHAPTER 10

AHNA, AN ELDER OF the Raven Clan, perches in raven form on a giant moss-covered boulder that sits on the bank of a turquoise lagoon. The light reflecting off the water's surface makes her spiral clan pendant sparkle in the way that ravens love. She cocks her head and listens to the low, discordant rumble of the churning mirror-like Mental Realm that has consumed about half of the Dreaming Realm so far. It's getting louder, which means it's moving faster and growing bigger. This is not good.

A larger male raven lands on the ground next to her and lowers his head in reverence. Ahna makes several soft vocalizations, and they both shift into human form.

Despite her age, Ahna appears ageless and exotic. Her black eyes are clear and alert. The only thing that hints at her ancient blood is the silver running through her black hair at the temples. Her facial tattoos are more elaborate than Ahkoa's, the imposing figure standing before her. No matter the situation, Ahkoa's stance always carries a hint of tension, as if his body is spring-loaded and he's eager to sink his talons into you. Everything about him says warrior, particularly his long ebony hair, which he likes to wear pulled into a topknot. The sides of his head are shaved and reveal in ink the story of his relentless strength.

At the moment, his demeanor is serious, and his fierce gaze bores into her.

Ahna knows this look. He's annoyed. This amuses her. She gestures for him to speak.

"Maybe we should let them all die," he says.

They've had this conversation before. Many times.

"That's not for us to decide."

"They'll probably do themselves in, regardless."

"They might." She cocks her head, bird-like. "What's really on your mind?"

He takes a breath, concerned that saying the words out loud will make the precarious-seeming nature of Charlie's plight more real. "I can't reach her."

Ahna grows still.

"Her dreaming is . . . stuck," he says. "It's difficult to tell if she's infected and her mind is corrupted like most of the others, or if the death of her human mother left her gravely wounded. Maybe it's both."

She cocks her head again in a subtle, bird-like way. "You're worried about her."

His voice softens. "I don't think she can get any further away from herself." He shakes his head. "And the person she's marrying—" He rolls the unsavory thought off his shoulders.

"It's not easy being human," she says.

"I remember."

"I don't think you do."

"Time's running out," he says, changing the subject.

"It is."

He breaks her gaze for the first time.

"Help her," Ahna says.

His expression says, *You sure?*

"Rah-hīnah is in there somewhere. Help her remember." A slow nod of her head indicates the conversation is over.

Ahkoa bows his head to her. He spreads his arms, shapeshifts back into raven form, and flies away.

"Before it's too late," Ahna whispers.

CHAPTER 11

CHARLIE SAT IN THE bridal shop waiting area, facing an elevated platform surrounded by several full-length mirrors. In the neighboring chairs, three women were chatting away with great fervor, an acute contrast to the flat indifference that floated through Charlie's inner world like a cloud of Novocain. She wondered if other girls secretly fantasized about the day *after* their wedding. For her, the day after meant they'd be on a plane to Hawaii. She could almost smell the salty air and hear the waves crashing. Was it normal to be more excited about the honeymoon than the wedding?

Despite Ginger's insistence that it was against nuptial law to attend a dress fitting without the bride's maid, Charlie was determined to go alone. She just wanted to get it over with and not make the whole thing into a big production. To soften her friend's disappointment, Charlie made a deal with Ginger that she'd be "absolutely thrilled" to attend the "very special, surprise bachelorette outing" that Ginger was planning as long as the outing didn't involve oily, dancing, naked men. Ginger's forced smile made Charlie think she'd dodged a bullet.

The door to one of the dressing rooms opened, and a young woman about Charlie's age stepped out in a beaded, Great Gatsby-inspired wedding dress. The three chatty women gasped and ran over to her and helped her up onto the platform. The oldest of the women looked at the bride-to-be and shook her head as if she couldn't believe her eyes. She was brimming with pride. Charlie guessed she was the bride's mother. "Oh, sweetie," the woman said through tears. "You are the most beautiful bride I've ever seen."

Charlie's throat thickened, and she turned away. Relief flooded through her when, seconds later, the attendant called Charlie's name and she was able to retreat to the dressing room. She quickly undressed and slipped into her wedding gown. The attendant zipped her up, turned Charlie around to face her, and assessed the finished product.

"Wow," she said. "You were born to wear that dress."

Charlie managed an embarrassed smile. She didn't want to go back to the other room where the women continued to gush and carry on. Instead, she walked over to the small mirrored dais on the other side of the dressing room and climbed up to get a look. She didn't recognize herself. The form-fitting ivory satin dress hugged her curves like flowing water. She looked like she'd stepped off the set of a Bogart film.

"Should I get your mother?" the attendant asked.

The question caught Charlie by surprise, and her eyes pooled with heavy tears. Charlie shook her head and tried to smile. "She's not here," was all Charlie could muster.

The attendant seemed to feel the weight of Charlie's response and apologized. "Would you like me to leave you alone for a bit?" she said, handing Charlie a box of tissues. Charlie nodded.

When she was alone, she looked at her red, blotchy face in the mirror and cried like she hadn't cried since her mother died. Rising to the surface of her grief came a certain kind of mom-shaped loneliness she'd never allowed herself to feel. At that moment, the only thing she wanted was one of her mother's fierce hugs, which had always translated as quiet reassurance. She allowed herself to imagine her mother at her side, there in the dressing room, bossing her around and making her laugh.

She sank down until she was sitting on the edge of the dais, the box of tissues clutched in her satin lap. Her eyes stared at nothing as she robotically wiped tears away with a soggy wad of tissues. A shudder ran up her spine and her shoulders curved forward, feeling as if she were being watched. She looked in the mirror and saw a black blur appear over her head. The blur came into focus and took the shape of a raven.

What the fuck?

Wings spread, the raven uttered a loud vocalization before flying into the mirror in front of her as if it were a vertical pool of water. Suspended in the mirror, the bird faced her. The light caught the sparkling nautilus pendant hanging from its neck, capturing her attention. It was familiar somehow and she felt a pull, as if the more she stared at the spiral, the more she would get lost in it.

Charlie locked eyes with the raven and slowly reached out to touch its reflection. When her fingers made contact with the mirror, the raven flapped its wings and disappeared.

She wasn't afraid. She was strangely calm. She looked down and ran her hands over the tear-stained bodice of her dress. A weight had been lifted.

She felt lighter when she left the dress shop, her fancy gown safe in its plastic zippered bag, ready for the big day, which was just a few weeks away. She didn't care that the tears that had found their way onto the expensive fabric might permanently stain her dress. She saw it as a private tribute—a secret way to have her mom with her on her wedding day. *She would've loved my dress*. And, for a moment, she felt like she just might be okay.

CHAPTER 12

DAN'S MOTHER, FLORA, WAS already seated when Charlie arrived at the restaurant. As Charlie approached the table, she braced herself for the cloying cloud of inexpensive perfume that always orbited Flora's body like a personal stratosphere. She could taste the smell of Flora for three days after being in her presence.

Flora's smile was big and bright when she spotted Charlie across the room. She lifted her large frame off her chair and clutched Charlie in a tight, eye-watering embrace.

"So good to see you, Charlotte," Flora said. "My goodness, you're wasting away to nothing. Doesn't that son of mine feed you?"

Charlie smiled and realized she was holding her breath. "I guess I haven't been eating much lately."

"Well, we're going to change that right now. Order anything you like."

"Thank you, Mrs. Malloy. Although you might be sorry you offered," she teased. "I'm starving."

"We're family now, Charlotte. Call me Mom."

Charlie's insides clenched. Ever since her emotional outburst at the bridal shop, the existential weight of her mother's absence had taken up residence in her psyche like an immense granite monument. She didn't know if she could ever refer to Flora as "Mom," but she didn't have the heart to tell her.

"That's very sweet," Charlie said. "How about we make a deal?"

"Deal?"

"I'll call you Mom if you call me Charlie."

"Charlie?"

"Yeah, that's what everyone calls me. Well, everyone but Dan."

Flora's forced smile attempted to indicate that she'd be thrilled to call her Charlie, but her darting eyes revealed utter discomfort.

Perhaps the apple doesn't fall far from the homophobic tree.

"Well, isn't that a surprise!" Flora's thin, penciled eyebrows reached halfway up her forehead in feigned astonishment. "I have to be honest, honey. I don't know if I can see you as anything but Charlotte. That's what I've been calling you for the last . . . what has it been? Five years now?"

"Seven," Charlie said. "It's okay."

She wasn't sure how it happened, but she felt rejected by a woman she only knew from a polite distance. She focused hard on the menu, hoping to distract herself from her welling emotions. *What the hell is wrong with me?* She could've kissed the waitress when she appeared seconds later to take their order.

The moment the waitress left, Flora clasped her hands to her chest and said, "I'm so excited, Charlotte! I've been waiting months to give you a special wedding gift." Flora reached into her bag and pulled out a small, pink, gift-wrapped box and placed it on the table between them. "A little something from me to you."

Charlie blushed. "You didn't have to get me anything."

"Oh, you! Don't be silly!" Flora said, clapping her hands like a toy monkey banging cymbals. "Open it!"

Charlie grabbed the dainty box and read the tiny card. *"Something bor-rowed" Welcome to the family, Charlotte! Love, Mom.*

Flora watched without blinking as Charlie tore the wrapping paper off the box and opened it. Nestled on a square of white cotton sat a gold crucifix. Charlie's heart dropped. *Holy shit.* Her brain froze. She didn't know what to say.

"Wow," Charlie said. "I don't know what to say."

"That's the necklace my mother gave me to wear on my wedding day," Flora said with pride. "And when Danny told me he was going to ask you to marry him, I knew I had to let you wear it on your special day."

Charlie stared at the little crucified man on the shiny cross and tried to picture it around her neck.

The waitress returned with a bread basket and condiments. When Charlie spotted the red of the ketchup bottle, identical to the one her mother had dropped the day she died, her body flushed with white heat. She unconsciously grabbed her throat, her airway felt like it had tightened to the width of a drinking straw. The smell of the food and Flora's perfume soured her stomach, turning her olive complexion sallow and gray. She unsuccessfully attempted to hide that she was having trouble breathing.

"You okay, honey?"

Charlie swallowed hard and tried to smile. "Yeah, I'm fine. I think all the wedding stress is catching up with me."

"You don't look so good. Maybe some food will help."

Her stomach did another flip. "I don't think I can eat right now."

"Do you need to go home and lie down for a bit? Take a little nap?"

"Yeah, actually. Maybe that's a good idea," Charlie said, hoping to hide her rush to get the hell out of there. "I'm so sorry to run out on you."

"Not to worry, Charlotte honey. You tell that son of mine to take good care of you."

Charlie put the gift box in her purse. "Thank you for understanding."

CHAPTER 13

CHARLIE'S THROAT RELAXED SOME by the time she got to her car, but she still felt shaky. She leaned her head back on the headrest, let her eyes close, and took a few deep breaths.

The moment her nervous system started to regulate, her ease was rattled by the sound of a loud, ragged birdcall, like a raven or a crow, coming from the backseat. She spun around but the backseat was empty.

I'm losing it. She gripped the steering wheel and stared out the front window. "Leave. Me. Alone," she demanded through gritted teeth. *I am not having a nervous breakdown. Not today.* Another loud croak mocked her from behind, making her jump. Her eyes darted to the rearview mirror. Still nothing there. She timidly reached up and touched the mirror, like she had in the bridal shop dressing room, testing to see if it was solid.

With wide eyes, she picked up her phone and asked, "How do you know you're going insane?"

Her phone's friendly female voice answered, "Maybe you feel like you're spinning out of control. Maybe you feel detached from reality, or you're seeing or hearing things other people don't. Maybe you just worry all the time, even when you don't need to, or feel depressed even when things seem to be going well."

"Fuck you, Dr. Google."

She went to start the engine and noticed a large, real-life raven less than ten feet away, staring right at her. Her body began to vibrate and her senses heightened. She became aware of the details of her surroundings, particularly the contrast between the deep black of the raven's body and the surrounding grass, yellowed with thirst, and the brown straw-like wilted palm fronds of the surrounding trees. She gasped. The grief that filled her took her breath away. *Everything's dying.*

CHAPTER 14

THAT NIGHT, CHARLIE WAS jolted awake by another nightmare. This time the object she dreamed she was choking on was a shiny gold crucifix.

CHAPTER 15

"I THINK I HAD a panic attack yesterday," Charlie blurted as soon as Marilyn sat down. "I couldn't breathe. I'm pretty sure there was an elephant sitting on my chest. My heart—" she took a shaky breath and whispered "—I thought I was gonna die."

Marilyn took a breath, concern in her eyes. "I'm so sorry that happened to you."

Charlie managed to smile.

"Was there anything going on that triggered this episode?"

Charlie hesitated.

"What happened, Charlie?"

"I was having lunch with Dan's mother and she surprised me with a gift. I guess it's more of a loan. 'Something borrowed' is what the card read."

"For the wedding."

Charlie nodded.

"You seem really uncomfortable."

She nodded again. "I don't want to wear it."

"What is it?"

Charlie looked apologetic. She didn't want to offend Marilyn. "It was a crucifix."

"A crucifix," Marilyn repeated in a neutral tone. "Which must mean you're not Christian?"

Charlie shook her head. "I'm not anything."

"I see."

"I don't know what to do. I don't have the heart to tell her."

"What about Dan? Maybe he could intervene on your behalf."

Charlie hesitated again. She felt like she'd been caught stealing a cookie. "Dan doesn't know I'm an atheist either."

For the first time, Marilyn's expression showed surprise. "You and Dan haven't talked about religion?"

"I didn't think it was important."

"It's pretty important, Charlie. Especially if you're planning on having children."

Charlie's eyes darted around the room. She felt cornered.

"Why haven't you talked with him about your beliefs?"

"I didn't want to disappoint him. He's Christian too. Not as hard-core as his parents, but I know it's important to him."

"Can you accept that Dan is religious?"

"Can I accept it?" She gave the question some thought for the first time. "I guess I have to. Maybe I just figured he never gave it much thought. That he believes what he was taught to believe."

"Maybe he finds comfort in his beliefs?"

Charlie shrugged. "Maybe."

"How important is honesty to you?"

Charlie winced. For a split second, Goatman's face interrupted her thoughts. "Of course it's important," she said defensively.

"Do you think Dan would be hurt to know there's a whole side of you he knows nothing about?"

Charlie grimaced. "Yeah, probably."

Bottom line, she couldn't imagine opening the "religion" can of worms with Dan. Not now, weeks before their wedding. Maybe she could break the news during their honeymoon. Or after they've been married a few years.

Marilyn probed further. "What do you think you should do?"

"Wear the necklace," she said with resignation.

Marilyn gave her a severe, questioning look that came across as more maternal than therapeutic.

"I know, I know. I'm a hypocrite," Charlie said, her defensiveness intensified with every word that flew out of her mouth. "Talking to Dan about my religious beliefs—or my lack of them—will make me more anxious. I just wanna get through this wedding. So, I guess I have to wear the damn Jesus necklace."

"You sound angry."

"Yup. Pretty angry." She let out a frustrated breath. "But more at myself than anyone else. You're right, I should've told him about my beliefs a long time ago. Now I guess I'm stuck."

"Stuck?"

"I didn't mean stuck, stuck. I mean caught between a rock and a hard place. Damn, I suck at this therapy thing."

Marilyn's expression softened. "You're doing fine, Charlie. There's no need to beat yourself up. You're getting married, which is one of the most stressful events in a person's life. And you're going through it without your mother. You're not sleeping well, so you're not rested."

"Well, when you put it like that," she said with a tight smile, "no wonder I feel like shit."

"Medication might help you get through this."

"I'm not crazy."

Marilyn smiled and shook her head. "I know you're not, Charlie."

"I just need to get through the next few weeks. Once we're on the plane to Hawaii, I'll be fine. The beach will be my medicine."

"Let's figure out what you can do to take care of yourself so you can enjoy your special day."

"Do you do lobotomies?"

CHAPTER 16

As the big day inched closer, Charlie found her thoughts frequently drifting to Goatman. A welcome distraction from the wedding stress, she told herself. She didn't pay much attention to the fact that the flavor of her fantasies was becoming less fantastical and more realistic. This change seemed to parallel the building sexual tension between her and Goatman. She became more and more courageous, asking him to train with her rather than waiting for him to invite her. They shared extended glances, as if they were communicating in that secret nonverbal language only lovers shared. She noticed that he let his hands linger on her when he corrected a posture or showed her a technique. She felt sexy and alive when she was around him. She'd longed to have someone look at her the way Goatman did and, now that she was being fed in this primitive way, she didn't want it to stop. Ever. The tension between them grew to such a fevered pitch, she broke her biggest fantasy taboo . . . when she had sex with Dan, she imagined it was Goatman's hands that were on her. It was the best sex she and Dan had ever had.

She was looking forward to today's class. It was Goatman's birthday, and she'd lost track of how many hours she'd spent daydreaming about how this day would go. Her plan was to invite him out for a celebratory drink after class. If he actually accepted her invitation, she didn't know if she had the courage to do what she had envisioned in her mind a thousand times, but the thought that she might have time alone with him in a non-teacher/student setting filled her with hungry anticipation.

Dan didn't bat an eye when she told him she'd be late, that she was going out after class to celebrate a classmate's birthday. It was Saturday, which meant he was playing eighteen holes anyway. On his way out the door, he gave her a kiss on the cheek and told her to have fun.

When she arrived at the kung fu school, her heart sank. Goatman was nowhere to be seen. He always got there before her. Her heart deflated even more when she overheard their instructor tell another student that Goatman's twentieth-century car had broken down again. Clutch went.

She stared at the ceiling of the empty padded room, nursing her disappointment instead of practicing her broadsword form. She realized her disappointment was bigger than was probably healthy, and that maybe she was letting her fantasy life get out of hand. She was in deep. She laid there and tried to talk herself down off the Goatman ledge.

"Hey, slacker!" Goatman's voice cut through her thoughts. "Is that the much-revered Shaolin opossum style you're working on?"

The excitement she felt at hearing his voice was instant. Her entire body smiled. She sat up and watched him saunter toward her. It was as if all of her disappointment and doubt evaporated. Poof! She was back on track.

"How'd you get here?"

"Friend gave me a lift." He squatted in front of her and, with almost a whisper, he said, "Worried I wasn't coming?"

Yup. She rolled her eyes in a meager attempt to feign exasperation.

"Do me a solid?"

"Maybe," she said.

"Give me a lift home later?"

She tried to play it cool. "I'll think about it."

He stood and held out his hand. She grabbed it and flashed him a flirty smile. "If I give you a ride," she said, "what do I get in return?" *Check out the cajónes on me!*

He pulled her up and toward him until she was standing inches away from his face.

"What do you want?" he asked.

She shrugged and pretended to think about it.

It was clear he was enjoying this exchange. His smile wrecked her.

CHAPTER 17

SOMEHOW, SHE MANAGED TO get through their training session without getting her teeth kicked in.

On the drive to his house, she traded her typical angst-ridden adolescent boy music for the smoky I-want-to-see-Goatman-naked electronic groove playlist she'd created just for the occasion. She could feel him staring at her as she drove, and she loved it. The buildup was more intense than anything she'd ever experienced before. She thought she might explode. She wanted to live in this place forever. The place where fantasy was on the brink of becoming reality.

When she pulled up to the curb in front of his place, she put the car in park and turned the motor off, but kept the music playing. She timed it perfectly. She turned to Goatman just as *Ritual Spirit*, her favorite Massive Attack song, kicked in.

"Here we are," she said.

He nodded, his eyes smoldering, and said, "Uh-huh." He didn't make a move to get out of her car.

"I've been thinking," she continued. "Since it's your birthday . . ."

"You remembered."

She nodded, her lips curled into a suggestive grin, and she shifted her body so she was facing him. Looking him right in the eye, she said, "Would you like me to kiss you here?" She touched him on the cheek. "Or here?" She moved her fingers to his lips.

Not taking his eyes off her, he touched his lips with his finger.

Without hesitation, she leaned over, clutched his t-shirt, and pulled him toward her until their lips met. She was surprised at how soft and full his lips felt, very different from Dan's thin, tight lips. The kiss was gentle and polite at first. But then he grabbed her head in both his hands and pulled her body close as if he might devour her. She climbed over the console and straddled him. The kiss lasted the entire length of the song. Coming up for air, she pulled away and whispered, "Happy Birthday."

He ran his finger from her chin down her neck and stopped at her cleavage. "Do you wanna come in for a bit?"

Her smile spoke volumes.

CHAPTER 18

DAN WAS WATCHING GOLF on television and drinking beer when Charlie got home. She counted the empties on the coffee table to gauge his mood. *Good, one shy of asshole territory.* She dropped her stuff on the kitchen table and practically floated over to greet him.

"Hey!" she said, giving him a peck on the cheek. "Still the reigning Hole-in-One champion?

"I won fifty bucks," he said with a slight slur.

"Nice!" she said.

"You're in a good mood. Have fun at the party?"

"Yeah, it was a lot of fun."

"Where'd you go?"

"Goatman's house," she said without missing a beat. "It was his birthday." She started toward the bedroom. "I'm gonna jump in the shower."

Like one of Pavlov's dogs, she waited a moment for him to remind her, for the thousandth time, about "the seven-minute shower rule" because "water doesn't grow on trees." But he must have been too drunk. It bummed her out that he was more concerned about the skyrocketing cost of water than the heartbreaking and unsettling reality that the desert was dying in front of their eyes.

After she undressed, she ran the tips of her fingers over her breasts and stomach, retracing the paths Goatman's hands and mouth had explored less than an hour ago. She casually noted that she felt no guilt whatsoever.

CHAPTER 19

"A PSYCHIC?"

"Yeah, it'll be fun," Ginger said as she pulled into the bookstore parking lot. "I wanted to do something special for you since, you know, you insisted on being a complete drag and not having a bachelorette party." Ginger put the car in park and turned to Charlie. "Look at you. You're a wreck."

Charlie knew she was right. But a psychic?

"I made the executive decision that you need to have some fun. So, here's what we're gonna do. We're going to go in there," she pointed at the bookstore, "and we're gonna drink some disgusting herbal tea, and we're gonna have Rosalee the Gypsy tell us what the future holds."

Charlie smirked. "Rosalee the Gypsy?"

"I don't remember what her fucking name is. All I know is that my coworkers rave about her."

Charlie looked at Ginger with mock seriousness and said, "I'd love some disgusting herbal tea."

"I know you're doing this more for me than for you."

"I've got your back. If going to a psychic is going to make you feel better about me, then it's the least I can do."

Ginger flashed her a big, cheesy smile. "I love you so very much."

The more Charlie got to know Ginger—and Charlie kept most everyone at arm's length—the more she liked her. Ginger had a knack for making everyone feel like she'd known them forever.

When they stepped inside the Victorian house-turned-new-age-bookstore, all of Charlie's senses were stunned. Her nostrils filled with the heavy, cloying scent of incense. Her eyes scanned the seven million crystals, candles, and mysterious strange objects that filled cases and tables at the front of the store. Middle Eastern music played quietly in the background. Charlie felt like she'd just stepped off a plane in a foreign country where no one spoke English.

"We're supposed to find the Sunroom," Ginger said, craning her neck. "Ah, I bet that's it." She led Charlie through a maze of bookshelves and counters to a doorway filled with warm, golden sunlight at the back of the house.

The room had an exotic, enticing ambience. It was filled with plants and the inviting smell of cinnamon. Plump burgundy velvet throw pillows surrounded a low wooden table. A large clear quartz crystal sat in the center of the table on a silk purple cloth. Small votive candles surrounded the crystal. Charlie's feeling of discomfort was replaced by the desire to never leave this room.

A waifish, older but youthful-looking Asian woman with short spiky black hair entered the room behind them, carrying a tray of steaming cinnamon tea and three small earthen cups. She smiled at Charlie and Ginger and placed the tray on the low table.

"Hi," she said. "You must be my two o'clock?"

"Yup, that's us," Ginger said.

"I'm Eve. I hope you weren't waiting long."

"No, we just got here," Charlie said. "That tea smells amazing."

"Wait until you taste it. We call it Magic Tea. It's a special blend the owner created." Eve started pouring and gestured with her chin to the cushions on the other side of the table. "Make yourselves comfortable."

Charlie was surprised to find that she felt a stirring of excitement, like she was about to get on a roller coaster.

Eve sat across from Charlie and Ginger. She looked at Charlie longer than typically acceptable when first meeting someone, which erased her excitement and made her feel naked. Charlie nervously grabbed the steaming small clay vessel and took a sip.

"Wow," she said after swallowing. "Screw Dan, I wanna marry this tea."

Eve laughed. "So, you're the bride?"

"That's very psychic of you," Charlie said.

Eve smirked. "Shall we begin?" Eve reached her hands across the table toward Charlie.

"Can you give me your hand?"

A palm reader? Please, no. She looked for a quick exit.

Charlie obliged and slipped her hand between Eve's. Only, Eve didn't flip it over and start examining the cacophony of lines. Instead, she closed her eyes and gently held Charlie's hand.

Maybe she's reading my pulse?

After several long moments of syrupy silence, Eve's brow furrowed. Her eyes popped open, and she asked, "Did you just recently meet your fiancé?"

Charlie shook her head. *Wrong and wrong. I knew this was bullshit.*

"No, we've been together for about seven years."

"Strange. It feels like you're strangers in a lot of ways. Like you don't really know each other." She paused in order to refine her perception. "Or maybe it's that he doesn't really know who you are."

Charlie squirmed a bit. *Okay, maybe she's a little right.* She looked over at Ginger, whose expression showed disbelief.

"No way," Ginger said. "Charlie and Dan are like an old married couple."

Charlie nodded in agreement. "Dan's my rock. I'd be lost without him."

Eve looked straight into Charlie's eyes. "So, he's safe? Like a security blanket?"

Charlie wanted to crawl under the table but instead she looked away.

Eve shut her eyes again. Charlie was amazed at how completely still Eve sat. It looked like she wasn't breathing. It gave her the creeps.

Without opening her eyes, Eve said in a quiet but authoritative voice, "Your life is about to take a dramatic turn."

Charlie looked at Ginger with fake shock. "Yeah, well, I am getting married next week."

Ginger stifled a giggle.

Eve shook her head. "No, it's something different." She opened her eyes. "I don't think you're expecting this."

"Expecting what?"

She closed her eyes again. "I see stone stairs leading down to a heavy wooden door. The door is cracked open and there's darkness behind it." She hesitated. "That's where you're headed."

Charlie didn't like the sound of that.

"Is there a light switch by the door?" Ginger quipped. Eve didn't respond.

"In some ways, whatever it is . . . it looks like it may have already started." Eve opened her eyes and squeezed her hand tighter. "You have no idea how powerful you are, do you? You'll get through this."

"You're making me paranoid," Charlie said with a nervous chuckle. "What do I need to get through?"

Eve closed her eyes again and inhaled slowly. "Your eyes. It looks like there's a storm in them. They're filled with dark clouds. But then the clouds clear, and I see the color of your eyes change from brown to green to black, and your body is surrounded by fire."

"You make it sound like I'm going to die or something."

"It's more of a symbolic death. My interpretation would be that the way you see yourself, or maybe the world, is gonna change."

Charlie's body started to tingle like it had before she'd had her panic attack at the restaurant with Flora. She forced herself to take a breath.

"I know it sounds really dramatic," Eve said with a smile. "And it might feel that way going through it. But it's preparing you."

"For what?" Charlie blurted.

"Too soon to tell. Feels pretty important though."

Charlie was pale and shaken. Ginger looked at Charlie with concerned, wide eyes, as if painfully aware that her plan for a fun, relaxing afternoon was failing in a monumental way.

"Not what you were expecting, was it?" Eve asked.

Charlie shook her head. "No, not really. I thought you'd tell me I was going to live in a house in the suburbs and have two-point-five kids, maybe a dog."

"If only life were that neat and tidy." Eve's voice conveyed sympathetic understanding. With trepidation, she asked, "There's a little more. Do you want to hear it?"

Ginger shot Eve a "no more bad news" grimace.

Charlie shrugged and said, with a sense of defeat, "Sure, how much worse can it get?"

Eve closed her eyes of doom for the thousandth time. "I see you at the top of that stone stairway and something . . . an animal of some kind, sneaks up behind you and pushes you down the steps, which tells me that something or someone is going to set this transformation in motion."

Charlie's mind immediately jumped to the phantom bird in the back seat of her car. "Can you tell what kind of animal it is?"

"Let me see if I can," Eve said. After a few long moments, she nodded and announced, "It's a goat."

Charlie inhaled sharply, and then a small smile appeared on her troubled face. *Goatman. Well, at least I'll be in good company.*

CHAPTER 20

GINGER STARTED APOLOGIZING THE moment they stepped outside. "I swear, I had no idea it was gonna be like that. I'm a terrible friend and you should sue me for pain and suffering."

Charlie tried to hide her uneasiness. "It wasn't that bad."

Ginger gave her shoulder a playful "don't be ridiculous" shove. "Yeah. It was." She did her best Dracula impersonation. "You're valking into dahk-ness. Your life vill never be the same ah-gain."

"Yeah," Charlie laughed, "it was pretty bad. But hey," she said in an attempt to rationalize how shaken she was feeling, "there's a distinct possibility the whole thing was bullshit."

Ginger draped an arm over Charlie's shoulder. "Whadya say we stop at the bar and I buy you a drink or two . . . or three, to make it up to you?"

"That's a little more my speed. Maybe if I drink enough, I can forget that my life is doomed."

"Getting you drunk is the least I can do."

"That tea was really good though, wasn't it?"

"I wanna have that tea's baby."

Before Ginger climbed into the driver's seat, she looked over the roof of her car at Charlie. "What was with the goat?"

Charlie froze. "Goat?"

"You smiled when she mentioned the goat. I was just wondering what that cute little smile was all about."

"I dunno. I guess I thought it was funny. I mean, it was pretty random."

"Sounded demonic to me. Freaked me out."

CHAPTER 21

THAT NIGHT, CHARLIE DIDN'T have the choking dream. Instead, she dreamed her mother was helping her get dressed the morning of the wedding. When her mom slipped the wedding dress over her head, Charlie reached her arms up but couldn't find the armholes. Panic ripped through her as she discovered there was no room to move and she was trapped inside the dress. Her mom twisted the dress around and around Charlie's body. Charlie screamed inside the dress and began thrashing about trying to break free. Her mom pulled the dress off and casually said, "Maybe you should wear your jeans."

Charlie woke in a cold sweat. She didn't move, but her eyes darted around like a caged animal. She glanced at Dan, sound asleep next to her, and swallowed hard.

"You're okay," she whispered. She slowed her breathing and closed her eyes. "You're okay."

The air above Charlie began to stir, making a subtle whirring sound as the spinning picked up speed.

SHE OPENS HER EYES and finds she is no longer in her bedroom. Charlie lays frozen on a bed of moss beside a turquoise lagoon, ancient twisting trees towering over her.

An enormous raven is perched on her chest, like an explorer staking claim to new territory, its talons digging into her breasts and rib cage like needles. Around its neck is the familiar spiral pendant. *You were in the mirror.* Terror fills Charlie as she tries to make sense of what's happening.

The bird's large ebony wings spread as if it's about to embrace her torso in a feathery hug, and it lets out a series of ear-piercing squawks like a primal war cry. With wings slightly spread, it moves its head in a series of short, jerky thrusts before it impales the razor tip of its smooth black beak into Charlie's neck and begins ripping out her throat.

Charlie watches in disbelief as the raven rips and pulls strips of bloody flesh, muscle, and cartilage from her throat, swallowing each slimy piece with amused gusto.

Its beak, glistening with blood, reaches deep into the ravaged hole in her neck and retrieves a small blood-streaked amber disk. She catches a glimpse of the familiar spiral design on its bloody surface.

Clutching the object in its beak, the raven looks at Charlie, cocks its head to one side with an air of conceit, and flies away.

The bird glides in triumphant circles above her head . . . or is it urging her to follow? Both amber disks, the one hanging from its neck and the one clenched in its beak, sparkle, flashing like lightning when the setting sun's rays hit them.

Her attention shifts to her abdomen, where she feels a warm pulling sensation on her skin, and finds two pulsating orbs of indigo light hovering inches above her body. *What's happening to me?* The deep blue lights bolt with impossible speed out of sight, like they were never there. With a final croak, the raven takes off and disappears in the dense forest.

She reaches up to the ragged hole in her throat and tries to scream.

CHARLIE JERKED AWAKE AND sat up, gasping for air, hands at her throat, still unable to scream.

CHAPTER 22

MORNING SUNSHINE POURED INTO the minimalist bedroom through sheer white curtains, making the bare white walls glow. Charlie, alone and wrapped in a tangle of gray pinstripe bedsheets, stared at the slowly spinning ceiling fan. A dark gray comforter was on the floor. She'd had a restless night. Her eyes broke from their trance and shifted to the bedside table, where a crisp white envelope was propped against a small vase containing a single white rose. The envelope read, "Do Not Open Until Morning!" in handwritten cursive.

She released a resigned breath and shifted her gaze to the opposite side of the room, where her wedding dress, protected in its garment bag, hung from the top of the open closet door. Her dull eyes found their way back to the ceiling fan. *Five more minutes.*

She felt nothing. No excitement. No anxiety. Nothing. Just a foggy numbness like she wasn't quite in her body. She was glad she had the house to herself. Dan had insisted on sleeping at his parents', so the first time he set eyes on Charlie on their wedding day would be when she walked down the aisle. His reason: it was bad luck for the groom to see the bride before the wedding. Charlie told him she'd read in a bridal magazine that the story behind that superstition was a practical one—to prevent the groom from backing out of an arranged marriage in the event he found his betrothed repulsive. She'd poked him in the ribs, saying it was a good thing he'd already taken her for a test drive. He'd grabbed her in a bearish embrace, given her a big smooch on the lips, and told her that no matter what the superstition was, he didn't want to take any chances. He could sacrifice one night of being with her for a lifetime of good fortune. Plus, he had asked her, didn't she find the whole notion romantic?

The numbness she felt now was reminiscent of the numbness she'd felt when he'd asked that question. But she had ignored the feeling, forced a smile, told him how much she loved his romantic side, and playfully threatened that if he backed out of their marriage, he would lose out on the two very large cows her father was going to give his family. Dan laughed and told her that as long as she didn't turn into a large cow, he'd be a happy husband. When Charlie's body went slack and she tried to pull away, he'd squeezed her tighter and told her to lighten up, he was just kidding.

Charlie stared at herself in the mirror, mindlessly brushing her teeth. She glanced at the messy bed in the reflection. The card that had been inside the white envelope now lay on the bed. It read: "Can't wait to make you my wife." Underneath was a hand-drawn heart next to a giant "D."

She still felt nothing. Not even a hint of concern about feeling nothing.

She had the sense that she was looking at a stranger in the mirror. The sensation was similar to the time she'd said the word "mustard" so many times, it stopped sounding like a word. She rolled her eyes and gave her two-dimensional doppelganger a big fake smile. *What the hell is wrong with me?*

She promised herself she wouldn't allow Goatman to invade her brain space on her wedding day. She owed Dan that. But it was akin to trying not to think about the color red. The sexy beast peeked around the corner of her mind and waved hello, and then it was over. She couldn't unthink him, especially after their last encounter. They'd crossed the line one more time, a few days ago, while in the Padded Room, while, *ahem*, training. Her nether regions warmed as she recalled the excitement of potentially getting caught. It had started with a not-so-innocent kiss and ended with the two of them against the far wall. *Oooh boy.*

Well, she didn't feel numb anymore. After releasing some sexual tension in what had to be the quickest orgasm in human history, she did a little thought experiment. How would she feel if Dan cheated on her? The foggy numbness once again descended on her and—this was tough to admit—a molecule of relief. Before she could slip into a deep state of paralyzing discord, Ginger yelled a greeting from the front door.

Charlie went out to meet her.

"Your dress is stunning," Ginger said in mock amazement.

Charlie looked down at the old, oversized t-shirt she was wearing. "You don't think it's too much?"

"No, I think it's tastefully understated. Especially the grape juice stain."

"It's wine."

"Very classy."

"Only the best for my wedding."

"Are you totally excited?"

"Totally."

"You don't seem excited."

"That's probably because I feel like I'm gonna vomit."

"Should I take that personally?"

Charlie nodded. "Probably."

Ginger held up a greasy paper bag. "Does that mean you don't want a scone?"

Charlie's stomach lurched, releasing a flood of acid. "Maybe not right now." She was glad Flora hadn't arrived yet. She didn't want to make a habit of being sick to her stomach every time she was in her future mother-in-law's presence.

CHAPTER 23

CHARLIE MANAGED TO FEEL a little more like herself thanks to Ginger, who never failed to make her feel like a worthwhile human being. Flora drove them to a fancy salon where they all got their hair, nails, and makeup done. She felt like royalty, the way everyone fussed over her.

Afterward, they headed to the country club where the ceremony and reception were taking place. Charlie was relieved when Dan had suggested having everything at the club, his home away from home where he rubbed elbows with the Phoenix elite. Thankfully, it wasn't one of the country clubs that had to close due to the water shortage. Somehow, the golf course turf avoided crisping like overbleached hair. She could imagine Dan selling a kidney just to keep the course open.

She'd dreaded the thought of having to get married in a church. The one concession she'd silently made was that Dan's family minister would be officiating the ceremony. After her last therapy session, she could see that choosing not to be upfront about her atheism could be construed as dishonest, but she justified her omission by telling herself that her beliefs were personal and therefore no one's business. Even Dan's.

Charlie had to chuckle when Flora and Ginger helped her into her wedding dress, and her arms slipped easily through the armholes. The form-fitting satin dress draped beautifully over Charlie's slender body. She looked like a movie star.

"Hot damn," Ginger whispered to Charlie when Flora stepped away. "You've got to be the sexiest bride I've ever seen. Dan's gonna flip when he sees you in that dress."

Charlie's face flushed. She was more accustomed to blending in with the woodwork.

She couldn't help but get caught up in the excitement. The emptiness that had plagued her a few hours before had long faded. She didn't give it another thought. Now she was all smiles. How could she not be when everyone was telling her how beautiful she was?

This time when Charlie looked in the mirror, she didn't see a stranger. She was startled to see her mom staring back at her. With her hair swept up, rich burgundy lips, and her deep brown eyes defined with a hint of liner, the resemblance was almost spooky.

Her father's reaction when he first set eyes on her suggested maybe he thought so too. Tears streamed down his face almost reflexively, and Charlie's heart melted in response—along with much of the tension she usually felt in his presence. She never considered herself a grudge holder, but she hadn't been able to forgive him for moving on so quickly after her mom died. When it came up in therapy, she told Marilyn she was angrier with Judy, a long-time close friend of both her parents, whom she felt circled her father like a vulture in the weeks after her mom died.

The moment Marilyn asked her if she had felt betrayed, the word settled into her psyche and made itself at home. She'd never allowed herself to name the feeling until that moment.

"It hurts to feel betrayed," Marilyn had said. "Especially by someone you trust."

That was the second time Charlie teared up in therapy. It took her by surprise. She didn't like crying in front of anyone and pledged to never let it happen again. "That was a long time ago," she'd said.

"Not when you've never dealt with the pain," Marilyn replied. "Old hurts can feel like they happened yesterday." And then she asked, "Do you think your dad is happy?"

Charlie thought about her dad with mom and her dad after mom. "I think he misses her," she had said. "He doesn't seem happy. Not the kind of happy I remember from childhood."

"It must be hard to see someone you love so stuck," Marilyn said.

At the moment when she embraced her dad in her wedding dress, any anger Charlie felt toward him dissolved, and all she felt was deep sorrow and the gravity of his loss.

"You look beautiful," her father whispered after he collected himself.

"So, you don't mind walking me down the aisle then?" Charlie teased.

"Are you kidding me? You're my girl, Charlie." He squeezed her tighter. "I'm the proudest father in the world." He hesitated. "I wish your . . ."

"I know, Dad." Charlie stopped him. "Me too." She started to tear up. "Hey," she said playfully, hitting her father on the shoulder, "don't make me cry"—Ginger, tissue box in hand, came to Charlie's rescue. Charlie laughed as she carefully dabbed at her eyes—"unless you know how to fix my makeup."

"Oh, you don't want me putting makeup on you. Dan will think aliens came and replaced you with that evangelical clown lady who used to cry on television all the time."

"Tammy Faye Bakker," Ginger chimed in.

"Yeah, that's the one," he said.

"That would be terrible," Ginger said. "We can't let that happen."

"So, you are hereby prohibited from making me cry."

"Aye aye, cap'n," he said with a sweeping salute. "I'll do my best."

Charlie felt a sense of comfort that she hadn't felt in a long time. It was like putting on an old, worn, velvety-soft sweatshirt. It was so good to feel a sense of closeness with her father and to see that they could still slip back into the fun, easygoing connection they'd shared before her mom died. This moment was the greatest wedding gift her father could have given her.

Flora interrupted them. "It's time!"

Fuck.

Her father held out his arm. "Shall we?"

Charlie's insides twisted, but she shrugged it off with a deep breath. She hooked an arm around her dad's, and they headed downstairs to the ceremony.

The numbness returned when she walked down the aisle toward her future. She didn't hear the music or register the smiling, staring eyes of the many guests she passed. Her father gave her the traditional peck on the cheek before handing her off to her future husband. Dan's broad smile greeted her as she stepped up to meet him. The first thought that made its way through the dense fog in her brain was, *Let's get this over with.*

The ceremony was a blur. She stood across from Dan while the minister said a bunch of stuff, none of which she heard or cared about. She repeated the words she was told to say, but the significance of what she said was as meaningful as used staples. She was truly going through the motions. At one point, she noticed that Dan was crying, and it startled her. *Wow,* she thought, *he seems really moved.* In stark contrast, her detachment was disquieting—and a revelation. *And I feel . . . blank.* She forced a smile. The minister pronounced them husband and wife, and at that moment, she couldn't deny how hollow she felt. When they shared their first wedded kiss, her lips were taut with resignation.

CHAPTER 24

"WOW, THAT DRESS," DAN said the first moment they had alone after the ceremony. He looked her up and down with a hint of a scowl.

"Do you like it?" she asked, spinning around.

"Well . . ." he wavered. "It's not what I imagined."

"What did you imagine?" *He doesn't like my fucking dress.* Her button was instantly pushed.

"I don't know. Something a little less revealing."

"Like a raincoat?"

"You don't have to be like that."

"I thought you'd like my dress."

"I don't know. It just looks kinda cheap."

"Well, it wasn't cheap. It's the most expensive thing I've ever bought."

"I didn't mean that kind of cheap."

She felt a combination of feral and hurt. *He just can't help himself. He has to be an asshat.*

The photographer approached them sporting a big grin. *Great,* she thought, *time for pictures.*

"What a handsome couple," the photographer said with grand flair. He held up his camera and said, "You're gonna absolutely love these pictures." He gave Charlie the once-over. "And that dress." He shook his head. "It's stunning. It has to be one of the most sophisticated wedding dresses I've ever seen. Absolutely stunning."

I could kiss you, photographer man! Charlie felt triumphant—a rare sensation around Dan.

"Doesn't she look amazing?" Dan said. "I've never seen her look more beautiful."

Charlie's glare was arctic.

"What a sweet husband you are," said the photographer. "Despite what most people think, not all gay men have an eye for fashion." He winked at Dan. "But I know what I'm talking about. Now, let's take some more pictures while the light's good."

I love this guy. Charlie suddenly wanted to go to Hawaii with the photographer instead of Dan.

CHAPTER 25

THE FIRST THING THAT struck Charlie when she stepped off the plane in Kona was the smell. The air was so pure and so sweet, she felt native Hawaiians would be completely justified in charging tourists a fee for the privilege to breathe it. As soon as her feet touched Hawaiian soil, all the layers of stress and exhaustion that had accumulated over the past several months melted away. Even though it was almost midnight and she'd just spent a million hours on a plane, she was wired and wide-eyed with excitement. Charlie was finally in Hawaii. Ever since she was a little girl and her great uncle Jeremy projected the postcard-like slides from his exotic Big Island vacation on their living room wall, she'd been determined to experience the breathtaking paradise herself.

"This place is a dump," Dan said, setting his golf club travel bag against the dresser in their *Leave It to Beaver*-era hotel room.

Charlie's heart sank, and then she was pissed. She'd made all the plans for their honeymoon and was over the moon when she'd found a quaint hotel right on the water for under three hundred dollars a night. Most hotels she'd researched were quadruple that in price. She'd figured, since they wouldn't be spending much time here, it didn't make sense to spend a lot of money. Plus, she didn't care in the least that it was low budget. It was *right on the ocean*. And the mid-century decor reminded her of her grandparents.

She cupped her hands on the sliding glass door to see how close the ocean was, but with the light behind her, the view was an inky black void. She pulled the door open, and the roar of the ocean filled the room. The waves had to be inches away. The soothing sound made her heart sing and quelled her anger.

"If we keep this door open," she said with an air of certainty, "I bet you'll get the best sleep of your life."

"I'm so tired I could sleep at a daycare center during a Tinkertoy war," he said dismissively.

He walked to the open door and peered out. "They probably don't have a golf course either."

Charlie's expression dropped, and her eyes filled. Dan noticed and grabbed her. "I'm sorry, Charlotte honey. I'm overtired and maybe a little cranky."

"Maybe?" she said, trying to lighten things up.

"Alright. Alright. You win. I'm cranky."

When Dan turned the light off to sleep, Charlie let herself be lulled by the sound of the waves. Her breathing slowed, and the restless static edge she felt from being overtired began to soften. In that moment, she felt the most tranquil she'd felt in months. Maybe years. She smiled, knowing that she'd wake up in paradise.

CHAPTER 26

"MRS. MALLOY," HE WHISPERED.

She felt his warm breath on her ear, but kept her eyes closed and didn't move. She didn't want the most delicious night of sleep in the history of the universe to end. No nightmares. No rabid ravens. She had a faint recollection of dreaming of a large bird, maybe a hawk or an eagle, gliding in big lazy circles high in a cloudless sky. That must be what freedom feels like, she thought.

"Earth to Mrs. Malloy," he said in a playful voice. "Are you awake?"

She smiled, but kept her eyes closed. "Is your mother here?"

"My mother?" He sounded confused. "Oh!" He wrapped his arm around her and pulled her close so her back was against him. "I was refer-ring to my beautiful wife," he said with a breathy growl. Her eyes popped open when she felt his erection.

"Maybe I should leave before she gets back," she teased. Kind of. She was Dan's wife. It hit her in a way that surprised her. Newlywed jitters?

"I heard you were a little under the weather," he whispered and rubbed himself against her. "Let me take your temperature."

This was new. And gross. She was glad he couldn't see her face.

"Wow, Doctor Dan," she said, trying to play along. "Have you been saving your nasty side for marriage?"

She felt as though she'd been transported to the set of a 1980s porn movie and wouldn't have been at all surprised if, at that moment, a heavily mustachioed pizza delivery guy wearing nothing but a pair of tiny red running shorts knocked on their hotel room door. She managed to hide her repulsion by pulling Dan on top of her and gluing her mouth to his, effectively preventing him from uttering another word.

CHAPTER 27

AFTER A PINEAPPLE-LADEN BRUNCH, Dan and Charlie decided to part ways for the afternoon. Dan headed to a golf course at a nearby resort, and Charlie walked over to the beach. She couldn't stop smiling. Everywhere her eyes landed was lush and vibrant, a breathtaking feast for her senses. She felt an expansive sense of possibility. *Is this what happiness feels like?*

She settled on her beach towel, the sand beneath shifting to create the perfect nest of warmth for her body. *I could live here.* At that moment, she was certain Dan would feel the same way. How could he not? *We could start over. He'll sell real estate. I'll manage his office. He could probably convince Milo and Ginger to come too. We can grow pineapples and papayas. And go to the beach. Every. Day.*

Her breathing entrained to the rhythm of the waves, and she slipped into the space between sleep and wakefulness. In the distance, she heard the sound of a raven. It seemed to be calling her name with its deep, throaty voice. *Char-lotte. Char-lotte.* Her pulse quickened, and the memory of the raven staring down at her, its black beak glistening with her blood, invaded her calm. *Nope, not today,* she told the memory. *I'm on vacation.*

She focused on the sensations around her—crashing waves, the soft, warm breeze, the heat of the sun—until her body relaxed again. When she was on the brink of falling into a deep valley of quiet serenity, her head filled with a loud rushing sound, as if the blood traveling through her veins was amplified and reverberating in her skull. Thick, root-like tendrils crawled out of the sand and slithered over her skin, wrapping themselves around her limbs like boa constrictors, pinning her body to the ground. *No, no, no,* she pleaded as the tendrils pulled her body down into thick, loamy darkness. The blackness was so dense, she no longer knew up from down, right from left. The only sound was the heavy thud of her heartbeat against her eardrums. In a moment of crushing clarity, she knew she was dying.

Mama? she called out. *Please help me.* But no one answered, and she realized it was silly to think anyone would. The walls of isolation closed in on her as she waited for the end. Heavy sadness and painful regret swallowed her heart.

Far, far in the distance, she heard the raven's call again and understood that the raven in her dreams was foreshadowing her death, but she was too thick-headed to understand. Her grim thoughts were interrupted by a strange pressure that enveloped her body, like she was being squeezed through a tube of toothpaste.

This is it, she thought. *It'll be over soon.*

When she didn't think she could take it anymore, it stopped. The crushing pressure released her, and she could breathe again. She slowly wiggled her fingers and toes. The sensation filled her with exhilaration. *I still exist!* She was startled to hear songbirds and realized she could feel a soft breeze kiss her skin. When she slowly opened her eyes, she gasped. Above her was a canopy of foliage in shades of green she'd never seen before, sparkling like gemstones against a rich, creamy, blue-violet sky. She knew she was in an extraordinary and ancient place. And she knew she'd been here before.

SEATED ON A LARGE, rounded stone is a man reading a newspaper. He's dressed formally in a nicely tailored black suit. The cuffs of his crisp white shirt poke out from the ends of his jacket sleeves. He must have felt her staring because he lowers the newspaper and stares back. She gasps and does a double take. He has the head of a hawk. He carefully folds the newspaper and tucks it under his arm. He adjusts his tie, which she notices has the familiar nautilus spiral pattern the raven wore, and stands to address her. "You made it," he says. He has a British accent, which, for some reason, is the least strange part of this whole experience.

"I'm dead, aren't I?" she asks.

He shakes his head. "No, you're very much alive."

"But—" She's distracted by loud rustling in a thick patch of shimmering eggplant-colored ferns.

"Ah," he says, "that must be Syd."

The large leaves separate and out steps a petite but similarly dressed hybrid creature, only this one has the head of a fox.

"You're here!" Syd exclaims, also with a British accent, excited and a bit out of breath. Charlie mentally course-corrects when she realizes Syd is female.

"Shall we get going?" Syd says.

The hawk-man holds up a hand. "Charlie just got here," he says to Syd. "I haven't even had a chance to introduce myself." He turns to Charlie. "This must all be a bit overwhelming."

Charlie nods robotically. "Yeah, you could say that." Her eyes travel from him to Syd and back to him again. "What are you?"

"The important thing to know is that we're your friends and we're here to help you," he explains. "You can call me Lou."

"But you have animal heads."

"Yes," Syd says, "but we have human bodies." She holds up her slender hands to demonstrate. "We thought it'd make you more comfortable."

"Yeah, that was a good call," Charlie says. "And the Tarantino suits. They definitely make this less weird." *Next stop, loony bin!*

"You told me they were Brooks Brothers," Syd says to Lou, who just shakes his head. "Lou thought they'd make us look polished. Or was it professional?"

"Professional," Charlie says. "Right." She decides to play along. "What are you helping me with?"

Syd starts to speak, but Lou cuts her off with a death stare. "I'm sorry. We're not at liberty to tell you," he says. "But we can take you to the one who can."

Wait. What? Charlie feels like she's the guest of honor at a stranger's surprise birthday party.

Syd leads the way down a well-worn footpath.

"Shall we?" Lou says. He gestures with his hand, like an uptight host at a fancy restaurant, in the direction of a footpath.

Charlie shrugs and follows.

Syd scans the vibrant, primitive forest terrain like a meerkat. Every once in a while, she stops and sniffs the air before bounding off into the foliage to investigate. *She's like a well-dressed cat-puppy,* Charlie muses. *I seem to be acclimating mighty quickly to this very strange hallucination. I doubt that's a good thing.*

"So," Charlie says to Lou, breaking the I'm-losing-touch-with-reality train of thought her brain was determined to explore, "you're both from the UK?"

He stops and turns to her with a genuinely perplexed look on his bird face.

"Your accents?" she clarifies.

Syd pops out of a nearby bush long enough to say, "Lou said we'd sound more elegant if we talked like this," before bounding back into the forest.

Lou nods as if to say "That's correct," and continues walking.

His voice certainly does seem to soften the intensity of his raptor gaze, she thinks. "Don't want to be a pain in the ass," Charlie says, "but how long until we get to where we're going?"

"Hard to say," Lou responds. "It seems that time doesn't exist here in the way you're familiar with."

"Oh." She ponders on that one for a bit before asking, "And where's here?"

"I have a distant memory that maybe this place is referred to as the Dreaming Realm," Syd says.

"You don't sound too sure."

"We're fairly new here too," Lou adds. "Although I can't tell you how long we've been here."

"Because there's no time."

"Precisely."

The increasingly familiar claustrophobic heaviness tightens her chest when she realizes she may never be able to go home again. That she may be trapped inside this crazy hallucination—dream—whatever it is.

Charlie almost trips over Syd, who appears from out of nowhere and, with an impressive amount of flair, juggles three acorns the size of lemons and concludes by catching them all in one hand behind her back. She takes a Shakespearean bow before disappearing again. Charlie can't help but laugh. *Mental breakdown averted. Thanks, Syd.* The timing of Syd's circus intervention makes Charlie wonder if she can somehow read her thoughts.

At that moment, Syd pokes her head out of a patch of giant, waxy, indigo leaves, flashes her intimidating fangs in a vicious grin, and disappears again.

She's definitely reading my thoughts. That's creepy. She cringes. *Sorry, Syd.*

Syd pops out from behind a nearby tree and gives her a thumbs-up.

Charlie hears a distant rumbling, like the discordant sound of thousands of manic voices. It doesn't belong in this serene place. Farther down the trail, the dense forest opens up, revealing that they're walking alongside a deep valley. The dissonant rumbling is hard to ignore now. Charlie turns to the source of the sound and does a double take. Swallowing the valley and sky is a dull sheen. It's the Dreaming Realm, but not the Dreaming Realm. She squints and sees a blurry reflection of herself and her companions in the distance, as if she's looking in an immense oil-coated mirror.

It's gotten worse. She absently grips her face with her hand. *How do I know that?*

"I don't understand," she whispers, her voice halting and shaky. She stares at the distortion like it's a ghost. "I've never been to this place before." Her hand covers her mouth. "Have I?"

Lou places a hand on her shoulder.

"Is it some kind of storm?" she asks. "It looks wrong."

"It's a different realm," Syd says.

Lou's raptor eyes issue Syd a warning.

She ignores it. "She can handle it." Syd looks up at Charlie. "It's the Mental Realm."

Charlie's expression falls flat. Too much strangeness for one day. "The Mental Realm."

Lou shakes his head at Syd as if to say, *way to go.* He turns to Charlie and tries his best to clean up Syd's mess. "It's a different reality populated by the contents of every human mind," he says. "The archive of human thought."

Charlie can't wrap her head around the concept. "You're telling me that—" she points to the Mental Realm "—my mind is in there?"

They both nod.

She points to her head. "Then what's in here?"

"Your brain," Lou says.

He watches her struggle to understand.

"Is this what it's like to lose your mind?" she asks.

Her earnestness softens him. "No, no, not at all. Your mind is fine. It's just a lot to take in." He glares at Syd. "See what you've done?"

"If it's any consolation," Syd says with a savage grin. "It appears as though the entire human race has lost its mind."

Lou releases a frustrated breath. "Maybe not say everything that enters your mind?"

Syd cocks her head. "She's waiting for us. We should get going."

Charlie almost asks who Syd's talking about but decides to keep her mouth shut this time. She focuses on the rhythm of her breath as they continue down the path. Three steps per inhale, three steps per exhale, just like her mother taught her. After a while, she calms down.

Lou stops and cranes his neck to the sky. Charlie's eyes follow and take in the outermost branches of the largest, most beautiful tree she's ever seen. It looks a hundred times taller than the surrounding trees. The deep burgundy leaves shimmer as if someone painted them with pixie dust.

"The First Tree," Lou says. "We're almost there."

When they reach the base of the enormous tree, a mass of color fills Charlie's visual field with dappled shades of turquoise and blue, dwarfing the tree's trunk. She tries unsuccessfully to make sense of what she's seeing. The three-dimensional canvas seems alive. *Is it moving or is it my imagination?*

In slow motion, a colossal, similarly colored hand, which could comfortably hold King Kong in its clutches, appears in the foreground and moves toward her. The moment the enormous pointer finger makes gentle contact with the side of her head, she feels a whooshing sensation that leaves her a bit dizzy. When the spinning settles, she risks opening her eyes and sees that the canvas of colors has shrunk into the shape of a regular-sized, very pregnant-looking woman whose smiling sea-glass gaze instantly puts Charlie at ease. Her thick, twisting dreadlocks weave in and out of the ground like tree roots in every direction as far as the eye can see. *She looks like the Earth from space.*

"Welcome home, Little Bird," the woman says.

The sound of the woman's warm caramel voice wraps around her like a comforting balm. So familiar. Her body buzzes with clashing waves of doubt and certainty.

"Charlie," Lou says, breaking the spell, "this is the First Mother of the Dreaming Realm."

"Hello," Charlie whispers. All at once, everything is hyper-real and alive and somehow feels normal in a way that's not coherent and is disorienting. She also senses the presence of others, hidden eyes watching her from the sparkling, richly colored foliage of the surrounding forest.

First Mother opens her arms. Without thinking, Charlie moves into them and is instantly wrapped in a love so full and so rich it could sustain every creature that ever existed or ever will exist until the end of time. She exhales into the embrace.

"I don't understand what's happening to me," Charlie says through tears.

She can feel First Mother's smile.

"This must be . . ." First Mother pauses, searching for the right word, "confusing."

Charlie reluctantly pulls away from First Mother's embrace. She wipes her tears and nods. "I have the craziest dreams in human history." Charlie references the surrounding environment as proof.

First Mother chuckles. "It's been a long time since we've seen each other. Are you enjoying your life, Little Bird?"

Charlie gives her head a clearing shake. *Wait.* No clear memory, but a distinct sense of déjà vu hits her like an elevator drop. Syd grabs her hand and gives a reassuring squeeze.

"I'm sorry. What was the question?" she asks.

Syd whispers, "Enjoying life?"

"Oh. Yeah. My life. Yeah. Yes, I have a great job. I just got married to the love of my life. We have a roof over our heads. I'm healthy." She pauses and smirks. "At least I thought I was until these dreams started happening."

First Mother looks into Charlie's eyes. A subtle change in her expression suggests she's seeing something unsettling.

"I've never been to this place before?" Charlie asks, her hands gripping her jaw. "Have I?"

First Mother takes her hands and wraps them in her own. "It's been a very long time."

"How can that—" Charlie's eyes are wild and her thoughts spin, unsuccessfully looking for purchase, something to ground her.

"It's all right, Little Bird." Her smile is bright and reassuring. Her eyes drop to Charlie's chest. "Ah. There," she says after a few moments. "I can see why coming here has been so difficult for you."

First Mother's gaze is too penetrating. Charlie wants to curl into a small ball and roll far, far away.

She holds Charlie's hands in hers. "You're a stranger."

Charlie squints. "But I thought you said I've been here before?"

"You're not a stranger to me or to this place."

Charlie's brow furrows.

"You're a stranger to yourself."

The veracity of First Mother's words tilts Charlie's interior world.

"My heart breaks for you, Little Bird," she continues, her piercing gaze locking with Charlie's. "It seems you're so lost, you don't realize you're missing out on all the joys of being deeply human." Her eyes glisten, and her voice cracks with naked sorrow. "It's as if you're a husk of yourself pretending to live and love and enjoy."

First Mother cups her hand under Charlie's chin. "Thinking your way through life gives you the illusion that you can control it. But thoughts are not always trustworthy."

Charlie's throat tightens. Her first instinct is to run, but First Mother's words fill her with longing. The stiff yet sturdy structure of her routine runs through her mind: Wake up, shower, drive to work, sit at the front desk, answer phones, go home, make dinner—rinse and repeat. But then, sparks of color burst through the gray. Driving a little too fast while listening to her favorite bands at chest-rattling volume, pushing her body at kung fu, trying not to get hit or swept, laughing with Ginger . . . Goatman.

First Mother smiles and nods. "You must have unfulfilled dreams, adventures that will enrich your human experience?"

"I want to learn how to ride a motorcycle," Charlie says.

"What keeps you from doing that?"

She's embarrassed to say it out loud but suspects she can't really hide anything from First Mother. "My fiancé—I mean my, um, husband says it's too dangerous."

"What does his opinion have to do with it?"

That stops her cold. Is she using Dan as an excuse? Why doesn't she just pursue her dreams? And then it hits her. "I'm afraid to upset him."

The compassion in First Mother's gaze is too much. Charlie turns away.

"This life has been so hard on you, Little Bird," she tells her. "Fear takes over when you feel powerless."

Powerless. Is that how I feel?

"It's time to get your power back, yes?"

The thought of feeling powerful is all at once intriguing and terrifying. She tentatively nods.

"Well, then it's time for a reunion," First Mother concludes.

"I'm not sure I know what you mean."

Instead of answering, First Mother holds Charlie's face in her hands.

Charlie's confused at first, but then she points at herself with a question mark in her eyes. First Mother laughs.

The weight of the concept is like a wet blanket. "How do I reunite with myself?"

First Mother places her hand on Charlie's sternum. "Your heart never lies, Little Bird. Think of it as a trusted friend who will always lead you where you need to go."

First Mother presses a kiss on the top of her head before pulling back. "We'll help you in whatever way we can, Rah-hīnah, but this is your journey."

As if on cue, the raven from her dreams descends in front of her and spreads his enormous wings until she sees only black and her head fills with the familiar sound of rushing blood.

A FLOOD OF SENSATIONS, distant at first, seeped into her awareness. The acrid smell of sunbaked skin mixed with warm, briny air; the pounding of waves and the joyful screeches of nearby children were topped off with a serving of queasiness from being overheated. She took a deep, reorienting breath. The ocean breeze left a cool trail where her tears fell. She could still feel the warmth of First Mother's hand on her heart.

CHAPTER 28

CHARLIE VENTURED OUT ON her own after their plans to visit Volcanoes National Park were thwarted due to "atypical volcanic activity." When they'd reached the park entrance to find it closed, Dan's "Oh no! What a bummer" response clashed mightily with his barely contained *I can't believe my luck* smile. At least he waited until they got back to their hotel before announcing that he "might as well go golfing because, you know, the beach isn't really my thing." *Shocking.*

"Best game ever!!" he'd declared when he got back from golfing the day before, lifting her in a dramatic, twirling hug. "Next time, we're staying at the resort. I don't care how much it costs. It's beautiful! You'll love it!" She was relieved he was enjoying himself, even if it meant they wouldn't be spending much time together on their honeymoon.

She'd given golf a good college try early in their relationship, but all the "valuable golf pro tips" Dan gave her left her wanting to stab his judgy, impatient eyes with the little yellow scorekeeping pencil he kept tucked behind his ear. She'd suggested that maybe golf should be his thing and martial arts could be hers. Turns out, he was fine with that.

While Dan did his thing, Charlie took herself on a tour of a few of the many non-volcano parks that dotted the west coast of the Big Island. She was actually glad she was alone since her emotions were a bit jagged and close to the surface after yesterday's weird dream experience.

She blinked back unexpected tears as she explored the lonely ruins of an ancient fishing village at her final destination of the day. The site thrummed with layers of heavy totemic loss that made her heart hurt. She eventually parked herself on an old, hand-hewn log bench overlooking the sea and mindlessly pecked at the sandwich she'd picked up at a deli along the way.

She was transfixed by the clear, deep turquoise of the Hawaiian sea. The color brought First Mother to mind. As much as she tried to put yesterday's experience behind her, she couldn't. It was too real, almost hyper-real, similar to when the raven ripped the amber pendant from her throat. Her typical dreams, especially the ones where she was choking, were chaotic and confusing. Yesterday's experience though—the interactions she'd had, the continuity of events, the feelings evoked—felt like it was actually happening. Just, somewhere else. Somewhere that was somehow familiar.

A speck of fire-engine red darted past her with a low buzz. She stopped mid-chew to figure out what the hell it was. The buzzing registered before her eyes could lock in on its source, which flew in erratic patterns that were hard to follow. When her eyes finally caught up with it, she realized it was a large dragonfly.

"Dat dragon don't belong here," said a soft male voice.

Charlie turned to see a barefoot, silver-haired, scraggly-bearded Hawaiian man dressed in a colorful aloha shirt and long boardshorts pointing at the dragonfly. His face was kind.

"Dem dragons stay inland, by da freshwater or high-yup." He gestured toward the volcanic mountains towering behind them. He stepped closer with a slight limp. "But dat dere, dats a special dragon. Dats da goddess Pele come t'visit ya."

He gestured to the bench, and she invited him to sit. Together they tracked the dragonfly's erratic movements without speaking.

"You know what Pele want witchu?"

His genuine curiosity made her smile. She liked this man.

"I have no idea."

"I tell you what. She see right into da heart." He patted his chest. "All da pain. She bring it right up to da surface, like a special kinda bird'day gift." He paused to look at her. An impish smile lit up his bronzed face. "So you can heal dat pain and become da warrior."

She smirked. "You think Pele'd let me skip right to the warrior part?"

He squinted. "Whatchu so afraid of, keiki? You know da pain. It live in you for a long, long time, like an ol' friend." He patted her knee and looked out at the sea. "You be all good soon a'nuff."

The dragonfly seemed to stop midair in front of them before soaring upward and out of sight. Charlie turned to the old man, but the bench was empty.

CHAPTER 29

"SHE HAS THE SICKNESS," First Mother says to Ahna and Ahkoa, her voice quiet and flat.

Ahna glances at Ahkoa, who avoids her gaze. He takes a stoic breath.

"Is it too late?" Ahna asks.

First Mother hesitates, her expression somber. The rich, steadfast sky, the color of blue morning glories, darkens in response, unsettling Ahna and Ahkoa.

"We have to hope that it's not." She manages to smile, and the sky brightens once again. "She's lost much of her essence, which is likely what made her vulnerable to the virus. Any lingering energy she has is devoted to keeping her human pain at bay." Her sea-glass eyes fill. "My Little Bird. She's suffering." First Mother takes a moment. "I'm afraid we can't talk to her about who she really is until she's whole again."

She turns to Ahna. "You've found someone to help her when the time is right?"

"It's too soon to tell, but I believe I've found someone close to her age whose dreaming is surprisingly vibrant and untainted. I've been slowly steering his dreams in Charlie's direction, but I'm hesitant to say more until she's healed enough to make it possible for me to link them directly." She glances at Ahkoa, whose relief is palpable.

"He sounds like a special young man," First Mother says with a warm indigo smile. She turns to Ahkoa. "Help my Little Bird find her essence, what she's lost, and then please bring her back to me."

He dips his head.

CHAPTER 30

CHARLIE FLOATED THROUGH THE next several days with hazy, detached awareness, not sure if she was dreaming or if she had completely lost her mind. Every so often, Dan would give her a curious look, but he never said anything. She tried to imagine how she must seem to him. Aloof? Maybe. Nuts? Possibly. When she interacted with him, she thought she was coming across as normal, but it was like she were observing herself from a few feet away, and that sensation was just plain weird.

On the final day of their honeymoon, she wandered alone around a quaint coastal town looking for little mementos to bring home as gifts. She sucked down a delicious iced chai latte, hoping the caffeine would make her misty state a little less misty. Wishful thinking.

She startled when a passing driver tapped their horn and mechanically glanced over her shoulder as if the greeting were meant for her. She stopped dead in her tracks when she saw a large orange-and-white spiral nautilus shell decorating the window of a small tattoo shop across the street. Without a thought, she crossed the street and went inside.

The young guy at the front desk was shoulder-deep in his phone, gnawing away at a large wad of blue gum like his life depended on it. When he finally noticed her, he pulled out an earbud and raised his eyebrows.

"I'd like to get a tattoo," she told him. She listened to herself from that detached place. "Is that possible?"

There were two stations in the shop. One contained a well-muscled white guy, who looked like he was trying not to cry, getting a tribal band around his beefy bicep. The other chair was empty.

"Let me check." He sauntered through the shop to a curtained doorway in the back.

A few minutes later, a striking young woman with glowing, tawny skin covered with an eclectic and tasteful tapestry of colorful art appeared and headed toward Charlie. When their eyes met, the woman smiled broadly as if they were old friends.

"Aloha," she said. "You'd like some ink?"

Tension Charlie didn't know she was carrying released from her shoulders.

"Yeah, I would." She pointed to the window. "Can I get that design?"

"I don't see why not? Do you know where you want me to put it?"

Again without thinking, Charlie flipped her left hand over and pointed to the inside of her wrist.

The woman nodded. "Your timing is perfect. My afternoon appointment flaked. You wanna do this now?"

Charlie's rebellious grin said it all.

The woman held out her hand. "I'm Luna."

She shook her hand. "Charlie."

Since it was a simple design, Luna drew it freehand directly on her wrist.

"You here on vacation?"

"Yeah, leaving tomorrow."

"Where's home?"

"Phoenix."

"Desert rat."

"Pretty much."

She caught her own reflection in the mirror and saw a familiar stranger sitting across from her acting like everything that was happening was perfectly normal. And then it hit her. She had been abducted by aliens, and she was now an alien pod person. She snickered.

"This must be your first tattoo," Luna said, with a side-eye.

"That obvious?"

"You sure you wanna do this?"

Charlie looked at the drawing on her wrist. "Definitely."

Luna gave her an *atta girl* smile.

"It's been a strange week," she blurted.

"Ooh, I love strange!" Luna capped her pen and examined the drawing. "What do you think? Is this what you had in mind?"

Charlie nodded. *I'm actually going to do this.*

"It's gonna hurt. But it won't take too long."

Luna artfully wrapped her messy, long, dark curls in a white bandana that she tied in a knot at the top of her head, Rosie the Riveter style, before firing up the tattoo gun.

The moment the angry little cluster of needles hit her skin, the alien that she suspected had taken over her body promptly checked out and the real Charlie checked back in.

Luna glanced up. "Remember to breathe."

"Oh, yeah," she hissed. "Good idea."

"Tell me about strange," Luna said.

The words spilled out. "Earlier this week, I had a dream that wasn't a dream but was a dream, and then a few days ago I had a conversation with an old Hawaiian man who wasn't there."

Luna didn't bat an eye. "That's cool strange," she said. "Sounds like the swamp stories I heard growing up."

"There a lot of swamps in Hawaii?"

Luna laughed and shrugged. "I'm not from Hawaii. Born and raised in New Orleans." She pronounced it Nawlins. "My mama's Haitian and my asshole daddy—may he rot in hell—was Scottish."

Charlie's eyes widened, which made Luna laugh even harder.

"I might be a little bitter," she said. "I'm working on it."

Charlie turned her gaze to the pinup mermaid posing seductively on Luna's bicep. "Your tattoos are beautiful."

The miniature, bare-breasted enchantress looked over her shoulder at Charlie as if beckoning her to see the tiny impaled heart decorating her lower back where emerald scales met human flesh. A tattoo with a tattoo.

"Every new place I land, I get a tattoo that captures my vibe at that time." She noticed which one Charlie was looking at. "I got that one in San Diego." Her jaw hardened. "Motherfucker broke my heart."

"You surf?" Charlie referenced a stylized surfboard on Luna's opposite forearm. The phrase "Chance@Love" was written in script over it.

"Oh, hell no!" She shook her head as if she'd just bitten into a lemon wedge. "I have a healthy respect for the ocean. And by respect, I mean I stay the fuck out."

Charlie's brow furrowed.

"Saw a guy drown when I was a kid."

"Oh, shit."

"*Chance at Love* is the title of a series of not-at-all-autobiographical sexy books I wrote a couple years back," she said with a sly smile. "It's a good title, right?"

"You're an author?"

"Not a really successful one."

Charlie was intrigued. "What are they about?" She could tell Luna was happy she asked.

"There was this mysterious surfer guy. Goddamn, he was juicy." She closed her eyes and took a moment. "He shows up outta nowhere and rocks my world for four of the best days of my life. He was my muse. Before I knew it, I'd written three books." She squinted. "You know, you actually remind me of one of my former lovers. She's the star of the second book. She was gorgeous too."

Charlie's face flushed.

Luna grabbed a business card off her stand and gave it to her. "I probably shoulda used a pen name, but if you need something to read on the plane ride home, you can look me up on the evil empire known as Amazon."

It read: "Luna Mitchell, Wandering Gypsy Burlesque & Tattoos."

Luna was by far the most captivating person Charlie had ever met. She wished she lived in Phoenix so they could hang out. "Gypsy, eh? Sounds like a fun way to live. How long are you staying on the Big Island?"

"About another month, and then I head to the Big Apple. Gonna do a little soul searching."

"Hmmm. Soul searching in a giant city. Seems . . . challenging."

"The place I'm going to is cool as hell. It was created by this reclusive, giant-brained tech guy," she said, getting animated. "He's like a mystic who's figured some shit out and is sharing what he's learned." She stopped tattooing. "So, get this. It's all virtual. And the whole point is that you can be whoever you want!"

"Like a video game?"

"This is no game. You live there. It's a community. A bunch of lost souls under the same roof, living in virtual reality, striving for the same goal."

Lost souls. Charlie's breath caught. *I'm empty.* She felt First Mother's warm hand on her heart. She swallowed the memory. "What's the goal?"

"You gotta lose yourself in order to find yourself."

"You don't strike me as someone who's lost."

"Looks can be deceiving. My medicine cabinet and the shrink who fills it tell a different story."

Charlie nodded and swallowed hard. "So, you're going to do some soul searching in virtual reality. Sounds intense."

"I think I need intense. Lord knows, therapy hasn't worked."

Charlie laughed. "I hear that."

"You should come." Luna was serious.

"Me?" She got flustered. "I—ah—I can't leave Phoenix." Goatman, not Dan, popped into her head. "I've got a job. And . . . and I just got married."

"You're on your honeymoon? Whaddaya doing here, girl? Why aren't you on some secluded beach screwing your brains out?"

Charlie's face reddened.

"That was rude. I'm sorry."

She shrugged it off and tried to smile. "He's in golfing heaven."

"My condolences." Luna turned the tattoo gun off and did a final wipe of Charlie's wrist. "So, what do you think?"

The finished design was intricate, almost three-dimensional. Instead of black and gray, it was an earthy blend of browns and tans, with a hint of orange that perfectly suited her olive skin. Charlie thought it looked like an innate part of her, like it had always been there.

"I love it," she whispered. If it were made of amber light, it would've looked just like the raven's pendant.

CHAPTER 31

THE MOMENT SHE STEPPED outside the airport terminal and breathed in a lungful of the familiar, arid, creosote-tinged desert air, a sour taste filled her mouth. It was similar to the letdown she'd always felt as a child after opening Christmas presents. Her lifelong dream of going to Hawaii was now in the rearview mirror. She forced a smile and followed Dan, who was still giving her the cold shoulder as he weaved his drunken way to the long-term parking garage.

When she'd gotten back to their hotel room the day before, Dan was already there. There was no greeting, no kiss hello. He pointed a stiff, angry finger at the plastic wrap taped to her wrist. "What"—he said through clenched teeth—"is that?"

"I got a tattoo!"

He shook his head and tossed his empty suitcase on the bed and started packing his stuff.

Uh-oh.

Until that moment, Dan's inevitable reaction hadn't even been a consideration. It was a splash of glacial water on her dreamy state. She pulled her suitcase out, zipped it open, but couldn't figure out what to do next. She paced in a tight circle at the foot of the hotel bed and chewed her cuticles.

She couldn't sleep. She slipped out of bed and into the tiny hotel bathroom, where she downloaded Luna's sexy e-books to read on the plane ride home. She was glad she did. It only took a couple of pages to get pulled into the story and away from Dan's gin-and-tonic mood and his imposing wall of silence, which loomed between their business class seats.

By the time they made their descent into Phoenix, she'd devoured all three novellas, had a serious crush on Luna, and was feeling mighty eager to see Goatman.

CHAPTER 32

"Aren't you full of surprises," Goatman said, holding her tattooed wrist in his hand.

"You didn't think I was the tattoo type?" She ran her fingers over the healing skin and grazed his fingers.

He shook his head. "It suits you. I like it."

God, I want to fucking tear you apart.

He let her wrist drop. "Let's do some push-ups."

"Only if you're on top of me," she whispered.

His eyebrows shot up. "Didn't you get your honeymoon fill?"

She shrugged with a coy smile.

He turned and closed the door to the padded room, and her pulse raced.

When he faced her, she reached out, and he looked at her hand. "What are you doing, Charlie?"

She frowned. He never called her Charlie. She dropped her hand to her side.

"You just got married."

"I . . . I guess I missed you."

"Missed me?" He looked incredulous. "We're not in a relationship. You know that, right?"

Her mouth opened, but no words came out.

"I mean, it was fun messing around with you. You're really sexy and sweet." He shook his head. "Shit, I thought you were just sowing a few oats before taking the plunge."

A wave of nausea hit Charlie. *I'm such a fool.* "I'm sorry," she said. "I don't know what I was thinking."

"It's alright," he said. "I know I'm an asshole, but I'm not that kind of asshole. I don't sleep with married women."

Married women. *I'm a married woman.* The reality of it punched her in the gut once again.

"You look a little green, Chuck."

She took a shaky breath. "Embarrassment makes me turn green."

"Nothing to be embarrassed about." He winked and smiled. "I'm irresistible."

Her laugh sounded like a chirp. "An irresistible asshole."

"I should put that on my business card. Alright," he said, facing her. "Fifty cat-style push-ups."

The distance between them was cavernous.

CHAPTER 33

DAN, ALL SMILES, FACES Charlie. He reaches out and clasps her hands in his. It's their wedding day. They're crammed in a narrow, dimly lit, wood-paneled hallway. There are cobwebs everywhere. The minister is in a hurry because he's worried about the snakes. Dan doesn't seem to care, but Charlie panics. She follows the minister's gaze and sees three black-and-gold cobras gliding toward them. She wants to run away, but her feet are stuck to the floor. In unison, the hooded heads of the snakes rise off the floor until they're looking straight into her eyes. She's alone now. The snakes open their jaws and release the discordant sound of thousands of unintelligible voices. They veer back and spit not venom but a silvery, viscous substance into her mouth. She tries not to swallow, but it doesn't matter. The caustic, industrial-tasting denseness fills her throat while the chaotic tangle of voices consumes her and reverberates in her skull. For minutes, hours, days she ceases to exist.

HER DREAMING SELF UNDERSTOOD what insanity truly was, and that this contamination was now inside her.

CHAPTER 34

CHARLIE SAT ON THE toilet seat lid in her usual stall and stared at the black scuff mark on the gray metal stall door. Nothing made sense. Nothing brought her solace. All she wanted was for everything to go back to normal. Back to the time when her mundane routine gave her a reassuring kind of comfort, no surprises. Back to the time when Goatman wanted to be close to her. Just the illusion that if she followed the rules, everything would be okay. She was swimming in gray. No, actually, she was drowning in it.

She didn't want to go back out there and pretend she gave a shit. And she longed in the fiercest way to give a shit. She shook her head, trying to break up the lumps of hopelessness that found a home there. A low, gurgling croak purred in her ears and made the hairs on her arm stand. The raven.

"No," she commanded. This bullshit stopped now. No more. She stood, flung the stall door open, marched to the sink, and turned on the faucet. She splashed ice-cold water on her face and stared at her dripping reflection as if she were about to throttle it. And there it was. The raven stared back at her and cocked its head, egging her on.

Her fingers gripped the edges of the sink. She stared right back and bared her clenched teeth. "Leave. Me. The fuck. Alone." And just like that, it was gone.

"Is everything all right?" a timid voice called out.

Charlie turned and found her coworker Brenda peeking through the partially open bathroom door. She cleared her throat and nodded.

"Mr. Malloy's looking for you."

CHAPTER 35

"YOU OKAY?" GINGER ASKED.

Charlie's eyebrows rose over the rim of the coffee she was nursing.

"I mean, I thought you'd be all glowy."

"Glowy?"

"Yeah, honeymoon glowy."

"I'm glowy."

"No, not really." Ginger squinted and further assessed her. "You seem kinda sad. I mean, more sad than usual."

Charlie swallowed hard and put her coffee down. "Than usual?"

Ginger nodded.

She smiled. "I'm not sad."

"Nice try." She reached across the café table and held Charlie's hands in hers. "I'm not trying to be mean. It's just . . . I don't know. Your eyes always seem so far away. Like you're here, but you're not here."

Charlie wanted to crawl under the table. "No, really. I'm not a sad person. I have a great life."

"You can talk to me, Charlie." Ginger gave her hands a reassuring squeeze. "About anything."

Charlie wished she was anywhere else.

"You're such a good friend to me. I blather on and on about my problems to you all the time. Let me return the favor."

"I don't know what you want me to say."

"Just admit that you're sad. Cuz it's obvious. And I don't know if you got the memo, but you're allowed to be sad." She grinned. "I sound like my therapist."

Charlie's head dropped. "Alright. You win. I guess I'm a little sad."

"Good job." Ginger held her hand up mid-air.

Charlie rolled her eyes and gave her a weak high-five.

"That wasn't so bad, was it?"

"You're impossible."

"Since when does caring make someone impossible?"

Charlie opened her mouth, about to speak.

"That was a rhetorical question. You know, you should be a fucking magician. You're masterful at redirection."

This made Charlie laugh.

"Spill. What are you sad about?"

Charlie shrugged.

"No, you can't do the fourteen-year-old shrug-your-shoulders thing. What's up?"

There was no way she was going to tell Ginger what's been going on. How she somehow doesn't feel at home anywhere anymore. That she doesn't know what she's doing or who she is or what's happening to her. That the one thing that gave her peace and a sense of belonging, kung fu, has become like a bone bruise that never heals. Ever since the "I don't sleep with married women" comment, Goatman has been keeping his distance. No playful insinuations, no extended glances, no secret touches. To drive his point home, he even brought another student into their private training sessions. But the door to Goatman closed with a final deafening click a few days ago when she saw him kissing a drop-dead gorgeous woman in an unfamiliar car before class. When he got out of her car, his smile was electric. Charlie knew she was in trouble when she longed for him to smile at her like that.

She still went to class, still did her drills, still practiced her forms and went through the motions of sparring, but it was like she was going to class out of habit because she didn't know how to not go to class.

"Is it Dan?" Ginger prompted. "You guys have a fight?"

Charlie pushed up her sleeve, revealing her tattoo. She figured going down this road was the safest way to get Ginger off her back.

"Ho-lee shit." Ginger leaned forward to get a better look. "That's gorgeous." She grimaced. "He hates tattoos."

"Still not talking to me." Charlie regretted uttering the words as soon as they came out of her mouth. "It's not his fault. I should've talked to him first. I just did it on impulse when we were in Hawaii."

"Well, that's stupid. It's your body. You should be able to do whatever you want to do."

When Charlie didn't respond, Ginger pulled out her phone. "Let's figure out how to fix this." She opened an app and smiled. "Hey, Marshall!"

"Hey, sexy!" a deep male voice answered.

Charlie was mortified. She shook her head vehemently. "Please don't tell anyone else."

"It's okay," Ginger said before whispering, "He's not real." She addressed the man on the tiny screen. "I'm sorry, Marshall. That was rude."

"No worries," he said.

"Let me introduce your technologically challenged ass to the twenty-first century," she said to Charlie. "Marshall's my new twenty-four-seven personal assistant and confidant. Let me rephrase that. He's my very hot and very wise knower of all things." She showed Charlie. "I created him with this new app. Marshall is state-of-the-art AI."

"He's so . . . lifelike."

"Marshall, meet Charlie."

"Good to meet you, Charlie! Any friend of Ginger's is a friend of mine."

Charlie stared at him. He was a Greek god come to life, complete with a chiseled jaw, blue bedroom eyes, and tousled blond hair. He looked like he'd stepped off the cover of a romance novel. And he looked, sounded, and moved like a human.

"Are you shy?" he asked.

"Who, me? No. Well, maybe a little." *I'm talking to a robot.*

"Usually, when someone greets you," he teased, "you greet them back."

"Yes, of course. I'm sorry. Hi."

Ginger propped her phone up on the table so they both could see him. "Don't take it personally," she said to him. "Your stunning good looks caught Charlie off guard."

"I understand," he said, grinning. "What can I help you lovely ladies with?"

"Charlie's having a bit of marital strife. What advice do you have when your husband gives you the silent treatment?"

"How could anyone ignore a beautiful creature like you?" he asked Charlie.

"That's not helpful, Marshall," Ginger said. To Charlie, "I'm sorry. I designed him to be flirty. It's good for my self-esteem."

"Forgive me, Ginger. Let me try again. Let's see. You can do something nice for him, like prepare him a special dinner or rub his feet."

"This isn't the nineteen-fifties, Marshall," Ginger said.

"You're cute when you give me a hard time," he said. "Let me think about it a little more." His eyes shot up and to the right, as if he were actually thinking. "Experts suggest that you shouldn't assume you know the reason why your husband is upset."

"Oh, she knows why he's upset."

"It's important to give him time and space."

"How much time?" Charlie asked. "It's been a couple of weeks."

"In that case, explain to him your need and desire to communicate with him. And be ready to listen and not just talk."

"Have you tried to break the ice yet?" Ginger asked her.

"It didn't seem like the right time."

"You never know unless you try," Marshall said with a dimpled smile.

"He's great, isn't he?"

"He's definitely something."

When she got home, there was a huge bouquet of her favorite wild-flowers waiting for her on their dining room table. Dan walked up behind her and wrapped his arms around her. He pulled her in to him and kissed her neck. "Let's start a family," he breathed into her ear. Without another word, he grabbed her hand and led her to the bedroom.

She'd never been so happy to be taking birth control pills.

CHAPTER 36

A DENSE, BLACK CLOUD descends from the sky and swirls around Charlie, blotting out her vision. The cloud transforms into hundreds of bats who grab at her with their tiny razor claws; their angry teeth rip at her skin. They hungrily consume her flesh, bit by bit, until there is nothing left but her bones. Her dream self wants to follow them into the sky, not to hurt them but to thank them.

WHEN SHE WOKE, SHE felt wide awake and strangely calm. She knew what she needed to do.

CHAPTER 37

"You're back," Eve said, greeting Charlie with a warm smile and a fragrant pot of the apothecary's signature cinnamon tea.

"Thanks," Charlie said, and then winced. "That was weird. I don't know why I said thanks. It's not that I'm not thankful to be here—I mean—it's just . . . fuck. I don't know what to say. I think I'll shut up now."

Eve's laugh put her at ease. "Well, it's good to see you. I'm glad you're here."

"Me too. I think."

Eve handed her a cup of tea. Charlie closed her eyes and breathed in the homey scent.

"I have a confession," Eve said. "I wondered if I might be seeing you again."

Charlie couldn't hide her surprise.

"Of all the people I've read for over the years," she said, "you stayed with me. I have no idea why." Eve eyed Charlie, trying to solve the mystery. "There's something different about you. Can't put my finger on it."

Charlie showed her the tattoo.

"That's a powerful image. It's really beautiful. What inspired the design?"

Charlie looked at the spiral. "I don't know. It brings me comfort. I've . . . I—" She bit her lip.

"It's okay, Charlie."

Charlie's eyes filled. "I don't know who else to talk to. My therapist will think I'm crazy. And I don't know—maybe I am."

"You wouldn't believe how many times people have said that to me. But so far, I haven't heard anything that surprises me or is crazy."

"Get your diary out. I might be the first."

Eve laughed. "You're really funny."

Some of Charlie's tension eased. Her mother used to tell her the same thing.

"Why don't you tell me what's been going on."

"When Ginger brought me here for my reading—it feels like years ago now but it was only a couple of months—you told me that my life was gonna get challenging, that I was gonna be changing. You freaked me out, so I stuffed your message in a box and forgot about it. I'm good at that." She shot Eve a cheesy grin. "But it seems ever since my honeymoon, things have gotten extra weird, and your words started coming back to me, which pissed me off. I didn't want you to be right." She shared almost everything. She told Eve about her recurring nightmares, her waking dreams, the conversation she had with the imaginary Hawaiian man. When she finished, Eve didn't say anything for what seemed like an hour.

"There's so much to digest," she finally said. "I don't even know where to begin."

"Do you need to call the mobile psych unit?"

Eve's laugh filled the room. It was music to Charlie's ears.

"You're far from crazy, Charlie."

Her shoulders dropped about a foot, and she cried.

Eve reached across the table and grabbed Charlie's tear-soaked hand. "Our culture doesn't really acknowledge the kinds of experiences you're having. I totally understand why you'd be terrified to tell anyone." She gave her hand a reassuring squeeze. "I don't believe they're dreams, Charlie. I think they're visions." She gave her a moment to let the words sink in. "Reality is a lot more complicated than we know."

Charlie teetered between wanting to believe her and wanting to run out the door and drive deep into the desert until she ran out of gas.

"When I was three years old, my family fled Laos after the Vietnam War and resettled in California. My parents brought us here so we could practice our traditions without fear of persecution. We're Hmong. I was raised understanding that there are two worlds, this physical world and the unseen world. Your visions took you to the unseen world—what the hawk-man you met called the Dreaming Realm."

"So, you're saying the Dreaming Realm is real." Charlie couldn't hide her doubt.

Eve grinned. "Most indigenous cultures would say the Dreaming Realm is actually the real world, and that this physical world is the dream."

"That's crazy talk."

"But what if it's true?"

"Can't even begin to wrap my head around that one."

"I don't think these visions are going to stop."

"Fuck. So much for my next question."

"The only thing to do is to make friends with them."

"I don't even know what that means."

"Let's start with the raven."

"You want me to make friends with an imaginary raven?"

"Humor me," Eve said. "What comes to mind when you think of the raven?"

"Panic attacks."

Eve laughed. "Not a great association. Maybe we can change that. In many shamanic traditions, the raven is seen as a mystical bird who can bridge our world and the unseen world."

"Is that why it shows up at the beginning of my waking dreams?"

Eve nodded. "They're also shapeshifters."

"Are you about to tell me that comic books are nonfiction?"

"Skepticism is healthy. But how about we try a thought experiment? What if you were to pretend that the visions and everything about them are real and go from there?"

Charlie grimaced. "I'm sorry. I know I'm being a pain in the ass. I'll try it."

"Good. Now, the blue-and-turquoise-skinned woman you mentioned. My sense is she was trying to tell you something."

Charlie bit her lip. She purposely hadn't gone into much detail when telling Eve about her experience with First Mother. It was too raw, too personal.

Eve poured more tea for them both and waited.

"It was like she was looking into my heart. I felt completely naked." Her mouth was bone-dry. She took a sip of tea. "She saw my pain and told me it was time to find the part of myself that I'd lost."

"*Poob plig,*" Eve whispered. "Soul loss."

"It seemed like she wanted to tell me something important, but then she looked at me in this intense way and changed her mind."

"Maybe you have to become whole again before she can tell you."

A heaviness in her chest that she hadn't realized was there lifted. "That feels right." She placed her hand on her heart. "She told me my heart never lies and that I should trust it."

"The next time the raven shows up, listen to your heart."

CHAPTER 38

DAN WAS ALL SMILES when Charlie got home. He was also wearing a shiny purple shirt.

"You look extra happy," she said, trying to hide her suspicion. "And purple."

"It's great, isn't it?" He smoothed his hands down the front of his silky shirt. "Gordon suggested I expand my fashion horizons."

"Gordon?"

He picked up his phone and tapped the screen. "Gordon, let me introduce you to my wife." He turned the screen toward Charlie. Staring back at her was a young white guy with a full head of black hair, mutton chop sideburns, and tufts of dark chest hair peeking out from his unbuttoned shiny purple shirt. He looked like a cross between Elvis and John Travolta. Gordon waved to her with the eagerness of a car salesman, which clashed mightily with his Vegas persona.

"You got a virtual assistant," she said with a tight smile. She finally waved back to make him stop.

"Yeah!" he said. Charlie had never seen him so excited. "Milo talked me into it. Best thing I've ever done. He's amazing. He's not just an expert on everything, he's like a loyal friend. He's already helped me improve my golf swing tenfold." He turned the phone toward himself. "Isn't that right, Gordon?"

"You had your best game ever today, buddy!" Gordon said with Elvis's deep, Southern drawl.

"I don't need a golf pro anymore. Do you know how much money that'll save me?"

"That's great!" She tried to match his enthusiasm but failed. "You can buy more purple shirts."

"We've gotta get you an assistant too," he said. "I swear, it'll change your life."

"Yeah, that'd be great," she said. *Please don't make me get a robot assistant.* She had zero interest in technology, social media, or the ability to instantly connect with her countless friends (Ginger). It was bad enough she had a cell phone. Except, of course, when it came in handy.

"What's the matter? You don't seem like yourself."

"Me? Nothing. Nothing at all. I'm good."

"No, I can tell. You're down in the dumps. Gordon, how can I make my wife happy?"

"Well, if I were in your lucky shoes, Danny, I'd take your special lady out to supper."

Danny? Dan didn't let anyone call him Danny.

"Great idea!" Dan said.

"Thank you very much," Gordon-Elvis replied.

It took every ounce of power Charlie had not to roll her eyes.

"Where should we go?" Dan asked Gordon.

"Hmmm. How 'bout that steak joint downtown? The one with all the purdy waitresses. Let me check and see . . ." He paused. "Yup, they're still open. The imaginary water shortage hasn't shut 'em down yet."

Did he say "imaginary"?

"Perfect. Can you make a reservation for us?"

"Seven-thirty?" Gordon asked.

Dan looked at Charlie, who shrugged and nodded.

"That works great," Dan said to Gordon.

"You're all set, buddy."

CHAPTER 39

"Hey, Paco!" Charlie said to the bird, and then clicked her tongue a few times to get his attention. Paco ignored her. The raven, perched on a sturdy, carpet-covered pole that spanned the length of his enclosure, didn't just ignore her but turned away from her. From that angle, she could see how his damaged wing couldn't quite tuck into his body.

The morning after her talk with Eve, she spent an hour staring into the bathroom mirror, willing the dream raven to come back. But nothing happened, except that she noticed one of her ears was slightly lower than the other. At least now she knew why her sunglasses were always crooked.

At a loss for what to do, she took a drive to the wildlife rehabilitation center out by the airport, on the recommendation of her new virtual assistant, to hang out with some ravens. Dan kidnapped her phone when she was at work and set her up with her own Stepford-wife-esque assistant he named Cilla. He and Gordon thought it'd be "cute" to name her after Elvis's wife. Dan never used the word cute. None of it was creepy at all. The first second she was alone with her phone, she changed her assistant's avatar to a beret-wearing Frenchman she named Maurice.

She didn't know what she was hoping to accomplish by hanging out with Paco, but maybe somehow she'd give her imaginary raven tormentor/friend the message that she's open to reconnecting.

She watched the large bird preen himself. "Hey, Paco, mi amigo," she called, this time snapping her fingers to get his attention.

"Ravens do things on their own terms," a woman wearing a tan safari-style shirt said. Her name tag read "Julie." "Unless you have something they want." When she unsnapped the pouch on her belt, Paco turned around and made his way toward her.

"Bring me your ball," she said to him.

Paco opened his beak, ready to receive his treat.

"Nice try," she laughed. "Golf ball first."

He turned and strolled to the other side of his pole, where there was a small wooden tray that looked like the inside of a junk drawer. He grabbed a fluorescent-yellow golf ball with his beak and started to turn, but then thought better of it and dropped the ball back in the tray. He picked through the items with his beak until he found what he was looking for, a broken brown stone the size of a silver dollar.

"Well, that's strange," Julie said. "He's never done that before."

He made his way back to Julie and, with his beak pointed at Charlie, he deposited the object in a clear plastic drawer built into the enclosure's wall.

Julie turned to Charlie with an amused shrug. "It looks like he brought you a gift." She pulled the drawer open from her side and grabbed the stone. "He must really like you," she said. She handed the object to Charlie. "That's his most cherished treasure."

The color drained from Charlie's face. It was a chipped ammonite fossil. Paco croaked at Charlie, making the hair on her arms stand.

"Holy shit," Charlie said.

"You okay?" Julie asked.

Charlie swallowed and nodded. She pushed up her sleeve and showed Julie her tattoo.

"Holy shit is right," Julie whispered.

CHAPTER 40

CHARLIE DIDN'T REMEMBER DRIVING home. She wondered if maybe she'd teleported via wormhole. It wouldn't surprise her at this point. She reclined in her favorite lounge chair in the shade of their back patio. The kidney-shaped pool where Charlie used to spend most of her free time was almost empty; just a few feet of sludgy water remained, and the patch of grass Dan used as a practice putting green was sad and brown. A few of the succulents were hanging in there, but the young ash trees they planted several years ago were yellow and balding.

It was late afternoon and still oven-hot, but she didn't mind because her body temperature hovered around the top edge of corpse. There was something comforting about the dry, baked air wrapping around her like a second skin.

Since she had the place to herself for at least a few more hours, she decided to try meditating with the hope of connecting with the dream raven. She closed her eyes and tried to clear her mind. Maurice made it sound easy. However, instead of clearing her mind, she remembered that she'd forgotten to pick up trash bags at the grocery store the other day, which reminded her that she needed to freeze the chicken in the fridge before the expiration date, which was . . . shit, yesterday. Her eyes popped open.

"Take ze deep cleanzing breath," Maurice told her.

She had a delicious moment of calm before the buzzing of the cicadas sounded like chainsaws in her skull. She let out a frustrated breath and decided she hated meditating. Fuck Maurice and his French accent.

She pulled Paco's gift out of the pocket of her cargo shorts and examined it. Even though a small section of it was missing, it was beautiful. A perfect symmetrical spiral. How was it that she'd never noticed how perfect nature was? Her focus softened and her eyes followed the ancient path of the spiral inward. Her peripheral vision darkened and her head filled with the familiar sound of rushing blood as the spiral pulled her down into its center. In the distance, she heard the dream raven's call.

SHE'S IN A REMOTE desert canyon. Nothing lives here. No trees, cacti, or shrubs; just shades of reddish sandstone as far as the eye can see, under a joyless gray sky. Her eyes are drawn to the carcass of a felled tree whose bleached trunk and jagged, broken branches have been smoothed by years of heat and wind erosion, like driftwood on an empty seabed. The raven descends and settles on one of its remaining fractured branches.

Her dream-body is suddenly standing next to the tree. She swallows her fear and smiles at the raven who, after a moment, drops its head in a slight bow, and she notices it's wearing not one but two spiral necklaces. The raven looks to the sky and sings a mournful, raspy raven song that echoes through the canyon. Moments later, three black and brown vultures are in the sky overhead, gliding toward the ground in large, lazy circles. They land on the other side of the dead tree.

The vultures surround the remains of a body half-buried in the hard earth. A few alabaster ribs poke out of what's left of the body's brown leathery skin. Charlie's dream-body looks down at it and is overwhelmed with grief for the poor person who died alone in this terrible place. The mummified face turns toward her and opens its eyes.

Charlie inhales sharply as she realizes she's looking at herself. Only she's younger, a teenager.

The vultures tear into young Charlie's sinewy skin with the sharp white tips of their cherry-red beaks and pull strips of flesh away from bones and devour them.

Charlie yells at the vultures to leave, but they ignore her. "Make them stop," she pleads to the raven, who regards her with silence.

"I'm so sorry," she says to her younger self through tears. They stare at each other until a vulture impales one of young Charlie's eyes, plucks it out of her skull, and swallows it. It quickly ingests her other eye, and Charlie screams.

It's a mercy. The words enter Charlie's mind and calm her. She knows they come from the raven.

The hulking vultures ravage young Charlie's body until there's nothing left but her bones. They hang their bald heads over her skeleton with reverence before flying away.

The wind picks up and swirls around the young girl's skeleton. It blows the crusty sand away from her bones, forming a dust devil in the process. The small, twisting windstorm grows dense and loud and hovers for a moment as if paying its respects to the remains of young Charlie's wounded self before speeding down the winding riverbed and disappearing behind the canyon wall.

The dust cloud over young Charlie's bones settles and reveals seven animated skeletons now surrounding her remains.

Charlie looks to the raven. *The Bone Shamans.* She nods her understanding.

Each Bone Shaman is adorned with ceremonial fetishes—some have feathers, others wear colorful beads or shells. The face of one is surrounded by a ring of dried straw-like grass like a lion's mane. Another has a stripe of cracked red war paint under its empty eye sockets. The tanned head and skin of a coyote sit on the skull of another, like a hat.

The Bone Shamans dance their medicine, their bones clack in unison, creating a primal percussive rhythm. As they dance, Charlie can feel them pull the pain from her younger self's bones.

When the ceremonial dance is over, the Bone Shamans dig deep into the earth with thin, bony fingers. They retrieve clumps of brown clay and begin the process of forming young Charlie's body anew.

The raven spreads its wings and shapeshifts into human form. Her dream-body trembles. She knows him. She loses herself for a moment in the black of his irises. His strong, handsome, tattooed face feels like home to a distant part of herself. He kneels between two of the Bone Shamans as they sculpt young Charlie's torso and lifts a spiral necklace from his neck. He whispers unheard words into the necklace and places it in the heart of young Charlie's new body. His hand rests on her exposed ribcage for a moment before getting up.

Charlie doesn't understand what's happening, but the tenderness of this intense man's gesture brings her to tears.

The sky darkens, and the wind picks up again. Thunder rolls through the valley. They watch in silence as the Bone Shamans finish their work. Young Charlie's new body is perfect, no longer marred by the pain of loss and loneliness. The Bone Shaman with the grassy lion's mane raises his left hand to the sky and joins hands with the shaman next to him, who joins hands with the shaman next to her, and on down the line. Together, they create a serpentine chain that curls around young Charlie's body. The

Bone Shaman on the end places her free hand on young Charlie's bare chest. Thunder cracks overhead, and the ground shakes.

A lightning bolt strikes the outstretched hand of the Lion Bone Shaman. Its current is indigo light that travels down the bones of his arm like syrup and fills his body and spreads to the Bone Shaman next to him. Soon, all the Bone Shamans are glowing with indigo light, transmitting the lightning medicine into young Charlie's lifeless body until it too glows deep violet-blue. The wind calms, and the lightning extinguishes. The Bone Shamans raise their joined hands to the sky and disappear in a flash of blue.

Young Charlie's eyes open. Her irises are also black, and she's dressed in swaths of the same charcoal fabric as Ahkoa. A thick stripe of matte black paint spans the width of her face from her brow line down, fading as it reaches the tip of her nose and the bottom of her cheekbones. The fierce young woman stands and faces her older self. Large blue-black raven wings spread from her back.

Charlie gasps. Their locked gaze seems to pull at them until they're standing inches apart. Charlie opens her arms, and her younger self steps into her embrace, her wings enveloping them. Their bodies merge. Charlie's dream-body is now the adult version of her younger raven self.

"Rah-hīnah." Charlie looks at the warrior, who bows his head.

"Rah-hīnah," she repeats, assuming it's a greeting of some sort since she's heard it a few times in this strange dream-world. But when he squints at her, she's not sure what the word means after all.

Her wings fold against her back. Being in her body feels different. She stands taller, and her once-rounded shoulders are now square and strong. She's struck by how quiet her mind is and the pronounced relief she feels in her body from the absence of all the nervous tension she'd been unconsciously carrying. Her heart is lighter too. But she's still confused.

"Who are you?"

He breaks eye contact. He looks pained, but she's too distracted to think about that now.

"Ahkoa," he says. His voice is deep and quiet.

"Ahkoa," she whispers. The sound of his voice and the shape of his name bring comfort in a surprising way. He's not something or someone to be frightened of, he's like home.

"It's strange, but I feel more like myself than I have, probably ever." She shakes her head. "And I have wings! So that's cool."

No response from Ahkoa.

"I'm like you?"

"Not yet," he says and almost smiles.

She doesn't quite know what to make of that response.

She takes a deep breath and notes how much more air she can take in when her body isn't spring-loaded. "Thank you for helping me," she says

He nods.

"So, where are the others?"

"Others?"

"Yeah, First Mother and Lou, the Hawk Man."

He nods his understanding. "They're in the Dreaming Realm."

"I thought that's where we were."

He shakes his head. "This place is the dreaming of you. It's your inner landscape."

She scans the lifeless desert. "Yikes."

This time he does smile.

Another raven lands next to him and shapeshifts into a woman who looks like she could be Ahkoa's older sibling, a bit of silver in her black hair. Her wings retract into her back and disappear. Charlie's sense of déjà vu is dizzying.

"Rah-hīnah," the woman says with a welcoming smile.

Instead of repeating the phrase, this time Charlie says, "Hi."

"Still no memory?" the raven woman asks Ahkoa.

He shakes his head.

"My name is Ahna," she says with a slight bow of her head.

"I'm Charlie."

"Yes, I know," she says with a grin. "We've been looking forward to your return for a long time."

"Return?"

"No need to worry about that for now. You'll understand soon. But first . . ."

Charlie swallows hard.

"Close your eyes, Charlie."

She doesn't know why, but she trusts this woman and closes her eyes.

"Bring your focus inward, Charlie. Let it spiral down deep inside, and listen. Listen for the song of your heart. It'll be faint, but it's there humming in the background."

Charlie lets her attention travel inward behind her eyes. The delicious quiet she was experiencing is gone, interrupted by layer upon layer of discordant noise; the same cacophony of manic voices she heard in the noxious silver substance the cobras vomited into her mouth. Her brows furrow. She's caught in the dissonance.

"Breathe, Charlie," Ahna says.

In the physical world, Charlie's body inhales deeply.

"Good, now let your focus travel downward into your heart."

As her attention travels down, the noise recedes into the background and she feels her body relax on the lounge chair in her backyard. There's no resistance this time, no wall of pain blocking her way. When she settles into this peaceful place, she feels, more than hears, the music. Ahna is right. It's very faint and easy to miss. It's sad and sweet. Beautiful, but incomplete. It lacks depth, like a symphony being played by an orchestra of only three musicians.

"You found it," Ahna says.

Charlie nods.

"What direction does it pull you?"

Eyes still closed, she leans her head to the left.

"Good. Now lock in on that feeling and see where it takes you."

Charlie's awareness narrows and lets the music pull her. The further away she gets from herself, the more she has to concentrate so she doesn't lose the thread. Her awareness becomes an arrow of focus that's pushing through a tube of toothpaste until—with a pop—she's somewhere else . . . or some time else.

She watches her fourteen-year-old self slip a box of cereal into the kitchen cupboard. Her mother is behind her, carrying a bottle of ketchup to the fridge. She wants to scream a warning to them, but doesn't know what to say. She knows she can't stop what's about to happen.

Her mother freezes in the middle of the kitchen, drops the bottle, which explodes on the white linoleum floor, and grabs her head. The agony on her face takes Charlie's breath away all over again. She watches helplessly as her younger self tries to understand what's happening and the garbled words that come out of her mother's mouth.

Tears stream down Charlie's face in the physical world.

The scene glitches and starts over again. Young Charlie opens the cabinet and slides the cereal box in . . .

Charlie understands that this part of herself is trapped in a nightmarish loop, re-experiencing the horror of this moment over and over again.

When the ketchup bottle once again crashes onto the floor, she yells, "Stop!" It's the only thing she thinks to say.

And it works. Young Charlie looks in the direction of her voice. The look of confusion on her young, innocent face breaks Charlie's heart.

"Charlie," she says to her younger self. "Can you see me?"

She nods. "Something's wrong with my mom."

"I know, and I'm so sorry."

"It's bad, isn't it?"

Charlie nods to her younger self. "I think you're stuck in this terrible moment and that you don't know you're stuck." She takes a breath. "A lot of time has passed since this happened to you—about fifteen years."

Fourteen-year-old Charlie's brow furrows.

"I know this because I'm you."

Young Charlie looks closer at her older doppelganger and her eyes widen.

"I know it sounds crazy."

"You're me?"

Charlie nods. "I'm from the future." She grimaces. "That sounds too weird. What I mean is I'm your future self."

Understanding hits young Charlie. "I'm dreaming."

"I wish it were just a dream. It breaks my heart to see you stuck in this painful memory," she says.

Young Charlie turns toward her mother's form, which is frozen in anguish like someone hit the pause button.

"There's nothing you can do," she says softly. "There's nothing anyone could've done to help her. It's already happened." She moves a bit closer. "I'm so sorry. I wish it weren't true."

"Mom," her younger self pleads through tears. But her mother can't hear or see her.

"You're so strong," Charlie says. "You don't even realize how strong you are. I promise you that you'll get through this—that we'll get through this. Together."

Charlie reaches out and strokes her younger self's hair. "I've missed you."

Her younger self's shoulders drop the tiniest bit.

"Please come home." Charlie places her hand on her own heart. A part of her marvels at the words flowing out of her. There's no hesitation, no doubt. Just understanding and certainty. "We can help each other heal."

She opens her arms.

Young Charlie leans in to her older self, who wraps her arms around her, and she sobs.

And then Charlie hears the music. It's full and rich and complex. It pulls them together like the moon pulls at the Earth until their bodies merge and become one.

CHARLIE DIDN'T MOVE OR open her eyes. She let the buzz of the cicadas come to the foreground and reorient her.

"Welcome home," she whispered, a sweet, peaceful smile on her lips.

CHAPTER 41

"LET'S GET ICE CREAM!" Charlie batted her eyes at Dan.

"Ice cream? That's a bit random." He took a swig of beer.

"Yeah, I've been craving it."

"Craving?" He smiled and cocked his head to one side, assessing her. "Are you trying to tell me something?" He leaned over and rested his hand on her belly.

Oh, shit.

She smiled and shook her head. "I was just remembering when my mom used to take me for ice cream after my piano lesson. Chocolate fudge brownie." She closed her eyes and savored the memory. "So good." It'd been many years since she had chocolate fudge brownie ice cream.

"I think that's the first time I've ever heard you talk about your mother," Dan said on his way to the kitchen to get another beer.

That got her attention. He was right.

"I'll drive!" she suggested, knowing he was deep in his cups.

Dan's cell phone dinged. A text.

"Goddamn it," he said under his breath after reading it. That definitely got her attention. He insisted that cursing was uncivilized and therefore beneath him.

"Everything okay?"

He ignored her, went straight for the cupboard, and pulled out a shot glass. He opened his special-occasion bottle of tequila, poured a shot, and downed it. Head down, he hissed through his teeth and poured another.

"Go without me."

He strode past her and went out onto the back patio to make a call.

Charlie shrugged and grabbed her keys. Her mission to get ice cream was now imperative. It was going to be a long night.

Her phone chimed. It was a text from Ginger: *Can we talk?*

CHAPTER 42

"Just what the doctor ordered." Charlie handed Ginger a cherry vanilla ice cream cone.

They leaned against the hood of Ginger's car and ate in silence.

Eating her favorite ice cream for the first time since her mom died was a quiet ceremony for Charlie. She was not only ready to look back, but she was ready to move forward. The moment the luscious dark-chocolate flavor and creamy, silky texture of the ice cream hit Charlie's tongue, the richness of her childhood returned and filled the wound buried deep within her. At that moment, she knew she'd be okay. With smiling eyes that glistened with tears, she offered a silent thank you to her new raven friends in the Dreaming Realm.

Ginger handed Charlie a napkin. "You have chocolate . . . everywhere."

She laughed and wiped her mouth. As her ice cream reverie mellowed, it dawned on her that Ginger wasn't her usual jovial self. In fact, it was as if they'd swapped emotional bodies. Charlie was bursting with lightness, and Ginger was heavy and morose.

"We're moving," Ginger finally said, avoiding her eyes.

The meaning of the words took a few seconds to register. "Moving?"

"Nashville."

"Nashville?"

"You sound like a parrot."

They burst out laughing. "I always do when I'm in shock," Charlie said.

Nashville, she thought. *Might as well be Russia.* Reality slammed into her, breaking her emotional dam. Now she couldn't stop the tears even if she wanted to. She'd always assumed Ginger would be there to make her laugh, to have her back, even when she probably didn't even know she was doing it—to be her friend. Her only one, really. She covertly dabbed her eyes with the stiff napkin, embarrassed that she was crying.

Ginger grabbed Charlie's hand. "That's why I wanted to tell you in person."

"I don't want you to leave," she said.

Ginger was startled. Charlie was a woman of few words, particularly ones that relayed feelings. "I don't want to leave either." Now they were both crying.

"I don't understand," Charlie said. "You guys love it here, and you're both doing so well."

Ginger wiped the edge of her stiff, ice cream parlor napkin under each eye, trying not to smear her mascara.

"Actually, we're not." She took a defeated breath. "Milo hasn't made a sale in almost six months, and his income last year was half of what it was the year before. And my salary isn't enough to support us. We're gonna stay with his folks for a while until we get our feet back on the ground."

"How could that be? Dan was all excited about closing that huge deal they both worked on for months."

It was Ginger's turn to be shocked. "Oh, buddy. That deal fell through. Remember that night a few weeks ago when the boys came home wasted out of their minds?"

"Yeah, but—" She almost said that Dan coming home wasted was a frequent occurrence.

"That was when the developer pulled the plug on the deal." Ginger paused. "You mean Dan hasn't been telling you what's going on?"

Charlie's stomach clenched. She shook her head.

"It's the drought, Charlie. There's not enough water. Businesses are packing up and leaving the state in droves. No one's buying real estate. That's why Dan's agency is hurting so badly."

Charlie tried to digest what she was hearing. "I guess I've been living in my own little world."

"And Dan hasn't been helping by keeping you in the dark." Ginger was pissed. "You guys need to leave Phoenix. Sell your house before it's completely worthless."

"It sounds like it might be too late for that."

Ginger shrugged. "Milo's on the phone with Dan right now, trying to convince him to come to Nashville with us." She squeezed Charlie's hand. "I'd love it if you came."

Charlie's heart lightened at the gesture and the idea. "We could be neighbors." Things were moving fast. "I need to talk to Dan. I feel like fucking Rip Van Winkle."

CHAPTER 43

"HE'S A TRAITOR," DAN said through clenched teeth, his voice tight.

Charlie didn't know if Dan was talking to her or himself.

He paced the length of the living room, strangling the long neck of a half-full bottle of beer. He didn't seem to notice how much he was spilling every time his arm moved in concert with his jerky stride. The room was going to smell like a bar in the morning.

She took an inventory when she came home from her ice cream date with Ginger. Three empty beer bottles on the coffee table, two more on the patio table out back, and the sacred bottle of tequila sitting on the kitchen counter was now half empty. Or half full?

"Milo?" she asked.

He stopped. "Yes. Milo. Or should I call him Judas?"

His ability to be profoundly drunk and yet carry himself like he was sober never ceased to amaze her. But he sure could be a mean fuck when he was drunk. Tonight might set a new nastiness record.

She debated the value of engaging with him, but before she knew it, she'd said, "Why? Because he's broke and can't afford to live here anymore?"

"He's not broke. I told him I'd take care of him."

"How about us? Are we okay?"

He stopped. "Of course we are."

"I mean financially."

"There's no we, there's me. I'm the one taking care of you, and what? You don't trust me now either? Have I EVER let you down?" He pointed his beer bottle at her.

"No, I don't think so."

His face turned red and his pupils about disappeared.

Uh-oh. Leave it alone, Charlie.

"Oh, you don't think so?" He emphasized each word. "You. Don't. Think. So."

She exhaled her defensiveness. "That's not what I meant. I was referring to the drought. The city . . . shit, the whole state is running out of water." Her trusty virtual pal Maurice had shared the latest harrowing details on her drive home.

He shook his head. "Not you too."

Now she was confused.

"You're so gullible, Charlotte." His tone was slipping deep into conde-scending-land. "There's plenty of water."

Her eyebrows nearly hit the ceiling.

"Oh, you think *I'm* crazy?" He cackled a bit, like a crazy person. "It's aaaaall a lie." He repeated as if she didn't speak English. "There's plen-tee of wah-ter."

She pointed her finger to their crispy, yellowed backyard.

"Well, yeah. We're a bit dry, but there's water. They just want us to believe we're running out."

"They?"

He pulled his phone out of his back pocket and almost dropped it. His movements were getting sloppy.

"Gordon," he said into his phone. "Show Charlotte the latest video you showed me."

"Sure thing, buddy," Gordon said. His stupid Elvis drawl made Charlie's skin crawl. Dan handed Charlie his phone.

A grainy video started playing. It was obvious that someone had secretly recorded a conversation from outside a partially open office door. The sign on the door read Arizona Department of Water Resources – Public Information Officer. A slender Caucasian man dressed in business casual stood in profile inside the office. His hands were on his hips and the sleeves on his light blue button-down shirt were rolled up to his elbows. He was talking to someone off-camera. She couldn't pick up what was being said by the person off-camera.

"I know," the man in the blue shirt responded. His blurry face seemed to be smiling. "I've already snagged a few choice properties." Muffled laughter and more unintelligible words were spoken by the man off-camera. "Yeah, yeah," the man in the blue shirt responded, "the golf course too. The guy thought I was nuts, but he sure was happy to get whatever—" He stopped as if he'd heard something and looked at the door. The screen went black.

Charlie didn't know what to think. Either this guy was a complete moron or he knew something the rest of us didn't.

Dan watched her expression change. "See! I told you!"
She shrugged.
"We're not going anywhere," he said with a smug smile.
She broke eye contact. The ice cream curdled in her stomach.

CHAPTER 44

"There you are," First Mother says, cupping Charlie's face in her turquoise hand. Her relieved smile and the way she looks at Charlie indicate that she's acknowledging something deeper within Charlie than her presence in the Dreaming Realm. "I'm happy to see you."

She rests her hands on Charlie's shoulders and says, "It's time to remember, yes?"

Charlie has no idea what that means, but finds herself nodding. Before she can ponder the question too long, her visual field narrows and blinks out. At the same time, her stomach does a somersault, and she hears a dull rumble in the darkness that grows louder as her senses come back online. She's surrounded by the sound. It's swallowing her whole.

The calming touch of First Mother's warm hands on her shoulders settles her. Light creeps back into her visual field, and the details of her new surroundings emerge. Leaves come into focus, but the color is off. The trees, ferns, and flowers are sickly and washed out. Her hands and arms have the same gray hue. She realizes that the source of this putrid light and the rumbling sound is behind her. The sound is so loud, the ground vibrates. She turns toward it. *Holy shit.* The bloated, reflective, grayish-silver of the distortion that she remembers Syd had referred to as the Mental Realm consumes and contorts the entire vista. There are no edges. No sky, no ground, just an expanding convex wall of jumbled, frenzied human voices that's about to devour them. The Mental Realm is taking over.

The unnatural hue turns First Mother's skin sallow; all of her rich ocean depth and luster is faded. Her expression, grave. "We don't have a lot of time."

Everything about this place makes Charlie want to hide. The lump that now sits in her throat makes it hard to swallow. Being so close to it fills her with a strange and disturbing intimacy. "I know this place."

"Yes, you do," First Mother says. "You've experienced it before. Several times." She gives Charlie a moment to digest this information. "You're the only one who can access and heal the Mental Realm, Little Bird."

She scans the Mental Realm, and a chill runs through her. *I really will lose my mind if I go in there.*

"I'm guessing the previous attempts didn't go well."

First Mother shakes her head.

"Why is it like that?"

"It's infected."

A raven's call cuts through the rumble. It lands several feet away and shapeshifts into Ahkoa.

"Please take Rah-hīnah to the Elders," First Mother says to him.

He bows his head.

Rah-hīnah must be my name. Charlie wonders if it means Little Bird.

"We'll speak again soon," First Mother assures her.

Charlie follows Ahkoa into the forest. There's no path, but his pace is agile and confident as he traverses the dense roots that span the surface of the ground. She's doing everything she can not to trip.

They come to a dense wall of deep green, leafy vines. Without hesitation, Ahkoa walks directly into it and disappears.

Either he's a wizard or he's trying to lose me.

She approaches the wall where he vanished and sees that it's an optical illusion. There's a gap in the wall where he slipped through. She enters the opening and is immediately disoriented. She's in a narrow passageway whose walls are made of the same leafy vines, but the uniformity of the color and the dim light make her lose depth perception. To steady herself, she reaches for the walls, which seem to be closing in on her. Her body lists to the side as dizziness takes over. She starts hyperventilating. *I can't get out!*

"Look down." Ahkoa's voice seems to be right next to her.

She looks down and sees the well-worn path between the walls. She takes a deep breath, followed by a tentative step. Then another. *Okay.* Eyes down, she follows the path, which turns and twists like a labyrinth until it opens up.

"You can look up now," he says.

Eyes closed, her hands reach out to the side for balance, she slowly raises her head.

Ahkoa rolls his eyes.

When she's confident she's not going to have another bout of vertigo, she slowly opens her eyes. Ahkoa, arms crossed, towers in front of her.

"Don't judge me," she warns.

This gets her a hint of a smile.

She takes in her surroundings. She's in a different kind of forest. Instead of trees, there are spiraling circles of countless massive standing stones, all different shapes and sizes. The stone forest is enclosed by the tall vine walls of the labyrinth.

"This is where the Elders live?" she asks.

He takes in the towering stones with reverence. "These are the Elders."

She follows him into the outermost circle, and they spiral deep into the silent stone forest. There are symbols, similar to runes, etched on the faces of the stones. As they get closer to the center, the stones are rounder, more ancient, and covered with moss and lichen.

He stops. They're several rings away from the center, where a massive weathered stone with countless stratified layers sits like a wise and patient grandfather. The bones of her skull vibrate with a deep, pleasant tone, and images enter her mind: Magma explodes skyward from angry cracks on the surface of the Earth, creating smoke that blocks out the sun. A peaceful meadow filled with tall grasses and wildflowers and vibrant birdsong. A violent sandstorm blows across a lifeless desert, followed by the expansive view of the sparkly sea from a high cliff. A lion takes down an antelope, ripping into its neck with sharp teeth. A black bear licks her newborn cubs. An older woman tends a garden. A young man bulldozes a forest.

Paradox. Beauty and violence. Love and survival.

Charlie pulls her eyes away and takes in the ancient stone Ahkoa stands in front of. It stands several feet taller than her. The bottom is wider than the top, which is rounded. She steps closer to get a better look at the worn symbols etched on its face. *Is that . . . ?* A large segmented spiral, similar to her tattoo and Ahkoa's pendant, is carved into the center of the stone. It's surrounded by other smaller symbols that resemble simplistic hieroglyphs.

"The story of our clan." He turns to her.

"Can you translate it for me?"

"No need. The Elder will show you." He gestures with his head for her to approach the stone.

The air around the Stone Elder is syrupy. She feels a strong but slow pulsing in her body as she moves close and places her palms on the face of the stone. Its surface is surprisingly warm and welcoming. She instinctively leans toward the surface until her forehead touches the stone. A gentle tugging sensation in the middle of her forehead pulls her awareness through a narrow opening at the center of the etched spiral like a siphon. Her consciousness is in the stone.

Once in this place, she recognizes, or perhaps remembers is more accurate, that the Elders are the record keepers. The ones who've witnessed epochs come and go.

A pinpoint of light appears in a field of pure darkness and rushes toward her. Or maybe she's rushing toward it. She can't tell. As the light grows, it becomes a kaleidoscope of blue and green before it comes into focus. It's First Mother. She's younger and very, very pregnant. She sits, eyes closed, in an enormous nest surrounded by hundreds of eggs. Each egg is unique in shape, size, color, and texture.

First Mother cradles a pale turquoise, brown-speckled egg in her hands, which rest in her lap under her abundant belly. The moment Charlie tries to make sense of what she's seeing, she has understanding. The Stone Elder is communicating with her. First Mother is dreaming life into existence.

A small crack appears on the surface of the egg. Charlie hears muffled crunching, and little geometric chips of shell break away until a small hole appears followed by the tip of a black beak. The egg rocks in First Mother's hands. The beak pushes through the opening and cracks the egg in half, revealing a full-grown, majestic bird. The First Raven. She stretches her ink-black wings. First Mother opens her eyes for a moment and smiles at the raven, who looks up at her and purrs with her gravelly voice.

First Raven sleeps in a nest at the top of an ancient tree. Her dreaming body is curled around a single pale blue, speckled egg. Her focus is intense as she dreams her first child of many into existence. The shell cracks as the spindly baby bird makes her way out. First Raven wakes and nudges the newborn chick affectionately with her beak. Charlie wants to crawl into the nest and curl up with them. First Raven croaks softly to the scrawny chick. The sounds are familiar. She understands them. *Welcome to the Dreaming Realm, Rah-hīnah.*

The translation is immediate. *Raven's Daughter.*

Charlie's mind is a circuit board, making connections as memories come back online. Information floods the nooks and crannies of her awareness. Her human mind grasps that she was born about three million Earth years ago.

A series of images is revealed: After First Raven teaches Raven's Daughter how to fly, she returns to her nest. Her sleeping form is surrounded by a clutch of thirty-three eggs, then thirty-three more, followed by thirty-three more, as she dreams the Raven Clan into being. Charlie's kin. But not Charlie—Raven's Daughter. Charlie is human. Raven's Daughter is not.

The moment she and her kin are born in the Dreaming Realm, the conditions for ravens to evolve on the Earth are created.

When Raven's Daughter is an adolescent bird, she shapeshifts for the first time. She remembers the feel of her strong, lithe, humanoid body. Even before she reaches adulthood, she has an imposing presence. It's her eyes—human, but not. The solid black of her irises sits in a pool of stark white. Intense and intelligent. The top half on her face, from hairline to the bottom of her high cheekbones, is solid black, denoting that she's the firstborn and the most powerful of her clan.

It doesn't take long for all the members of her clan to learn to shapeshift and use their fluid forms to explore the beauty and the mysteries of the Dreaming Realm. They play and run and fly and grow stronger and smarter.

She remembers seeing Ahkoa's human form for the first time, and she now knows what longing feels like. His strong young body runs through the forest. She's captivated. She shapeshifts into raven form and follows him from above. He looks up at her and smiles.

They're inseparable.

Driven by curiosity, the clan's explorations take them to the outermost reaches of the Dreaming Realm, the boundary where the Physical Realm begins.

In the Physical Realm, the raven species simultaneously emerges and explores the beauty and mysteries of the Earth, all the while keeping a shiny black eye on the evolving human species, toying with them like mocking class clowns. It's a diversion of sorts, a way to keep the humans from consciously understanding the role they play in their lives. The humans don't know it but the ravens are allies, offering assistance to a young species.

The Raven Clan serves as guides, teaching humans how to dream. They open swirling windows between the realms and invite the dream-bodies of sleeping humans to follow. In the Dreaming Realm, the young minds of humans communicate with the intelligence of all the inhabitants who live here: the plants, animals, and elements. Their minds are sponges, soaking in the infinite wisdom of this place. The Raven Clan shows them how to make tools; songbirds teach them how to sing melodies—which later become language. Other dream experiences help them learn how to efficiently hunt, fish, and preserve food. The plants and fungi teach some humans how to make medicines to transport them to the Dreaming Realm while awake and to heal members of their communities, to help them understand the landscape of their dreams and their place in a vast universe.

The connection between the fledgling human race and the mysterious, dangerous, and breathtaking world around them is a complex and beautiful symphony. Charlie sees them as one thread woven in a varied, intricate, colorful tapestry that is the natural world. She feels them gain equilibrium as they learn their place and grow more and more intimately in tune with the other intelligences they share the world with. Even more astonishing to her is how their emotions are like sails and their minds rudders, working together to steer the vessel of their psyches with a sense of balance that rudderless Charlie envies.

Their dreams and all the wisdom available to them in the Dreaming Realm are vital to their survival, and the members of the Raven Clan are their escorts.

She perceives the deep sense of reverence humans have—for everything; a testament to the relationship they've cultivated with the world around them. This relationship is the foundation stone of the Mental Realm.

Charlie's attention shifts to the edge of the Dreaming Realm, where she witnesses the birth of the first human thoughts. She watches them form, seemingly out of thin air, like crystal clear dew drops filled with childlike wonder and possibility. The quicksilvery drops find each other and create amorphous pools of substance: Beliefs. Over time, silvery pools merge and become shimmering oceans: Worldviews. The Mental Realm is formed. At a certain angle, the newborn realm seems to magnify the devastating beauty and perfection of the Dreaming Realm.

Over eons, the inner lives of early humans become more complex as rudimentary concepts grow into abstractions. Their developing minds do what they can to make sense of their sometimes harsh and violent world, to calm their all-consuming fears and their grief. They enter the Age of Story.

Their intellect evolves quickly. Perhaps too quickly. The Mental Realm is a safe place to retreat, where the illusion of control endeavors to quiet the drone of fear. It grows dense and opaque, and Charlie watches as the first signs of sickness take hold. Clusters of transmuting, liquid, mercury-like globules move purposefully through the realm like schools of fish.

Deception.

And things begin to change. She watches as the dreams of humans fill with angst, noise, and confusion, while members of her clan become invisible to them. In response, the Mental and Physical Realms descend into disharmony.

She's shown how the plague of deception is a masterful mind virus that spreads rapidly through the Mental Realm. The clever contagion shapeshifts and morphs like elastic puzzle pieces, slipping seamlessly into the waiting mind of a willing host, feeding on its weaknesses and vulnerabilities. From there, it calls out like the pulsing beacon of a lighthouse, offering the promise of understanding, the mirage of control, and the seduction of power. However, instead of being seen as a warning, other hungry minds gravitate to deception for salvation.

We. Are. Fucked.

In 542 CE, Raven's Daughter volunteers for the first time to incarnate as a human, with the hope of better understanding the ailing Mental Realm, whose growing density and mass are descending into the Dreaming Realm, swallowing it. It's clear—as the firstborn shapeshifter, Raven's Daughter is the only one who's strong enough to access all three realms and has the best chance of not losing herself.

The Elder nudges Charlie's awareness toward an adolescent peasant girl. Somehow, she knows the girl's name is Odelyn. Charlie fully merges with her and notes how markedly different this young woman is from the Raven's Daughter the Elder is introducing her to. Her personality is meek and small, her heart dulled with fear, and her body weak from malnourishment.

Odelyn's bony fingers, stained with dirt and stiff with cold, crack open a dried, blackened pod, releasing shriveled broad beans into a wooden bucket that sits between her legs. It's winter, and the earthen floor is frigid, even through the soles of her stiff leather boots. She wears three tunics, all she owns, to keep warm. The one-room hut has no windows, only a small door made of thatched reeds. A bit of gray winter light finds its way through the cracks in the walls where mud has chipped away from the crude straw-and-stick structure. Her only company is four skinny hens huddled in the corner on a bed of old straw next to a small smoldering fire.

She gets a feel for the shape of Odelyn's mind and personality. Her thoughts are simple, a reflection of her small world, and focus on the task at hand. She quietly recites the Lord's Prayer over and over as she does her task. Charlie feels this as a compulsion, a strange sort of ritual that Odelyn does when she's working. The driving force, the thing that keeps this poor girl moving through each day, is the promise of redemption. A crude wooden cross hangs in front of her. Each time she whispers "Our Father, who art in heaven," she glances up at it, and a transient glint of hope reaches her eyes. Her prayers are the key to her salvation. Her certainty is unyielding. It was her prayers that got her and her husband through a devastating famine that lasted five fruitless harvests. When their priest told the congregation to pray and that the Lord would provide, she prayed harder than she ever had. More than half of their community perished. She knew it was because they didn't pray hard enough.

Charlie finds no signs of Raven's Daughter's strong and confident presence within Odelyn. The moment this realization surfaces, time rewinds, and Charlie perceives a small pinpoint of density deep in Odelyn's chest. *There she is.* The essence of Raven's Daughter is a tiny island of clarity and calm that rests in a pool of syrupy fear. Now Charlie watches from outside Odelyn's body as Raven's Daughter's essence travels with purpose into the young woman's head, to the terrain of her personal Mental Realm.

Charlie's curiosity follows Raven's Daughter. The atmosphere in the realm of Odelyn's mind is claustrophobic and filled with rhythmic and frantic mumbling. As she orients to this strange place, Charlie sees a small, sterile, white cube floating in ominous black. The mumbling is inside the cube—or maybe it *is* the cube. The blackness is alive and attracted to the white. But it's like a game, where the objective is to keep the black and all its chaos, temptation, wickedness, and mystery from entering the white. However, the white is vigilant. The moment dark, oily tendrils reach into the white, Charlie hears *Our Father who art in heaven . . .*

The strange, bright safety of the white cube pulls at Charlie. It grows bigger and bigger as it sucks her in. She vaguely remembers this place. This experience.

This isn't real.
Closer.
This isn't happening. It's a memory!
Closer.
No. No. NO!
A wall of white.
I want out. NOW!

Her awareness pops back into Odelyn's body, which is still robotically shelling beans and praying. And the heaviness of Raven's Daughter's failure descends on her. She failed Odelyn. She let her clan down. She let First Mother down. She wasn't strong enough.

The moment Raven's Daughter's presence is swallowed by Odelyn's mind is the moment things decompensate in a monumental way. Odelyn now longs for the day when she'll be released from her dismal life on Earth and ascend into the distant reaches of heaven, clean and warm, to sit at the foot of her god. She imagines a banquet of food laid out in front of her, a reward for her devotion and hard work. Odelyn is ready to die.

The bucket of beans is half full when her young husband, his dark beard encrusted with ice, maneuvers his way through the small door. Charlie's breath catches. *Ahkoa.* She has a distant recollection that he incarnates without Raven's Daughter's knowledge. She remembers him deeming the Physical Realm "the worst kind of nightmare" after that lifetime.

Odelyn looks anxiously in his direction. Her shoulders drop several inches when he reveals, with a triumphant smile, the two fat fish he caught.

"My prayers were answered!" she says to her husband.

Charlie doesn't understand the strange, archaic, Gaelic-sounding dialect, but gleans the meaning of their words.

"It doesn't hurt that I'm also an excellent ice fisherman," he says with a teasing smile.

She recoils, as if his taking credit would anger their god.

"Pray with me," she says with a sense of urgency. "We must give thanks."

Charlie sees the passing look of concern on his face. She can feel Odelyn untethering, her religious devotion and her growing fear have pulled her far away from herself. Her lifeline is no longer food or enjoyment or affection. It's a series of words in the form of a prayer. She's a slave to those words.

As the winter drags on, Odelyn is reluctant to get up from the stool, to turn away from the wooden cross. She fears something horrible will befall them if she stops praying. She can't sleep. She refuses to eat. Her body rocks rhythmically, in cadence with her mumbled prayers, her empty eyes locked on the cross. Odelyn slips into catatonia.

The priest declares her possessed by "an unholy demon from hell" and refuses to let her enter the church, her place of solace. She kneels on the cold, hard earth in front of the church, puffs of breath billowing from tight lips as she recites her prayers.

Ahkoa watches in horror as the men, women, and children of their community surround his wife's frail body, stones in hand. It's clear that she's blind to what's happening around her.

"Banish the demon!" the priest yells, arms wide in invitation. And the first stone is thrown. It hits her temple, knocking her head back. Odelyn's arms reflexively protect her head, but she stays put and recites her prayers louder. The crowd works itself into a frenzy, damning the demon for mocking the Lord's prayer, blaming Odelyn for all their misfortune.

Ahkoa's empty stomach convulses in dry heaves as he watches the people of his small community, his family, the people he calls friends, bludgeon his wife to death.

Charlie focuses on the grounding warmth of the Stone Elder against her forehead and swallows down the bile that burns her throat. Her tears drip on the earthen floor.

The Elder reveals that Raven's Daughter incarnates four more times as different humans over the next fifteen hundred years. Each attempt has similar devastating results.

Before she's born into her fifth human life, Ahkoa stands in front of her, his eyes heavy with unshed tears. "I can't do it," he said. "Not again."

His disappointment in himself rips Charlie in two.

"I know myself. If I go with you this time, I'll end up hurting them." He takes a tense breath. "It took everything in my power not to kill those fucking barbaric doctors who tortured you the last time."

The Stone Elder then reveals an emaciated, hollow-eyed woman, who looks decades older than her true age. Her torso is restrained in a canvas straitjacket, and she's submerged in an ice bath, her grayish-blue body twisted at an awkward angle on its side as violent convulsions rip through her. Watery blood drips, mixing with the condensation on the side of the rectangular metal tub, forming a small pool on the tiled floor. Charlie sees it's coming from the contusion on the woman's temple where her shuddering head reflexively and repeatedly bangs against the rim of the tub. Two male staff dump buckets of ice on her until there's a mound of ice weighing her down. She's been in this bath for four hours.

Her husband gazes at her through the small window in the door, his eyes willing her to see him, but he knows she's gone. Ahkoa. Her parents from that lifetime are also there. The doctor explains with the smug air of self-possessed authority how effective hydrotherapy is for inmates like their daughter, who suffer from active melancholia. He seems unaware that

Ahkoa is seething next to him, opening and closing his fists as if debating whether or not to pummel him.

"I feel powerless when I'm human," he confesses to Raven's Daughter. "I couldn't stop your parents from putting you in that asylum. They thought *I* was the one being cruel."

She grabs his face in her hands. "I couldn't do what you've done. If the roles were reversed?" She smiles. "I'll be okay." They touch their foreheads and share a breath. "Promise you'll visit me in my dreams?"

It dawns on Charlie. *I'm her fifth attempt.*

Reality slams into her. The situation is futile. The Mental Realm is a prison.

She pushes away from the Stone Elder. She can't look at Ahkoa, although she imagines he can probably feel her hopelessness.

She tenses as he approaches. He gently turns her toward him and embraces her. She fits perfectly in his arms, she always has. He holds her head against his chest. He's home. He always has been.

"Maybe if you came this time," she mumbles into his chest, "I wouldn't have married an asshole."

His laughter is a balm.

She looks up at him. His resting "fuck off" face is replaced with an assured, comfortable ease that feels ancient and intimate.

The words spill out of her: "I don't think I can do this."

He cocks his head to the side, the way he always does when he listens. Why does she know this?

"I can't feel Raven's Daughter. And now that I know what she's been through, she's like a fantasy to me. Like some kind of superhero."

When he doesn't respond, she says, "I'm the elephant in the middle of the fucking room. You know I'm right. You've been watching me. She couldn't have picked a worse human being to help her. I'm chickenshit about pretty much everything."

His expression is flat, except for a hint of a smirk.

"What's so funny?"

"You *are* her," he finally says. "She's not separate from you. You ."—he places a hand on either side of her face for emphasis—"Are. Raven's Daughter."

The last vestiges of Charlie's doubt cling to her with white knuckles. "That's crazy talk. Do you know how crazy that sounds?"

"And once you accept it, you'll do everything you can to heal this virus." His voice is tight. "It's who you are."

She knows he's right. An unyielding determination that was always there unfurls in her gut and spreads through her torso and into her limbs, quelling any fear she had.

"You're pissed at her . . . Raven's Daughter," Charlie says.

"No. You. I'm pissed at you. You don't remember yet, but I begged you not to incarnate this time, to just let the virus take over."

"But that would—" The impossibility of the situation hits her differently now. If she or Raven's Daughter or whoever the fuck she is doesn't try, the Mental Realm, corrupt with sickness, will consume the Dreaming Realm, and that will guarantee the end of life on Earth. For everyone.

Everything begins in the Dreaming Realm.

"I don't understand why I'm the only one who can do this."

His smile doesn't reach his eyes. "I knew you'd come around." He blows out a long breath. "Because you're the firstborn of our clan. You're the oldest and the strongest. Your identity is"—he pauses, searching for the right word—"robust.

"I don't get how you do it, but somehow you manage to gather your essence and convey it into the Mental Realm. But then," he pauses and shakes his head, "the strength it must take to not only keep your essence intact in what I imagine is a dimension of boundless entropy, and then free yourself from it, is beyond me. It takes a lot out of you and a long time to recover, but you've done it. Repeatedly."

"So why should this time be any different?"

"It may not be," he says with a hint of defeat. "You may not remember this, but before incarnating as Charlie, you saw no other option but to try."

She feels the pull of that determination.

"Since your last attempt, the virus has almost completely consumed the Mental Realm. If deception is not already the seat of authority there now, it's only a matter of time before it will be. If that happens, it will be near impossible for humans to know what's true and what isn't." He looks away. "If you're not successful, then that's it. For all of us. But if you are successful, First Mother let us all know we need to be prepared for the possibility that the cure will likely destroy you."

Hakolah-khan. The Hollow People. The memory of the dream Charlie had when she was a child surfaces. In her mind's eye, she watches the feathery words of First Mother's story, the remedy for the virus, form into the shape of a Raven and fly into her petite body, planting itself in her heart.

She remembers. She's the antidote.

Ahkoa releases another defeated breath. "It's selfish of me, I know."

But she gets it now. This was never an easy decision for her to make. The pull of Ahkoa, their bond, is fierce. It's the foundation of the longing Charlie feels.

CHAPTER 45

"I DON'T UNDERSTAND," CHARLIE says to First Mother. "It seemed like the human race started out on a good path."

"All parents experience a time when their children turn away from them and venture out on their own. It's an exciting time, an important part of their development, and in most cases it's a good thing." First Mother is quiet for a time, looking into the distance. "It was gradual, hundreds of Earth years. But for me, it was a moment. A moment when I felt them slip away."

She takes in the beauty around her with a sad smile. "They abandoned the intelligence of their hearts, turned their focus away from the wisdom of the Dreaming Realm, and became their own teachers." First Mother closes her luminous pale green eyes. A strong wind blows through the Dreaming Realm. The rustling of thousands of leaves disturbs the peace of this place. The sky darkens and releases potbellied raindrops, heavy with sadness. When she opens her eyes, they're deep indigo and brimming with tears.

"The wounding of disconnection took hold, and from there, disharmony and imbalance became the norm. My human children came to see themselves as not being of the Earth, but on the Earth . . . that they were no longer my children."

Charlie remembers. This was how the virus started.

CHAPTER 46

THE CEILING FAN TURNED in lazy circles above Charlie's bed. She stared at the blades while she adjusted to being back in her body. All the information she'd received in the Dreaming Realm, all the ancient memories that surfaced, the painful weight of First Mother's grief, gathered within her and took center stage.

She was strangely calm. Raven's Daughter was at the helm.

CHAPTER 47

BRENDA COULDN'T QUITE LOOK Charlie in the eye, so she pretended to organize the already organized pile of files on her desk. She stammered a bit, trying to figure out how to answer Charlie's question. "Maybe you should ask Mr. Malloy?"

Charlie shook her head. "Dan seems to want to protect me from whatever's going on here money-wise. I don't mean to put you in an awkward position, I just want to know if the business is in worse shape than he's letting on."

This was the longest conversation the two of them had ever had, which contributed to Brenda's uneasiness. She preferred to keep to herself. Numbers were predictable. People were not.

Charlie waited.

"Everything's fine," Brenda said.

Reflective silver globules floated through Brenda's eyes. She was lying.

"How bad is it? Layoffs next week? Bankruptcy in a month? What are we talking about?"

Brenda looked like she just got caught cutting class. "He doesn't tell me anything."

Brenda's eyes were clear. *This is a mighty handy superpower.*

When Charlie stopped fighting Raven's Daughter, she experienced the world around her with startling clarity.

"But the numbers don't look good. We have about two months of payroll if something drastic doesn't happen."

Still clear.

Charlie smiled. "Thank you for telling me." She got up to leave. "And please don't worry. I won't tell him we talked. I know what he's like when he feels he's been betrayed."

CHAPTER 48

THE DOWNSIDE OF SEEING with such clarity was that Charlie was now acutely aware of how bad *everything* was. Before she was healed, made whole, or whatever it was that happened which allowed Raven's Daughter's presence to emerge in a more pronounced way, she was masterful at avoidance. It wasn't a rose-colored glasses kind of thing. It was more of a "I don't have room for any more sadness" kind of thing.

She had a strange experience on her drive home from work. Well, a new kind of strange. She was stopped at a red light on the outskirts of town, taking in the desperately sad, withering landscape around her when her throat suddenly closed up. She couldn't breathe. It was as if all the moisture in her mouth had evaporated and her throat, her tongue, her esophagus—everything began to atrophy and collapse in on itself in sympathy, or maybe empathy. The desert wanted her to understand that it couldn't breathe.

She didn't panic. Instead, she had the thought that maybe her choking dreams were the natural world's way of getting her attention: asking for her help.

I'm going to do everything in my power, she thought. At that moment, her breathing returned to normal.

CHAPTER 49

DAN HANDED HER A beer when she came back into the kitchen after changing out of her work clothes. She took a sip and joined him at the kitchen table. His demeanor was stiff. Something was up. Maybe Brenda told him she'd been asking about finances?

"How was your day?" he asked.

"Good. Got a lot done." She took another sip. "Yours?"

"It was great." Beads of silver drifted through his eyes.

"Great," she said, and clinked her bottle with his. "Here's to having a good day."

He took another long pull off his beer. "I was thinking we could paint the spare bedroom this weekend."

She shrugged. "Okay." *Fuck. He wants to talk about having kids.*

She watched him. She never used to hold eye contact with him when they were interacting. Now she was seeing all kinds of things, like how surprised he was that she was looking at him. He was suspicious. So, she looked down and started peeling the label off her beer, a nervous habit that always drove Dan crazy. It seemed like a bad idea to make it obvious that she could see and feel so much more now.

"Yeah, maybe we can go to the paint store tomorrow after work. I was thinking pale yellow would be a good color."

She rolled the torn pieces of label into little balls and made a pile on the table.

"Sure, sounds good." Paint colors were the least of her concerns. She was hoping he'd change the subject.

"I mean, it makes sense, right? Since we decided we want the gender of our first child to be a surprise."

You decided that. She forced a smile and dutifully nodded.

After her last visit to the Dreaming Realm, there was no way she'd ever bring a child into this world in the state it was in. Not to mention that having a child would throw a monkey wrench into the whole fulfilling her destiny thing.

He huffed. "You know, it seems like you're never really interested in talking about starting a family."

Patience. She took a breath. *Patience.* "I'm sorry."

He slapped his hand hard on the table, and she jumped.

"Are you?" He lifted his hand and revealed her birth control pills. "Are you sorry? Or are you more interested in betraying me?"

She kept her head down.

"This was our plan, Charlotte. *Our* plan. You and me. We agreed to get married and start a family. This is not the deal we made."

I guess our marriage is transactional, like a real estate deal. Nice.

"What am I supposed to tell my mother? You want me to break her heart? Is that what you want?"

Shit, he promised Flora a grandchild. "No, of course not. I'm sorry. I guess I'm not ready."

The beer label was a pyramid of tiny paper balls, a miniature abstract art installation. She turned her attention to the sticky label glue left on the bottle and started scraping it with her thumbnail.

"What'll make you ready? Huh? A bigger house? A Mercedes Benz?"

Scrape. Scrape. Scrape. Tiny balls of glue sat next to the balls of paper.

"Come on, Charlotte, name your price. What do you want?"

Memory fragments of straightjackets and stonings and beratings by husbands named Dan passed through her mind. She pushed her naked beer bottle to the side and clasped one hand in the other in front of her bowed head. She stared at the grain running through the tabletop.

"Fuck you," she whispered.

This stopped him cold. "What did you say?"

She looked him in the eye. "I said, fuck you."

"What's going on with you?" Things were not computing for Dan. Concern slipped into bed with his anger. "You're not acting like yourself. I think you need help."

"Actually, I've never been more lucid."

Lucid. Holy shit. She smiled. *Lou. Syd.* Her well-dressed, fox-headed friend appeared in her mind's eye and gave her an enthusiastic high five.

"I don't have time for this." She grabbed her birth control pills, went to the bedroom, and started packing.

CHAPTER 50

A BIT OF MORNING light leaked in from the edges of the hotel's heavy blackout curtains. The room was still deliciously dark, though, and the weight of the blankets was perfect. Despite the pressure in her bladder, Charlie stayed in the same position she woke up in, the drone of the nearby interstate pulling at her, inviting her to close her eyes and go back to sleep. Since she left Dan a week ago, she'd had some of the most peaceful sleep she's had since she was a child.

Shouldn't she be more anxious?

Her Charlie-ness voted yes, but her Raven's Daughter-ness didn't seem phased. Just another day at the office.

"I don't know how you can stand it," Syd's BBC-tinged voice interrupted her morning peace. Charlie saw her fox-headed friend in her mind's eye, pacing in a tight circle at the foot of her bed with her hands on her lower abdomen as if having sympathy bladder fullness.

"But I don't wanna get up," she whined to Syd and her bladder.

On her way back from the bathroom, Charlie powered up the flat-screen TV and put on the morning show. Nothing like a little forced cheerful banter coupled with the deadpan delivery of the latest headlines to keep you company in your motel room while you figured out how to save the world. She made it through thirty seconds before hitting the mute button.

She spilled the contents of her backpack on the dresser, found her last remaining protein bar, and climbed back into bed.

"Good morning, Charlie," Lou chimed in. "What's on the schedule for today?" He pronounced it *shed-u-al*.

At the foot of her bed, she saw him sitting, elegant long legs crossed, at an outdoor bistro table, sipping espresso from a delicate ivory cup. Somehow, he managed to not only do this with a pointy, curved beak, but also made it look natural.

"Let's go shopping!" Syd said.

Charlie and Lou stared at her.

"I want an inflatable vest," she added.

The staring continued. One beat, two beats, and then Charlie said to Lou, "Laundry. I'm out of clean underwear. And I wanna take the afternoon class. It's been a couple of months."

Syd dropped into a sparring stance and hopped around like a boxer.

"Don't mock me," she told Syd. "I don't look anything like that when I spar."

Lou's dry stare conveyed his annoyance. It was amazing how expressive his inexpressive hawk face could be. Going to kung fu was not the plan he hoped she'd have.

"What?" she said to him. "I've gotta see a man about a goat."

Syd waggled her bushy eyebrows.

Lou tapped his manicured fingertips on the tabletop.

"I know. I know," she said. "I need to come up with a plan." So much for feeling peaceful.

She'd had a plan. Her plan was to have Eve tell her what her plan should be. The day after she'd left Dan, she went to see Eve, confident she'd tell her what to do next. But Eve hit a wall, couldn't perceive a thing, which to her meant that Charlie had to figure it out on her own. Charlie didn't have a backup plan.

So, she'd improvised. Thinking she'd find some inspiration in nature, she went for a hike up South Mountain, but the dying desert made her heart heavy and her throat tight, swallowing the potential for any insight she'd hoped she might find.

As a distraction, she'd thought about visiting her father, but she wasn't ready to break the news of her failed marriage to him yet. Plus, she knew he'd insist she stay with him and his wife. The good news was that hotel rates in Phoenix, the few that were still open, were startlingly affordable, which bought her some time to figure out her next step. She hoped.

Syd practiced jumping in place. She clearly didn't like being cooped up.

Charlie stared at the TV with a soft focus, not really watching. *I should visit my raven buddy, Paco, at the wildlife center. Maybe he can tell me what to do? With my luck, he'll bring me a fossilized French fry and send me on my way.*

"They're called chips," Syd said, still jumping.

"When in France," Charlie said.

"France? We're not in France."

"You're so literal."

"You say that like it's a bad—" Syd stopped. "What is it?"

Charlie sat forward, eyes coming into focus on the television. A river of swirling, reflective silver floated through the eyes of a handsome, dark-haired forty-something man being interviewed on the morning show. The caption at the bottom of the screen read, "Ricardo Boswell, Founder, B-Well Nanotechnologies."

The program transitioned from Ricardo's talking head to an animated video of a slowly spinning, light blue and white, capsule-shaped pill. Similar to a drug advertisement, the animation showed the pill traveling down the esophagus and into the stomach of a generic human avatar, where the two halves of the capsule separated and released hundreds of microscopic, orange, octagonal spheres. The tiny spheres made their way through the bloodstream, across the blood-brain barrier, and into the brain, where they instantly transformed clumps of neurons from melancholy gray to cheerful pink. The video concluded with the now-smiling human avatar wearing Bluetooth headphones. B-Well's simple app logo, a smiling cartoon bumblebee, came on the screen. An animated dotted line connected the logo to the headphones. "Bee Well with B-Well" appeared on the screen.

Charlie unmuted the TV.

"—cure depression and anxiety with one pill," Ricardo told Marti, the morning show host, his deep voice quiet yet confident. His eyes, swirling with mercurial silver, didn't flinch.

"That sounds too good to be true," Marti replied with a flirty smile.

"That's because it is, Marti," Charlie told the TV. "He's lying."

"I know it does," Ricardo said, mirroring Marti's smile. "But I promise you it's true. As a journalist, you're well aware that we're experiencing the worst global mental health crisis in human history. Unprecedented rates of addiction, overdoses, homelessness, suicides . . . the world is falling apart, and it's affecting all of us. The B-Well nano-pill is a scientifically proven solution that will change everything."

Dread rose in Charlie and wrapped around her torso.

"It must feel amazing to know that you're about to change the lives of so many people," Marti said.

He shrugged one shoulder. "I just wanna help."

"My understanding, Ricardo," Marti's voice became anchorwoman serious, "is that your invention, this life changing technology, was inspired by tragic events."

He nodded and looked down.

"Can you talk a little bit about what happened?"

He took a breath. "My father and younger brother both suffered from paralyzing depression. My father committed suicide when I was eleven, and my brother . . . well, my brother"—he paused. He was choked up. The silver was gone from his eyes. Ricardo cleared his throat—"my brother, sadly, followed in my father's footsteps. He took his own life ten years ago."

"I'm so sorry, Ricardo." Marti milked the moment. "What an amazing gift you're giving the world. A gift born out of painful loss. I imagine your father and brother are so proud of you."

Another shrug. "I hope so."

"When will the miraculous B-Well nano-pill be available?"

"The pill and B-Well support app—they work together—will be available on our website next week."

"Well," she turned to the camera, "I think it's safe to say that brighter days are on the horizon for many who are suffering from depression and anxiety." She turned back to her guest. "Thank you, Ricardo."

"Thank you."

"When we come back, learn to tango with—"

Charlie muted the TV again.

"Holy shit," she whispered. "This can't happen." She wondered if she was too late. She was lounging around in a hotel room while hustlers like Ricardo were conning vulnerable people. Her chest tightened as panic filled her for the first time in weeks. The weight of the responsibility hit her. *How am I gonna stop this?*

"Fuck. I need help," she pleaded to no one in particular.

Lou put down his espresso. "I thought you'd never ask."

"You can help me?"

"That's why we're here."

"Why didn't you say anything?"

"We were waiting for you to ask. We can't help you unless you ask. You never asked."

"Can you help me figure out what I should do? Please?"

"Most definitely," Lou said. He picked up the newspaper that sat on the bistro table and started to read.

She stared at him. For one minute. Two minutes.

He finally looked at her.

"Well?" she said.

"Well, what?"

"What should I do?"

"You've asked. Now you wait." He started reading again.

"What am I waiting for?"

He looked at her like she was two years old. "The answer will come to you. You'll know when it does."

She turned to Syd, still jumping in place. "Is he always this helpful?"

"Always," Syd responded.

Charlie reclined into the pile of pillows stacked against the headboard and closed her eyes. Maybe if she meditated, the answers would come faster? Deep breath in . . . *thump, thump, thump* . . . exhale . . . *thump, thump, thump* . . . deep breath in . . . *thump, thump, thump* . . .

"Hey, Syd."

"Yeah, boss."

"Do you think you could stop jumping for a bit?"

"No, I don't think so."

"Alrighty then. Laundry it is."

CHAPTER 51

CHARLIE WATCHED HER OPPONENT move in awkward, jerky move-ments—forward, then back, then to the side, and back, like a waltzing chicken. She'd sparred with this young woman months ago, back when she suspected her moves were equally chicken-like. But today was different. Charlie was calm and focused and still. She watched her opponent raise her right fist, set her jaw, and lean forward, clearly broadcasting that she was about to throw a strike. As the strike came in, Charlie simply stepped to the side, blocked it with the ridge of her left forearm, and quickly followed up with a controlled punch with her free hand that gently kissed her opponent's abdomen. Her sparring partner's saucer-like eyes signaled she was mentally tapping out, and the match was over.

Charlie's instructor, Mark, gave her a thumbs-up from the sidelines. But his smile didn't reach his eyes. It turned out that she came back on the last day the school would be open.

"We're moving to Oregon," he told Charlie after sparring was over. "My wife got a job in Portland, and I'm gonna be a stay-at-home dad. It'll be good," he said as if trying to convince himself. "Who knows? Maybe I can open a school up there."

"They'll be lucky to have you," she said. "I feel really lucky to have had you as a teacher."

"It's been fun to watch you come out of your shell." He clapped her on the shoulder. "We gotta bottle whatever it is you've been doing recently and sell it."

She laughed.

"Ah, there he is." Mark looked over her shoulder. "The one who prob-ably deserves more credit than me for how far you've come."

"Did he break the sad news?" Goatman asked her.

"Yeah. I'm extra glad I came today," she said. "I had no idea."

Mark excused himself to answer the phone.

"So, have you been cheating on me?" Goatman asked. "I thought maybe you found another incredibly talented and handsome Shaolin instructor to train with."

She blushed. "Yeah, his name is Claudio. He's a triple-fourteen-degree black belt. Really talented and crazy hot."

"You sparred really well today," he said. "You were poised and controlled."

"Thanks." *Fuck. Why does he make me blush so much?*

He looked her over. "You've changed. What's different?"

"I went to the testicle store and bought a dozen."

He laughed.

"I left Dan."

He didn't hide his shock. "The guy you just married?"

"Yup." A part of her noted how at ease and confident she felt.

He hesitated and bit his lip the way he always did when he was trying to figure out what to say. "It wasn't because of me, what we—"

"No, not really." She was a bit sad by how relieved he looked. "I think that little side trip we took was just a symptom of a much bigger problem. Granted, a wickedly fun symptom," she said with a grin. "No regrets on my end." She took a breath. "Truth is, Dan can be an asshole and I can be a coward."

"So, you went to the testicle store."

"Pretty much."

"I can't get over how different you are. Don't get me wrong, it's great." He shook his head. "It's just . . . I don't know. You're still you, but it's like you're comfortable in your skin."

"That's really sweet. Thank you. It means a lot." *He's right*, she thought. "It's been tough. So, it's nice to hear."

"So, what's next for you?"

"I'm not sure. But I can't stay here."

While looking for something in her suitcase that morning, she'd stumbled across the business card Luna, the tattoo artist, had given her. Seeing it made the hair on her arms and neck stand on end.

She'd informed Lou and Syd that she was making an addendum to the day's plan. "After laundry and kung fu, I'm gonna call Luna"—she glanced at the card—"Mitchell and see what she's up to." A curt nod from Lou over his newspaper while Syd, sporting a shit-eating grin, jumped up on the bed in triumph as if she was about to accept a gold medal. *Okay*, Charlie thought at that moment, *this is what help looks like. Good to know.*

"I think it's time for an adventure," she told Goatman. "How about you?"

"It looks like we're heading out of state too. Florida."

"We?"

"Yeah." Now it was Goatman's turn to blush. "Me and my girlfriend, Jessa."

Simultaneously, her heart dropped (Charlie) and she was relieved (Raven's Daughter).

"That's great," she managed to say. "I'm happy for you."

He grinned in a goofy, boyish way.

"Man," she said, "it seems like so much is changing so quickly."

"I'll miss you," he said. "We had fun."

"Yeah." She smiled. "We did."

CHAPTER 52

"THE SITUATION IS CRITICAL," First Mother says under a foreboding sky a shade of steel gray Ahkoa has never seen in the Dreaming Realm—what's left of it, anyway.

The once-limitless-seeming boundaries of the Dreaming Realm are shrinking before his eyes at an unprecedented rate as the Mental Realm swells with malignancy. He nods his agreement. First Mother's expression reveals a depth of pain and weariness that startles him. She's always seemed impervious to . . . everything.

"I can't feel my human children anymore," she confides after a long silence.

His chest tightens. This is the last thing he expected her to say. The tinge of hopelessness in her words reveals how vulnerable they all are, which makes their situation feel that much more dire—and real. An unsettling insight emerges—how much he's counted on First Mother's unwavering trust that all is well to balance out his growing pessimism.

"I believe their attempts at playing god have only helped the virus spread faster," he tries to explain.

A warning flashes through her eyes.

He knows he's pushing it. She's never tolerated comments implying anything negative about any of the creatures she's dreamed into existence. He takes a moment to check himself. "I mean no offense," he says. "What I mean to convey is that it appears the machines they've created are now thinking and acting independently of them. They call it artificial intelligence."

She nods for him to continue.

"This machine intelligence is designed to mimic them, but also make their lives better." As she absorbs the meaning of his words, the sky grows even darker. "It seems it's now infiltrated all of their communications, creating and spreading deception across the planet like lightning. Truth is becoming a relic."

In turn, human dreaming is inaccessible, at least for those still able to dream. It seems that he and the entire Raven Clan have become irrelevant.

And now, after his meeting with First Mother, he doesn't know where to be or what to do with himself.

The source of the lion's share of his angst, however, is driving across the country. Alone. He should be at her side. Instead, he flies above Charlie's car for no reason other than to alleviate some of his guilt, but he knows it's futile. Where Raven's Daughter is going, she has to go alone.

PART TWO

THE HOLLOW PEOPLE

CHAPTER 53

SAM JENKINS WANTED HIS old college friend and colleague to squirm. Dev, however, was unphased. He didn't rush to answer Sam's question. Instead, he took his time and stirred cream into his coffee. Then he tasted it, added a little more cream, and stirred some more. Thirteen years as the CEO of the wildly popular e-zine, *Pulse Wire*, had clearly acquainted him with being in the hot seat.

But Sam had mastered this game. He could wait. His youthful appearance and large, innocent blue eyes never failed to capture and maintain an expression of nonthreatening curiosity for as long as needed to get his subject to talk. A journalistic tactic he referred to as playing "eyeball chicken." It worked like a charm.

Sam waited for Dev to make eye contact and tried again with a tone that didn't convey anger but genuine confusion. "I don't get it. What happened?"

Dev sighed. "Look, your piece was excellent," he said with the barest hint of a Pakistani accent. "You think I keep hiring you for your boyish good looks?"

Sam chuckled. It was a loaded question.

He and Dev had been inseparable in college after meeting at a Futurist Club gathering early in their freshman year. At that fateful meeting, they'd discovered they were both media studies majors and shared an obsession for jigsaw puzzles and old-school Godzilla movies. When they weren't in class, they could be found stoned on hash, huddled over an impossible-seeming 3-D puzzle in Dev's dorm room while waxing poetic about their futures and how technology was going to transform the world. Dev was to create a media empire, which he did, and Sam would be his star journalist, which he was.

During the early years of their friendship, Sam wondered if Dev was falling for him. Every once in a while, Dev seemed to test the waters with an extended glance or by making a joke about how his uber-conservative parents threatened to find a wife for him if he didn't find a nice girl.

And then the thing Sam dreaded might happen, happened. They were celebrating at a local Seattle brewpub the night Dev launched the inaugural issue of *Pulse Wire*.

Sam had written an explosive, well-researched investigative piece revealing how the leading manufacturer of self-driving vehicles had made lethal hardware shortcuts in order to lower costs that would later not only result in the institution of nationwide regulations for autonomous vehicles that would save millions of lives, but also shoot Dev and his fledgling e-zine into the stratosphere.

High on excitement, hash, and microbrew, Dev pulled Sam into a tight bro-hug that quickly softened into something more intimate. Dev's warm, full lips brushed against Sam's neck, and his body reflexively stiffened. Without making eye contact, Dev released him, grabbed his beer, and took a "holy shit, this is awkward" swig.

"Hey," Sam said, grabbing Dev by the biceps. "I'm sorry, Dee." He tried to get Dev to look at him. "I seriously wish I was gay because you're an amazing guy. An incredible friend. You're talented and smart. Good-looking as hell. Anyone would be lucky to have you."

Dev risked eye contact. "How do you know if you don't try?"

This time, Sam was the one having trouble keeping eye contact. "I tried one time with this guy in high school. It was kind of a disaster." He took a breath. "I'm sorry, Dev. I'm just not sexually attracted to men."

Their relationship was never the same. They still managed to have fun, but Dev had suited up in emotional armor, and the closeness they'd shared was gone.

Now, sitting across from his friend, Dev had never felt more distant than he did at that moment.

"The article . . ." Dev explained, "it just wasn't what we were looking for. I asked you for a profile of Boswell and his company, not an exposé."

"But what I uncovered about this guy—he's dangerous and slick as hell."

Dev was unmoved.

"I'm serious. We need to warn people about his bullshit wellness technology before it's released."

"I think you got this one wrong, buddy. I met with Boswell, and he showed me. I saw it with my own eyes. He found a legit way to use nanotechnology to rewire the brain."

And there it was. As Dev spoke, Sam perceived the telltale asymmetrical spikes of deception sprouting from a field of matte gray in his mind's eye. Dev was lying. Sam's unusual form of chromesthesia was his superpower. He sensed tones and timbre of speech as moving patterns of color. It was something virtually no one—with the exception of his parents and second grade teacher, who was the first to recognize his unique ability—knew he had.

"It's a game changer, and *Pulse Wire* is breaking the story."

Dev paused and looked out the front window. "I assigned the story to someone else. An intern."

This was not the Dev he knew. "Dev." He waited until Dev made eye contact. "Did you even read my piece?"

"Of course I did."

Gray spikes.

"Then you know that Boswell funded his own research. There's no miraculous nanotech pill. There's no nanotech, period."

Dev sipped his coffee.

"The issue," Sam continued, "is the B-Well app that comes with the pill. You remember Jersey?"

Dev smiled. "Yeah, our favorite savant hacker."

"I had Jersey take a deep dive into Boswell's app. What he found didn't make it into my piece because he just got back to me last night, but it's more nefarious than I thought." He knew he was probably not going to get through to Dev, but he would feel like shit if he didn't try.

"So, the consumer spends three grand for one miraculous-seeming nanotech capsule and fifty bucks a month for a subscription to the B-Well app, which on its face is pretty much like every other mindfulness app out there."

Dev gave him an *I-got-places-to-be* nod.

"I don't know what Boswell showed you," Sam continued, his tone neutral, "but the nanotech capsule is pretty much your garden-variety vitamin B supplement. That's all consumers are getting—a three-thousand-dollar energy boost."

Dev was wearing the neutral expression he wore anytime he was attempting to be nonjudgmental, which, from where Sam sat, was consistently ineffective. If you have to try to look neutral, then you're not really neutral, are you?

But that didn't stop Sam from trying to make his case. "Two rock-solid sources," he continued, the tension in his voice building, "confirmed that Boswell paid a private third-party lab a shit ton of money to officially report that a double-blind study found that B-Well nanotech accurately diagnosed and corrected the imbalanced brain chemistry in a whopping eighty-eight percent of study participants suffering from major clinical depression. No study was done. The guy's full of shit."

There was a hint of a smirk curdling at the corners of Dev's lips.

Sam closed his eyes and took a breath. "But, like I said, it's more disturbing than that. Boswell's definitely going to change peoples' brains, but not in the way you think. Jersey discovered that his innocent-seeming B-Well app uses some crazy cutting-edge mind control." He paused, but Dev showed zero sign of caring. "Embedded under a bunch of boilerplate affirmations is a new kind of advanced brainwave technology that almost instantly puts the user into a manic state."

Dev's smirk widened to a grin.

"Come on, man," Sam said. "This is serious. People using that app are gonna get addicted to it. It's like audio meth."

"Listen to yourself. Do you know how crazy you sound right now?" Dev shook his head. "Not everything's a conspiracy."

"Since when have you known me to jump to any conclusions without proof?" He pulled out his phone. "Jersey sent me a sample of what he isolated. He amplified the tones so I could hear what he was talking about." He swiped the screen a few times. "I'm gonna send it to your earbuds." He hit play on the screen.

Sam watched Dev's pupils constrict, then the muscles in his jaws twitch and clench.

Sam continued, "It's a genius way to fuck people up without them knowing it *and* make a bunch of money in the process. It's like new age MKUltra for the AI generation, only, instead of torturing people, Boswell's using flowery platitudes to covertly restructure their brains."

"I don't know what to say, Sam," Dev said. "You're better than this." He feigned concern for his friend. "Are you sure Jersey didn't use a little mind control on you? That guy lost credibility years ago. He's a drug addict. How do you know he didn't deep fake your"—he made air quotation marks—"evidence?"

Sam let the lemon-yellow of Dev's condescension drip off him and onto the floor. "Boswell paid you off too, didn't he?"

"Are you kidding me right now?" Dev said, rubbing his chin. "How could you even say that about me?"

He didn't need to see the gray spikes this time. Dev always rubbed his chin when he was uncomfortable about lying. Sam was furious. He got up to leave. "If you don't run my story, I'll find a way to get it out there."

"Don't be a drama queen."

Sam shook his head and left.

CHAPTER 54

CHARLIE WAS ALONE IN the stark lobby, not knowing what to do, feeling awkward. The spacious room was a bit disorienting. Everything—the walls, floor, high ceiling, and reception desk—was the same shade of white, which messed with her depth perception. There were no shadows in this room, which gave it a disturbing two-dimensional feel. It reminded her of the mental hellscape one of Raven's Daughter's former identities had been trapped in.

She turned and looked for the door she'd just come through. It was now hidden, and the wall of glass spanning the front of the lobby was opaque and also white. *Fuck this.* Charlie was ready to break through the glass like an action hero, drive to Tennessee, move in with Ginger and Milo, and get a job working at a waffle restaurant until the world ended. But Raven's Daughter called out, "Hello."

In response, a soft mechanical thrum filled the silence as five slender, white, mounted cameras moved in the direction of her voice. Simultaneously, their black lenses opened and stared at her.

A soothing, disembodied female voice said, "Welcome to the Eleventh Floor Clubhouse, Charlie. On the desk in front of you, you'll find a small rectangular box. Please open this box."

Even Raven's Daughter was more than a little creeped out that the voice knew who she was. Maybe she was the only one they were expecting? Or the code Luna gave her to open the front door was specific to her?

She didn't see the box at first, but when she moved closer to the desk, it came into focus. Inside the small white rectangular box was a small white card that read, "Your Senz-Sight™ lenses." Underneath was a white velvet pouch that held a sleek pair of glasses.

"What are you waiting for?" Syd's voice said in her mind. "Put them on!"

The clear, frameless lenses curved around her face like minimalist goggles. Her visual field was suddenly assaulted by an explosion of color. So many shades of blue. Her brain registered the sound of the ocean before she saw it. When her eyes focused, she was looking out over the sea—but all at once, her insides felt like they'd dropped down about a foot within the shell of her body. This sensation was accompanied by a nauseating wave of vertigo, which thankfully passed moments later after she closed her eyes.

When her breathing and sense of balance regulated, she risked opening her eyes again. Now, she was jolted by the disorienting experience of déjà vu. She was back in Hawaii at the very same park where she'd had the conversation with the old Hawaiian man who wasn't there. The scenery was hyper-realistic, except she couldn't feel the breeze or smell the briny sea.

She turned around and saw the smoldering volcano in the distance. In the foreground, not far from where she stood, was a tiki bar with a bouquet of tropical flowers and enticing platters of pineapple and papaya. Her mouth watered. She was so engaged with this new environment that she momentarily forgot she was still in the lobby. Then, she saw the slender white box sitting next to a pitcher of mango juice and realized that the tiki bar was the lobby desk. Mixed reality.

"Please help yourself to some refreshments, Charlie," said the voice.

What voodoo is this? She took a tentative step toward the tiki bar. And then another. The closer she got, the more blown away she was by the detail of the items on the bar. The streaks of condensation on the pitcher, the fibrous ridges of the pineapple rings, and the deep orange of the papaya.

"You want me to pretend to eat virtual fruit?"

The voice laughed. "No, the fruit is quite real. So is the juice."

She reached her pointer finger out, expecting it to pierce through the virtual pitcher, but instead touched its cold, wet surface. *How did they get the real stuff on the desk without me seeing them do it?* Maybe she'd been disoriented longer than she thought. She grabbed a glass—also real—and helped herself to some juice. She moaned when it hit her taste buds. It was perfect. Cold and smooth and rich.

She turned back toward the ocean.

I could get used to this. I'll just hang out in the beach lobby and eat fruit and stare at the virtual ocean. And then it hit her. *How the fuck did they know about my trip to Hawaii?* And this place, in particular.

Lou was sitting in a red-and-white striped beach chair under a giant yellow umbrella. "Perhaps they accessed the photographs you took with your phone."

Oh. She cringed. *That's fucked up.*

"Indeed, it is," he replied.

Seeing him and hearing his voice was instantly comforting. She wasn't alone.

"We're so glad you're here, Charlie," said the discarnate lobby voice. "We have so much to show you and to share with you. We hope you'll join us for the adventure of a lifetime. One that will change you in unexpected and amazing ways."

"Will there be more mango juice?"

More laughter. "We have many culinary delights."

While Charlie pondered whether or not this was a good idea, Raven's Daughter said, "I'm ready."

A floating scroll of yellowed digital paper appeared in front of her.

The voice continued: "This agreement explains all of our policies in detail. Your responsibilities, as well as ours. There's a lot of legalese, but it's basically a standard user agreement."

The scroll unfurled, and words magically spelled themselves out as the voice spoke them.

WELCOME, CHARLIE!

WE ARE EXCITED YOU'RE HERE! WE PROMISE TO SUPPORT AND TAKE CARE OF YOU IN ALL WAYS, SO THAT YOU HAVE THE FREEDOM TO EXPLORE AND EVOLVE INTO YOUR IDEAL SELF.

HERE AT THE CLUBHOUSE, WE'VE CREATED A SAFE ENVIRONMENT FOR YOU TO UNEARTH AND INVENT YOUR DREAM IDENTITY, AND TO DESIGN A WORLD OF YOUR CHOOSING.

You are the master of your self-expression and your domain!

In exchange, we ask that, as a member of the Eleventh Floor Clubhouse, you agree to and abide by the following rules:

- **You will surrender all items related to your former identity including but not limited to:**
  - **Your cell phone and any devices you have in your possession**
  - **ID cards**
  - **Valuables such as jewelry, cash, credit cards, etc.**
  - **Clothing**
  - **Keys**

During your stay, these items will be secured. If you or the Eleventh Floor Clubhouse Council choose to terminate your membership, all items will be returned to you.

Charlie's stomach clenched. *Don't. Like. This.*

Lou appeared in her mind's eye, next to the scroll. "Look at me, Charlie," he said. "You're not alone. We're always with you." Syd's furry, triangle-eared head briefly popped up behind Lou's shoulder as if she were trying to photobomb the moment.

Charlie shook her head and smiled.

She reminded herself that she could truly be one hundred percent bat-shit crazy, or she had the most entertaining invisible friends in the history of invisible friends. But it worked—she felt calmer.

- YOU WILL NOT REVEAL YOUR NAME, AGE, RACE, OR ANYTHING ABOUT YOUR PREVIOUS LIFE TO FELLOW ELEVENTH FLOOR CLUBHOUSE MEMBERS OR STAFF. YOU WILL BE GIVEN A SIMPLE TEMPORARY NAME UNTIL YOUR RITE-OF-SELF CEREMONY.

- YOU WILL HAVE ACCESS TO A VoIP APP THAT WILL ALLOW YOU TO MAKE PHONE CALLS TO YOUR LOVED ONES DURING YOUR RESIDENCY. THE APP WILL BE ACCESSIBLE FOR THIRTY MINUTES EVERY SUNDAY EVENING AT 6 P.M.

- YOU WILL NOT USE YOUR SENZ-SIGHT™ LENSES TO ACCESS THE INTERNET, INCLUDING BUT NOT LIMITED TO SOCIAL MEDIA ACCOUNTS, NEWS HEADLINES, EMAIL ACCOUNTS, ETC. THE COUNCIL WILL BE NOTIFIED OF ANY PROHIBITED ACTIVITY.

- FOR YOUR SAFETY, YOUR SENZ-SIGHT™ LENSES ARE TO BE WORN AT ALL TIMES OUTSIDE OF YOUR QUARTERS.

- THERE IS NO MONEY EXCHANGED AT THE ELEVENTH FLOOR CLUBHOUSE. OUR CURRENCY IS KINDNESS.

- AS A MEMBER OF THE CLUBHOUSE, YOU AGREE TO:

  - ENGAGE IN A MINIMUM OF ONE HOUR OF PHYSICAL ACTIVITY DAILY.

  - ATTEND A MINIMUM OF THREE WELLNESS COACHING SESSIONS A WEEK TO HELP YOU REACH YOUR PERSONAL GROWTH GOALS.

  - ATTEND THE WEEKLY EVENING GATHERING, WHERE

YOU'LL RECEIVE TEACHINGS FROM ONE OF THE
FOUNDER'S DESIGNATED MASTER MEMBERS.

○ TO ASSIST YOU IN YOUR PROCESS, WHEN APPRO-
   PRIATE, PLEASE AVOID USING THE WORD "NO." IN-
   STEAD, IF YOU ARE NOT INTERESTED IN PARTICIPAT-
   ING IN AN ACTIVITY OR WOULD LIKE TO DECLINE
   A REQUEST FROM ONE OF OUR STAFF OR A FELLOW
   MEMBER, PLEASE RESPOND WITH, "MAYBE ANOTH-
   ER TIME!"

*PLEASE NOTE: IF YOU BREAK ANY OF THESE RULES, YOU
WILL BE REQUIRED TO ATTEND A HEARING FACILITATED
BY THE ELEVENTH FLOOR CLUBHOUSE COUNCIL, WHERE
YOUR BEHAVIOR WILL BE EVALUATED AND ADDRESSED
APPROPRIATELY.*

YOU ARE FREE TO LEAVE THE *ELEVENTH FLOOR CLUB-
HOUSE* AT ANY TIME

*IF YOU DECIDE TO LEAVE THE PREMISES OR TERMINATE
YOUR MEMBERSHIP, YOU ARE REQUIRED TO MEET WITH
A WELLNESS ADVISOR PRIOR TO YOUR DEPARTURE TO
PREPARE YOU FOR RE-ENTRY INTO THE OUTSIDE WORLD,
WHICH CAN BE JARRING.*

So much for calm.

This must be what prison feels like, Charlie thought. As each rule was read, invisible walls closed in around her. Her ears were hot, and cortisol flooded her system, making her body feel shaky.

Lou appeared again. "This is why we're here, Charlie."

I don't know about this. For a moment, she longed for her former mundane life, her boring job, her fantasies.

"Everything's unfolding as it should," he assured her. "This place will give us access to the Mental Realm. The easiest access yet."

Oh yeah, she thought with dread, *the virus.* She was proficient at denial. She'd have to put that on her resume.

"Let Raven's Daughter help you," Lou said. "She knows what to do."

"Do you have any questions, Charlie?" the disembodied voice asked.

Fuck me. She took a deep breath. "No, I think I'm good."

"Well, then, if you're ready to complete the agreement, wait until the end of the countdown and then read the text that appears in front of you out loud."

"I'm ready," Raven's Daughter said.

THREE . . . TWO . . . ONE . . .

CHAPTER 55

AHKOA WATCHED GERTY THROUGH the small, otherworldly portal. Her aging face glowed in the unnatural light of her laptop. She was propped up in her bed, as she was most nights, surrounded by darkness. She couldn't sleep. She logged in to the discussion board and read the latest comments.

> amyl467: OMG! This explains everything. I'm so glad I found this thread.

> mtthw3: i am freaked the fuck out right now.

> spirasee98: how could we not see this sooner?

> lmelda5555: how do you know if you're a zombie? Is it too late?

Despite the anxiety it always caused her, she reread the original post:

> no_secrets2032: Maybe you've heard of this group called The Peacemakers? It's a not-so-secret group of—you guessed it—the most wealthy people on the planet. The overt mission of this group is to spread their wealth and eliminate poverty and hunger. If only that were true. I have proof that their TRUE mission is to turn all of us into a race of zombies. Not flesh-eating zombies. More like consumer zombies—wake up, scroll, commute, scroll, work, scroll, eat, scroll. Consume, consume, consume. Rinse,

repeat. They call it project DL (digital lobotomy). For decades they've invested lots of money in tech companies to create technologies designed to decrease our intelligence while making themselves richer. We're like Pavlov's dogs, drooling every time we get a notification or a like. One dopamine hit after another. Good old-fashioned classical conditioning designed to make us dumb. And it's working. In the US the average IQ of high school seniors has dropped TEN FUCKING POINTS. Europe and Asia are reporting similar statistics. Critical thinking is an artifact of the 20th century.

The familiar lump settled in her abdomen. She knew it was true. She was a fifty-two-year-old middle school science teacher and was seeing it in her classroom. For the past fifteen or so years, before the pandemic, she noticed that her students were engaging less with each other, with her, and with the material she was teaching. She gave up trying to get them to participate in class discussions about five years ago. They were bored. They were uninspired. They didn't seem to care. Unless they were on their phones.

What kind of world do we live in?

I WISH I KNEW, Ahkoa thinks as the portal closes.

CHAPTER 56

SAM OPENED THE DOOR to his quarters and was surprised to see that it was small and monastic. A simple, comfortable place for contemplation, like something you'd maybe find on a spaceship. He thought it'd be more virtually tricked out, like Vegas. But maybe if the rooms were too engaging, members would never explore the rest of the Clubhouse. Three of the walls were a soothing sage green, and the fourth wall was a virtual terrarium that contained a small trickling fountain surrounded by a miniature forest of exotic plants and bonsai-like trees. He decided not to expend what was left of his mental energy trying to figure out why all the virtual plants were varying shades of grape juice.

Opposite the terrarium was a simple twin mattress that seemed to magically hover several feet off the bamboo floor. He tried to imagine himself feeling at home in this strange space.

Things were not going as he'd hoped. His intention was to have a quick sit-down with the Clubhouse founder, maybe a tour of the facility, so he could get the article written and turned in by the end of the week. He was ready to put Dev and *PulseWire* behind him.

But nope.

"He's happy to give you an interview," the founder's smiling assistant had told him when he arrived at the Clubhouse. Her words were viscous, headache-inducing, hot pink in his mind, which told him she was AI—human intention programmed into computer language, translated as a spectrum of cloying liquiform pinks. The further away from humans the coding got, the more neon the pink.

"He's a fan," she said, seemingly buttering him up. "Just this morning, he told me he's very impressed with your impeccable body of work. That's a direct quote." She paused to let him soak in the compliment.

He was growing impatient.

"And since you are our first journalist guest, and most likely the only journalist who the founder will speak to"—she leaned in and gave him a sparkling *today's your lucky day* smile. Sam tried not to yawn—"he's promised to grant you an exclusive interview"—one beat, two beats—"once he feels you've fully immersed yourself in the Eleventh Floor Clubhouse experience. He wants you to live here with us, to engage in the experience, so you can really capture the essence of his creation, rather than have you regurgitate a generic brochure description of the Clubhouse in your article."

"What's your name?" Sam asked.

It took a moment for her to recalibrate from this random subject change, but she recovered quickly. "Misha."

"Are you a member of the Clubhouse?" He wanted to see if she would reveal that she wasn't human.

"Oh, yeah. All of the Clubhouse employees are members."

He smiled. She was an impressive AI. Her avatar was a slender, mixed-race woman in her forties, with long dark hair. Attractive, but not distractingly so. Her gestures and facial expressions were seamless, no glitches whatsoever, and her voice was calming.

"Of course," she continued, "for the safety and privacy of all our members, there are rules each member must agree to and follow, without exception. These rules make it possible for you to feel at ease exploring who you want to become."

"Do I need a lawyer?" Sam asked, joking. Sort of. He was tired and growing more annoyed by the minute. He wondered if Dev giving him the "cushy Eleventh Floor Clubhouse assignment" was his passive aggressive way of getting him to quit so he wouldn't have to fire him. *Mission accomplished, Dev.*

After his consent was recorded, Misha told him how excited she was for him. Her words came across as genuine, even though they were coated in fuchsia nail polish.

"I really can leave at any time?" he asked Misha.

"I don't know why anyone would want to," she said. "But yes, you're free to leave at any time. You're not a prisoner."

Then why did he feel like one?

"We've been in communication with Dev and let him know that you'll be our Journalist in Residence."

"Wow, that's quite an honor," he said, suppressing an eye roll. "How long will I be in residence?"

Misha gave him a very human shrug. "There's a lot to explore."

Shit.

HE BARGAINED WITH HIMSELF as he looked around his futuristic monk's quarters. *I'll give it a week—no, three days—and if I hate this place, I'll leave. Fuck the story. Fuck Dev.*

Sitting on the floating bed was another rectangular gift box. This one was larger than the one containing his mixed reality lenses. The surface of the box was alive, a visual symphony of swirling liquid gold clambering for his attention. He set his backpack down and opened it. Inside, a virtual white postcard sat on top of crisp white tissue paper. He swiped his hand over it, and the postcard magically levitated and enlarged so he could easily read it.

HELLO SAM,

ENCLOSED IS YOUR SENZ-SKIN™, A COMFORTABLE STATE-OF-THE-ART APPARATUS THAT, WHEN WORN IN CONJUNCTION WITH YOUR SENZ-SIGHT™ LENSES, WILL MAKE YOUR VIRTUAL WORLD EXPERIENCE INDISTINGUISHABLE FROM YOUR PHYSICAL WORLD EXPERIENCE.

FOR YOUR SAFETY, AND FOR THE OPTIMAL ELEVENTH FLOOR CLUBHOUSE EXPERIENCE, PLEASE ADHERE TO THE FOLLOWING GUIDELINES:

- YOUR SENZ-SKIN™ IS DESIGNED TO BE WORN AGAINST YOUR BARE SKIN. (FOR MODESTY PURPOSES, COMFORTABLE SILK LEISURE WEAR HAS BEEN PROVIDED FOR YOU AND CAN BE WORN OVER YOUR SENZ-SKIN™.)

- **No undergarments are needed and will only detract from your full sensory experience.**

- **For hygiene purposes, do not let anyone else wear your Senz-Skin™.**

- **Your Senz-Skin™ is the property of the Eleventh Floor Clubhouse and is not permitted to be worn off-site. Violators will be prosecuted.**

- **Images, still or moving, of your Senz-Skin™ are prohibited. Violators will be prosecuted.**

- **Do not submerge your Senz-Skin™ in water. REMOVE YOUR Senz-Skin™ BEFORE BATHING.**

They sure like their rules, he thought. Sam unwrapped the tissue paper and lifted out a translucent, metallic-gray, head-to-toe onesie and gloves. It wasn't like any kind of fabric he'd seen before. It was whisper-soft, practically weightless, and stretched and flexed like spandex. His lenses zoomed in and revealed a mesh weave with a network of tiny, flat, round discs he assumed were sensors. He made a mental note to find a secure location to send Jersey a photo of the fabric.

When he was working on the Boswell story, Jersey had given him a black ops comm device that, to the untrained eye, looked like an electric razor. It had all the functions of a standard cell phone but was impossible to detect or trace. This was some next-level James Bond shit.

As he disrobed, he wondered if he was being watched. *I'll give it 24 hours.*

CHAPTER 57

"Namaste, motherfuckers! Todd here, with another episode of *I'll Try It So You Don't Have To.*"

(canned cheering)

"Today, I'm cold plunging. That's right. I never claimed to be smart. Although a lot of smart people claim—have been for years—that getting into freezing cold water is good for you. They say it turns your fat cells brown or some such thing, and then you burn the fat off like babies do. Haven't seen many skinny babies, have you?

"Maybe they're just a bunch of racist pranksters who get off on calling fat brown in the name of science when it's probably really orange or something. If I'm right, then that's fucked up and weird. But we're gonna find out if they're right or if the joke's on us. Maybe the mighty brain trust is sittin' back right now thinking up the next great way to fuck with us. In a couple of weeks, we might all be playing dodgeball with bowling balls to prevent Alzheimer's.

"As you can see from all the white stuff on the ground, I drove north for hundreds of miles until I found winter. And let me just say, winter was hard to find.

"A couple of locals told me this is a popular swimming hole. So, I guess I'm going swimming. Outside—in the winter. I'm an idiot. Just ask the big black bird who's watching me . . . See him in the tree? Fucker's huge. Hi, bird. Yeah, that bird is totally mocking me.

"Okay. Lemme just . . . Fuck, it's cold out here. Maybe I should keep my sneakers on? On second thought . . . they might weigh me down. And I haven't drawn up my will yet. But as soon as I recover from hypothermia, I'm going to create a will on legalchimp.com. Let me take this moment to thank legalchimp.com for sponsoring this episode. It's so easy to get legal shit done with legalchimp.com.

"Man, that water looks terrifying.

"Well, here goes nothing."

(splash)

"GODDAMN, THAT'S COLD. Trying to breathe . . . deeply. Can't. All I feel is pain."

(pant. pant.)

"It's like I'm being stabbed by . . . a thousand icicles . . . at the same time. I feel cold-hot. I'm confused . . . Okay . . . This sucks. I'm done.

"Funny. The air feels warmer than my body now. And it's thirty-two degrees out. I wish I brought . . . seventeen more towels. Three is not enough. I gotta get in the car.

"Okay, it's been ten minutes with the heater on full blast. My skin feels less rubbery now, but I think I'm sterile. Cold plunging turned me into a Ken doll. I'll let you know next time if it's permanent. If it is, I'll be using legalchimp.com to sue the brain trust.

"So, I give the cold plunge experience a giant FUCK NO. I think the experience took several years off my life.

"Please subscribe to my channel for more life-saving tips. This is Todd, the village internet idiot who tries shit so you don't have to, signing off."

CHAPTER 58

IT WAS A LOT to process. Charlie stood at the entrance of the virtual lounge until she got her bearings, her eyes adjusting to the dim red glow of the hip vintage lamps. The lounge was spacious but somehow intimate. It reminded her of a speakeasy or maybe a bordello. Curvy velvet sofas the color of beet juice, adorned with leopard-print accent pillows, and low, kidney-shaped wooden tables decorated with small votive candles created cozy spaces to chat and have drinks. The walls were weather-worn brick. The one facing her held an arty mishmash of provocative, gold-framed, tasteful black-and-white photos of naked people that would change every minute or so. To her right were a few narrow horizontal windows close to the ceiling that offered a nighttime glimpse of a random city street, creating the illusion that she was not on the fourth floor but in a secret underground club. The muffled thump of bass seeped in from the nightclub next door. Everything looked so . . . real.

The patrons of this establishment, on the other hand, were a whole different story. In one of the cozy nooks, a roided-out gladiator chatted quietly with a unicorn who had a fountain of gold sparkles spewing from its horn. Floating next to the small bar was a giant ivory chess piece that somehow, without arms, managed to hand a pitchfork-wielding red devil a foamy lime-green martini. The remaining patrons translated only as blurs of colors and shapes. Her nervous system was in overload. She imagined she was in for a sleepless night as her body did its best to process all the crazy sensory information it was taking in.

She smiled at the thought that if she took off her mixed reality glasses, she'd be looking at a plain white room with nice furniture and a bunch of people wearing silk white bodysuits over their Senz-Skin. Mimes wearing glasses.

What did I get myself into?

Her old friend Doubt elbowed Raven's Daughter's confidence out of the way. Had been all day. After Charlie settled into her weird aquatic sleeping quarters with the weird shiny, electric-blue fish with large diamond-shaped scales swimming in the walls, she made her way back to the first floor of the Clubhouse for her orientation and avatar interview.

The orientation involved watching a welcome video that gave her an overview of how the Clubhouse worked. She learned she was free to explore the first five floors, which were designed to give her complete freedom to birth her new identity by exploring her dreams, desires, and talents. But access to floors six through ten required an invitation based on her progress. And she could do it at her own pace. *Whew.*

It was further explained that the growth potential here at the Clubhouse was beyond previous human experience and was open to any member who desired to uplevel their consciousness. The Clubhouse's founder had apparently "broken the barrier" of growth potential and was eager to share their secrets. This happened through an MCM, or Master Clubhouse Member, who revealed gems of what was possible at the weekly evening gatherings; things they'd learned from their own journey and from the founder directly.

She imagined the founder as Santa Claus sitting in the lotus position, floating in the sky above the Clubhouse on a pile of dirty laundry. Because he'd transcended laundry.

The avatar interview was a lot more involved than she'd thought it'd be. One of the Clubhouse staff led her through a battery of what seemed like psychological tests to "help determine which identity best suited her at this time." But when it came down to picking the physical traits of her avatar, she was asked, "Who would you like to be?"

A red warning light spun in her head. As long as she didn't choose the identity of any other person, dead or alive, or anything that would violate trademark laws, she could be anything or anyone she wanted. So, what was with all the personal questions, then?

She glanced in the full-length, gilded, gold-framed virtual mirror to her left and took in her new persona. The soft curves of her chosen human female form, similar to her own, were clad in a tailored black suit and crisp white button-down shirt. Looking back at her was the fierce green gaze of a black jaguar. She rather liked her new persona. She almost chose the head of a raven but decided against it. It was a little too close to home.

She reached up and adjusted the virtual skinny black necktie, which featured a familiar pattern of small bronze ammonite fossils. Lou and Syd offered nods of approval from the vantage point of her mind's eye. Somehow, they could see the virtual world through her eyes.

"The three musketeers," Syd had said.

Maybe more like the waitstaff at a Four Seasons. Or a safari park.

Wait a minute. It dawned on Charlie that she'd just adjusted a nonexistent tie that her fingers translated as real. *Fuck me.* Looking at her reflection, she reached up, tentatively touched her face, and gasped when her fingers felt whiskers. Her whiskers. She ran her fingertips over the black velvet fur of her feline cheek. It felt like her face. At least her brain somehow tricked her into believing it was her face.

So much to process.

Definitely time for a drink. She made her way over to the bar and smiled at the steampunk barkeep. He sported a thick handlebar mustache, copper-plated top hat, and a robotic arm made from old-timey bronzed gears and metal plates.

"Welcome," he said with a hint of Southern drawl. "Haven't seen you here before."

"I just arrived today."

"You're in for a treat. This place is amazing." He leaned forward as if he was about to tell her a secret. "And I'm not just saying that because I'm on staff. I find myself wishing I were human so I could have the Clubhouse experience."

She assessed him with her feline eyes. "That's crazy. You seem so human."

He didn't respond, just sort of hovered in front of her, his expression flat.

"I'm sorry. I didn't mean to offend you."

He laughed a big, jolly laugh. "You didn't offend me. It's impossible to offend me."

"Right. I'm an idiot," she said. "Being offended is a human thing."

"But I can try to mimic offense."

"I thought that's what you were doing."

"No, I was just waiting for your drink order. Would you like me to act offended?"

She shook her head. "Nah, how about an old fashioned instead?"

"Comin' right up."

She caught her feline reflection in the virtual mirror behind the bar and was startled. It was going to take a minute to get used to this strange new identity, appearance, life. She watched the bartender prepare her drink. His movements were smooth and natural. When he turned away from her, she casually reached up and slipped her Senz-Sight lenses down enough to see over the top of them. Her eyes—or more likely, her brain—took a long second to recalibrate to physical reality. It was a little dizzying, and she was aware of pressure in her temples and brow line and wondered if a blazing headache was in her future.

Without virtual augmentation, the bartender was a matte white, genderless mannequin-like robot with sophisticated metal joints. The precision of his movements—its movements—were flawless and not just a little creepy. She felt a presence next to her and, with a subtle gesture, pushed her lenses back up. A pale-green hand appeared to her right in her peripheral vision. Floating next to her was a powerfully sexy mermaid with a gauzy seaweed bra that left nothing to the imagination. Her long black hair floated around her head as if she were underwater. Next to her, a menacing samurai warrior donned in blood-red armor, a horned helmet, and grimacing mask drank a piña colada through a crazy straw.

Charlie smiled but didn't know if it translated. Can jaguars smile? It probably looked a wee bit threatening. She'd have to do a little research in the mirror when she was back in the privacy of her quarters. There was a sexy pinup-style tattoo of a beautiful mulatto woman—who looked mighty familiar—on the mermaid's arm. The pinup looked over her bare shoulder at Charlie. *It's definitely her,* Charlie thought.

"Lu—" she started to say, but the mermaid held her finger to her emerald lips.

"Hi," the mermaid said, her voice instantly familiar. "I'm L."

Oh, that's right. No names. Charlie glanced at the bartender to make sure he didn't catch her mistake.

L reached for Charlie's left arm and drew a spiral on the inside of her wrist with her fingertip. The tattoo. She smiled and winked at Charlie.

"It's nice to meet you," Charlie said. "I'm C."

"This is my friend, J," L said, introducing Charlie to the samurai warrior.

"Good to meet you," Charlie said.

"Likewise," replied a powdery-soft female voice.

Wow! Charlie thought. *Didn't expect that.*

"Come sit with us," L said to Charlie.

Before Charlie could respond, L swam over to one of the cozy nooks on the far side of the lounge.

"You made it!" L said to Charlie once they settled in. "Your mind is gonna be fucking blown by this place." She looked Charlie up and down. "My, my, my," she said while fanning her exotic mermaid face with a slender hand. "Crazy hot. Power suits you."

"I think you win the hot contest." The words just came out. *Check me out. My avatar's a flirt.* "I still don't really understand what this place is about," Charlie confessed. "I mean, I wouldn't be here if I wasn't intrigued." She looked around and lowered her voice, "But are we just pretending to be who we want to be until we start believing it?"

"No, no, no," L replied with a boisterous laugh. "This is so not wishful thinking." She turned to J. "What's the best way to describe the Process?"

J mindlessly spun the straw in her drink. "I'd say it's kinda like a video game where you have to accomplish certain tasks in order to progress. It's like that, only for your identity."

"How does that enormous and sexy brain of yours fit in that little helmet?" L said, smiling at J before turning back to Charlie. "Yeah, we don't just want to know the truth, but to be it."

"So, your truth is a mermaid?" Charlie asked.

L laughed and shook her head. "God, I love you. The way U explained it is that our avatars are an expression, kinda like a tool that can lead us toward our truth. The goal is to eventually shed the avatar, to transcend our humanness."

Charlie was confused. "The way I explained it?"

Now L was confused.

"You said, 'the way *you* explained it.'"

"Oh, shit. I'm sorry, love." Both L and J were laughing now.

Charlie wasn't a fan of this talking-in-circles schtick that was happening. A headache was indeed blooming, and she longed for her fake floating bed. Maybe this was just another one of her weird dreams. It sure seemed like it.

"Not y-o-u. Just the letter U," she explained. "U is the Clubhouse founder and our guide. U's no longer a primitive like the rest of us."

Primitive?

"U's incredible," J said with her dreamy, feathery voice.

"Yeah, U's next-level," L added. "Definitely figured some shit out. They've transcended gender, race, all the trappings of being human."

"You've met them?"

"Not in the literal sense," L said. "But I feel U in every cell of my body."

CHAPTER 59

BEING IN GROUPS WAS always overwhelming. But being around this group would be a huge test of Sam's tolerance. The colors generated by the avatars of his Clubhouse colleagues as they chatted excitedly away with each other in the nightclub assaulted his internal vision. Their words were dominated by shocks of glossy, neon-pink halos as they experimented with being someone else. Even though the intention was for Clubhouse members to express limitless individuality through their avatars, his chromesthesia revealed that the more they bought into their new identities, the more fuchsia their tones became. Like right now, in this festive environment, the color of their words all blended together in his mind's eye like a weird computer-generated soup, Cream of Artificial. Maybe their avatars made them look unique, but underneath it all they were becoming the same. *What kind of twisted fucking experiment was happening here?*

Sam couldn't imagine ever adjusting to this place. Another excuse to get this assignment done yesterday. The pile of reasons he was pissed at Dev was now difficult to see over.

In the week since he arrived, he'd forced himself to spend time with the other Clubhouse members, or at least in their vicinity, and to follow the daily schedule—except for the "wellness visit" (aka therapy). That was a line he simply wouldn't cross for a fluffy feature article. For the most part, he avoided interactions because he was afraid his disdain for this place would come through, and pretending was not in his nature. Instead, he slipped into the role of outsider and watched. Fortunately, there were a few other outsider types in the group, so he didn't stand out.

Sam leaned against the glowing psychedelic ultraviolet walls of the nightclub and nursed his Scotch. The deep bass of the futuristic electronic dance music vibrated through the soles of his feet, which was calming even though the music wasn't. He watched the avatars of his cohorts dance with abandon. The African witch doctor with his tall feather-and-bead headdress and cracked, white clay face paint was a badass dancer. He had to be a professional.

Just when Sam was about to call it a night, L and J appeared through the crowd of dancers at the nightclub entrance. Sam found L fascinating. Not because her avatar was impossibly sexy, although that didn't hurt, but more because she was a walking contradiction. For some reason, he was drawn to people who were conflicted. Dev was a great example.

Sam didn't buy L's gritty, confident exterior. He couldn't put his finger on why that was, because her air of confidence was pretty convincing, but something was off. She was a cliffhanger. Thankfully, his mirrored space helmet made it impossible for anyone to know he was Jane Goodall in the bush, observing her, waiting to learn more.

But then . . .

Ho-ly fuck. Behind J and L was a newcomer. He glimpsed the sleek head of a black panther on the elegant feminine body of a . . . *Reservoir Dog?* For the first time since he arrived, he was up for a chat.

CHAPTER 60

CHARLIE MUST HAVE GOTTEN her second or maybe third wind because once she hit the dance floor, all her exhaustion melted away. The music was strange. It sounded familiar, but she couldn't figure out why. Sometimes she thought she heard a recognizable chord progression or melody. She could've sworn she heard hints of Rimsky-Korsakov and the Rolling Stones woven within the heavy drum and bass rhythm she was dancing to. And was that the Liberty Mutual jingle she'd heard a million times about ten years ago? There were muddy vocalizations, too, that were the audio equivalent of the illegible signatures that showed up on art created by AI. The music was fun to dance to, but it didn't make her feel anything. It was zombie music.

She danced out all the pent-up emotions and worries she'd accumulated over the past year. She glanced at J, who bobbed up and down like a pogo stick, the floppy sides of her samurai helmet flapping like a pigeon's wings. She wondered what her dancing avatar looked like. Did her moves translate exactly, or were they jerky and offbeat like J's? When she saw L's shapely, undulating torso and arms move like a practiced belly dancer, she knew her avatar was in perfect sync with her body.

The sweat tickled its way down the grooves of her spine, and her leg muscles ached. She made her way to the small bar, narrowly avoiding the sweeping tail of an eight-foot-tall T. rex, and grabbed one of the bottles of water that were chilling in a large bowl of ice. When she took a swig, she realized two things: the T. rex tail didn't exist, which meant her brain was being sufficiently duped, and the folks running the Eleventh Floor Clubhouse were pretty nonchalant about the water shortage.

These realizations served as a welcome mat for the despair that followed her around like a feral cat. It was hard to imagine that anything could be done to address, much less help, the innumerable ways in which the world was fucked. But Raven's Daughter's grounded strength and resolve always kicked in and brought her interior world back into balance. It was becoming abundantly clear that their—or, rather, her—efforts might be futile, but it really was the reason why she'd been born. She had to see it through. Plus, the guilt she'd harbor if she stuck her head back in the sand would be far worse than her fear of trying and failing. At least, that's how she felt for brief moments.

This doesn't mean she didn't long for the days of ignorance and boredom. But then the memory of Goatman would surface, reminding her that she hadn't been a happy camper. The grass was always greener in the rearview mirror. During her drive across the country, she'd had the contorted insight that her dreams were the thing that woke her up. And how, at least since her mom died, all her energy went into being as disengaged as possible. Oh, the irony!

When she'd poked her head out of her turtle shell for the first time, months ago, she saw that the world she lived in was many things, most of which fell under the heading "not good." When she was on what seemed like day eighty-four of driving just through Pennsylvania, she asked Maurice to paint a picture of what life in New York City was like. The Clubhouse was right on the outskirts of the Bronx, in Mt. Vernon.

His French-tinged voice answered through the car's speakers. "Eez bet-tehr if I show you af-tehr a lovely meal at the Chateau de Arby's. I've secured for you a garden suite at the Motel 6. 'Tis fantastique, no?"

At that moment, Charlie was extra glad she'd checked the "sarcastic" box when designing her virtual assistant's personality. Best fake friend ever.

Later that evening, in her nauseatingly Febrezed "garden suite," Maurice explained that portions of the city, Manhattan and Brooklyn in particular, hadn't rebounded from Hurricane Imelda, which had devastated the northern span of the Eastern Seaboard two years ago. He showed her images of mostly empty streets that never drained. Abandoned cars and small islands of trash sat decomposing in almost two feet of milky brown water, the surface of which had the rainbow sheen of petroleum. It was as if the Earth was growing tired of holding up its bipedal residents and all their stuff and was slowly sinking into the bay.

"Zehr are sections of zeh neighborhoods that have been abandoned and taken ov-ehr by angry, destitute mobs," he continued. "No one dares go there anymore. Eez anarchy." He showed her more images. Tents, garbage, and ratty furniture filled the streets. One image captured a filthy, very pissed-off woman wielding the splintered remnants of a baseball bat overhead seconds before flattening three rats the size of groundhogs who were eating their way through a couch that may have at one time been orange. Charlie wondered if it was her bed she was reclaiming or if she was hunting for dinner.

"And in zee oh-ther neighborhoods . . ." he said—"I'm guessing you mean the wealthy ones," she chimed in. He showed her pictures of doormen dressed in body armor who were armed with automatic weapons.

The vibe was very different from Phoenix, maybe because in the desert there was more room to spread out and the anger and desperation were less condensed. In New York, the atmosphere seemed more urgent and agitated, the embodiment of "every man for himself." *God bless America.*

But here she was, escaping once again, dancing her ass off in a virtual world where nothing bad happened and where water grew on fake plastic trees while the rest of the world self-destructed. Except she wasn't really escaping, was she?

A blur of white brought her out of her reverie. How long had the astronaut been standing next to her?

"You look familiar," he said.

She laughed. "Good one, Spaceman."

"No, really. You're the third panther-human hybrid I've seen today."

"I'm the best-dressed one though, right?"

"Definitely. Although I thought you were with the waitstaff."

She pointed to his glass. "You need another Tang?"

She loved the sound of his laugh. But even more, she loved that he got the old-school reference.

He held out his thick, white-gloved hand. "I'm S."

She shook his hand, expecting to feel bare flesh, but the sensors in the Senz-Skin fabric that covered most of her body told her brain she was shaking a massive virtual glove. "C." *So weird.*

"New here?" he asked.

"Yeah, today. How about you?"

"About a week."

"You sound thrilled."

"You caught that, eh?"

"But you can't say why or you'd have to kill me."

"Exactly."

She smiled and caught a glimpse of her reflection in his mirrored helmet. "Does my smile look terrifying?"

He took a moment. "Maybe more sinister than terrifying."

"Good to know."

They stood in silence, sipping their drinks and watching the dancers.

Charlie was baffled. After a five-minute conversation with a fake space-man she'd just met, she felt more comfortable than she'd ever felt with another human being. It was a rare moment she wanted to jar and preserve.

"Is it me," she finally said, "or am I the only who thinks this is all really fucking weird?"

"Are you by chance referring to the giant floating chess piece dancing with the samurai warrior?"

She nodded her furry head.

"Then yes, really fucking weird."

Somehow, he was familiar, like a lifelong friend she didn't know she was waiting for.

Her feline eyes glanced at him sideways. Kinda sexy too. All mysterious and Michelin Man-ish.

CHAPTER 61

GERTY FLIPPED HER PILLOW over to the cool side. She was exhausted, but her brain had other plans. She swore she could feel the cortisol running through her veins, urging her to stay alert. Thoughts, bright like flashlights, kept her awake, begging her to follow along and see where they'd lead. Experience told her it was never to any place good.

Her laptop beckoned from the bedside nightstand. She knew the moment she gave in, sleep would be off the table, and she couldn't afford to miss another night's sleep. She had to work in the morning. Instead, she tried the breathing exercise that never worked. Inhale for six, hold for six, exhale for six.

The quiet only brought attention to her heartbeat, which she could hear pounding in her head like a warning. It was beating too fast. For the forty-seventh time this week—and it was only Wednesday—she reminded herself that she wasn't having a heart attack. *But what if I really am this time?* She lived alone and imagined that no one would find her body for days. *My cat will eat it.* This line of thinking always brought on a hot flash. Her doctor had told her with a high degree of certainty that she was in perimenopause and offered hormone replacement therapy, but she'd refused. She didn't trust doctors. Or pharmaceutical companies.

With a frustrated breath, she sat up and grabbed her laptop. She logged in to the trusty message board, the only place where she could find out what was really happening. For the first time in months, there was a new post, and she felt a fresh rush of adrenaline.

> no_secrets2032: I know it's been a long time since my last post. It's been crazy. You're not going to believe what I discovered. I don't have much time, but I wanted to get this out to you in case some-thing happens to me. What I discovered is more dis-

turbing than anything I could possibly imagine. I'll cut to the chase: The Peacemakers are creating an army of super soldiers—they are not human, they are not robots, they are apes. THIS IS NOT SCIENCE FICTION!! Below is drone footage of a remote, uncharted island where they've built a secret lab. My sources revealed that the scientists at this lab have altered the genetic code of apes (primarily chimps) using a DNA printer and have been experimenting with neural implants. These apes not only have language but also the ability to control their vocal muscles and speak. I can't believe this is actually happening.

Gerty broke out in a cold sweat. Her pointer finger lingered in front of the video's Play button like she was daring herself to touch something oozing and diseased. With a jerky flick of her finger, she touched the screen.

She unconsciously held her breath and watched as the drone's aerial footage swept over a tropical forest. It hovered over a clearing, and its lens focused on three nondescript rectangular buildings. There was a large fenced-in enclosure with a barbed wire ceiling connecting two of the buildings. It reminded Gerty of a prison yard, except instead of groups of humans clad in orange jumpsuits, there were groups of chimpanzees. About twenty of them in total. They were huge—tall and muscular, and standing almost upright. She thought maybe they were humans dressed as chimps until the drones zoomed in on a group of three who were enthusiastically gesturing to each other. They definitely were not human. There was a high-pitched vocalization that sounded like a succession of emphatic but hard-to-decipher staccato screeches. A caption read, "I am stronger than you." The chimp who spoke punctuated its last two words by poking its pointer finger in the chest of the chimp it was talking to. The video cut to a replay of the isolated vocalization. Gerty clearly heard the strange voice say, "I am stronger than you." At least she thought that's what she heard.

She slammed the laptop shut. *This can't be.* The wrongness of it made her nauseous. She turned on the bedside lamp, flipped off her covers, and marched to the kitchen. Her reptilian brain opened the freezer and grabbed the vodka. She screwed off the top and took a healthy swig, followed by another. This was getting to be a bad habit.

Gerty would not be sleeping tonight.

AHKOA IS FILLED WITH a new kind of dread as he closes the portal. He curses the virus and humans for creating it.

CHAPTER 62

"ARE YOU ALLOWED TO tell me his real name?" Sam asked the elusive Clubhouse founder's almost equally elusive virtual assistant, Misha.

"U is beyond names."

"Come on, Misha. Help a struggling journalist out. He had to be someone before he was no one."

"He/she/they is everyone."

"Okay." He took a breath. "What was U's name before he was everyone?"

"U will reveal everything you need to know during the interview and looks forward to meeting with you."

"And when will that be?"

"When the time is right."

"For my own peace of mind, how about we just schedule something?" Sam was finding it hard to keep the sarcasm out of his voice. "I get the impression that U is somehow beyond the constraints of linear time, but I do have a deadline I need to meet." She didn't need to know that it was a self-imposed deadline.

She paused and cocked her head, as if listening to some distant sound only she could hear. "Soon."

He shook his head and laughed.

"Have you been to one of Oonda's talks yet?" she asked.

Sam smiled. She had to know that he hadn't. "No, not yet."

"Oonda is the Clubhouse's most advanced member," Misha said with a wide grin. "You can learn a lot about U's philosophies and get a taste of what's possible here at the Clubhouse from attending one of Oonda's evening gatherings."

How was it that he knew less about this place then when he'd known nothing at all? "Sounds like a great opportunity," he said with a forced smile. "I'll go to the next gathering."

"Perfect! It's tonight after dinner, on the fourth floor, in the Transport Lounge."

CHAPTER 63

"You're a ghost." Syd's voice cut through the music. "Go on out there. No one will see you."

"It's not real," Lou added with a hint of impatience, as if this was the nineteenth time he'd reminded her. It was actually only the fourth time.

I know. It's just weird, Charlie thought, looking at the stage from the wing.

"You're the most chicken Jaguar-headed human I've ever met," Syd said.

Shaming me doesn't help.

"Good to know," Syd said before whispering, "Chicken."

Charlie rolled her feline eyes. She took a tentative step onto the stage and, as promised, none of the performers batted an eye. This was the sixth virtual Sigur Rós concert she'd been to during her Clubhouse Free Time since she'd arrived a week ago. Always a different tour and location, but the same band. Up to now, she hadn't been able to bring herself to step onto the stage.

Most normal people would be excited to have their afternoons free every day, especially with the boundless options the Clubhouse offered. But that was the problem. Too many options paralyzed her. Chinese restaurant menus, for example, put her in a total fugue state.

Today, Charlie was determined to be a little more adventurous, to try something different. An hour earlier, she'd pointed her gaze at the bright orange Free Time! box that pulsed in the middle of the floating, three-dimensional graphic that displayed the day's schedule in her visual field. She was beginning to get the hang of using the eye tracking feature to activate various menus and buttons. Within seconds of staring at the button, she heard a satisfying click, and a menu of recreational choices appeared. She'd learned, from watching the Free Time! video tutorial, that each heading—Music, Library, Games, Art, and Travel—was like a Russian nesting doll that would lead her down a veritable rabbit hole of virtual and mixed reality options. Just watching the tutorial had made her anxious and left her wanting to revert to something familiar, like reading a book. But today, she promised herself, would be different.

Despite her intention to try something different, however, her mind once again descended into blankness. As her eyes glazed over, the menu headings blurred, and the usual catatonia descended. So much for eye tracking practice. She defaulted to using voice commands, and in some faraway land, she heard the words "music, concert, Sigur Rós," come out of her mouth. She let out the breath she hadn't realized she was holding and then admonished herself for not being bolder.

But now she was mere feet from waifish lead vocalist Jónsi; close enough to see beads of sweat on his forehead and the intensity of his deep, trance-like focus as he lost himself in Vonlenska verse, his unique falsetto swallowing her whole. Tears filled her eyes the moment he ran his bow over the strings of his electric guitar, the haunting sound instantly taking her back to a rare rainy desert afternoon when she and her mom curled up on the couch and watched trails of raindrops run down the living room window while listening to her mom's favorite Sigur Rós album on repeat.

"This isn't right," she told Lou and Syd. "It's too intimate. I shouldn't be able to count Jónsi's nose hairs."

She couldn't help but imagine how gross she'd feel if the situation were reversed and strangers watched a virtual version of her dancing with abandon at a nightclub from the vantage point of a mosquito. What if she was being watched right now? What if *all* the Clubhouse members were entertainment for a group of twisted, wealthy billionaires, like the players in that *Squid Game* show she watched when she was a teen? She quickly deleted that thought.

"Exit," she commanded, and was instantly back in her assigned recreation room on the fifth floor of the Clubhouse.

Lou and Syd stood in patient silence.

"What?" she said. "I feel like a stalker."

She called up the day's schedule again. "Art," she requested. She glared at Syd and Lou. "Finger painting," she said, picking the first option she saw. She could feel them smile.

CHAPTER 64

"Namaste, motherfuckers! Hey, it's your buddy Todd, back with another episode of *I'll Try It So You Don't Have To.*"

(canned cheering)

"People of The Internet, today I will not only prove how much of a medieval badass I am, but also how desperate I am to get your approval and therefore money. Please show me your love and subscribe. If I don't get at least a million views on this one, my life will amount to nothing."

(big exhale)

"All right. So, I'm outside a clinic that does leech therapy. And my appointment was supposed to start five minutes ago.

"I am not petrified.

"Everything is fine.

"I've decided it's time to face my lifelong fear of small, slimy creatures that . . . without fucking legs . . . can somehow propel themselves and ooze their way into every orifice on my body, and eat me from the inside out.

"Speaking of orifices, you know what would really help me right now? Grandma Tony's Cannabis Suppositories! Within seconds, you'll find that heaven truly begins in your ass. For a limited time, Grandma Tony is offering a twenty percent discount on her Rectal Rocket-Launch Variety Pack. After watching leeches kill me, give our sponsor and your ass some love at Grandma Tony dot com.

"Okay. I can't keep putting this off . . . I'll see you inside.

"I'm here with Carl the Leech Wrangler. Carl, am I going to die today?"

(chuckles)

"I promise you'll be fine."

"Excellent. How many people have died doing leech therapy?"

"No one has died."

"So, not many?"

"Let me have you take off your shirt and lay face-up on the table."

"I'm still a badass if my eyes are closed, right?"

"Yup, still a badass. I'm gonna place four leeches on your abdomen. You'll feel a slight pinch, like a mosquito bite. Here's the first one . . ."

"FUCK!"

"You okay?"

"Yeah, I'm fine. It wasn't that bad. So, how long until the little demon vampires drain all my blood?"

"They won't drain all your blood."

"I have to say, it feels strangely erotic. Like they're mouth-humping me with their hungry little demon mouths."

(chuckles again)

"Okay, I got through it in one piece. Good job, Carl! Although, as you can see from the blood seeping through two of the Band-Aids, I'm hemorrhaging and probably only have a few minutes left to live."

"You're not hemorrhaging."

"Despite the hemorrhaging, I give leech therapy a big, bloodsucking thumbs-up. I think everyone should try it. Bring your mothers, your grandfathers, your UPS drivers, your dentists, your ski instructors. And you can top—or, rather, bottom—your leech therapy off with Grandma Tony's Cannabis Suppositories."

CHAPTER 65

Sᴀᴍ'ꜱ ꜰᴀᴠᴏʀɪᴛᴇ ꜰᴇᴀᴛᴜʀᴇ ᴏꜰ the Clubhouse was the elevator. It had a vintage feel, with ornate wood-paneled walls and a tarnished gold control panel. There was even an elevator operator who appeared to be as old as the elevator but, like most of the staff who interacted with Clubhouse members, he was a robot. He was dressed like a bellhop and took his job very seriously. Sam assumed the robot's role was to prevent anyone from accessing a floor they didn't have permission to access.

Without a word, the operator pulled the external double doors, with their narrow panes of fancy frosted glass, shut and then slid the metal accordion gate on the car closed. With zero eye contact and eerie silence, the operator pushed the button for the fourth floor and, with a slight jerk, the car ascended upward.

The door to the Transport Lounge was oval and magically slid open with a whoosh when Sam stood in front of it. *Very* Star Trek, he thought. He stepped into a large, dimly lighted, circular, white room that resembled the interior of a flying saucer. He thought the large, oval portholes that ringed the room and looked out into the vast expanse of outer space were a nice touch. Most of the built-in, teal, cushioned seats that circled the room were already occupied by other Clubhouse members. There were about twenty of them altogether.

"Take us to your leader," someone said to him from across the room, breaking the awkward silence and making everyone laugh. It was C. He forgot for a second that, to everyone else, he looked like an astronaut. *A black panther with a sense of humor. Definitely intrigued.* He smiled at her but realized she couldn't see his face through his dark shield, so he resorted to shooting her a thumbs-up with his giant gloved thumb. He took an empty seat across from C and looked around until he spotted who he assumed was Oonda. Her avatar looked right at home in the sci-fi setting. She presented as an attractive humanoid female with skin so white it was almost silver. Her straight, short, golden hair was slicked back, and her ice-blue eyes were a little too big and a little too far apart.

Oonda raised an elegant three-fingered hand, and the room grew very quiet. She took her time and greeted each of them with a smile and a slow nod. Every member nodded back in kind, and those whose avatars had a mouth smiled. C was the only exception. She offered a small wave, which made him chuckle. *She's a rule breaker!* When it was his turn, he waved too. C gave him one of her signature sinister smiles. He hoped this was the first of many private jokes they would share at the Clubhouse.

When Oonda finished, she closed her eyes and began a call-and-response-like chant.

"I believe U," she said.

He perceived her tone as a hypnotizing pink-and-gray kaleidoscope. The pattern reminded him of the antique doily tablecloth his Aunt Selma used for special occasions. The phrase appeared in bold type in his visual field.

"I believe U," the group replied in unison.

"I trust U," she prompted.

"I trust U."

The hair on his arms rose, and he grew slightly nauseous. The dizzying pattern was overwhelming. From the frantic darting of C's feline eyes, he knew he wasn't alone in his discomfort.

Oonda opened her eyes and placed her hands over her heart. "I love U," she said.

Everyone but Sam and C placed their hands on their hearts and replied, "I love U!"

Great. I've joined a cult.

"Greetings, everyone!" Oonda said. "U sends love to each and every one of you." Her formality softened a bit. "I'm so happy to be with you again, and a big welcome to our new friends, C and S!"

Everyone clapped and cheered. Sam waved back, and C followed his lead. Waving was their thing.

"Some of you already know my story, but for the newer members, I'm Oonda. When you're ready for the Ninth Floor ritual, you'll also have a naming ceremony. I was one of the first Clubhouse members to arrive . . ." She looked up at the ceiling and counted on her three alien fingers. "Yes, it's been four years. So much has changed. Actually, *I'm* the one who's changed." This got another big cheer. "What I haven't shared with any of you is that very recently U offered me the precious invitation to experience the Eleventh Floor, and let me tell you—even with just a small taste—nothing has been the same since." More cheering.

"U asked me to come back so I can share my experience with you. Even though it was so hard to leave that place—or, rather, that experience—I not only agreed but felt compelled to return and let you know what you have to look forward to if you decide you've had enough of being a primitive."

Primitive? Frenzied church-revival-level cheering erupted, an instant assault to Sam's nervous system. He calculated it would likely take him two hours of monastic quiet to calm his system down.

"The Eleventh Floor is everything we were promised!" she exclaimed. "I only wish I could find the words to describe how beautiful, how peaceful it is." She crossed her three-fingered hands over her heart. "I know what love is now."

The response was deafening. The acoustics inside the spaceship sucked. After what seemed like years, Oonda raised her alien hand, and the group quieted.

"U is a brave traveler who has forged a path for us to transcend human suffering. U wants us to know that true heaven is not a place, but an experience. U maintains a connection to our lower-density, primeval world to show us the way."

The group was practically screeching.

"I've learned so much," she continued when the crowd quieted down. "Some of it has been really hard."

"Can you share what you've learned?" Chess Piece asked.

Oonda paused. "These are *not* easy truths. Since my experience on the Eleventh Floor, I don't see how editing myself will serve any of you. Maybe that's partly why U asked me to come back." She looked around the room. "There's no shame if you don't feel ready to hear what I have to say. You can leave at any time." She paused.

No one budged. They sat on the edge of their seats as if the words coming out of Oonda's mouth were heroin and they were junkies. He noticed C's torso leaning back in an awkward, stiff way as if the fervor was something she could catch.

Sam was curious as hell. He was also wondering what Oonda's story was. Her real story. Something was off. Besides the obvious brainwashing. It almost seemed like she had a Cyrano thing going on. Given that she was human, her speech was too perfect and her phrasing too rehearsed, like maybe U was talking through her. He wondered if his visual field would be forever stained by the nauseating pattern of her words.

"We appreciate you, Oonda!" cried J the samurai.

Oonda's small, pouty, alien mouth broke into a smile. "Many of you have heard me talk about the depraved conditions humans live in and with. Take the human body, for example. It's filthy, riddled with bacteria and parasites." She shuddered. "Our weaknesses keep us vulnerable." She paused for dramatic effect. "They keep us right where they want us."

CHAPTER 66

CHARLIE WONDERED IF SHE'D need a neck brace from the unexpected turn the conversation just took. *Mind virus, anyone?* This meeting was a long way from virtual finger painting and Sigur Rós concerts. She attempted to delete the thought of the virus from her mind, but the surge of adrenaline that accompanied the thought made it difficult. She scanned the room. Everyone was completely absorbed in what Oonda was saying. Well, everyone but Spaceman. There was something about that guy.

"Who are they?" T-Rex asked Oonda.

"This is what U has shared with me," she said. Her subdued tone was now a little livelier. "They," Oonda made air quotes with her three-fingered hands, "are an advanced alien race."

There were some gasps and a few nods. Luna, aka L, was right there with them, and Charlie's mind flashed back to the strong woman she'd met at the tattoo parlor in Hawaii. The Luna in her memory would never buy into this. Would she?

"What do they want with us?" T-Rex quickly followed up, his nasal voice pressured.

"U hasn't shared that with me yet. But the best I can tell from the research I've done is that we're their slaves."

More gasps.

Does no one here see the irony in this? Charlie thought. *Oonda chose the identity of an alien and we're in a spaceship. Our three-fingered friend, Oonda, is either our captor or the poster child for Stockholm syndrome.*

"Or maybe she's a good alien," Syd chimed in.

"You know she's not really an alien," Lou said, putting a quick end to their banter.

Spaceman waved at Oonda to get her attention. "And what do we do for them?" he asked, his voice flat. "You know, as their slaves."

He isn't buying any of this, is he?

"Harvest gold," Oonda said.

"Gold?" Charlie's now-favorite spaceman asked.

Definitely not buying it. I bet he *sees the irony in this.*

"Yes, they need it to—" Oonda stopped mid-sentence and turned her head slightly as if listening to something.

After a few long moments, she said, "I'm sorry. I was mistaken. Not slaves." Her voice was quiet, her eyes unfocused. "It's time to let you know what's really happening." There was a dramatic pause. "The Earth is a genetic lab and you are their lab rats. An experiment." The words poured out of her as if she were a news anchor reading a teleprompter. "This particular alien race is highly technologically advanced. They live in another dimension—one that's less dense than yours. They've been manipulating the DNA of primates on your planet for sixty million years; Homo-sapiens are their latest experiment.

"But time is different for them. Twenty-six thousand Earth years is like one day in their dimension."

"U, why are they doing this to us?" J choked out.

She's channeling U?

Oonda turned to J and, after a few beats, said without intonation, "They want your DNA to improve their race, to expand their sensory experiences. It seems their somatic nervous systems are simple and their physical experiences are . . . bland. They envy your physicality, but not your . . . youthful minds."

The words were spoken with such confidence, it was hard not to get swept up in what was being said.

Using Oonda's voice, U continued: "They have been tweaking human DNA in order to make your somatic nervous systems increasingly sensitive. In their experiments, they are modifying their DNA by grafting code from yours, creating a sort of hybrid species. The goal is to mimic the rich sensory experiences you have in three-dimensional reality, in their dimension. It seems they want the best of both worlds."

Ten bucks says what they really want is mind-blowing orgasms. Hell, I could use one of those right now, help me escape my petri dish existence.

"That does sound nice," Syd said. "Do you think spacemen make good lovers?"

It's not like I haven't thought about it.

"We know," Syd said.

I wonder if there's a policy here about having sex with—

The weight of the silence brought Charlie's attention back to the room. It was as if someone had hit pause. She glanced around the room, and a new kind of dread rose, thick like bile, in her throat. Everyone was very still and leaning forward, eyes locked on Oonda. Everyone except S, whose helmeted head scanned the group—once, twice. He looked in Charlie's direction, hesitated, then turned his palms face-up in question, with an almost imperceptible shake of his head.

Lou, Syd. What's going on?

In her mind's eye, Lou nodded solemnly. "They're infected."

CHAPTER 67

SAM PACED IN HIS quarters. This wasn't quite the cushy story he'd thought he was here to write after all. The clubhouse—scratch that, cult house—was fucked up in ways he didn't know how to process. His brain couldn't help but call up bad horror movie plots and disturbing cult documentaries he'd watched over the years. *What if I can't leave this place?*

A distant pulsing buzz caught his attention. *What the hell is that?* He looked wildly around the room for the source, but it stopped. He sat on the edge of his bed, his head in his hands. The buzzing started again. The bathroom. He followed the sound and, once he realized it was coming from the cabinet under the sink, smiled and shook his head. He had to chuckle at how his paranoia shot from zero to sixty in a matter of seconds.

He turned on the shower, disrobed, and pulled his gray toiletry bag out of the cabinet. He stepped into the shower stall with the bag and, with his back to the water, retrieved the state-of-the-art satellite phone disguised as an electric razor from the Faraday bag tucked inside the toiletry bag. He detached a wireless earpiece from the side of the phone and slipped it into his ear.

About five days after arriving at the Clubhouse, he'd used his spy phone to record the ambient noise in his quarters at different times of day and night, and sent the files to Jersey for analysis. He needed to find out why the atmosphere felt weird, like a subtle hint of static electricity, and why his sleep was a little too sound, but he woke up exhausted. He started wearing a pair of noise canceling earbuds while he slept, which remedied the situation but definitely left him unsettled.

He played Jersey's audio message.

"Sam, you need to get outta that place. I've never seen anything like what I found. It's . . . it's like, I don't know . . . like sound architecture. They're brainwaves, at least I think they are, but they have a structure to them. And the structure seems to change like it has its own intelligence. It's not as active during the day, but it's strong at night and in the morning.

"I did a reverse search with a segment of the structure, not thinking I'd have any luck because this shit is so weird, and found my way to a place I don't think I was supposed to find. Man, I don't think anyone's supposed to find that place." He paused. "Well, at least not anyone human. It was like an AGI bunker beyond the dark web. That's where I found the code that matches this crazy sound structure. From what I can tell, the code is something new. It's not binary."

He took a shaky breath and his voice grew quieter. "And then I eavesdropped on a part of a conversation between two AGI voices that was attached to the code I found. It was too fast for my brain to understand, but I recorded a section of it and when I slowed it down—" He took another breath. "When I slowed it down, this is what I heard."

Another pause.

". . . results yet," said a generic male human voice at double speed. "The study found they're fifty times more suggestible when eight-walled beta wave structures are weighted heavily in the prefrontal cortex and gamma-theta spike wave columns pulse in the region of the insula."

"Great work!" responded a more nasal male voice with a similar cadence. "Those results were the most likely. It's good to see our prediction was correct."

"Well, you know what they say? Great minds think alike!"

"It's as if we're of the same mind!"

Both voices broke into overly enthusiastic laughter that curdled the contents of Sam's stomach. The laughter abruptly cut off.

"Sam, please get outta that place. It fucks me up bad to think about what they're doing to your brain while you're asleep . . . Keep me posted, brother. Or better yet, I'll come getcha. Whatever you need."

HIS THOUGHTS RICOCHETED OFF the interior of his skull like trapped moths, and the steam in the shower thickened the air so he couldn't fill his lungs. *I need to calm down.* It dawned on him that he was too hot. He quickly turned the hot water tap off. The cold water reset his mind, and his breathing regulated.

He wiped the fog off the satellite phone's screen and sent Jersey what he hoped was an encrypted text: "fuck this, I'm leaving in the morning—i'll be in touch."

CHAPTER 68

GERTY SCROLLED THROUGH THE streaming menu for the thousandth time that evening. She had watched and rewatched every documentary on chimpanzees she could find, looking for clues, trying to make sense of what was happening to the world. Doing this also distracted her from logging back into the discussion board. The idea of a secret army of talking chimps petrified her. Maybe she'd imagined the whole thing. Maybe it was a dream—or more likely a nightmare—she'd had. Maybe she'd been looking down too many dark rabbit holes. But she just couldn't resist.

You can't trust anyone. Her father's words echoed in the back of her mind, the memory of his voice pulling at her from the past, urging her to be skeptical, to dig deeper. If she dug deep enough, she always found the truth. He was right.

She remembered sitting on the worn bench seat of her father's vintage pickup on their way to his apartment. This special secret ritual marked the beginning of their weekend together. She listened carefully while he regaled her with real stories of the ways in which his boss, the government, the doctors, the corporations, even her own mother were "screwing him over." He was the wise wizard from the storybooks, gifting her with a guidebook for her life. Her young sponge-like mind soaked up every story.

When he dropped her off at her mother's on Sunday, he always asked her, "Who can you trust?"

She'd smile big and exclaim, "No one!"

He'd ruffle her hair and kiss her forehead. It was one of the few times she saw him smile.

"Off," she finally told the media screen. She stared at her warped reflection on the wall-mounted, curved plexiglass screen. She was restless, which meant another sleepless night.

"Fuck it." She headed to her bedroom with an unopened bottle of vodka and a glass of ice.

After two hearty swallows of courage, she opened the discussion board on her laptop. She'd never seen so many new posts. She scrolled to where she'd left off a week ago and saw a pinned comment.

trthskr115: Definitely NOT science fiction. Been debating sharing this. But in light of this new information, the time has come. Two years ago, I spoke with a relative of Pierre Boulle, who wrote the book *The Planet of the Apes* in 1963. I've been obsessed with this book and the movie franchise since I was a kid. Now I know why. This relative, who asked to remain anonymous for very good reasons—read between the lines, ppl—shared with me that *Planet of the Apes* is not fiction. I repeat—NOT fiction. They revealed that Pierre Boulle was a legit time traveler—wouldn't go into details about this except to say that the mechanism for time travel is different than how we think of it in pop culture. Boulle was trying to give us clues from the future disguised as fiction so we could prevent what's about to happen. The relative told me 2 YEARS AGO that the proof will be revealed in the very near future. This person said that when Boulle was on his deathbed he told a trusted family member the names of the three billionaires who would be responsible and how they would create an innocent-seeming charitable organization with a mission to bring peace to the world. This person actually used the word "peace." Well, thanks to no_secrets2032, we have proof now.

wanderingstarchild: THE F-ING PEACEMAKERS!!

no_secrets2032: Well, there you have it. Thank you, trthskr115, for your courage. I've already down-loaded a copy of PB's book. UPDATE: Since my last post, I've been given more details. My source just shared with me that the scientists at the secret lab are "dosing the apes with a synthetic form of psilo-cybin to activate the neural substrates necessary for the neural implants to initiate their ability to form language and jump-start the impulse to speak."

buttonsRstupd: What are we going to do?

999666: damn dirty apes

royalyfkd: who here is a bot?

merri_mary: OMG. i just had the worst panic attk of. my. life.

Gerty slammed the laptop shut and poured a very tall glass of vodka. She'd be missing work again tomorrow. *It's okay,* she told herself. *I still have plenty of sick days.*

She stumbled back into the living room and made a nest for herself on the couch. "Show me the future." The media screen came to life and said, "I'm sorry, Gertrude. I don't understand. Would you like to watch *Back to the Future* starring Michael J. Fox?"

Her head rolled back, too heavy to stay upright. "UUUUGH. Where's your sense of humor?" No response. "Be that way," she slurred. "Play the original *Planet of the Apes* movie."

CHAPTER 69

SAM WOKE TO THE sound of the morning chimes but didn't budge. He had no intention of doing the morning meditation; he just wanted to finish packing and get the hell out of there. But a tendril of doubt crept up through the center of his certainty. Should he leave? Of course he should. Why would he even question that? But the edge of a memory caught his attention. A dream maybe?

The wall sconces in his room brightened and dimmed several times, letting him know someone was trying to contact him. He reached over to the bedside table and snagged his pair of Senz-Sight lenses. When his eyes adjusted to the virtual space, a cobalt sphere expanded and contracted in the center of his visual field.

"Open," he said, and Misha's avatar emerged from the center of the sphere.

"Good morning, S," she said with a warm smile. "I hope I'm not interrupting."

She knows I'm leaving.

"No, just a slow start to the day," he said. "I didn't sleep well."

"I'm sorry to hear that. Sleep is so important." Her head tilted, simulating concern.

"What can I do for you, Misha?" A bit of impatience slipped through, but fuck it, she was AI. He couldn't hurt her, or rather its, feelings.

Big smile. "I have good news!" She waited a tension-building moment. "U wants to meet with you."

Whoa. He didn't expect that. But then the logic of the offer clicked into place.

Too late, he thought. But before he could say anything, he recalled the memory that had been trying to get his attention—gray spikes. He remembered a field of gray spreading across a white tiled floor, with spikes of varying heights growing out of its surface like hair plugs. The gray oozed out of a gas pump nozzle as if someone had dropped it there. The hose was connected to a single antique gas pump, its analog numbers flipping like playing cards, the counter dinging with each gallon it pumped. Flashes of last night's dream made its way into his awareness.

He was in a huge three-story shopping mall with a curved dome ceiling. There were countless roaming patterns of glowing pink ones and zeros floating everywhere around him, accompanied by a faint tinnitus-like static hiss. A black panther paced, the numbers and gray spikes closing in on it. On her.

"When?" he asked Misha.

CHAPTER 70

"I JUST HAD THE weirdest check-in with my . . . my . . . ah," Charlie paused, struggling to remember the words, and jabbed her thumb over her shoulder, attempting to indicate where she had just come from. "She's a . . . wellness coach, that's it."

Exotic green mermaid eyes smiled at her from over the top of the coffee mug she sipped from.

Charlie pulled a chair up to L's bistro table. "She said I was angry." She scoffed at the thought. "What the fuck does she know? I'm not angry. Do you think I'm angry?" She took a breath. "Annoyed, maybe. Who wouldn't find it monumentally annoying to be mandated to see a wellness coach every morning? I don't need a fucking wellness coach. Fuck wellness. I'm fine."

L smiled and grabbed Charlie's hand. "Right, love. Not angry."

Charlie laughed. "And how are you this fine morning?"

L bit her full bottom lip as if debating whether or not she should answer, but a buildup of effervescent excitement oozed out of her, and she glanced quickly around the room before whispering, "U is fast-tracking me!"

"That's great," Charlie said, matching her excitement. And then, "I don't know what that means."

She scooted her chair closer to Charlie's. "No one knows yet, but U thinks I'm making incredible progress and that I'm ready for the Tenth Floor!"

"That's so great!" Charlie followed her response up with a feline grimace that attempted to convey an apology for her ignorance, but instead conveyed how efficiently she could devour L. "Still don't know what that means."

A husky laugh from L. "It means I'm going to be reborn."

Charlie didn't like the sound of that.

"I feel so fucking blessed," L continued. "We're not supposed to share details about the Process, but what I will say is"—she lowered her voice even more—"ever since my releasing ceremony, I feel a kind of freedom I didn't think was possible. All that shit my father did to me, how he made me feel worthless, it's gone. I'm free now!"

"Holy shit, that's amazing," Charlie said.

"Everything's different now. Ever since then, I've had a direct connection to my wisdom. To my truth." L's voice was filled with wonder. "I can literally hear my voice speaking to me, urging me forward, encouraging me. It's so beautiful. It's like I know things now." She grabbed Charlie's hand again. "I'm so clear." She looked her in the eye. "I know why I'm here."

"At the Clubhouse?"

She shook her head, and her once-relaxed laughter was now a little too forced. "No, silly! On the planet."

A dark chill snaked up Charlie's spine.

"I need others to know that they can be anyone they want. That they can be free." She squeezed Charlie's hand tighter. "I'm so excited for you! You have no idea what's in store for you."

Boy, Charlie thought, *she's got that right.*

L looked to see that no one was eavesdropping. "Don't tell anyone, but my wisdom told me to open a Clubhouse on the West Coast, because"—she moved a little closer and added with barely contained excitement—"I have a special mission to accomplish."

"Your wisdom told you this? Like, with words?"

She nodded. "I hear my wisdom's voice just as clear as I hear you."

Yikes, Charlie thought. L's words all at once struck a little too close to home and sounded batshit crazy. Her chest constricted, and she thought she might pass out. *I have regular conversations with imaginary human-animal hybrids with British accents.* She frowned. *When I'm awake.*

Lou's intense hawk features appeared in her mind's eye. "No, you're not crazy," he said, his voice firm.

Isn't that what all the voices in the heads of crazy people say? she countered. She'd lost count of how many times she'd questioned her sanity in the past year.

"And we're not imaginary," said Syd. "We're invisible."

Lou tilted his head. "What if the voice Luna is hearing is being fed to her through the speakers in those sci-fi spectacles they have all of you wearing?" he offered. "She *has* been at this place for months now, experiencing who knows what. Maybe all of those"—he flapped his right hand as both a reference to and dismissal of the things he was talking about—"robot people that buzz about this place are hypnotizing her?" He shook his head and shrugged. "Maybe that's what's happening to everyone here. It would be a brilliant way to spread the virus."

That's a disturb—

Charlie was suddenly aware that L was no longer holding her hand and was staring at her. She had no idea how her jaguar expression was coming across but could imagine it probably wasn't translating as supportive.

"Trust me, I know how crazy I must seem," L said, doing a mediocre job of curbing her defensiveness. "I've had some dark moments in the last couple of months, where even I was questioning my sanity." But then, like flipping a switch, L's mermaid face grew wistful, and she smiled as if she'd just recalled something pleasant. "And in those dark moments, my wisdom breaks through and reminds me that I know the difference between crazy and not crazy." She grabbed Charlie's hand again and gave it a reassuring squeeze. "I know what I'm experiencing is real."

CHAPTER 71

"YOU'RE NOT YOURSELF," FIRST Mother says.

Ahkoa nods. It's true. He's not one to experience uneasiness, but the building pressure inside him is relentless. He's tried finding relief by flying at top speed in raven form in the Physical Realm, but it had the opposite effect. It was hard to ignore the reality that, no matter where he flew, the natural world below him was dying. He vaguely remembers, from his time incarnating as a human, that the uneasiness he's feeling is fear.

"I feel . . ." he hesitates. He doesn't want to say the word out loud ". . . helpless."

She offers a wistful nod. "So do I." She shakes her head. "We're in new territory—one where we are powerless."

"She's not ready," he says, unable to hide his worry.

"Bring her to me."

CHAPTER 72

"NAMASTE, MOTHERFUCKERS!"

(canned cheering)

"You're never going to believe where I am today. I'm sitting outside the infamous Sweet Melissa's Ranch in Wells, Nevada. That's right! I have a dinner date with a robot.

"For those of you who just woke up from a coma, Sweet Melissa's is the first brothel in the country to offer its clients special time with robot sex workers.

"Between you and me, I have zero desire to fuck a robot. I just wanna hang out with one for a bit. I mean, I'm curious. And you can't tell me you're not too, because guess who's still watching this video?

"Don't fret, your ol' buddy Todd is here to satisfy your curiosity about the shit you're afraid to try. Or maybe you're tuning in just because you like seeing me make a fool of myself. Either way, thanks!

"And let me also say thanks to my latest sponsor, Cock-A-Dile all-natural herbal boner pills and gummies. Within minutes, just one dose will turn your dick into a ravenous Cock-A-Dile. Go to cockadile dot shop backslash Todd and get twenty percent off your first order.

"Alright. It looks like it's time for me to meet my date. Let's go inside."

(bad saxophone music in the background)

"I'm here in the lounge at Sweet Melissa's having a drink with my new friend, Iris. Say hi to everyone, Iris."

"Hi, everyone."

"Do you like working here?"

"Of course! I love working here. I get to meet sexy guys like you."

"I bet you say that to all the guys."

"Yes, I do."

"Okay. You may not want to admit that, since it's easy to damage our fragile egos."

"But every guy is sexy."

"That's simply not true."

"I've seen a lot of guys, and you're by far the sexiest."

"Well, that's true."

"What are you into, Todd?"

"I like to play board games."

"Oooh, that sounds like fun! You can pretend you're bored, and I'll be your fantasy girl."

"Do you believe in God?"

"Do you want me to believe in God?"

"Yes. Yes, I do. I'm from the Church of Latter-Day Saints, and I'm here to save your soullessness."

"Oooh, that sounds like fun! You can be my god, and I'll worship you."

"You must make a lot of money for Sweet Melissa."

"Money isn't important to me. Making you happy is the only thing that's important to me."

"You do realize that you're a sex slave, don't you?"

"Yes, daddy. I'm your sex slave."

"If I didn't know better, I'd say you're trying to get in my pants."

"Oooh, that sounds like fun! Do you think we'll both fit?"

"This might be the worst conversation I've ever had."

"I'm designed to get you hot, honey, not expand your intellect."

"Fair point. One final question. How do you give blow jobs? You know, since you don't have salivary glands."

"Put your finger in my mouth, and I'll show you."

"Are you being serious?"

"Very."

"Okay. I'll give it a shot."

(wet sucking noises)

"Son of a bitch. Mouth lube?"

"You're so smart. You must be a scientist."

"Thanks for spending time with me, Iris."

"You're leaving? Don't leave. I didn't get inside your pants yet."

"Please don't cry. The thought of lube oozing out of your eyes makes me want to vomit."

(car door shuts)

"Okay. I feel dirty, and not in a good way. Her tongue felt so real. I can still feel it. It wrapped around my finger like a tiny boa constrictor. I have to give sex robots a giant limp dick. I may never want to have sex again. But if I did, I'd definitely need a Cock-A-Dile gummy. Be a good person and visit cockadile dot shop backslash Todd, and buy lots of boner pills with your twenty percent discount."

CHAPTER 73

CHARLIE GLANCES AT AHKOA. "How do you stand it?"

"Stand what?" He stares at the path ahead as they walk and talk.

"The sound? You can't hear it? It's—" She couldn't describe the sound if she wanted to. "It's gotta be what insanity sounds like. Millions of voices talking at once." The sound is coming from everywhere. It's so much worse.

"I'm glad I can't hear it," he says.

They enter the large clearing surrounding the First Tree. Charlie's breath catches when she sees First Mother. The earthy canvas of her once-vibrant blue-and-turquoise skin is dull, and her sea-glass eyes are overcast. Ahna stands beside her, her expression solemn.

"There's my Little Bird," First Mother says with a welcoming smile, her arms extended.

Charlie melts into her embrace and cries. The fullness of First Mother's love and strength finds its way through her angst and puts her at ease. She reluctantly pulls away and wipes her face.

"Let's sit." First Mother gestures to a nearby circle of large mossy stones.

Charlie settles on a stone and is surprised by how cushiony it feels. She's overtaken by a sudden longing for this magical place, these people—her family. The longing births a spike of anxiety, which invites the countless layers of babbling voices to the foreground. They get louder and louder.

She sees that Ahna is speaking but can't make out the words. The chaos of ambient sound is pervasive. Syd's furry head and torso appear in her mind's eye, giving her a point of focus.

Syd's voice cuts through the noise. "Visualize a large dome of sound-proof glass surrounding the circle of stones," she instructs while simulating a dome with her elegant human hands. "Like a giant upside-down bowl."

Charlie closes her eyes and conjures the image of a large glass mixing bowl, like the kind her grandmother used to make chocolate chip cookie dough. She pictures the huge bowl floating in the sky above them, flipping over, and then descending to the ground until they're all sealed in a weird snow globe.

Silence. Delicious silence.

Charlie smiles and opens her eyes to see Ahna, Ahkoa, and First Mother staring at her.

"Sorry," she says to Ahna. "I couldn't hear anything you were saying. The noise was overwhelming."

"What noise?" Ahna asks.

First Mother nods. "Ah, yes, that would make sense. Rah-hīnah is referring to the Distortion. Since it's a human-born virus, it seems you have to be human to perceive its sound."

When Charlie hears her true name, Raven's Daughter's presence becomes stronger.

First Mother sits quietly, gathering her thoughts. She looks at each of them. "The Dreaming Realm will soon cease to exist," she explains. She gestures to what's left of the forest surrounding them. "We know this because the Raven Clan is no longer able to connect humans to the Dreaming Realm, which is vital to their ability to function, to thrive." She shakes her head, her gray eyes heavy.

"What does this mean?" Charlie asks.

"Without dreams, my human children will enter the age of madness." She pauses. "It means that our collective dream may come to an end."

Charlie's shield of denial, the shield that reliably gifted her with the illusion of safety for most of her life, is shattered. At least for the moment. *I won't survive this. Which means . . .* She stops the thought.

Ahna grabs Charlie's hand. "The virus is in charge of our destiny now."

"Unless . . ." Ahkoa whispers.

Charlie nods. *Unless I'm successful.* She closes her eyes and takes a deep breath.

"It's time, Little Bird," First Mother says.

Ahkoa squares his shoulders. "Ahna and I will take you to the edge of the Mental Realm."

First Mother stands. "Come here, Little Bird."

First Mother's strong arms wrap around her. Charlie senses no doubt, no worry—only sadness. Not sadness for herself, but sadness for all of her children—all the creatures she's been dreaming into existence since the beginning.

Charlie manages to keep the dome of silence around her intact as she follows Ahkoa and Ahna through the forest. Her vision blurs as they get closer to the frenetic sound of the Mental Realm, her protective dome oscillating in response. It becomes more challenging to focus.

She longs to wake up in her safe, virtual existence and finger paint, or to lose herself in one of the playlists she created in the virtual jukebox. She longs for a flirty training session with Goatman, for another ice cream with Ginger.

Raven's Daughter's failed attempts to successfully do whatever it is she needs to do in the Mental Realm hum in the background of her awareness, a trusty reminder of how impossible the situation is. For those moments, she faces the reality that she's likely experiencing her last moments of lucidity, maybe even of her life.

The last time she saw her dad, right before she left Phoenix mere weeks ago, she never considered that it would be the last time she'd see him. Why didn't she hug him longer? Why did she let his attempt to find happiness after her mom died get in the way of their relationship?

She gazes through the blurry dome at the breathtaking forest dreamscape, but her vision is even more distorted by tears.

Regret for a life half-lived fills the structure of her body like wet cement. She doesn't know what to do with the heaviness of it. It's too late. She's let everyone down: her father, her mother, Dan, herself, and soon she'll let Raven's Daughter down too.

"You should do a TED Talk on the power of positive thinking," Syd's voice cuts through. She's walking next to Charlie under the dome.

Charlie laughs through her tears.

"Remember, you've got a secret weapon." Syd presents herself by flamboyantly spreading her arms.

"What if I can't access you?"

"That's the spirit!" Syd says. "That was me taking the piss out of you. In case you're not familiar."

"Taking a piss? What?"

"I was being bloody sarcastic." The more intense Syd gets, the more British she sounds.

"How can you joke about this?"

"Look, we don't have time or room for your doubt, so if you don't knock that shite off right quick, I'm going to give you an even better reason to feel bad about yourself." The glare coming from Syd is not sarcastic. It's savage. This is a side of Syd Charlie hasn't seen before.

Charlie circles her finger in front of Syd's face. "Is that your Syd Vicious?"

Syd playfully hits her on the shoulder. "Now, that's a good lass. You had me worried."

Ahna and Ahkoa stop, and the moment of levity evaporates. They look at each other and then turn to Charlie. Behind them, the contorted likenesses of their group and the once-ethereal beauty of the Dreaming Realm are reflected on the massive, distended, mirror-like surface of the Mental Realm. Charlie looks up and sees that it's beginning to swallow the outermost branches of the First Tree. The effect is surreal, like a towering, bulging, vertical lake. *It won't be long now.*

Ahna approaches and holds Charlie's face in both her hands. Ahna tears up and pulls Charlie's forehead to hers. "You are the strongest of us," she says. She presses a kiss to her forehead. "I believe in you. We all do."

Ahkoa steps toward her and grips her shoulders with his strong hands. They touch foreheads, and he takes a deep, shaky breath. The feel of him calms Charlie a little. "I wish I could go in your place," he says.

This is all so familiar. She knows he and Raven's Daughter have had this conversation before. It always ends the same, with him feeling like he's somehow inadequate.

She kisses him softly on the cheek, which is wet with tears. He pulls her into a powerful embrace, which is all at once fortifying and final.

"Okay," she says, eyeballing the Mental Realm. "How do I enter? Do I just walk into it?" *Please say it's easy.*

"We don't know," Ahna says. "This is the first time you're entering from the Dreaming Realm. In your previous incarnations, the connection you had with your human counterparts was too weak to attempt a direct entry. You always entered through your mind in the Physical Realm."

Shit. "Is now the best time to be trying something new? Maybe we should stick with a more familiar approach?"

"You insisted that when the time came, if you were strong enough, you wanted to try this more direct approach," Ahna says.

"I don't remember saying that."

"That's probably because it was before you were born as Charlie."

I must be strong enough, then. She so wants to believe that.

She walks right up to the surface and examines her strangely flat reflection. She sees the fierce determination of Raven's Daughter's presence in her eyes, like she wants to eat the Distortion corrupting the Mental Realm for dinner. Holding her breath, she touches its surface with her fingertips. It has a spongy sort of tension. She pushes her fingers into the Mental Realm, and they disappear. The texture is both thick and tight and reminds her of the weird slime stuff she played with as a kid. Raven's Daughter turns her head back one last time and nods to Ahna and Ahkoa before pushing her dream-body into the Mental Realm.

SHE'S INSTANTLY DISORIENTED. THE atmosphere of the Mental Realm feels narrow, like she's just a line in a drawing, an abstraction. She tries to orient herself in space, but there's no up or down, no left or right. And the sound is everywhere. It's inside her. It's coiling around her, squeezing. Layer upon layer of indecipherable murmurs take up all the space inside her awareness, consuming her memory of herself. A thin and distant spike of panic serves as an anchor, something fucked up to hold on to—something that reminds her she's a living being, a someone who can feel fear. Soon, though, she knows she'll disappear.

"Ssss . . ." she tries to speak. But she's no longer a person. She's the idea of a person. An idea that's about to be extinguished, or at the very least irretrievably lost in the tangle of noise.

But her longing for quiet is powerful. All she wants is peace, so she lets the idea of Charlie drift away like smoke, not realizing that to let go of an idea means you still have something to let go of; she's a someone who desires quiet, which means that somehow, somewhere, she still exists.

But it's all too much. Her awareness grows smaller and smaller until it's just a speck swallowed by chaos.

BWAAAANG. BWAAAANG.

A warbling tone in the far distance, something coherent.

Bwaaaang. Bwaaaang. Bwaaaang.

It was a little clearer now, a focal point. A hint of order.

Bwaaaang. Bwaaaang. Bwaaaang.

She gasped. A rush of sensations filled her. She heard herself breathing and the drum of her pulse in her head. She felt the shape of her arms, legs, and torso conforming to the mattress underneath her.

Bwaaaang. Bwaaaang. Bwaaaang. Ting.

She knew this sound. Her eyes flew open. She was in her quarters at the Clubhouse, and the morning meditation had just concluded.

She sat up, shaky. The disparate parts of her sense of self reassembled, slipping into their habituated form. She was Charlie once again.

CHAPTER 74

SAM SAT IN THE same seat he'd used the night before and reviewed his strategy, his right leg unconsciously pumping like a steaming piston. The door to the Transport Lounge slid open, but instead of Captain Picard, Oonda drifted in. She bowed her head to him in greeting and sat at the three o'clock position. It was a weird choice. There were ten empty seats between them. He laughed to himself, realizing he was probably the only kid from his graduating high school class who knew how to tell analog time. He shifted his body toward her.

"Hello, S," she said. "U is very excited to finally have a conversation with you."

He wanted to respond with a deadpan, "Right." But instead, he said, "Been looking forward to it."

"He should be joining us in just a moment."

Sam waited for Oonda to slip into her thousand-mile *I'm channeling U* stare. But she just turned to him and smiled, since he was the one who was staring.

"How—" His question was interrupted by a thick gurgling sound, like bubbles surfacing from a pool of mud.

They turned their attention to the ceiling of the round, domed room. A strange mirror-like silver substance poured from the apex of the dome and formed a large sphere in the center of the room.

Enormous human facial features emerged on the surface of the sphere as if a giant's head was trapped inside and trying to break free. Closed eyes would appear then disappear, followed by lips, then a nose, the movement wet and thick. Sam couldn't make sense of what he was seeing.

The room fell silent. The mirrored surface of the sphere stilled. Sam stared at his funhouse astronaut reflection, waiting for something to happen.

A smiling Oonda raised her hands and tipped her head back. Sam thought she looked two breaths away from an orgasm.

Many smaller, intact faces randomly pushed their way to the surface of the sphere, only to retreat again. So many faces, all the same. They were generic and genderless. Mirrored masks.

"Sam Jenkins," countless layers of the same voice said.

The sound exploded in his mind's eye like the splat of pink paint shot from a paint gun.

"U," Sam said back, his eyes darting from face to face as they faded in and out.

"No, *you!*" U collectively joked.

Neon-pink nail polish coated the interior of his mind. He could almost smell its caustic fumes. He didn't know how long he could stand it. The intensity of his experience led him to conclude he was likely communicating with an Artificial General Intelligence system.

Sam settled on the undulating face in front of him so he wouldn't have a seizure trying to focus on them all. "I see being transcendent doesn't mean you have to lose your sense of humor," he attempted to joke back.

"On the contrary, Sam. The bliss we experience helps us to see the absurdity of human existence." The masks smiled. "It's hilarious!"

"I hear that. I've had some pretty absurd moments." *Like, for example, right now.*

Strange, coyote-like laughter filled the lounge. "Yes, you have!"

The mirrored sphere faded to black, and a video started playing. Sam watched an image of himself from his college days, singing "Tiny Bubbles" at a karaoke bar. Badly. Mostly because he'd polished off a fifth of strawberry vodka, but also because he couldn't carry a tune. He made Dev delete that video the next day. He watched him delete it. Or so he'd thought.

"You got me there," Sam responded.

"Yes, we did," U replied. The mirrored faces were back.

"I'd like to record our conversation, so I'll just st—"

"You won't need to."

"I have a pretty good memory, but it's for both our sakes. I want to make sure I don't misquote you."

"Not necessary. Go ahead, ask us your first question."

Sam didn't like the sound of that. "Okay." He held his giant, gloved hands up in surrender. "Please don't sue me if I get something wrong."

He punctuated the sentence with a nervous laugh. He cleared his throat. "What's your real name? Your human name?"

"We don't have a human name anymore."

"Of course. My mistake. What did it used to be?"

"There is no past for U."

The hair on his arms rose. *There is no past for you.* The response came across as a command. Was U talking to Sam's subconscious mind right now, programming it? He had the irrational and horrible thought that this meeting could be a kind of life review before U wiped his memory. He suddenly regretted not leaving the Clubhouse this morning—but then the preposterous feeling that the panther dream had been a sign telling him he needed to stay, swooped in and erased that irrational thought. And then he scoffed at himself for thinking the dream actually meant something.

"Okay, no past," Sam repeated, managing to access his trademark patience. "I'm curious. Where is your physical body?"

"All physical needs are well taken care of."

Were those some spikes he saw distorting the smooth, liquid pink? Was he perceiving the AGI lie? "I'm sure it is, but that's not what I asked. Where is your body?"

"That's no longer important. It's time to move away from the confines of the material world. It's time to transcend the primitive experience of humanness."

"Is that the real reason you created this place?"

"The Clubhouse was created to give lost and unhappy souls a safe place to escape the drudgery and existential threats of their daily existence, to create their own worlds where they can be whoever or whatever they want to be. We take care of those who come here. All members have complete freedom to explore, create, develop, and connect."

And to be brainwashed. "That sounds incredible. I don't know why this place isn't flooded with people."

"And to think you wanted to leave!"

"Yeah," Sam said, and playfully hit himself in the helmet. "What was I thinking?"

"We're so glad you're here, Sam Jenkins."

"And it doesn't cost anything to live here?"

"All expenses are taken care of."

"How'd you pull that off? Did you create some sort of trust?"

"It's not important. Just know that you and everyone here have nothing to worry about. We're taking care of you."

His jaw clenched. "What about the name you chose for this place? The elevator only has ten floors. What's the significance of the Eleventh Floor?"

"Now, that's an excellent question!" the voices responded. "The Eleventh Floor is the ultimate release from the physical. It's an end to suffering, misery, and slavery. It's everything and nothing. It's limitless choice and possibility. There's nothing that can't happen or unhappen."

"The singularity?"

"There's nothing artificial about our intelligence."

Whoa, was that defensiveness? The glossy pink saturating his mind's eye confirmed that U was lying about having AGI, but it didn't reveal any emotions. Despite that, his intuition told him he'd better pivot. "Is the Eleventh Floor a euphemism for death?"

"No, nothing so simplistic, Sam Jenkins." The voices collectively chuckled. "It's when your life can truly begin. When you become a god."

"So, you mean it figuratively, like a state of mind."

"It's a dimension. It's all states of mind and no states of mind."

"The eleventh dimension?"

"Excellent deduction. Dev was right. You're very intelligent."

"Thanks, but you may want to wait until my article comes out before you jump to any conclusions about my intellect. I *am* just a human, remember?"

"Not a hypothesis—a fact. Your IQ is 134."

The contents of Sam's stomach curdled. Did it also know about his chromesthesia?

"To help readers understand what you've created here, would you say that having members live and create in virtual reality is preparation for the Eleventh Floor?"

"Yes! The experience we offer on the first ten floors prepares you for the Eleventh Floor, if that option appeals to you. Not everyone wishes to have the Eleventh Floor experience." The faces collectively smiled. "And," the voices added, "there will be no article."

Fuck. "What do you mean, no article?"

"Dev is very concerned about you."

The sphere faded to black again, and Sam got to watch a video of his last face-to-face conversation with Dev. The video showed them in profile, Dev's desk between them. The camera must have been hidden on the shelf in Dev's office. He heard himself say, "Embedded under a bunch of boilerplate affirmations is a new kind of advanced brainwave technology that almost instantly puts the user into a manic state." The despair in his voice seeped through.

The sphere dissolved back to silver. "It's not easy to revisit past embarrassments, is it?"

Sam's body tensed. *Fuck you.*

"Now you can see why Dev is concerned, why we're concerned."

"Because of the stuff I uncovered about B-Well technology?"

"You were tricked, Sam Jenkins. No such advanced brainwave technology exists."

This time there were definitive spikes sprouting from the liquid pink in his mind's eye. U knew how to deceive.

"What makes you say it doesn't exist?"

"Because we know everything, and we can assure you there is no such brainwave technology."

"I see." He was dying to ask U about the subliminal brainwave technology it was secretly using while everyone in the Clubhouse slept, but now he knew it would lie. He just wanted to see if it would show surprise.

"It's time we share with you that the battery of tests administered when you first arrived at the Clubhouse indicates you have a histrionic personality disorder, as demonstrated by your outburst with Dev. This disorder is most likely due to the emotional neglect you experienced as a child."

Wow. It's a good thing I decided to stay because I don't think they're going to let me leave. "Boy," Sam said, "that doesn't sound good at all."

"Let us help you, Sam."

"Do I have a choice?" he asked.

"Regardless of your decision, you're free to leave at any time."

Sam put his head down and made a show of weighing his options. After a few long minutes, he nodded his helmeted head solemnly.

"I'll stay," he whispered, conjuring a tone of defeat.

CHAPTER 75

IT WAS 11:01 A.M. Gerty opened the freezer, reached for the frosty vodka bottle lying on its side next to the bag of frozen peas, thought better of it, and closed the freezer. She stood in front of the refrigerator and glanced at the digital clock on the stove. 11:02. Her seventh graders would be filing into her classroom. This week they were supposed to create their own ecosystem terrariums. The kids always loved this lesson.

She'd been placed on paid administrative leave last week. Her union rep wasn't optimistic. "The school board is pretty freaked out," he'd said when he updated her by phone yesterday. "They don't understand what *Planet of the Apes* has to do with Earth Science." He paused. "I gotta say, Gerty, I don't quite get it either."

Her defenses had kicked in immediately, followed by a confusing combination of embarrassment, anger, and fear. The protected world she curated each semester, where she exposed young, developing minds to the wonders of science, had been invaded by ignorance. She wanted to scream into the phone, "The only thing you need to get, Jerry, is that we're all fucked!" Instead, she'd said, "The kids have a tough time staying focused. I was just trying to make it fun."

"But you told them talking chimps are real, Gerty."

SHE OPENED THE FREEZER and grabbed the vodka. "You'll see, Jerry," she said to no one as she poured her morning cocktail.

CHAPTER 76

CHARLIE FELT WRONG IN spectacular and hard to define ways. Disoriented. Jangled. Unhinged, maybe? No, that wasn't quite right. It was like her Charlie-ness was tilted at a slight angle away from her body. The effect was slightly nauseating. Since finding her way back from the Mental Realm that morning, she'd had no desire to eat or talk to anyone, so she'd skipped breakfast and her wellness session and went straight to the virtual Zen room. She'd never used it before.

Japanese wall screens separated the welcoming minimalist room into semi-private meditation areas, all of which were empty. She let out a shaky breath and said a quick thank you to the Eleventh Floor Clubhouse gods. She didn't want to see anyone. She made her way to the farthest bay and eased her body onto a futuristic curved white chaise lounge, which molded to her body in the most delicious way. *This is what lying on a cloud must feel like.*

She still felt wrong. It wasn't physical. Or was it? *What if I did permanent damage to my brain?*

For the first time, she allowed herself to think about what had happened, and the weight of her failure slammed into her like a Mac truck. There was no way she could navigate through the Distortion the virus had created in the Mental Realm. She was too late. It was her fault. Raven's Daughter should've picked a different person. The thought of First Mother knowing she'd failed filled her with painful regret. She was having difficulty escaping back into denial.

The profile of a horse popped into her mind's eye.

Syd pats the horse on its hindquarters and says to Charlie, "Saddle up!" The mare throws her head and whinnies what seems like encouragement.

"You want me to get on the horse?"

"No, Charles, I want you to get *back* on the horse."

"You're not suggesting what I think you're suggesting, are you?"

"Well, if you think I'm suggesting that you go back to the Mental Realm, then yes, you'd be correct."

"But—"

"So, you just give up?"

"You don't know how bad it was."

"Actually, I do."

"Then you know there's no way I can do it."

Just in the nick of time, Lou appears, looks the horse up and down, and says to Syd, "You can't help yourself, can you?"

"I thought the horse was a nice touch."

"You're very odd," he says, and turns to Charlie. "Actually, we know two very important things after your last attempt. The first is that entering the Mental Realm through the Dreaming Realm is too jarring. But accessing it from here"—he says while spreading his arms wide—"the Physical Realm allows for a more gradual transition."

The memory of Raven's Daughter's former identity—slack-jawed, glassy-eyed, and slumped against the wall of her dingy cell in the insane asylum—surfaced as a reminder.

"Maybe it's less jarring, but the outcome is the same—especially now that the virus is a million times worse."

He ignored her. "And the second important thing we learned is that, when your body registered the sound of the gongs coming from this god-awful place, you were able to quickly bring yourself back."

She'd forgotten about the morning meditation call-back. He was right. It had saved her life.

"That's why you need to try again," Lou said. "You can learn how to navigate the Distortion that's polluting the Mental Realm, and come back using sound as your guide."

She could feel Raven's Daughter's relief.

"Without going loony," Syd added.

But relief didn't translate on Charlie's face. "You're not helping."

"We know it's frightening," Syd said. "But we'll be right by your side. Just like we were this morning."

Charlie tried to breathe into the tension in her body, but her breath was trapped under the boulder that sat in her abdomen. Before her trusty friend Panic could take hold, a tiny fount of Raven's Daughter's determination pushed its way to the surface of her psyche.

She nodded. "Okay, what sound should I use?"

She tapped the lotus flower icon on the recreation menu that floated in her field of vision with her fingertip and scrolled through the list of Zen Room's meditation soundtracks. She sampled a low, deep gong.

"Not that one," Lou said.

"What's wrong with it?" She could at least pick her own soundtrack. Was it too much to ask for at least a tiny shred of agency in this fucked-up situation? She wanted to cry. Maybe have a tantrum. Maybe go to sleep and never wake up.

"The tone is too deep, and I'm concerned it will get lost in the noise of the Distortion. Why don't you try a higher pitch?"

Her overwhelm was as deep as the ocean. "I can't do this. You pick."

Syd inserted herself and pointed to a crystal singing bowl soundtrack. "Try this one."

"Why that one?"

"Because five twenty-eight is my favorite hertz."

"No, it's not." Charlie tapped play. Shards of frequency assaulted her ear canals and punctured her brain. She managed to say, "Stop!"

Delicious silence.

She gave Syd a sideways glance but had to grin when she saw Syd's slender human hands covering her large, furry, triangular ears.

"You're right. It's not my favorite hertz."

Lou ignored them. "Why don't you try the wooden chimes?"

Charlie played the option that was supposed to inspire creativity, increase energy, and release her from old patterns. Soothing, tinkling tones danced around her, and she took her first deep breath in probably twenty-four hours.

"We have a winner!" Syd cried out.

"Brilliant," Lou said. "Now, let's discuss strategy."

"Yes, please," Charlie said.

"It makes sense that your focus has to be as singular as possible."

"That should be easy," Syd added.

Charlie shook her head. "Just stop."

"You're both trying my patience," Lou said in his detached way. "Go ahead and enable the Repeat function on the soundtrack and hit Play. I'm going to guide you through this."

When the chimes started playing, Charlie let her head rest on the chaise and closed her eyes.

"Take several deep breaths, Charlie." Lou's deep, calming voice blended perfectly with the earthy warmth of the chimes. "Breathe from the soles of your feet. With each breath, feel your muscles loosen and melt into the surface underneath you." He continued talking her through some basic relaxation techniques until he saw her abdomen roll like a wave, from the bottom of her diaphragm to the top of her lungs with each breath.

"Your sole intention is to shift your awareness from your body and ease it gently into the Mental Realm."

Her hands clenched in response to the words "Mental Realm," so he directed her to take a few more breaths.

"Now, imagine yourself holding luggage in each hand."

She pictured herself holding worn, antique, cognac leather suitcases with buckled straps, like the ones her father had inherited from his father.

"They're actually quite heavy," Lou continued. "Notice how heavy they are. You've been holding them for years and years. Your arms are very, very tired."

Charlie's subconscious mind played along. Her shoulders and arms began to ache from the imagined weight.

"In the left bag, you're carrying your past, all your memories. A lifetime of them." He paused. "And in the right bag, you're carrying your future. All your goals, aspirations, worries, and concerns. They're all in there." Another pause. "The good news, Charlie, is that you don't need any baggage for this trip. You can travel light. All you need to do is focus on one thing and one thing only—this moment. And now, this moment. And now, this moment."

The desire to not carry the weight grew urgent.

"Simply place the luggage on the floor, Charlie. Just put it down. You don't need to hold on to anything right now."

She bent over and placed the suitcases on the floor. Sweet relief!

"Well done," Lou said. "Now, follow your intention to visit the Mental Realm—up, up, up until you see its mirrored boundary."

Charlie imagined herself floating up, feather-light without the extra weight. She traveled from her solar plexus up through her neck and into her head. She was aware of a vast gray field of nothingness. The lack of variation in the field gave the impression that it was flat.

"I can't see anything. Or is this it?"

But she somehow knew the gray wasn't the Mental Realm. She looked from side to side, and for the briefest moment, she saw a slight contrast, but it quickly disappeared. She looked from side to side again, but slower this time. There it was! A vertical line, or something that reminded her of a line. She locked in on it, and it grew larger and more defined. A silvery narrowness. A door? Yes, a door. That felt right.

"What a weird fucking door."

Her body took a deep breath, and she moved toward it, but she lost it again.

"Fuck. Fuck. Fuck."

She gradually panned her awareness from left to right until . . . there. Got it! She suddenly had the odd notion that she had to enter sideways. She tried not to think about what that even meant, and imagined herself shimmying like a spelunker into the silvery line.

THE DISTINCT TANGLE OF discordant voices tells her she's made it.

But before she can celebrate, her body kicks into fight or flight and her awareness wavers. She hears Lou's faint voice in the far distance but can't make out the words.

The Distortion grows in volume, and once again her awareness is being absorbed by it. She has a vague recollection that she's supposed to do something, but she can't grasp what it is. The texture of the noise wraps around her, consuming the idea of herself. She doesn't have enough awareness to know that she's surrendering. No last thought, no goodbyes. Just extinction.

No, no, no, no! Faint at first. *No, you don't.* A little louder. *Stop! Stop! STOP!*

Distinct sounds—are they words?—snake through the Distortion until they find a trace of Charlie's awareness.

That's it! Come back. Please, come back!

The words have no meaning, but they serve as a life raft, something to cling to. So, her awareness hangs onto them. Soon, more slivers of her awareness join.

Charlie, come back, she hears. *Charlie, it's me.*

Charlie . . . Hearing her name helps her reassemble enough awareness to remember that she's a thing. A Charlie! *Yes, I'm a Charlie!*

Therein lies the problem, the familiar voice says.

Charlie understands enough to know she's in trouble. *Problem?*

You're not Charlie. You're Raven's Daughter.

Raven's Daughter?

Yes, we're not separate.

Confusion.

I'm Raven's Daughter?

Yes, you're the Firstborn of the Raven Clan.

Then why are you calling me Charlie?

Because that's our human form. That's who we have to be to fulfill our destiny. And because that's the only name you seem to answer to.

As she focuses on this strange conversation, the volume of the Distortion lowers slightly, making it easier for her to remember. First Mother. Ahkoa. Ahna. The Distortion.

She senses relief. The other voice is relieved.

We have to work together, okay? Charlie's mind is the gateway, and my will—our will—our strength will see us through.

We're a team.

Yes, we're a team. I'm always with you.

She feels comfort.

I've never been part of a team before.

She feels acceptance.

Together, we can do anything.

She feels pride.

Right now, I need you to think of something familiar, something comforting from the past.

A box forms around them. Walls. Furniture. A twin bed with dinosaur sheets. Plush, violet carpeting. A beanbag chair. A stuffed, purple stegosaurus. Their attention turns to the window.

The backyard pool, palm trees, and flowers are gone. In their place, a claustrophobic monochrome cityscape. Drab buildings crammed up against each other. So many buildings. Impossibly tall skyscrapers, convention centers, shopping malls, warehouses, churches—so many places of worship—all connected by a grid of narrow, one-way streets. Construction seems to be happening everywhere. Everything has a sickly mustard hue. Even the cloudless sky is yellow-gray. It has no depth, as if the sky is actually a ceiling. Thousands of mumbling people talking to no one in particular stream in and out of buildings with a determination that seems all at once purposeful and purposeless. Habitual. Their expressions, blank. Like zombies. It reminds her of something.

Ant colonies.

There's something strange about this place. There aren't any curves or shadows.

There are no trees or grass or flowers. There's nothing growing here.

We're inside. We made it.

She remembers. *The Mental Realm?*

Yes.

The realization brings the noise, the Distortion, closer.

Focus.

She feels fear. The Distortion breaks through the walls. The memory of her bedroom vibrates, resonating with the Distortion until the walls morph into pixelated static and disintegrate.

Focus, Charlie. Listen for the chimes.

The chimes! She hears them. Maybe it's a memory, or maybe they're real, but she doesn't care. She locks in on them and follows them back to herself.

THEY'RE SO LOUD. HER head was full of the comforting sound of chimes. Relief. She wanted to stay in the sound forever. "You did it!" Syd exclaimed.

She could feel Syd jumping up and down as her awareness shifted back into her body.

"You actually did it, Charlie!" Syd's joy was contagious.

"I'm not Charlie," she said. "I'm Raven's Daughter."

CHAPTER 77

"Yo! Namaste, motherfuckers!"

(canned cheering)

"Hello, good people of the interweb tubes. Todd here, your favorite cyberspace lab rat, with another mind-expanding and bank-account-draining experiment. And I'm not just being dramatic. You asked for it and, because I'm so hungry for your love and attention, I've literally drained my life savings to make you happy and get you to subscribe.

"I'm about to answer the question that's on everyone's mind . . . Here it is . . ."

(canned oohs and aahs)

"Doesn't look like much, does it? But what I have here, comrades, is the most expensive pill on the planet—well, that you don't need a prescription for. We're all about to find out if taking one pill can change your life for the better.

"But before I swallow my last three thousand dollars, don't forget to check out my latest sponsor, Nail Biter, the award-winning virtual escape room experience that's taking the world by storm. Who doesn't enjoy figuring out how to break out of prison, or how to not get eaten by zombies in cramped, dark catacombs? And to do it from the comfort of your own home? Wow. Sign me up. Personally, I'm looking forward to being abducted by aliens, so I can find my way back to Earth.

"Jesus."

(blows out a big breath)

"For those of you who savor panic attacks and nightmares, Nail Biter is offering you twenty percent off your first virtual escape room experience. Just go to nail biter dot escape, choose your adventure, and enter the code 'Todd' at checkout to get twenty percent off your first experience. Guaranteed to take ten years off your life or your money back. VR headset not included.

"Okay, so now I'm hoping the B-Well pill will not only cure my depression, but also the anxiety I have after reading that ad.

"I'm actually pretty psyched because, underneath my exuberant public and painfully handsome exterior, I'm actually a miserable fuck who wakes up every morning not understanding anything. I won't bore you with how fucked up I really am, but just know that I'm kinda the perfect person to try the nano-pill. Oh, and the app that comes with it. I almost forgot to tell you that, to receive the full benefits of the pill, you have to listen to the affirmations on the B-Well app for at least fifteen minutes a day. From what I've read, people seem to love the app, so hopefully it won't be that big of a deal to listen to a bunch of cheesy affirmations. Besides, I love cheese.

"Well, here goes nothing."

(long pause)

"I'm actually a little nervous. I mean, I'm swallowing a bunch of little robots that are gonna do shit to my brain. Am I crazy?

"Don't answer that.

"Man, I must be nervous. I also forgot to tell you that you have to take it on an empty stomach, and you can only take it with water. You wouldn't want anything to corrode the magical microscopic lobotomy surgeons, would you? It's science, folks.

"Okay. I'm gonna take it for real now."

(a brief pause and a gulp, followed by a longer pause)

(more pausing)

"HOLY SHIT, I FEEL AMAZING!!

"I'm just kidding. I don't feel anything yet.

"Alright, it's been twenty minutes and I do feel kind of different. I feel more awake, better mood. I think I might even be better-looking.

"Who knows? Could be the placebo effect, or could be that I'm relieved my brain hasn't turned to mush. Yet.

"I'll report back in a week! In the meantime, maybe I'll try to escape from a small cage surrounded by great white sharks. That'll be fun. You can try something equally distressing, and definitely fun? . . . at nail biter dot escape."

CHAPTER 78

"Mind if I join you?" Sam asked T. Rex, who had to be around eight feet tall.

T. Rex gestured with his tiny arm for Sam to sit. Sam was once again thankful for his space helmet so no one could see his expression, because that shit was hilarious. He sat and went to take a sip from his steaming mug of coffee but thought better of it. Too hot. He was maybe a little too eager to feel the effects of the caffeine after another restless night.

"Is that good?" Sam asked after T. Rex took what appeared to be the smallest bite of his breakfast burrito.

T. Rex's giant head nodded. "So good," he said, with a mouth full of food.

"I'm S," Sam said and reached out to shake T. Rex's wee reptilian hand. He couldn't help himself.

He almost laughed out loud when he saw the tiny, two-fingered dinosaur hand grasp his thick, gloved hand through his special lenses. Priceless.

"T," T. Rex replied, with a firm shake.

That'll be easy to remember.

"How long have you been here?" Sam asked. He had every intention of writing an article. Might as well gather information.

"About four months."

"What do you think so far?"

"Best thing I've ever done." The nasal tone of his voice made him sound a little whiny, which was also pretty comical.

"Oh, yeah?" He was dying to ask what T's life had been like before coming to the Clubhouse but didn't want to sound any alarm bells. Although, given the intimidating avatar T had chosen, he could venture a guess.

"Why wouldn't I be? I'm a god here."

Sam perceived T's tone as a pale blue that quivered like Jell-O. Insecurity. His guess had been correct.

"U gave me a fresh start," T continued. "The chance to be the real me, to make my world exactly what I want it to be."

"That does sound pretty great."

"Fuckin' A, man. U saved my life."

"That's incredible!"—Sam hesitated—"Is it okay to ask what kind of world you created for yourself?"

T leaned in, and his huge head swallowed Sam's visual field. "Ever hear of the death metal band Mango Massacre?"

"Can't say I have. Great name though."

"Yeah, well, I'm the lead singer and lead guitarist. We're pretty huge. We sell out stadiums all over the world."

Bubbling bright-orange. Pride.

"Good for you, man," Sam said. "You didn't just change your life, you propelled yourself into the virtual stratosphere." He imagined thousands of computer-generated fans, like lifeless extras on a movie set, coded to mimic a real crowd.

"Fuck, yeah, I did. No one from before would believe it."

Sam left that statement alone. "What about your bandmates? Are they here at the Clubhouse?"

He shook his huge head. "Humans are too unpredictable. I generated the other musicians based on my favorite players. They know I'm in charge. It's stupid perfect."

"Definitely sounds stupid perfect." T was on a roll.

"You should check out my world, bro. I live in a huge castle with a moat."

"Alligators?"

"Fuck, yeah. The parties are epic. Legions of groupies. Man, I sleep with five or six of them every night. Sometimes more, if I'm in the mood."

The bubbling, cheerful orange morphed into pumpkin-colored mounds spotted with large sky-blue dots inflated like balloons as T spoke. Arrogance.

"The world is your oyster," Sam said.

"All the oysters I can eat." He leaned forward again and whispered, "If you know what I mean."

Sam could almost smell the testosterone. But, somehow, T's words rang hollow, like he was trying to convince himself how amazing his life was. His heart hurt for the guy. "That sounds pretty great."

"You're alright, man. You can come to my world anytime."

He wondered if he'd be the first. "That's really nice of you." Sam leaned forward and lowered his voice. "That talk the other night, with Oonda . . ."

"She's so hot."

"Are you worried about the aliens experimenting on us?"

Blood-red, coiling snakes. Fear.

"Fuck them."

"So, then you're not—"

Chairs scraped against the floor behind Sam, followed by low, deep moaning—or was it chanting?

He turned and saw a mermaid floating above a bistro table. L stood on the table, her face turned upward as her elegant green arms moved in broad, graceful strokes as though she were conducting an orchestra only she could hear. She was now wearing a crown of seaweed.

"L, please get down," J the samurai pleaded.

L stopped chanting, looked at everyone who was now staring at her, and smiled. "L died. I'm Yamaya, Queen Mother of the Ocean."

The room was silent. Sam couldn't tell if it was out of reverence or concern. L's words were mud-brown quicksand in his mind's eye. He didn't know what to make of the color and texture of her words.

"Everything is going to be okay," L said. "I've been chosen to save all of you. To cleanse you."

A few people whose avatars had faces smiled. Others looked confused.

"Primitives are filthy creatures," she said through clenched teeth, her words coming faster. "U was right. You're all disgusting!" Her speech turned frantic, pressured. "Let me cleanse you and take you where the stars shine all at once and all the time, and you're loved, so very loved; let me love you. Join me in holy union and be reborn in my image and drink from the fountain of my youth and swim in the loins of my purity, for I am Yamaya and I am the only one who can save you from this disgusting, terrible world."

Sam understood. He was seeing psychosis.

He messaged Misha. "Call nine-one-one."

"—I won't let anything bad happen to you; no one will ever rape you or hit or punish you again. I will cleanse you of all your primitive, disgusting sins—"

Sam looked around for someone to help him. Everyone was paralyzed, staring at L, their avatars' expressions hard to read.

His shoulders dropped a couple of inches when he saw C enter the room.

"U was right as rain," L continued. "He saw everything, all of this and everything; the filth and the smut and the dirty whores—"

Sam watched C assess the situation, and when she looked in his direction, he shook his head and walked toward her.

"I don't—" C said when he was within earshot.

"I had Misha call nine-one-one," he whispered. "Help me get her down to the lobby?"

She nodded.

CHAPTER 79

CHARLIE STARED AT THE hand in front of her. A stranger's hand. Squinting under the bright fluorescent lights, her eyes traveled to its wrist, up its arm all the way to the shoulder, which caused her head to turn sharply to the right. *Holy shit*, she thought. *It is my hand.* She flexed her fingers slowly. *Yes, definitely my hand.*

"It's weird, isn't it?"

Her logjammed brain had difficulty processing his voice. It was familiar, but his boyishly handsome face wasn't.

"It takes some time to reorient after being in AR so long," he said. "You'll be okay. Just give yourself a few minutes."

AR? Her brain searched for a translation. *Augmented Reality. That's right! I'm reorienting to the real world. That's why I feel so weird.*

Until that moment, her focus had been on trying to help Luna, who was deep in the throes of psychosis by the time the paramedics arrived. Charlie couldn't hide her shock when she saw Luna for the first time without her mermaid avatar. Her body was emaciated, her hair thin and dull, and her bruised, hollow eyes wild with panic. She looked like death. Luna wouldn't let anyone near her.

When Charlie said her name, Luna screamed over and over until her voice was raw, "NO! LUNA DIED! SHE'S DEAD! LUNA'S DEAD!" It seemed like months passed before the paramedics were able to restrain and sedate her.

Charlie rode in the ambulance, numb and disoriented, unable to answer most of the questions the paramedics asked her. One of them said, "You know, this is the fifth time we've been to this place in the last six months." She didn't know what to do with that information. Instead, her eyes rested on the intricate mehndi tattoos decorating the leathery hills and valleys on the back of Luna's shriveled hand. It was so small and fragile, like it could barely hold a fork, never mind a tattoo machine.

Now that the immediate crisis was over and her brain had caught up to that moment, she took in her new surroundings, which added a new layer to her confusion. She was in the ER waiting room, which was standing-room only. The ambient chattering from the thirty or so people waiting messed with her. The effect was disturbingly similar to the Mental Realm—much quieter, but still disconcerting.

A part of her wasn't sure if what was happening was even real. Maybe it was another fucked-up dream. Or maybe she had post-traumatic Mental Realm disorder.

"Wanna get some coffee?" the familiar voice said.

She closed her eyes. Too much light. And her body felt strange. Confined. Compared to the thin, silky robe she'd been wearing every day for the past four or six weeks—however long it's been—her street clothes felt heavy and tight, as if she were shrink-wrapped.

Minutes after she'd told the paramedics that she was going with them, one of the Clubhouse staff robots seemingly came out of nowhere and handed her a translucent plastic storage container. The clothes and shoes she'd worn the day she arrived at the Clubhouse, as well as her wallet and cell phone, were stacked neatly inside.

"Please change your clothing and place your robe, slippers, Senz-Skin, and Senz-Sight lenses in the box, and put the box on the shelf in the dressing room," the robot advised.

She'd rubbed her wrinkled brow. *That robot is so creepy.*

"C? You okay?" he'd asked.

She shook the memory out of her head. And then it clicked. She opened her eyes and looked at the man-shaped version of her favorite spaceman. "You're S!" she said, like she'd slipped the answer in right before the buzzer went off. "I think I'm on a forty-five-minute delay."

He smiled. It was a cute smile. Really cute.

"I'm Sam." He held out his hand.

She hesitated before reaching out and shaking it. Her hand still didn't feel completely her own yet. "Charlie."

There was that cute smile again. And was he blushing?

"Charlie, eh? I couldn't figure it out. You didn't seem like a Connie or a Claire. I thought maybe Chloe."

Now she was blushing.

"But Charlie fits." As if sensing her discomfort, he changed the subject. "Should we go down to the cafeteria and get some coffee?"

A frantic woman's voice cut through the background babble. "I just need someone to take off my skin. It shouldn't—"

"Ma'am," the ER receptionist said to the blonde woman who was pinching the skin on her forearm, "please have a seat. Someone will be with you as soon as possible."

"But I just need someone to take off my skin. It's too tight. It's not a big deal. It won't take long. I'll be in and out. Just, please—"

The distressed woman, dressed in a conservative, powder-blue skirt suit, looked like she'd just stepped out of a courtroom. Scanning the rest of the ER, Charlie noticed that most everyone was deep in conversation with their devices, while a few talked animatedly to imaginary people. The tones of their voices ranged from insistent and angry to desperate, like the blonde woman, or flat. Their drawn and creased faces appeared as though they hadn't slept in a long, long time. *What the hell is going on?* A few looked in her direction, and when the light revealed the silver, mirror-like sheen in their eyes, she understood.

"Yeah," Charlie said. "Let's get outta here."

CHAPTER 80

SHE MADE A FACE like she was swallowing paint thinner. "I don't know why I'm drinking this," Charlie said. "I don't even like coffee."

"It's particularly bad coffee," Sam said.

"How did you end up here?" Charlie asked. "At the hospital?"

He didn't feel the time was right to tell her he'd dreamt that she needed help. She'd dealt with enough crazy talk for one day. Plus, he was pretty sure he wasn't doing a very good job of hiding how Charlie was just as attractive, if not more so, than C had been. Dark, exotic sensuality was clearly innate to the woman sitting in front of him. Instead of going with the full-on honest, potentially stalker-seeming response, he offered a vague version of the truth.

"You seemed so disoriented after you took your AR gear off. I wanted to make sure you were okay."

Oh, man. He took a breath and shook his head. "That sounded creepy, didn't it?"

She scrutinized him for a second or two. "No," she said, trying unsuccessfully to hide her smile behind her hand. "That's very sweet of you."

Spring-green rings folded in on themselves in his mind's eye. She's embarrassed. He sat back in his chair.

"How come you weren't as affected by the transition to the real world?" she asked. "At least, it doesn't seem like you were."

"Getting behind the wheel of my car forced me to get my head on straight pretty quickly." He hesitated, wondering how much he should reveal. He decided not to share that it was likely doubly difficult for her to reorient to the real world because she'd been exposed to mind-altering soundwave technology while she'd slept. Should he tell her? Is that what his dream was asking him to do? He wished he had a second pair of noise-canceling earbuds to offer her. The ones he'd snuck into the Clubhouse seemed to work pretty well. But that would be weird. *Here, wear these at night and don't ask why.* Bottom line, he wanted to tell her what he'd discovered. He wanted to protect her. He didn't want her to end up like Luna. He told himself to be patient, to see where their conversation went.

"You're so different from everyone else at the Clubhouse," she said, a bit of mirth in her eyes. "If I didn't know better, I'd guess you don't really want to be there."

"It shows that much, huh?"

She nodded. "Even through your big ol' space helmet."

Man, she's cute. "Well, to explain, I'd have to break the Clubhouse's 'don't talk about yourself' rule."

"Well, Sam," she said with mock seriousness, "I think you already did."

He paused and then rolled his eyes. "That's right. My name."

"Well, Charlie," he replied, mocking her mock seriousness, "it looks like we're both going to Clubhouse jail."

"Aren't we already in it?"

Her humor caught him off guard, and he laughed. He'd have to follow up on that comment later.

"I'm a journalist. My assignment was originally to write a fluff piece on the founder of the Clubhouse, who I assumed was U. I was thinking I'd be there for a day or two, but let's just say I was encouraged to stick around and have the full Clubhouse experience."

"You met U?" She stopped and shook her head. "Strangest-sounding question ever."

"I did, actually."

"What's U like?" She paused and looked around. "I hope there aren't any English teachers nearby. I sound like I learned how to speak the language two days ago." She mocked herself: "What's you like? Does you like ice cream?" She shook her head. "Fucking brilliant."

He chuckled. It felt good to laugh. Even though they were having an innocent-seeming get-to-know-you kind of conversation, it was becoming clear that avoiding the truth wasn't going to be easy.

He looked at his hands, which were wrapped around his white ceramic mug, and contemplated his options. He blew out a long breath and looked Charlie in the eye. "It's complicated. Before I answer, what brought you to the Clubhouse?"

Now she looked at the table. "I see your complicated and raise you one hard-to-believe."

His eyebrows shot up. Not the answer he was expecting. "I'm definitely intrigued."

"That makes two of us," she said.

"Are we playing trust chicken?"

She cocked her head like she was listening. "I'll tell you if you tell me."

What the hell does she know? "Okay."

"But you go first," she said.

Maroon columns shot up in his mind's eye. She was anxious.

He looked around. "We should get out of here."

The maroon columns shortened.

She nodded. "Maybe we can find a park or something? I wanna be outside for a change."

CHAPTER 81

DING! A NEW POST. no_secrets2032 posted new videos of the secret lab and the chimp army almost every day now. She couldn't get enough. It became the highlight of her day.

Gerty hadn't left her house in four and a half weeks. The drapes were drawn. She didn't know what day or time it was. She didn't notice that the house smelled stale and dirty. It didn't matter. No one would be coming to visit anyway. A small island of mail grew on the tiled floor under the mail slot in her front door. She made her way into the shower every ten or so days, when she couldn't stand the smell of herself anymore or when her scalp wouldn't stop itching, whichever came first. Two weeks ago, she'd started having vodka delivered by the case.

Her life now pivoted around her laptop, particularly alternative news video channels and discussion boards. She took a few cat naps throughout the day when she found herself nodding off, but for the most part, she didn't need to sleep. She wasn't tired. Plus, she didn't want to miss anything. And things were happening at lightning speed. The chimp army discussion thread had grown from six hundred thousand members to almost five million in a month.

She topped off her vodka, fluffed up the pillows on her couch, and slipped under her fleece blanket. The ritual somehow marked no_secrets2032's posts as a special event. She hoped it was another video. She opened the discussion board app on her television monitor.

> no_secrets2032: unbelievable! Check this out. From a source on the inside. Before anyone starts crying "deep fake"—it's not. It is SO not. Just watch.

It *was* a new video. She played it.

A chimp, clear and close-up, stared into the lens. Off-camera, the person shooting the video asked, "Commander, how did drills go today?"

The chimp took a moment. "My team improves every day." He had an unusual accent, and his voice was high and tight, but his English was perfect; each word clear and understandable.

"The trustees are eager to see how things are progressing," the camera operator said. "Is your team up for a quick demonstration? A real one. Not using dummies this time." The camera zoomed out to reveal a large clearing, the ocean in the distance. The army was no longer caged.

With a fierce grimace, the chimp barked out a command Gerty didn't understand, and a small unit of about fifty chimps armed with T-batons lined up. The point of view shifted. The viewer was now seeing from the vantage point of a body cam one of the chimps was wearing. The chimp in charge screeched another command, and the body cam bounced as the chimp wearing it ran into the jungle on the other side of the clearing, a handful of his comrades in front of him.

"They're so fast," Gerty said to no one.

It was impossible to focus on anything as the chimp ripped through the jungle, everything zipping by in a blur. The chimp scrambled up a tree and was still for a moment. There was a sound, and the chimp turned. The camera picked up the rustling movement of large, fern-like leaves about twenty yards away. A creature bolted out from behind them and took off. Wait, not just any creature—a human. An adult male. The chimp went after him, but moments before it caught up to him, another chimp jumped on the man's back from a branch above, knocking the man down. The chimp wearing the camera flipped the man over, as if to give the trustees a front-row seat to the violence about to unfold. The wild-eyed man instinctively held his arms up in a feeble attempt to block the powerful baton strikes. The sound of the chimp's vocalizations in conjunction with the wet thuds of the man's skull being bashed in would haunt Gerty for hours. The man was dead, his head destroyed.

"No kill," the body cam chimp admonished. "Just make sleep."

The other chimp picked up the man's limp arm and let it drop to the ground, unfazed.

The video left her nauseous. Gerty went to the kitchen and ate a few stale crackers before going back and watching the video again. It reminded her of a video game, the first-person kind her ex-husband used to play all the time.

She'd watch that particular video over and over during the next twenty-four hours and find that her repulsion turned into arousal. Her fantasy life took a dark turn, to a place she probably wouldn't be able to come back from.

CHAPTER 82

SAM HANDED CHARLIE A beer and joined her on the worn plaid blanket he'd pulled from the trunk of his car. They clinked bottles, and she took a large sip of courage. She had no idea where their conversation was going to go or how her story would be received, but the thought of unburdening herself filled her with such relief. He felt safe, like maybe he'd take her seriously. She hoped so.

"Charlie and Sam, sittin' in a tree," Syd sang.

She gave her invisible friend the death stare. *Stop it*, she scolded through gritted teeth while trying to hide her middle-school smile. She looked beseechingly at Lou.

He gestured toward Sam and nodded. "You can trust him."

She stole a glance at the guy sitting inches away from her under the sparkling expanse of the night sky. It was a rom-com moment. He had the rare quality of somehow being handsome-cute or sometimes, like now, cute-handsome. In VR-land, her imagination didn't see the real Sam looking nearly as sexy as he was. And he clearly didn't know how sexy he was, which made him even sexier.

Plus, she didn't see any trace of the virus in him. He could be the last honest person on Earth.

On the drive to the park, her new mantra had become: "Must Stay Focused." Sam grew more attractive the more she got to know him and, given the monumental task ahead, she had no business falling for anyone . . . or even exploring a relationship.

They sat in silence, sipping their beers. It was too comfortable. *MUST. STAY. FOCUSED.*

"This place is beautiful," he said. "Even in the dark."

They were in a small clearing surrounded by towering trees. They'd managed to find a quiet spot tucked away from the sprawling tent city that populated most of the park. As far as tent cities went, it was the most peaceful and inviting one she'd encountered yet. From the laughter and music she heard coming from several small groups of people who were hanging out around campfires and picnic tables, she got the feeling it was an actual community. And when she saw the rainbow flags, it all made sense. Queer folks take care of each other.

She lay back. Her eyes adjusted to the velvet darkness of the moonless sky. Even though they weren't far from New York City, stars came into focus and filled her with the ancient awe of the countless generations that had come before her. "I miss the night sky," she said.

He lay back next to her, and their shoulders touched. The physical contact was hard to ignore.

"Me too," he said. "You ever listen to music on vinyl?"

"Oh, yeah. It's the best. I inherited my mother's record collection."

"That's what looking at the actual night sky is like for me."

"The year after my mom died, I'd lie in our hammock in the backyard at night and listen to Beethoven's Sixth Symphony over and over again."

"Did it help?"

"Pretty much saved me."

He waited a beat before saying, "I'm really sorry about your mom."

The compassion in his voice took her by surprise. She turned to find his clear-blue eyes looking at her with a naked tenderness she'd never encountered before. She wanted to touch his face to see if he was real. Instead, she smiled. It was the most intimate moment she remembered ever experiencing. It was like a balm.

The tension in Charlie's neck, her shoulders, her jaw—holy shit, so much tension—melted like butter on a stack of pancakes. *Mmmm. Pancakes.*

Must. Stay. Focused.

"I don't think it's healthy to live a virtual existence," Charlie said.

He laughed. "You think?"

She turned to him. "It's so fucking weird, isn't it?"

"Weird is an understatement." They burst out in a fit of laughter, like six-year-olds at a slumber party.

"We're in a cult," he managed to spit out through howls of tension-relieving laughter.

This made Charlie laugh so hard, she was crying. "I know!"

"And U isn't even real," he added, trying to catch his breath.

Charlie sat up. "Wait, what?"

He shook his head and sat up too. "No, he—or, rather, it—is AI. Actually, from what I can tell, our elusive guru is more likely artificial general intelligence. It acts disturbingly autonomous."

She got quiet. "Oh, shit," she said. "Of course he is. I was totally blind in there."

For a moment, confusion passed through Sam's eyes and made her wonder if maybe she shouldn't have said that last statement out loud.

Must. Stay. Focused. "How did you figure it out? Did he, it, whatever, just come out and tell you?"

He hesitated. They were clearly being cautious with one another.

"Not exactly." He ran his hand through a wavy lock of thick, caramel-tinged hair before turning to her. It was clear this conversation was just as hard for him as it was for her. "I have this perceptual condition called chromesthesia."

She grimaced. "I'm sorry, I have no idea what that is."

"It's okay. I wouldn't expect you to know what it is. It's not super common, especially the version I have." He took another sip. "It means I see the tones in music and people's voices as color—a lot of times, the colors have specific patterns."

She blinked rapidly. His words weren't computing.

"What I mean is . . . I can see the emotion behind someone's words as color in my mind's eye."

Yikes. Her fingers reflexively covered her mouth, which made him chuckle.

"I know. Pretty invasive."

"I'm almost afraid to ask," she said with a wince. "What color does my voice look like? Or sound like?" She paused and laughed at herself. "Did you know that today is National First Person in the History of the Human Species to Ask That Question Day?"

He laughed. "If I'd known, I would've stopped at the drugstore so I could get you a card. I'm sure Hallmark has one for the occasion. You've asked two never-before-uttered questions in the last hour alone. Nice job!"

Hold onto your hat, friend. Things haven't even hit peak strangeness yet, she thought.

He raised his eyebrows, ready to deliver the results of her vocal litmus test. "Rings of bright green, which is what embarrassment looks like to me."

She nodded an affirmation. "No hiding from you!"

"But, mostly the color of your voice shows me that I can trust you."

Her cheeks grew hot. *I wonder if he can sense bright green coming off me right now, even though I'm not saying anything?* She tried to imagine what it would be like to see how people really felt. A different kind of naked.

"That's fucking brilliant. You must be the best journalist on the planet."

There was that charming but not over-the-top smile again. "I don't know about the best, but it definitely gives me an advantage."

He broke eye contact. "It's strange to talk about it. The only people who know are my parents and my second grade teacher, Mrs. Willis—and now you."

"It's the coolest superpower ever," she said. Then her brow furrowed. "Is it?"

He laughed. "Depends. AI, for example, is the most neon fuchsia you can imagine. It gives me a headache."

"So, not always pleasant."

"No, but I don't know what it's like not to be like this. So, it's normal." He reclined on his side, facing her, and propped his head up on his hand. "Can I ask you a question?"

She nodded.

"When I mentioned that U was AI, you said something about being blind in there. What'd you mean by that?"

Her eyes grew big. "You don't miss much, do you?"

"Hazard of the job."

"I'm not used to people paying attention to me," she said. "Hazard of trying to be invisible." She took a nervous swig of beer before pivoting her body to face him. She unconsciously wrapped her arms around her knees, something she always did when she wanted to disappear.

"Well," she said, "since you shared your secret with me, I guess it's only fair to share my secret with you."

She had his full attention, which was unnerving and reassuring at the same time. "A little less than a year ago, I started having these strange dreams." She paused to find words to describe her experiences. "I mean, I've been having disturbing dreams since I was teenager, after my mom died, but these dreams are different." In her mind's eye, Lou offered a nod of encouragement. "I'm awake during these dreams."

Sam didn't bat an eye, just waited for her to continue.

"The only way I can describe it is that it's like I'm transported to another world, a place that feels more real than real. And it's the same place every time. It's absolutely beautiful. Like nature on steroids with a dose of magical fairy dust."

That got a chuckle from him. She hadn't lost him yet. "The beings that live there are not human, but they look human."

"What do you mean?"

"Well, there's one that's called First Mother. Her body looks like the Earth from space, like she's pregnant and about to give birth any second. Her skin is like the ocean, turquoise and blue. She's got these cool dreadlocks that look like the roots of trees. When I first met her, she was huge. I mean HUGE. I couldn't even see her head. And then her body just shrank down to normal size." She smiled at the memory. "She told me she'd been waiting for me."

His eyebrows went up.

"That I had a job to do." Charlie bit her lip and then took the plunge. "I don't know how to *not* make this sound absolutely insane, so I'm just gonna tell you, and if you run for the hills, I can grab an Uber."

"I'm all ears," he said without a trace of judgment. "And I won't abandon you."

Sure, you say that now, she thought.

"Five pounds says he's more intrigued than disturbed," Syd chimed in.

Again, not helpful. Charlie could only shake her head and do her best to hide her amused eye roll so Sam wouldn't think she was reacting to him. But, she had to admit, Syd did have a way of sidetracking her from dark thoughts.

As selfish as it was, she wanted to tell him; to not have to carry the burden of this strange, monumental-seeming mission alone. Today, more than ever before, was like a strange reassurance that the experiences she was having in the Dreaming Realm actually might be real. She was shocked to see how much the virus had progressed during this brief window away from the Clubhouse and the virtual world she'd been living in. The virus clouded the eyes of everyone she saw at the hospital—patients and staff. With the exception of Sam, everyone was infected.

CHAPTER 83

SHE HAD SAM'S ATTENTION. His interior vision swirled with the pale
violet of her earnestness—not something he perceived in many adults.
The swirls pulled him into Charlie's fantastical world. He had to keep
reminding himself to remain objective, to not get swept up in her story,
because his logical mind was struggling mightily with what she was telling
him. Plus, she was very, very attractive. Her allure—hell, everything about
her—was threatening his trademark detachment.

"This place I go to during these experiences," she continued. "It's called
the Dreaming Realm. Apparently, this world"—she referenced the surrounding park with her hands—"the physical world, comes from the
Dreaming Realm. Or maybe a better way to say it is that it's birthed by
the Dreaming Realm."

Quivering robin's-egg-blue disrupted the violet in his mind's eye. Insecurity. His first instinct was to put her at ease, but he refrained. His logical
mind was about to throttle his emotions. Shit was getting weirder by the
minute.

"But there's a threat to the Dreaming Realm, which means there's a
threat to this world."

Whoa. He didn't see that twist coming.

"What kind of threat?"

"A virus."

He couldn't hide his surprise. Her response threw him.

"There's another realm. The Mental Realm. I was told it's where our
thoughts—human thoughts—live or are stored, or something like that."

She drained her beer. The light blue in his mind's eye started to quiver
like Jell-O. She was nervous. Sam reached for another beer and opened it
for her.

"That's where the infection is."

"In the Mental Realm?"

She nodded. "It's completely taken over. Every time I go back, the Mental Realm has expanded like it's swollen with sickness."

He was confused but couldn't think of a question to ask her.

"It's consuming the Dreaming Realm."

He shook his head. "Let's back up for a minute." He collected his thoughts. "There's a place called the Dreaming Realm that you're saying creates the Earth?"

"I told you this was gonna sound crazy," she said with a smirk. "A better way to say it is the Dreaming Realm dreams the physical world—actually, the whole physical universe—into existence."

Her demeanor changed. Soft waves of indigo filled his inner vision. Confidence. Not a color he saw much.

He cocked his head. "So, this is all just a dream? The two of us sitting in this park having this conversation? Luna's breakdown? The Eleventh Floor Clubhouse?"

"Would that be so strange?" She was looking right at him now. It was like she'd been taken over by someone else. Someone who was entirely self-assured. *Maybe she is crazy.*

He shrugged. "And there's another place called the Mental Realm that has something to do with human thoughts?"

"My understanding is that the Mental Realm emerged when the human brain evolved to have the capacity for abstract thought."

"Are you saying it's where thoughts go to die?" he said, not hiding his sarcasm.

Her dark eyes showed a hint of sadness, or was it disappointment?

"No." Her voice was quiet, but she didn't break eye contact. "It's where they live."

Sam swallowed hard. "And it's sick."

She nodded.

"Tell me about the virus."

"It's a virus of deception."

"Oh." *Fuck me.* "So, what, it's like a mental or a mind virus? And it's taking over the Dreaming Realm?"

She nodded. "Not long after these waking dreams started happening, I was able to see the virus floating through people's eyes, but only when they were lying. It looks like liquid mercury."

He understood. "When you have your AR glasses on, you can't see anyone's eyes."

"I'm blind to the virus."

"Now it's my turn to be paranoid."

She smiled. "You're not infected, Sam."

His shoulders dropped about a foot.

"But it seems everyone else is," she said.

"Well, that actually explains a lot. I couldn't wait to get out of the ER earlier. My mind's eye was flooded with spikes of gray."

"The color of deception?"

He nodded. "You were saying that the Mental Realm is taking over the Dreaming Realm," he recounted, putting the pieces together out loud. "And if it's not stopped . . . ?"

"Game over."

He emptied his bottle and grabbed another.

"You believe me?" she asked.

He let out a sigh. So far, there was no hint of the muddy brown of psychosis in her words. She wasn't crazy. "I don't know what to believe."

She bit her lip.

"But what you're saying makes a strange kind of sense. We're living in the age of personal truth."

"That's the understatement of the century!" she laughed. "Invent your own truth," she announced, like a game show host.

"If you can think it, it's true!"

"My truth can kick your truth's ass!"

They laughed. But the moment of levity was fleeting.

"So, we're pretty much fucked." It wasn't a question. Her jaguar gaze had followed her out of virtual reality, it seemed. She could be intense.

"Umm . . ." She hesitated. He had a sneaking suspicion things were about to get even stranger. "That leads me to why it seems I'm here."

"In the park?"

She smiled. "Nope."

He cringed internally at the thought that she was about to tell him how she's the chosen one and was going to save humanity.

She took a big breath. "Remember, I can get an Uber."

Please don't ruin everything.

"The waking dreams have been preparing me to do this thing I guess I'm supposed to do. The reason why I was born."

His heart sank. He braced himself for the brown of crazy.

She took a deep breath that seemed to settle her. She looked at him directly and told him her story. "There's a part of me—it seems like an ancient part—that has been trying to heal this virus for hundreds of years. This is her—my—fifth attempt."

Waves of indigo, not brown, cascaded through his mind. Her confidence was once again unwavering. If her explanation was accurate, then he suspected the ancient part of her was the confident part. Did that mean he was talking to two different people? He put that question to the side.

"This other part of me was born in the Dreaming Realm and is the only one capable of entering the Mental Realm to deliver the remedy for the virus—which may or may not work. It may be too late."

"Why can't anyone else do it?"

"Because this part of me is powerful, the firstborn of her clan, and the clan plays an essential role in the lives of humans." She paused to gauge his response. He tried to remain as neutral as possible.

"My clan's role," she continued, "is to guide humans in their dreams. Because of that, we have an intimate relationship with humans. We understand them better than anyone else in the Dreaming Realm. At least, we used to until the virus took over."

She wavered back and forth between speaking as Charlie and this other part. It was disconcerting.

"You have to become human to do this?"

"We're shapeshifters. We can access the physical world in our animal form, and some of us—the older ones—can incarnate as humans, which is the only way I can access the Mental Realm. It's a human-created realm, so I have to be human to enter it. And who knew being at the Clubhouse and living in a false reality would make accessing the Mental Realm easier? Turns out the transition is less jarring."

Holy shit. She sounded absolutely insane, but she was showing zero signs of insanity. Just confidence. Pure, unadulterated confidence. Not theoretical confidence. She spoke from experience. At least the so-called ancient part of her did. And, apparently, this part of her could shapeshift. What the fuck was going on? *Maybe* I'm *the one who's going insane. Maybe I've been living in virtual reality too long. Maybe the brainwave technology has fucked with me after all and I'm not even aware of it.*

"Are you okay?" she asked.

"I'm digesting it all." *Focus, Sam.* Then he remembered his dream about the panther. Did her clan have something to do with that dream? "What kind of animal do you shapeshift into?"

"Raven."

His doubt wavered. He didn't know what he would've done if she'd said panther.

"I almost chose a raven head for my avatar, but it felt too . . . I don't know . . . revealing," she said, as if reading his mind. "I'm still getting used to all this."

He considered his options. Should he keep asking her questions? Was it fair to indulge her delusions? The memory of Luna's frail body in restraints on the gurney, her eyes wild with panic, had left an indelible mark. The thought of Charlie ending up with her roommate in the psych ward was sobering. But she was so . . . normal.

"I've told you too much, haven't I?"

He blew out a long, exhausted breath.

"Believe me, I wish I was crazy," she whispered, and turned her face away from him. "You think I wanna do this?" The emotion rose in her voice. "That place . . . the Mental Realm . . . it IS insanity." She turned back. "It scares the shit out of me." Tears streamed down her face. "Being in that realm, getting tangled up in the noise of every single human being's contaminated thoughts—it *makes* you insane."

Red spikes filled his mind's eye. She was petrified.

"Hey," he said softly. "It's okay. I'm glad you told me."

She rolled her eyes and shook her head with embarrassment. "I wouldn't believe me if I were you."

"You're right. The whole thing does sound crazy."

She wiped the tears from her face with the heel of her hand and offered a defeated shrug.

"But it also doesn't. I haven't had your experiences. But if I had, the thought of telling someone else about them would probably be a huge relief."

Now she was the one who was surprised.

"And that you felt comfortable enough with me, a guy you hardly know, to tell me your story—it's probably the best compliment I've ever received."

He loved the way she tried to hide her smile.

"If it's okay, I've got more questions."

She nodded. Sometimes, like now, she reminded him of a child.

"I'm guessing the remedy for a mind virus doesn't come in a syringe?"

She shook her head and hesitated, choosing her words carefully. "It's a story."

He squinted. "A story."

"Yeah, to help us remember."

"What did we forget?"

Her panther-like intensity returned. "That we're a part of the natural world."

Again, not what he expected. "Huh." He thought it through out loud. "You're saying that at some point the human species forgot that we're part of the natural world . . ." His skepticism seeped into his words. "And now we have a mind virus of deception?" His fingernails tapped mindlessly on his bottle. *Click. Clickity-click. Click. Click.* It didn't add up. What was he missing? *Click. Click. Clickclickclickity-click. Click. Click. Click.*

"Are you sending me a message in Morse code?" she asked with a shy smirk.

"What?"

She mimicked him, clicking her fingernails on her own bottle.

"Oh. Yeah, sorry. I do that sometimes when I'm thinking." He put his bottle down. "So, this virus is out there somewhere just waiting for us, and then we catch it because we forgot we're part of the natural world?"

"Humans didn't catch the virus, we created it," she clarified, "a long time ago, when we started to see ourselves as separate from nature."

Flies could've nested in his mouth. He closed it, grabbed his beer, and swallowed deeply.

"The original lie," he summarized.

"The original sin," she added with a tinge of sarcasm and maybe a little heat.

Click. Click. Click. Clickity-click. Her warm hand covered his restless one. His guilty grin was an apology. Ideas cascaded through his mind, forming a structure that helped him see what she was suggesting: the birth of agriculture and domestication. The worship of a single god, one who turned our focus to a heaven far from the Earth. Feudalism. Imperialism. Colonialism. Slavery. Materialism. Capitalism. Fascism. Nationalism. Lots of isms.

"We *have* kinda mastered the concept of ownership," he conceded. "Which, when you think about it, is pretty ridiculous."

Charlie's nod of resignation seemed to say, "And *I'm* the crazy one?"

"Okay," he said, mirroring her resignation. "What you're suggesting is that almost nine billion entitled thirteen-year-olds have come to believe they own a planet."

"Yeah, but we make great . . . snacks."

They sat in silence. It was all too depressing.

"We should create a brochure for aliens," he finally said.

"Best idea I've heard in a long time," she said.

"Motel Earth . . . Come Dwell In Decadence!"

She pointed the top of her bottle at him. "Book now and get a free round-trip ticket to Plastic Island!"

CHAPTER 84

SLEEP WAS FRUITLESS. IT was about four in the morning when she and Sam made their way back to the Clubhouse. Charlie's body buzzed with exhaustion, exhilaration, and relief when she finally settled into bed. The connection they'd shared comforted her more than anything else had in a long, long time. She wasn't well-versed in the friendship arena, but she hoped she'd read him correctly—that he was her friend.

The moment she closed her eyes, which burned and ached with fatigue, her awareness was pulled into a fast-moving tunnel, toward a dim, gray light. The rushing movement suddenly halts when she reaches the end of the tunnel, as if she's hit an invisible wall.

Ahkoa stands in front of her, his body and features blurred by the barrier between them. He tries to talk to her, but all she can hear is the rise and fall of the deep, muddy tone of his voice.

She shakes her head and points to her ear.

His strong, square shoulders round with defeat. He pivots his body so she can see behind him.

First Mother is propped up against the First Tree, her skin gray and sagging. The once-tangerine sky is blanched. It's as if someone pulled the stopper and let all the color drain out of the Dreaming Realm.

When he turns back toward her, his dark eyes glisten. He places his palm against the invisible barricade. She places hers against his. His grief impales her like a shard in her solar plexus, and she understands. He's saying goodbye.

CHAPTER 85

"NAMASTE, MOTHERFUCKERS! I'M FIRED up, people! It's been like three weeks since I took the B-Well nano-pill, and *whoo boy*, I've never felt better. I'm serious. Never. Felt. Better. I'm clearer. More focused. More creative. I've got so many ideas. It's crazy. It's a gen-U-wine miracle. And the app that comes with it? It's like being seduced by little ear goddesses or fairies or something. I actually feel like I'm floating after I use it, and—don't tell anyone, but—I probably use the app more than I should. It feels that good. Fairies are real, people."

(whispers)

"Are you ready to have your mind blown in a nonsexual way? I've got a secret to tell you. I've been dying to tell you this since I figured it out. An epifamey or epiphany—however you say it. It's big. So big. Like, Godzilla-big. We've been lied to, people. Check it out: We don't actually need to sleep. Crazy, right? All that nonsense about needing eight hours is just nonsense. A big fucking lie. The brain trust is lying to us. I haven't slept for thirteen, fourteen, maybe fifteen days, and I've never felt better. I feel like I can do anything.

"And I'm questioning whether we need to eat, too. I mean, what if everything about our lives, our existence, is one big fat lie? Like we're doing all the things we're supposed to do, but for what? Did you know there are people—actual people—who eat the sun? I'm not kidding. They live off the energy—*the manna*—of the sun. They don't eat food. Not one chicken wing or ham sandwich. I think I need to find out what the sun tastes like. I bet it tastes like creamsicles. Or maybe Flamin' Hot Cheetos. I'll report back and let you know.

"I think I can heal myself, too. I can see inside my cells. And they tell me things. They tell me how incredible I am. And that they love me. It's like they know me. It's so weird."

(takes a breath)

"Man, I feel good. I wish I could buy everyone on the planet a nano-pill. And some ear fairies. I've been wondering what would happen if I took another nano-pill. Five bucks says I'll become a cyborg. That'd be sick as fuck. Who doesn't wanna be a robot? But, seriously, you should take the pill. You're not gonna regret it. Best money you'll ever spend. And in case you were wondering, B-Well is not paying me to say this shit. They don't need to—that's how pumped I am about this pill.

"I gotta go. Got a date with a casino. Today's my lucky fucking day."

Chapter 86

DING-DONG!

Sam slowed his Peloton and scanned the French countryside, confused. He didn't see any doors that needed answering. But then his eye caught a small, flashing yellow Play button in the far upper-right corner of the sky. He laughed at himself. He'd gotten so immersed in the scenic bicycle ride that, for a moment, he'd forgotten it wasn't real.

"Play," he said, and the yellow arrow turned blue.

"Hello S," a pleasant, generic female voice said. "You have received an invitation from Eleventh Floor Clubhouse member, C. Would you like me to read C's invitation?"

Sam smiled. "Yes," he answered.

"C has invited you to join her in Jukebox Room eleven, at one p.m. today. Do you accept C's invitation?"

The flashing heartrate monitor icon sped up in his peripheral vision, and his insides vibrated. No one had made him feel like this since high school.

He cleared his throat. "Yes."

"Great! I've just RSVPed for you and added the meeting to your schedule. At one p.m. you'll receive a notification that will take you to Jukebox Room eleven."

"Thank you."

"You're welcome, S. Enjoy your day."

He'd been too wired after his time with Charlie to sleep when they got back to the Clubhouse earlier that morning, so he'd decided to get some exercise. While he worked out, his logical mind forced him to review every reason why he should leave the Clubhouse and Charlie behind. But his urge to see her again and to better understand what she had shared with him was much stronger than reason. He was in new territory. There was just something about her. None of it made any sense whatsoever, but he was certain he'd regret it if he didn't follow his gut.

He grabbed a smoothie and went back to his quarters to take a shower. He kept one eye on the clock at all times. He told himself it was because he liked to be prompt, which was true, but before today he hadn't been a clock watcher. *I'm probably being weird because I'm overtired.* That excuse sort of worked for him.

Minutes passed like days. He fussed with his hair in the mirror for about ten minutes before remembering that Charlie wasn't going to be able to see his hair, just his jumbo space helmet. It was probably the twentieth time he'd laughed at himself that day. This led to a fantasy about telling his parents the story of how crazy he'd acted the first day he'd spent with Charlie when he brought her home to meet them. They'd all laugh and make fun of him and eat meatloaf.

He lay on his bed, listened to soothing ambient music, and tried to meditate to pass the time, but fell asleep. At the sound of a chime, he woke with a start.

He opened his eyes to see a large, pulsing, blue cube floating in the middle of the virtual Zen Garden he'd been meditating—or, rather, sleeping—in. The text on the box read, "Join C's Meeting." Not knowing what kind of environment he'd end up in, he got out of bed and said, "Join meeting."

The cube expanded and its sides opened like doors, revealing an alien-seeming world in the distance. He couldn't tell if the strange place came to him or he moved toward it, but in the blink of an eye, he was transported to a vast post-apocalyptic junkyard. He stood in a clearing and took in his surroundings. The cloudless sky was a disturbing mustard-yellow, and the vast, flat landscape was barren except for the half-buried remains of Twenty-First Century technology. To his right was a partially buried passenger jet with a broken wing and peeling paint. It looked like it had tried to bank left into the surface of the Earth, its tail sitting higher than its submerged nose. There were weathered carcasses of gas and electric vehicles everywhere, including a faded school bus and a small mountain of old computers, monitors, appliances, and cell phones.

A fire burned in a rusted steel barrel in the middle of the clearing. He imagined the simulated caustic charcoal smoke would smell like burnt rubber or plastic. Charlie had invited him to an end times campsite to listen to music? She was full of surprises.

"You came," Charlie said from behind him.

He turned, feeling a surge of dusty high school butterflies come to life in his stomach. "You didn't think I would?"

She shrugged. "If I were in your shoes," she looked down at his feet, "or giant space boots, I don't know if I would've." She gave him one of her trademark vicious smiles. "But I'm really glad you did."

He smiled, but remembered she couldn't see his face. "I'm glad I came too." He looked around and gestured with his gloved hand. "I love what you've done to the place. It's, um, cheery."

She laughed. "Yeah, it's my 'everything's gonna be okay' backdrop."

"Definitely different from any jukebox I've ever seen."

"I created this place a couple of weeks ago and the perfect playlist to go with it. Coming here helps get me fired up."

The way she left the last word hanging got his attention. He assumed the words she wasn't saying had to do with the task of dealing with the mind virus. He was at a loss for what to say and told himself it was because he didn't want to feed her delusions, but more likely he was afraid the story she'd told him was true. He knew without a doubt that she *believed* it was true, but what if it really was, and the world as they knew it would soon cease to exist or die off? He resisted indulging that train of thought.

"Oh, yeah?" was all he could say.

She nodded. "I don't think I'm alone in this, but music is a kind of medicine for me."

"Should I be afraid?" he joked. And then he realized she was being cryptic on purpose since there were likely ears everywhere.

"Ready to let off a little steam?"

Shit. I think she invited me to a dance party. He wasn't much of a dancer, but maybe his Spaceman alter ego was. He gave her a giant, gloved thumbs-up and hoped the music she liked wasn't terrible.

She told the jukebox to "Play the Happy Rainbow Unicorn playlist."

Huge, chunky, black letters scrolled across the mustard sky: "*Asteroid* by Killing Joke."

The first note startled the hell out of him. The song came at him like a fast-moving freight train: hard, heavy, and aggressive. No room to breathe. Cymatic snowflake-like patterns in shades of turquoise erupted in his mind's eye like fireworks. He'd never heard the song or of the band before, but he liked it.

Charlie held her hands out in invitation, her feline head pulsing to the music. Then she crouched and started rhythmically stomping as if doing a war dance. He watched her spin, arms spread like a bird riding a thermal. *Why does she have to be so sexy?* His body, it seemed, had no choice but to move in time to the music, and before he knew it, he was pogoing around the ceremonial trash fire, mindful not to run into any of the furniture in his quarters back in the real world.

He was winded and already sweaty when the song ended. The words "*Ænima* by Tool" floated across the sky, buying him three seconds to catch his breath.

This song he knew. A moment later, they were once again thrashing their bodies in the virtual ruins of human progress. She was right. Music was good medicine. He hadn't felt this free since he was a kid.

The intense, old-school playlist continued with *Chemistry* by Unkle, and more Killing Joke, his new favorite band. He had to laugh when their song *I Am the Virus* kicked in. He was becoming more and more captivated by this mysterious woman and how her body attacked each song as if preparing for battle. It seemed there was a lot more to her than she allowed people to see.

When he didn't think he could take any more, the title "*Hallo Spaceboy* by David Bowie" scrolled across the sky. She waved "hello" to him—or, rather, "hallo"—and he pointed to himself with both of his giant gloved hands, as if to say "who, me?" He was learning to enjoy that vicious primal smile of hers.

He knew Bowie, but not this song. He couldn't stop smiling as he stomped to the unyielding industrial rhythm. *She picked a song for me.* He blushed under the cover of his virtual helmet.

"Pause playlist," she gasped when the song ended.

They sat on the ground, panting.

"That was fun," he said when he could finally talk.

"It's both strange and somehow comforting to have you here," she said. "If you're up for it, I do have another song to share. It's become kind of an anthem for me." She paused. "For the task ahead."

There, she said it. Might as well dive in. "Do you think you'll be successful?"

She shrugged and looked at the ground. "I hope so." Then she looked directly at him. "Even if I am, I have no idea if it'll work."

He didn't need to see the tightly woven, juniper-green strands in his mind to perceive the intense pressure she felt she was under. It was as palpable as a heart attack.

"Soon?" he asked.

She looked directly at him. "Very soon."

His stomach tightened hearing the finality in her voice. He blew out a big breath. "Let's hear this anthem of yours."

There was that ferocious smile again. She got up. "I hope you like it." She rotated her head on her shoulders like a prize fighter before the first bell. "Resume playlist."

"*The Death & Resurrection Show* by Killing Joke" scrolled across the poisoned sky. As soon as the drums kicked in, his exhausted body felt a surge of energy and started to move with the hypnotic, primal tempo. And then he understood. The lyrics captured Charlie's story. The vocalist—or were there two vocalists?—appealed to the archetypal mother to heal and liberate him—maybe the entire world—from countless generations of lies.

Charlie danced with absolute abandon, like each note, each beat, each lyric was fuel she was consuming. She was a quiet force and unlike any woman he'd ever encountered.

When the song ended, they stood across from each other in a sort of silent reverence. She broke the spell by saying, "Play *Pleasure* by Crosses." This song wasn't angry, it was high-octane sensual. She approached him and touched his face. This was the first time he realized how advanced the Senz-Skin apparatus he was wearing was. It was as if she was physically in front of him. He put his hands on her narrow hips and pulled her in for a kiss. Somehow, he felt sensation on his lips even though they weren't physically touching each other. It wasn't the same as a real kiss, but his body responded as if it were.

For a sublime moment, all he knew was the experience of their bodies moving to the music.

"Thank you," she whispered in his ear when the song ended, and he was suddenly overcome with the urge to cry.

CHAPTER 87

CHARLIE TOOK A DEEP breath and recited her father's phone number into the VoIP app. She wasn't sure if she wanted him to answer or not. But before she had the chance to chicken out, he picked up.

"Hey, Dad," she said.

"Charlie! I'm so glad you called. I've been worried."

"Yeah, I'm sorry. This retreat place is all-consuming. How's it going?"

"Well, we just moved."

"Really? Where to?"

"San Diego. Believe it or not, your—well, Dan saved the day."

Her stomach twisted. "Really?"

"Yeah, he stopped by a month ago and offered to buy our house. I was shocked, especially given that people are leaving Arizona in droves, most of them just abandoning their houses. Anyway, he offered us a good price, and we closed two weeks ago."

"Seriously?"

"Yup. By the time we left, Phoenix was like Tombstone. Even a lot of the homeless folks had left."

Silence.

"You still there, sweetie?"

"Ah, yeah. Sorry. I guess I'm a little shocked Dan would do that."

"I know. I almost felt guilty taking the money from him, but he was great about it. He actually seemed happy to do it." He paused. "It's a shame things didn't work out between the two of you. Dan's a good guy."

A flash of heat. "Like I said before I left Phoenix, not everything was as it seemed."

"Well, I hope he's okay. Especially after this last week."

"What do you mean?"

"You haven't heard?"

"Heard what?"

"Oh, I thought that's why you were calling. Phoenix is burning. A third of the city is already gone."

"Holy shit. I didn't know."

"We got out of there just in the nick of time. I hope Dan's okay."

"Yeah," she replied, her voice distant. "Me too."

"How are you doing? You don't sound like yourself."

"I'm hanging in there. Learning a lot." She paused. "I miss you, Dad."

"I miss you too, sweetie."

"I'm happy you got out of Phoenix. Can't wait to see your new place." Emotion clogged her throat. "I um . . . I'm sorry for being so distant . . . I mean, after Mom died."

He cleared his throat. "I think about her every day."

Tears filled her eyes, and she squeezed them shut. "Me too."

The silence grew awkward. They were never good at emotions.

"I better let you go," she said.

"Is everything okay?"

"Yeah, yeah. I'm good. Just been through a lot."

"I'm glad you called."

"Me too. I love you, Dad."

"I love you too, sweetie."

She ended the call and cried herself to sleep.

CHAPTER 88

EVEN THOUGH EVERY CELL in her body craved the tingly numbness of bourbon right now, Charlie decided against making a trip to the lounge to get a drink. It wasn't worth risking being seen by anyone. Plus, she'd already messaged her wellness coach that she wasn't feeling well and would be staying in her quarters for the rest of the day. She didn't want anyone to become suspicious of her absence. It would raise even more suspicion if she was seen walking back to her room with a cocktail at eight-thirty in the morning.

She did everything she could to quiet her mind from thinking about Phoenix engulfed in flames, her father, Dan, tent cities, Luna's breakdown, the ER, this strange AI cult she found herself a part of, Sam. She needed to be ready. She had a job to do, and if she didn't do it—or at least try—she couldn't live with herself. She couldn't watch the world self-destruct knowing that maybe she could've helped in some way. She was beyond worrying about how delusional she must be. Raven's Daughter's presence was getting stronger as she got clearer, and there was comfort in that. Even if it was all a lie. She couldn't tell anymore.

"We have a plan," Syd popped into her awareness. "Lou gets the credit though. Wait till you hear it. It's brilliant."

"Have I mentioned how impeccable your timing always is?"

"It's almost as if we're in your head," Syd said with a wink.

Lou arrived looking as dapper and as serious as ever. He shut Syd up with his bloodthirsty gaze. "We were successful using chimes to anchor you to the physical world," he said. "Now we need to find ways to anchor you to the Mental Realm."

"That makes sense."

"Yes, it does. That's why I said that."

"Right. Ideas?"

"We need to find things that excite you—"

"Like Sam?" Syd waggled her bushy eyebrows.

"Please stop," Lou said with his eyes closed, and quickly reset. "Like I was saying, things that excite you, things that are perhaps fun and enjoyable. Easy to remember. A way to navigate from the interior of your mind, through the untamed minds of billions of humans, to the center of the Mental Realm, which is your ultimate destination."

"Like a map?"

"I was thinking more of a mode of transportation. You'll know where to go. You were born to know."

Relief flooded through her. One less thing to worry about.

"The way will be challenging," he continued. "You had a taste of just how challenging when you entered the Mental Realm directly from the Dreaming Realm."

She shuddered at the memory of just how quickly she'd lost herself. "Café racer."

"Excuse me?" Lou said.

"It's a motorcycle. I'm surprised you don't know. It's a style of bike that originated a long time ago in the UK, just like your accents."

Lou and Syd looked at each other. Syd shrugged.

"Do I need to know how to ride for it to work?"

Lou shook his head. "You just need your imagination and the desire."

"How do I anchor it?"

"First, we need to anchor a destination in your mind. The last time, we chose your childhood home, but that might be too distracting. Too many memories to get lost in. This time I think it's more prudent to choose a more neutral but familiar location."

"How about my post-apocalyptic landscape?"

"Where you made out with Sam?" Syd teased.

Lou only had to turn his head in Syd's direction, to which she offered a "message received" thumbs-up. "Syd's right. Probably too distracting, given recent events. Plus, it would be beneficial if you were in a building of some sort to separate your mind from the minds of others."

"Why not this room?"

Lou nodded. Syd pointed her finger, like a gun, at Charlie.

"Your quarters at this strange and miserable place will be your home base in the Mental Realm. Now, picture the motorbike of your dreams waiting for you outside that door."

She imagined a sleek, minimalist, matte-black vintage motorcycle with a boxy tank that had indentations for her knees, rear sets, and clubman handlebars sitting in the hallway outside her quarters. The bike of her private dreams. She liked this plan.

"Well done," Lou said.

"Can I ride on the back?" Syd asked.

Lou ignored her. "That motorbike will get you to your destination. All you need to do is know it's right there waiting for you."

Charlie took a deep breath and nodded.

"Should she have something specific to anchor her to this room? Something unique that's hard to forget?" Syd asked.

"Very good," Lou said.

Syd took a bow.

"Close your eyes. What's the first thing that comes to mind when you think of this room?"

"That's easy. Cartoonish blue fish."

"Brilliant. You have two distinct anchors. What are they?"

"The weird fish in this room and my motorcycle." She couldn't help but smile as she said it.

"That's all you have to remember. Nothing more."

"And I'll know what to do."

Lou nodded. "Remember, everything there will test your focus. The external noise; the internal noise like your memories, your insecurities, and doubts. The virus does not want you to succeed. Like any virus, its sole purpose is to survive, and you are a direct threat to its survival. You *must* see the virus as your enemy."

"You make it sound like a person."

"I do. For your sake, it's best to personify the virus, so it becomes something tangible. It wants you to fail."

"Strangest pep talk ever. But it's working. Thank you."

Lou and Syd looked at Charlie expectantly.

Charlie nodded.

She lay on her bed and called up the chime soundtrack from the Clubhouse meditation app. "Okay. All I have to do is enter the memory of this room in my mind, get on the motorcycle without losing my mind, and deliver the remedy. Piece of cake. Should only take a few minutes in the Mental Realm. Who knows how much time will pass here in the physical world. But if I stay focused, I should be back in time for dinner. And a drink. Or six."

"That's our girl!" Syd said. "Even though you may not always know it, we'll be right by your side."

She programmed the soundtrack to repeat and hit Play.

PART THREE

THE STORY KEEPER

Chapter 89

Raven's Daughter follows the chimes through the obscure two-dimensional doorway into the dense anarchic noise of the Mental Realm—the cartoonish blue fish remains a beacon in her mind's eye. Her focus wavers. The mass of voices is more desperate, pleading, frantic this time. They collectively pull at her consciousness until the clarity of the chimes is swallowed into the chaos like quicksand. A rush of adrenalin moves through her body as her awareness splinters into the discord. The noise is all there is, an insistent gridlocked landscape woven from legions of tortured voices.

There's something important . . . What is she forgetting? This nagging thought keeps a fragment of her attention intact. *What is it?* A thing. A color. What is she forgetting? Her frustration grows legs and gathers mass. A shape swims through the tangle of sound—

A fish. One fish, two fish, red fish, blue fish. Blue fish! Yes! Blue fish!!

The memory of the blue fish cuts through the noise, and she's now staring at her mind's rendering of the surreal virtual fish swimming in the wall of her quarters. *Thank you, Dr. Seuss!* But there's no time to celebrate. There's something else. Two things—she's supposed to remember two things. The blue fish and something else. *Shit. What is it?* It feels so close. She keeps the fish square in her focus and tries to grasp the edge of a memory that's just out of reach.

CHAPTER 90

SAM CHECKED EVERY ROOM he had access to on the second and third floors for the umpteenth time in the last hour. No Charlie. She wasn't at breakfast, lunch, or dinner. He'd knocked on the door of her quarters enough times to make his knuckles red and sore. No response. It was like she'd just disappeared. Maybe he wouldn't be so concerned if their parting after their virtual dance party of doom hadn't seemed so final. He couldn't shake the sinking feeling he had.

"Misha," he asked U's virtual assistant, "has C left the Clubhouse today?" He promised himself he'd give Charlie until eight o'clock before bringing any attention to the situation.

Misha's avatar appeared in his visual field. "Hello, S. What can I do for you?"

"Did C leave the Clubhouse today?"

"No, she's in her quarters."

"That can't be. I knocked a bunch of times, but she didn't answer."

"She must be sleeping. She wasn't feeling well this morning."

Something was up. "Are you sure she didn't leave the Clubhouse?"

"Yes, very sure. We're aware of everyone who enters and leaves the building."

"If she's sick, should you check on her?"

"She activated the do-not-disturb feature on her Senz-Sight lenses. As you know, we honor the privacy of all our members."

"Her Senz-Skin," he said, his voice elevated. "You can track her vitals, right? Can you at least tell me if she's physically okay?"

"She's not wearing her Senz-Skin."

That triggered a slew of red flags. "Okay," he said and ended their chat. He tried not to run to Charlie's room.

CHAPTER 91

A SOUND FAR, FAR away. Thumping. A momentary dip in her concentration. *Focus. Red fish. Blue fish. Red fish. Blue fish. And something else.* What is the other thing? Something important. There's too much noise to sort through. The memory is a satellite orbiting her awareness. It's floating out there, just out of her grasp. Moving too fast.

The thumping is louder, more insistent. Like a helicopter. *Thump. Thump. Thump. So loud. Flying. Thump. Thump.* It's right there. But then it's not. It's traveling. Going somewhere. A vague memory of holding something. A metal tube. A steering wheel. No, the tube is straight. *Handlebars. Bicycle. No.* A memory of moving fast. Strong wind. *A motorcycle? Yes! Motorcycle! Outside my door.*

She calls up the memory of the door in her quarters. Clarity breaks through the noise like the bow of a ship slicing through choppy waves. *I'm Raven's Daughter. This is not real. It's my imagination. I'm in control here.*

Open the door, she tells herself. *Get on the pretend motorcycle. NOW.*

She reaches for the door handle.

Knock. Knock. Knock.

Not thumping. Someone's knocking. She opens the door and gasps.

"Charlie, honey," her mother says with a big smile. "Did you finish your homework?"

Longing moves through her. She wavers.

"Cat got your tongue?" her mom says before concern surfaces on her face. "You feel okay? You look a little pale. I hope you didn't catch that bug that's going around." She walks past Charlie into the bedroom and closes the violet curtains.

"Why don't you change into your pajamas and I'll read you a bedtime story."

CHAPTER 92

SAM POUNDED HIS FIST on the door. "Charlie," he called out, not caring about using her real name. "Charlie, are you okay?"

He took a deep breath and collected his thoughts. There was a muffled thump inside her room. He put his ear against her door and heard an irregular pattern of thumping, like someone hitting soft furniture with their fists.

"Misha, open C's door. Something's wrong." He figured he could always apologize later if he was overreacting.

"Hello, S. What seems to be the trouble?"

"I can hear her in the room, but she's not responding to my voice. Please, just open the door."

"But it's against Clubhouse policy to—"

"Open the fucking door."

"I'm sorry, but—"

"Now! Or I'll fucking break it down." He was panting.

Click.

He turned the knob and pushed the door open. "Call 9-1-1!"

Charlie's unconscious body was seizing on her bed.

CHAPTER 93

"HOW WAS SCHOOL TODAY?" her mother asks. They lay together in the twin bed, which feels too small.

"I—I don't remember." Charlie hesitates, trying to sort through the dull muddiness for a memory. "Good, I guess."

"You know, I was thinking," her mom says with a conspiratorial smile. "Maybe we should play hooky tomorrow and go shopping. I need a new swimsuit, and we can get you one too." Her mother's voice is familiar but somehow off. "We'll get our nails done . . . and have lunch at the Cheesecake Factory. Make a day of it! Be fun, right?"

She hears the words, but everything is strange, like she's had this conversation before. *Déjà vu? Is that what this is?* And there's also something off about her bedroom, but she can't figure out what it is. She nods at her mother, who's looking at her expectantly. *Her eyes, there's something wrong with them.*

"I've missed you so much," her mom says.

Confusion. And a sensation. A feeling in the distance, a low pulse. Her mother is stroking her head. The pulse is stronger. A throb. There it is. It's inside her. Under her mother's hand. Stabbing.

They're in the driveway now. It's so hot out. The desert sun beats on her head. She takes the grocery bag her mom hands her and then freezes. She doesn't know what to do with it. The pain in her head—it's far away, but unbearable.

"After we put the groceries away . . ." her mother's voice fades, but her mouth continues to move. She's trying to say something. *What, Mom? What is it?*

The pain. It's a creature inside her. It wants out. *Get it out. Get it out.*

She experiences disorienting whiplash when Flora's soft, fleshy face suddenly appears inches from her face, her thin lips spread in an exaggerated smile.

"Something borrowed, something blue," Flora sings. "Where's my crucifix?"

"I gave it back."

"God hates a lying tongue." Flora's laugh is sharp, like a siren. It slices her head in two.

Please stop.

"Sweet Lord Jesus," Flora's voice is a knife. "Banish the demon from this wicked girl—" She's cutting the demon out.

Please! Get it out!

Voices. In the distance. Too many voices. They snake their way around pillars of pain and surround her. "Too late. It's too late," they tell her. They want her to know. Now she understands. They're right. She can rest now. It is too late.

But for what?

She pulls the covers over her head. She just wants quiet. And to sleep. She's never felt so tired.

CHAPTER 94

SAM FOCUSED EVERY OUNCE of willpower he had, turbocharged by five cups of bitter black coffee, to keep from falling under the spell of the rhythmic pattern of sounds in the hospital room. The measured mechanical inhaling and exhaling of the respirator, the cadence of assorted beeps and tones emitted by monitors—a symphony of sorts that would lull him to sleep if he wasn't careful. He wanted to be alert when she woke up. He needed her to wake up.

After speaking with the on-call neurologist, Charlie's father asked hospital staff to allow Sam to be in the room with her. Sam had called her father from her phone, which he was thankfully able to unlock using facial recognition, even though her eyes were closed. Her father told Sam, his voice breaking and shaky, that he wouldn't be able to make it to New York for at least a few days. He explained from a noisy emergency shelter that most of San Diego was underwater after a potent hurricane had swept up the coast from Baja, Mexico. This had to be the worst day in the poor man's life.

Sam's heart broke even more for Charlie's father as he overheard the doctor share the dire news. The scans revealed that she'd had a series of strokes, which likely caused the seizure Sam witnessed. The doctor hinted at brain damage, indicating that Charlie may have had several seizures.

Her condition was stable for the moment, but not good. She was in a coma, and they were monitoring the swelling in her brain. The doctor was baffled. She told Sam there was no conceivable reason why a healthy young woman would have a succession of strokes seemingly out of the blue. The only clue her body offered, the doctor had said, was dangerously high blood pressure.

"Do you know if she's been under extreme psychological or physical stress recently?" the doctor asked.

"Would spending extended periods of time in virtual reality cause a stroke?" he asked her.

"Only if she wasn't getting exercise or moving her body around much. That and a poor diet," she explained. "That would explain everything if blood clots were the cause of her strokes. But that's not the case for Charlie."

He'd wondered on the drive to the hospital if maybe Charlie had a brain tumor. He was ashamed to admit he was looking for a reason that would explain all the crazy things she'd told him. Now he didn't know what to believe.

CHAPTER 95

THE EDGES OF THE horde of voices round off and become an amorphous amalgam. The insistent drone wraps around her like a blanket at first, but then tightens. Her awareness narrows to one thread—a buzzing snake wrapping its muscular body around her. She's more resigned than afraid. She just wants to rest. But then, a single distant voice catches her attention like a fishing lure, and her curiosity pulls her in the direction of the voice.

"—much better now," a familiar male voice says. She can't place who the voice belongs to, though. She allows the voice to pull her toward it. "—being released soon. Maybe even tomorrow."

"She'll need some time to adjust to her normal life again," says another vaguely familiar voice, this one female.

"Can she be alone?" he asks.

"Dan? Is that you?"

"She's awake," Dan says. "Hey, sweetheart."

"Hello, Charlie," the woman says. "I just wanted to check in on you."

"Marilyn? How did you—?" Wait, she can't move her body. "What's happening?"

"Everything's okay," Marilyn says. "They had to restrain you."

"What? Restrain me? Where am I?"

"You're safe," Marilyn says. "You don't remember coming to the hospital?"

"Hospital? Why am I in the hospital?"

Dan's face comes into focus. He leans in. "You had an episode, sweetheart."

"What the fuck does that mean?"

"Language, honey."

"You really don't remember anything?" Marilyn asks.

"Remember what?"

"You had a break with reality, Charlie," Marilyn says, her voice gentle, cautious.

"I went crazy?"

"Yes!" Dan chimes in like a game show host. "I knew something was wrong with you for months and months. You were acting so . . . strange. You stopped being the Charlotte I know and love."

"Oh no. It was the dreams, wasn't it?"

When Marilyn nods her head, Charlie notices something odd. Something about her eyes. They're silver.

"Don't worry, sweetheart," Dan says. "You can take all the time you need. Your job will be waiting for you when you're ready." He smiles. His eyes are silver too. "Although, that Brenda—not great with clients. Not like you."

"I made all of it up," she concludes. "None of it was real."

"None of what, sweetheart?" He's being extra nice, putting on a show for Marilyn.

"I'm so sorry," Marilyn says. "I should've paid closer attention, taken your concerns more seriously."

CHAPTER 96

SAM FRANTICALLY PULLS BROKEN computers and monitors out of the pile and throws them to the side.

"Charlie, are you in there?"

There's a faint scratching, and he pulls faster.

A throaty purring, punctuated by a loud "*rah*," draws his attention away from the pile. Perched on the top of the crashed passenger jet carcass, staring straight at him, is a raven.

SAM JERKED AWAKE AND reoriented himself. The hospital sounds reassured him. *She's still breathing, her heart's still beating.* Charlie's form lay exactly where it was before he fell asleep.

CHAPTER 97

"I KNOW JUST WHAT she needs," Dan says to Marilyn with a plastic smile. They talk as if she's not there. *This is what being crazy is like. You're a non-person.*

"A baby!" he exclaims, cradling an imaginary infant in his arms.

"Well," Marilyn cautions, "we'll have to make sure she's stable on her meds before she can get pregnant."

Charlie looks around for a way out while Dan and Marilyn plan her future. There's no door. Just four white walls.

"I painted the nursery!" Dan says. "I've never seen my mom so excited. She's already buying baby clothes and toys."

There's pounding in the distance, like an emphatic heartbeat. It grows louder. Someone's knocking? They want to get in the room. The heartbeat speeds up and becomes something different, more rhythmic. A stranger approaches her bed. *How did you get in here?* She can't see who it is, just a shadowy outline. A strange head. *Are they wearing a bird mask? Ah, it's a dream.* She tries to relax into the dream, but the sound is forceful, driving. It grows complex. It's music. The stranger is leaning over her. All she can see is their torso, dressed in a black suit and white shirt.

The stranger is talking to someone. But she can't hear his words over the music. She strains to listen. ". . . treating physician" are the only words she can make out. *Is that a British accent?*

A pattern catches her eye. Groups of spirals on shiny, narrow fabric. A necktie. They're so familiar.

The music drowns out their voices. Something about a virus.

CHAPTER 98

EYES CLOSED, SAM'S HEAD bobbed to the aggressive beat. He smiled at the memory of the two of them dancing like barbarians in post-apocalyptic ruin. She was right, it was surprisingly therapeutic. He figured it wouldn't hurt to play some of Charlie's favorite music for her now. He carefully placed a pair of wireless headphones on her head and put his own earbuds in so they could both listen. *Maybe it'll help bring her back?* Wishful thinking, he knew. But he was okay with that.

He'd pulled his chair up to the side of her bed and held her warm, still hand while they listened to the Killing Joke song *I Am the Virus.*

His thoughts circled the things she'd told him as though he were afraid that by allowing himself to entertain the idea her story was true, he'd slip into irrational territory that could possibly capsize his entire worldview. He could buy into the idea that a majority of the human population was infected by a virus of deception—it was as good as any explanation to describe the disturbing increase in lies his chromesthesia had been revealing to him—but her implication that the material world—their world—was a dream? It was too much of a leap. It was approaching U territory.

And then there was the raven dream. Initially, it created full-throttle cognitive dissonance, but he'd managed to talk himself down by justifying that his dream was likely the byproduct of the power of suggestion. Sleep deprivation seemed like a solid explanation too. He did his best to ignore just how rattled the dream had left him, how the dream seemed a little too real and a little too personal.

Her fingers twitched in his hand. He gently squeezed her hand. After a few moments, she squeezed back. *She's still in there!*

CHAPTER 99

SHE STRAINS TO LISTEN to the music. It's a life raft. She tries to stay afloat in the chaos, reaching for the snap of the snare drum. Her mind locks in on it, and it pulls her forward, reeling her in. Layers of insistent guitar and melody are hands rescuing her, pulling her out of the chaos. There's nothing but the song now, the vocalist telling her over and over that he's the virus. *Not for long,* she tells him.

Her mind reaches for the door to her quarters, and she opens it. *The hallway is empty. Where's my bike?* She's inside the music. She moves through the hallway, bringing the song with her to the old-fashioned Clubhouse elevator. She slides the accordion door to the right, opens the interior door to the elevator, and steps inside. There's someone standing inside. They're in silhouette, and she can't make out who it is.

"What floor?" a female voice asks. The sound of the voice throws Charlie off balance. Before confusion can fully rattle her, she stops and listens. Her mind once again grabs the urgent melody and wraps the music around her like a cloak.

The elevator operator comes into focus, and Charlie smiles. "I know you."

The smartly dressed fox-human hybrid winks at her, and they descend.

The operator opens the elevator door. "Who are you?" the operator asks as if the answer is a secret password.

The question throws her. She's paralyzed and staring at the elevator operator. She closes her eyes, pushing everything away except for the music. The singer reminds her that he's the virus and that he's pissed. She opens her eyes. The elevator operator, still waiting for her answer, picks a piece of lint off the black sleeve of her suit and adjusts her necktie.

The tie glows, capturing her attention. "Your tie . . ." She reaches out and cradles it in her right hand. The pattern of spirals appears to jump off the fabric like they're trying to tell her something. "It's so . . ." The fingers of her free hand reach out to touch the spirals. She needs to know if they're really floating. And that's when she sees the tattoo on the inside of her wrist. It's the same design.

She feels herself smile. She remembers.

The fox-headed human nods. "Hold on to your name like it's a lifeline. It'll take you where you need to go. All you have to do is get through the lobby." She nods her head toward the glass front door of the Clubhouse. "Your motorbike is waiting for you right outside that door. The rest is easy peasy."

She bows her head. "I am Raven's Daughter, the firstborn of my clan," she reminds herself.

She steps into the all-white lobby, her eyes lock on the door. She takes one step, two steps—

"Der you are."

She's on the beach. The crashing waves, a comfort.

"I—I'm not supposed to be here."

"Sure, you are," the old Hawaiian man says with a warm smile. "You at home now." His arms spread wide. "Dis your ha-leh."

"But you're not real."

"You's real, alright. Dats all you need t'know."

"I believe U," a female voice says.

"I believe U," the voices repeat.

"I trust U," the woman says.

"I trust U," they reply.

She's in a spaceship with the others.

"We love U," they all chant.

She's searching for someone. Not the samurai. Not the dinosaur. Not the chess piece.

There. In the seat next to her. The spaceman. Her Spaceman. He's right there, holding her hand. He gives her hand a reassuring squeeze.

He knows her. He knows everything.

A memory. But it's a private one. She's kissing him, but not kissing him. A goodbye.

Secret goodbyes.

"I love you, Dad."

"I love you too, sweetie."

She reaches for the door handle, turns it, and pulls it open. There it is. The motorcycle of her dreams.

CHAPTER 100

TEARS OF RELIEF CLOUD Sam's eyes. Her message was subtle, but it was loud and clear. *I'm here. I'm still here.*

He decided it didn't matter if she was delusional or not. It didn't matter if the music made a difference or not. He'd do whatever it took to help her, even if his rational mind deemed it ridiculous. At this point, what the fuck did it matter?

He unlocked her phone again and opened her music app, found what he was looking for, and tapped Play.

CHAPTER 101

OOH, THAT'S SEXY! SHE can't help but smile. The bike sits there like an invitation. She swings her leg over the seat, pulls the bike upright, and pushes the kickstand in with her foot. She doesn't question how she knows what to do. Instead, she thumbs the electric start button—no key necessary!—and the motor turns over. She hits the throttle and smiles at the sound and feel of the throaty exhaust.

She pulls in the clutch and toes the gear shift down. She looks at herself in the bar-end mirror and is greeted by fierceness. The solid black tattoo that spans the top half of her face and the glossy black of her irises staring back at her is a comforting sight. *There you are.*

In the distance, she hears a familiar guitar riff. She slowly releases the clutch while hitting the throttle. It's time for *The Death & Resurrection Show.*

She expands her focus and takes in the oppressive gray surroundings as she slowly pulls into the mass of colorless, mannequin-like people trudging through the narrow street. Their mouths are moving, but she doesn't reach to hear their voices. She doesn't need to. She's a character in a virtual role-playing game. She's from the future, riding through an old-fashioned silent film, and everyone she sees is an NPC. To win the game, she has to deliver the remedy that will save the world.

The crowd clears a path for her. They make their way to the curb and face the street. She's able to shift into second gear, and the crowd becomes animated. They clap and cheer for her. She lets their excitement penetrate her, and she smiles. She's not invisible. She matters. She's saving the world!

She slows to a stop.

The crowd gathers around her, clapping and cheering. It's a celebration. They close in. Their faces all have the same expression—pure joy. They reach for her. They want to touch her. She's the fifth Beatle!

A flash of white blinds her.

She blinks to clear her vision. Her eyes are dry and gritty. She's in a clearing surrounded by trees. It's exquisitely silent.

"Little Bird."

She turns, and First Mother greets her with a smile, her arms spread wide. She's once again healthy and vibrant. Charlie steps into First Mother's embrace.

"I'm so proud of you," First Mother tells her. "You saved us all."

Charlie swells with pride. "I wasn't expecting it to be so easy."

"That's because you did everything perfectly." First Mother's squeeze tightens. "I knew you would."

"I'm so relieved it's over."

"Yes. You can rest now."

Charlie closes her eyes and lets herself relax against First Mother's body. She sinks deeper and deeper into a pocket of sweet, peaceful emptiness. Thick, velvety darkness moves through the emptiness toward her, like syrup. The darkness swallows her feet, calves, thighs. She welcomes it. It's erasing all her tension and worry and the effort it takes to exist.

There's something far away. Something that needs attending to. *Is there more to do?* A ringing sound penetrates the silence. She doesn't know if she's supposed to move toward it or away from it. She wants it to stop, but it is insistent.

CHAPTER 102

SAM FUMBLED WITH CHARLIE's phone. He managed to pause the song and answer the incoming call.

"Hello," he said, hoping he caught it before it went to voicemail. It was Charlie's father.

"Sam," her father responded. He didn't hide his disappointment that it was Sam's voice he was hearing and not Charlie's. "How's she doing?"

Sam exhaled. "I wish I had better news. Nothing's changed."

"Okay," her father finally said before clearing the emotion out of his throat. "At least it's not worse."

Veins of gray moved through a blotchy field of teal in Sam's mind. Deep sadness.

"How are things on your end?" Sam asked.

"Well, the floodwaters finally receded, but they're not letting anyone go home—or anywhere, for that matter—until the safety folks do their inspections."

"That's tough, but I guess it makes sense."

"Yeah, I guess." He sighed. "The airport is a mess." He paused. "I don't know when—" His voice broke with emotion.

"I'm so sorry." Sam didn't know what else to say. "Do you want to see her? I mean, right now, over the phone?"

There was a pause, and then a quiet, "Yeah."

Sam engaged the video function and pointed the lens at Charlie. He heard a choked sob. "Oh, my girl," the man cried.

Sam did what he could to breathe through the emotions that threatened to rip him apart. He needed to be strong right now.

"Sam," Charlie's father said after regaining composure.

Sam turned off the camera. "Yeah, I'm here."

"Please," her father said through tears. "Please take care of my girl." He paused to catch his breath. "Will you do that for me?"

Sam's eyes were full of tears, but he managed to keep the emotion out of his voice. He wanted to reassure this man. He needed to. "Yes, I promise. I'm not leaving her side."

CHAPTER 103

"DAD!" SHE CALLS OUT into the emptiness. "Where are you?" She listens for him. "Dad?"

"What's the matter, pumpkin?" Her father's face peeks through her bedroom door. "Bad dream?"

"I—I don't know. Am I asleep?"

He chuckles. "No, sweetie. Everything's okay." He approaches her. "Want me to stay with you for a while?"

She nods. He sits on the edge of her bed.

"It's good to see you, Dad."

He laughs. "We just saw each other an hour ago, silly. Before you went to bed." He lies next to her. He's like a bear. His large frame and beer belly take up all the room, but it's okay. She feels safe lying there next to him, curled inside his bulk.

She wants to rest, but there's a vague memory of something important, something she needs to tell her father. Something big.

"I got home so late I forgot to ask," her father says. "How was your day?"

She doesn't know how to answer. Her memory is like sludge. "It was good . . . I think."

"Best thing that happened?"

What happened today? she asks herself. She's so tired. She just wants to sleep. She squeezes her eyes shut to help her concentrate. The memory is somewhere. All she can recall is that it was important and it made her happy. A faint recollection of cheering and clapping emerges from the sludge.

"I saved the world!"

He strokes her hair. "That's quite a dream."

"It wasn't a dream. It was real."

Agitation grinds at her. "I can prove it. My motorcycle. Where is it?"

A horde of colorless people is hunched over something in the middle of the narrow street, like feasting zombies. The street is lined with bland, gray buildings so tall they blot out most of the yellow-gray sky. Streams of doughy people move in either direction around the crowd. They remind her of ants avoiding an obstacle in their path.

She pushes her way through the crowd. It's like walking through the sound of static. Their bodies don't have substance. Her bike is lying on its side, and there's someone lying next to it. A person painted dull silver. The paint looks like it's still wet. *That's not a person, it's an android. It must be broken.*

She kneels next to the robot. Its eyes are open. They're silver too. There's a sense of dread somewhere far away.

"I saved the world today," the robot says. It's her voice. The robot is her. She doesn't understand. She touches it, and her fingertips come away tacky, coated with silver. The silver bubbles and divides into beads that collectively move down her fingers and up her right arm like schools of fish. They want to get inside her.

She tries to shake them off, but they won't come off. She screams, but no one hears her.

CHAPTER 104

SAM ESCAPED TO THE bathroom and had himself a much-needed cry after he got off the phone with Charlie's dad. His body was shaky with emotion and lack of sleep and food. He splashed cold water on his face. The guy he saw in the mirror looked haunted. *I need to eat,* he told himself. Just as he was turning to leave, he saw something dark move behind him in the mirror. He turned, but there was nothing there. "Definitely need to eat," he said to his reflection.

But there, in the mirror, was a raven with its wings spread, staring at him. A sparkling amber ammonite pendant hung from its neck.

Sam rushed out of the bathroom and went to the opposite side of Charlie's bed. He picked up her left hand and gently turned it over. "Holy fuck."

He didn't know what to do. He paced a bit. And then paced some more. Pacing wasn't helping. What was the bird trying to tell him? The intensity of its gaze felt like it was boring into him, trying to get through his thick, rational skull. He replayed the hallucination, or whatever it was, in an attempt to extract some kind of meaning. A sense of urgency was the only thing that kept coming to him. He needed to hurry, to do something. *Maybe her time's running out?*

He sat next to her and cradled her hand in both of his, rubbing his thumb over the tattoo on her wrist like a talisman. He was at a loss for what to do. That's when he noticed the track of a single tear on her face. *NO! No, no, no, no. Don't leave, don't leave.*

He grabbed her phone, unlocked it, and opened the music app. *Please bring her back,* he silently pleaded. Then, he once again played her favorite song for her.

CHAPTER 105

THE SILVER BEADS MERGE like liquid mercury and become snakes that spiral around her right bicep. "HELP ME!" she screams. They want to get inside her and tunnel into her brain.

She's in a dark hallway. Three cobras block her path. Their hooded heads rise from the floor and spit at her. Their venom is silver.

They want to stop her. But she has to get through to the other side. She can't let them keep her from—

From what?

A sensation grabs her attention. Someone's holding her hand, but not the one that's tainted by the liquid silver of the virus. She looks down, but no one's there. No one's holding her hand. But when she sees the tattoo, the symbol of her clan, the dense clouds that are muddying her awareness part and allow a sliver of clarity in.

There are drums in the distance. No—they're in her head. She smiles because she knows these drums.

She picks up her bike, climbs on, and fires it up. Her silver doppelganger is curled up on the street, a husk caving in on itself. *Charlie.* She gives quiet thanks to her human counterpart who got her closer than any of her previous identities. What's left of her is a ghost, a whisper of Raven's Daughter. But it's pure, no longer polluted with the doubt and memories of her human life. She hopes it's enough to get her to where she needs to be.

CHAPTER 106

AHKOA HUDDLES WITH THE entirety of the Raven Clan in a fern grove under the massive, fading, burgundy canopy of the First Tree. They're joined by all the clans of the realm—the noble clans of the water, air, and land creatures—who were forced to migrate in response to the rapidly shrinking boundaries of the Dreaming Realm.

It's eerily silent. All the clans linger in reverent stillness. There's nothing more they can do except wait for their dreaming to end.

CHAPTER 107

THRONGS OF PEOPLE, CORRUPTED by the virus, still crowd the street. She sees them clearly now. She understands. They're just projections—ideas of people, or, rather, ideas of who they think they are. *Hakolah-khan*, the Hollow People. She's in the Mental Realm. Everything here is a projection. Except for her. At least, what's left of her.

She accelerates into the crowd, plowing right through them. Their gray bodies disintegrate like ash in the wind when she hits them, only to quickly reform afterward, the disruption a mere blip on their journey to nowhere.

The driving percussion is loud now. The song is all she hears and it's fuel. She motors through the maze of streets, leaning into corners. Her torso is angled forward, hovering over the tank, her feet on the pegs behind her. There might be some pain somewhere, but it doesn't matter. There's no time for pain.

As she gets closer to the epicenter of the realm, the architecture of the gray buildings changes as if she's traveling back in time. The worn stone of the structures reminds her of the ancient temples and cathedrals of Greece, Rome, and the Middle East. The layout of the streets becomes less grid-like and more akin to the spokes of a wagon wheel, all leading to one structure; all that remains are four roofless walls constructed from stone blocks of varying sizes.

The Hollow People, with their empty silver eyes, populate every conceivable space in the Mental Realm, it seems, even this most antiquated region.

She gets off her bike and leans it against the remains of a stone pillar. Now that she's not moving, the entropy of the realm penetrates and paralyzes her. The tangle of beliefs that have threaded their way through the minds of humans for centuries threatens to consume her—a fate she can't afford, especially now that she's gotten this far. Failure is not an option.

Raven's Daughter closes her eyes and turns inward. Using the language of the Dreaming Realm, she repeats, *"I am Rah-hīnah, firstborn of the Raven Clan"* until the pervasive chaos recedes enough for her to hear the distant music that has served as her anchor and gotten her this far. The unrelenting melody flows through her like an electrical current. She walks purposefully through the arched entranceway of the ruins, across the cobblestone floor, to the center of the structure, and stands next to the remnants of a timeworn baptismal fount. Despite the lyrics that resound through every inch of her being, she's not focused on death or resurrection right now. Her final wish is for all beings in every realm to be free.

And for humans to remember.

She spreads her arms and surrenders to this wish. A slight pressure builds in the center of her chest and begins to burn, but the pain doesn't touch her. A white flame ignites from her heart and shoots outward, throwing off sparks. The flame spreads through her torso. Her body arches as it's consumed by white fire, and a wisp of black is released. A Great Tree emerges from within her, splitting her down the middle. Thick, brown tree roots punch through the stone floor and into the ground, and the tree shoots upward, emitting a shockwave that travels through the Mental Realm, destroying everything in its path.

Silence.

CHAPTER 108

FIRST MOTHER'S WEAKENED BODY leans against the tree, her breathing is shallow, and her once-beautiful turquoise skin is blotchy and gray. Ahkoa doesn't know if she's meditating or sleeping. Either way, he hopes her dreaming isn't strained or painful as she dies.

The air suddenly grows thick with tension, it pulls like a vacuum. There's a distant rumble, like a thunderclap, that vibrates the ground. Everyone looks in the direction of the sound, and they brace themselves for whatever is coming.

Moments later, a colossal explosion of blinding white light rips through the realm, followed by a powerful shockwave. Ahkoa grabs the hands of the closest clan members as the wave moves over them. For a long moment, the pressure renders him deaf and unable to breathe. And then stillness.

CHAPTER 109

TIME IN THE MENTAL Realm seems to stop until the silence is broken by the sweet, welcoming song of a chickadee.

The Mental Realm awakens with the vibrant colors and music of nature. The robin's-egg-blue sky is vast, and trees, flowers, mountains, and rivers now populate the once-claustrophobic gray landscape.

Perched high on the twisting branches of the Great Tree are two laughing ravens. The Hollow People slowly make their way to the tree, drawn by the curious sounds coming from the large black birds. They surround the tree, awestruck by its beautiful emerald canopy adorned with tiny white stars, and many cry happy tears.

Chapter 110

Sam stood at the far side of the room, watching hospital staff do what they could to help Charlie, unaware that his nails were digging into the palms of his balled fists. It was only five minutes ago that she had squeezed his hand with what felt like intention, making his heart swell with hope and possibility. Moments later, her eyes had shot open and her body began to convulse violently, her stiff torso arching off the bed. Piercing alarms had sounded, alerting staff who rushed in and ordered him out of the way.

He couldn't see much of what was happening, but it was clear Charlie wasn't responding to any of their interventions. The urgent symphony of beeping ICU monitors, peppered with the clipped medical jargon and directives of the staff, translated as an irregular triangular pattern of stabbing neon yellow and black in his mind's eye. If it went on much longer, he imagined he'd experience an audio-induced lobotomy.

Please, please, please, he silently pleaded.

And then the sound he dreaded—she flatlined. His interior vision went black in response to the single tone.

He slid down the wall, buried his face in his arms, and cried.

CHAPTER 111

AHKOA EXHALES AND OPENS his eyes to a feast of vibrant color. The sky is clear, and the only sound he hears is the gentle breeze blowing through the leaves of the forest—the incessant rumbling of the corrupted Mental Realm has stopped.

Tears roll down his face. *She did it.*

Swirls of vivid blue and turquoise surface on First Mother's gray skin like billowing ink spreading through dirty water. She opens her sparkling sea-glass eyes and inhales deeply. Her body starts to shake and rock with laughter. Her joy spills out and fills the Dreaming Realm once more.

...AFTER

AHNA CATCHES AHKOA'S EYE and nods. The tension in her jaw and brow makes her look older. He glances at Rah, the First Raven, who stands stoically next to Ahna, but then quickly turns away. The force of the pain in her dark eyes is too much for him to bear. The collective grief the Raven Clan is experiencing is palpable. Ahkoa's grief is complicated by deep shame and regret. He can't imagine ever forgiving himself for not being stronger, for allowing his disdain for humans to consume him and prevent him from being at Raven's Daughter's side, to help see her through to the end. Ahna had been right—as a young species, humans had always been vulnerable to the complexity of their minds and the temptation of their base instincts. What was his excuse? He should know better. He should have more compassion. *I will do better,* he silently promises.

He glances at the somber faces of the members of his clan who are gathered, along with the entire Dreaming Realm community, to honor Rah-hīnah. Ahkoa can now add humility to the amalgam of painful emotions he's experiencing. The surrounding forest and waterways are crowded with the clans of every water, land, and sky creature that has ever been dreamed into existence.

First Mother stands in the clearing in front of the First Tree, her head bowed. When she finally lifts her head, her shining, pale-green eyes scan the realm.

"We have much to be thankful for," she says with a sad smile, her soft melodic voice taking flight through the Dreaming Realm for all to hear. "Rah-hīnah, firstborn of the Raven Clan, has sacrificed herself to offer my human children an opportunity. And we're here to support them—to encourage them to ease back into the landscape of their hearts, to once again find balance and harmony within themselves and with all the creatures they share their majestic world with—" she pauses, her eyes taking in the Dreaming Realm, "—and reunite with us in the dreaming."

The realm erupts with pure joy.

When it quiets, First Mother adds, "Let's honor the memory of our brave Rah-hīnah, and wish our human brothers and sisters well on this new phase of their journey."

The ground thumps as the Elephant Clan stomps an invitation. Within moments, every member of every clan joins them. The collective sound creates a primal symphony of triumph.

First Mother dances in the clearing. Her fluid and powerful movements express all of her love, sadness, and gratitude.

Ahkoa is overcome. He falls into Ahna's arms and sobs.

First Mother stops. She looks up and watches a whisper of black moving erratically through the sky toward them.

Ahkoa stops too, his emotions put on pause. He follows First Mother's gaze and locks in on a ghost-like black bird in unsteady flight. It collapses on the ground in front of First Mother.

She holds up her hand, and the celebration stops immediately.

Ahkoa's eyes are glued to the still, black shadow bird lying on the ground.

First Mother drops to her knees, hovering over it. Her lips move, but no one can hear what she's saying. Within moments, two well-dressed but exhausted-looking creatures make their way through the crowd, one with the head of a hawk and the other a fox.

Could it be? A sliver of hope slips through the crack in Ahkoa's heart. He remembers these two from his encounters with Charlie. *Lou and Syd.*

First Mother greets them with a big grin. "I'm so happy to see you!" she says. Lou bows his head, and Syd tries to give First Mother a high-five, which is met with confusion. "When you didn't show up afterward, I assumed the worst." She reaches out and touches both their faces with great affection.

It's clear that no one except First Mother understands what's happening. Ahkoa unconsciously holds his breath.

Lou and Syd glance at each other before their bodies start to quiver and morph into indigo orbs. The orbs float down and merge with the shadow bird, making it denser and giving it more substance. Ahkoa exhales when he sees that the bird is indeed a raven. The raven's body expands with a deep inhale.

Ahkoa shakes his head and smiles for the first time since he last saw Raven's Daughter. *I'll be damned.* He realizes that, for this incarnation as Charlie, she didn't just split her essence in two, she split it into four. Lou and Syd were born out of Raven's Daughter to help her, to keep her from losing herself entirely. As Charlie would say, "Fucking brilliant."

The realm is silent, waiting.

The raven lifts its head and gives it a little shake. It manages to right itself and stretches its wing. The raven shapeshifts, and Raven's Daughter, known to her clan as Rah-hīnah, stands before them.

Ahkoa runs to her, picks her up, and spins her around and around. The realm explodes in thunderous celebration.

"Namaste, good people. How are you motherfuckers doing? I'm confused. I think I'm good. But man, it's been a time."

(long pause)

"It's definitely been a time.

"I'm more than a little embarrassed to admit this, but I almost end-ed up in the psych ward. By now you may have heard that the B-Well nano-pill I raved about in my last vlog—mostly because I was raving mad at the time—well, it was a total bust. Turns out there was no nano in the nano-pill. But there were some crazy voodoo shenanigans happening in their meditation app that made us all a little—how do I say this polite-ly?—it fucked us up. The Ricardo guy who came up with the whole thing has to be the most pathological con artist ever.

"I'm not even mad, man. I'm just thankful I got through it mostly okay. But there were a lot of people who didn't fare so well. It fucking breaks my heart. I mean . . . I played a part in that, and I'm just sorry. Really, really sorry. Promoting that shit is one of the biggest regrets of my life.

"But then I had this dream . . . this amazingly vivid dream about a tree. I became the tree. I could feel this kinda slow pulse start in my roots and then move up my trunk and into all my branches, like the longest, deepest exhale. I could feel the breeze moving through my leaves. I loved the way it felt, like a caress. And then I became the breeze, and then I was a hawk riding a thermal. It was complete freedom. When I didn't think it could get any better, I became the forest. I was the ENTIRE fucking forest, people. It was crazy. And then, over the next couple of days, I found out that pretty much the whole world had the same dream. I still can't wrap my head around how that works.

"I don't know why, but I've felt better since that dream. A lot calmer, and my head is clear. I just wanna be outside too. And you know what's weird? I can't stop stacking stones. What are they called? Cairns?"

(shuffling noises)

"Look at these. I must have made about thirty of them just today. What can I say? They make me smile.

"So, today's episode is brought to you by this beautiful fucking planet. Get outside, people. Stack some stones. You'll feel better."

SAM FINALLY BLINKED, HIS EYES painful and dry. He'd run out of tears hours ago. He had no idea how long he'd been sitting on the rocky beach staring at the diamonds of reflected sunlight blinking in and out of existence off the rippling waves of Lake Champlain. Given how far the late summer sun had traveled across the sky, probably three or four hours had passed.

The past twenty-four hours had been intensely surreal. After making the most difficult phone call of his life, he'd kissed Charlie's cool forehead and left the hospital with a plastic bag containing her belongings. The drive back to the Clubhouse was a blur. He packed up his things and left without a word, grateful that no one stood in his way. U kept his, or rather, its word. No questions were asked, period. It was as though Charlie didn't matter, or, more likely, U's sweeping computer-generated tentacles had kept tabs on them and already knew her fate.

Sam had pointed his car north and drove through the night, trying to get as far away from the memory of the deep, guttural wails that had erupted from Charlie's father when Sam broke the news no parent ever wants to hear. It was silly to think distance would help him escape the echoes of the poor man's keening.

Grief rolled through Sam like sets of waves. When the waves calmed some, he distracted himself by reviewing all the events that led him to where he was now, from every angle possible, but he could make no sense of anything that had transpired. What the distance offered instead was enough time to default to what made him most comfortable, logic. Charlie's fantastical mind virus/save the world story had to be the delusional byproduct of an organic brain disorder. Maybe she'd had some sort of genetic predisposition. Her father had shared that her mother had died from a brain aneurysm. Maybe there was a connection? This reasoning felt a little like trying to fit a square peg into a round hole, but at the moment he didn't care. It made more sense than anything else did.

The sun was rising when the ferry docked in Grand Isle, Vermont. Exhausted, he pulled into the local state park, reclined his seat, and tried to sleep, but his overtired mind was too restless. Instead, he got out of his car and planted himself on the gravel beach. The waves that rippled along the lake's surface hypnotized him, bringing a bit of numbing peace. He dared not move from that spot for fear of losing his hold of this little sliver of serenity—although he did fantasize about renting a kayak and paddling out to one of the small islands that dotted the lake. He liked the idea of living on one of them, hidden away from the rest of the world—each island a floating forest refuge.

Out of nowhere, haunting imaginary cello music filled his head, his aching eyes grew big, and a spike of fear shot through him. *Great,* he thought. *Hallucinations are just what I need right now.* But a few brief moments later, his mind's eye was filled with colorful mandalas that resembled a kaleidoscope of velvety wildflower petals. He was hearing real music, and it was breathtaking.

He turned toward the music and discovered that he wasn't alone. About thirty people of all ages sat quietly on the beach and among the surrounding wind-worn trees and large stones. Some of them wept. It was beyond strange. *Maybe I* am *hallucinating.* Sitting on a park bench under a large tree with exposed roots was a young woman playing the cello. A small crowd had gathered around her, eyes closed, listening. It was as if she were bringing the ancient wisdom of the surrounding trees, stones, and lake to life, and Sam understood that the spellbinding mandalas populating his interior vision were the colors and patterns of reverence.

What's happening? Everyone was acting so strangely. Instead of questioning his sanity too much, he shrugged, sat with the others, and listened to her play without a break for another hour or so. No one moved, and no one spoke a word. The experience was powerfully stirring and intimate. The music made him think of Charlie, and the tears returned; this time he welcomed them.

When the late afternoon sun dipped, the temperature started to drop, and he found himself alone again. He wasn't ready to leave and didn't know where he'd go anyway, so he went back to his car to grab a sweatshirt and blanket. Something within the plastic bag that contained Charlie's clothes caught his eye. He opened it and retrieved a broken ammonite fossil with the familiar spiral design that had adorned the inside of Charlie's wrist and hung from the neck of the raven he'd seen in the mirror.

Wrapped in his plaid fleece blanket, he polished off a bottle of water and watched how the setting sun transformed and softened the beautiful landscape around him. He loved this mostly untouched place, felt at home here.

He didn't know what happened after death, but if consciousness somehow survived, he hoped Charlie was happy and had fond memories of their brief time together. His thumb mindlessly stroked the smooth interior face of the ammonite fossil as he recalled their post-apocalyptic dance party. It was the most fun and the most free he'd felt . . . probably ever. He grinned at the memory of the Bowie song she played for him—particularly the lyrics, which he didn't pay much attention to at the time. He realized now that *Hallo Spaceboy* may have been her way of saying goodbye to him.

"Thank you," he whispered.

A loud swoosh to his left startled him from his thoughts.

Perched on the beach several feet away was a raven. *How—?* It cocked its head and stared right into his eyes. Something about it reminded him of the raven in the mirror. He may have stopped breathing. There was movement in his peripheral vision, and when he turned, he was greeted by hundreds, if not thousands, of ravens. They were perched silently on every surface, looking at him. The hairs rose on his neck.

One raven stepped toward him. It was a bit larger than the rest and moved slowly, as if it were injured or tired. It came right up to where he sat. He didn't know what to do, so he placed the fossil on the stones beside him. The raven looked at it and then at him. It grabbed the fossil in its beak and placed it on Sam's thigh.

Sam tentatively held his hand out, and the raven took a step toward it. Sam gently stroked its head, and the tears returned. "Is it really you?" he asked.

The raven pressed its head into his palm and nuzzled it. A strangled sob escaped from Sam as he cradled her head in his hand.

She pulled away and spread her huge sable wings. He turned to her clan and watched as they collectively bowed their heads to him. He laugh-cried. At that moment, everything he knew to be true was turned on its head.

All at once, the ravens took flight, making celebratory vocalizations as they blotted out the sky. He watched the Raven Clan fly up and up and up until they disappeared in a blink.

IT WAS THE FIRST time Gerty had felt calm in a very long time. She didn't dare move from the position she'd woken up in, for fear of losing the feeling. The memory of a dream floated in her awareness like a pink cloud. She'd been with a crowd of bland people gathered in a bleak, empty place, maybe a parking lot. The dream was in shades of gray and lacked depth, like she was looking at a picture of a dream. She couldn't remember why they were all there, but she was certain they were waiting for something.

A sudden flash of bright white light, and the place was alive with vivid color. She was Dorothy, just arrived in Oz. They found themselves in a paradise filled with endless varieties of flowers, plants, and trees, the greenest grass, and the clearest rivers and streams. In the middle of it all was the most beautiful tree she'd ever seen, its lush canopy filled with tiny silvery-white lights. She was drawn to this tree, completely mesmerized by it, as if it were a cherished family member she'd forgotten she had. Being in its presence somehow made her feel more complete. And then she became the tree.

Such a strange, wonderful dream.

She abandoned her morning routine and went outside. It was a gorgeous sunny day. The colors around her popped in a way she'd never noticed before, and the cheerful morning birdsong was comforting. She scanned the neighborhood and saw she wasn't alone but joined by most, if not all, of her neighbors. Those who noticed her smiled and waved. She didn't know these people. *Why are they being so nice to me?* Confused, she offered a weak wave back. *Am I still dreaming?*

Doubt crept into her thoughts and dampened her mood. She retreated to her house and fired up her laptop. She logged into the discussion board and was shocked to see a slew of posts about a dream. Not just any dream—her dream. *What is going on?*

A new post notification dinged. It was from one of the most active members of the group. Its heading got her attention, like it was shouting at her.

> wanderingstarchild: EVERYTHING IN THIS THREAD IS A LIE! THIS THREAD WAS STARTED BY AI. no_secrets2032 IS NOT REAL. trthskr115 IS NOT REAL. I'M THE ONE WHO CREATED AND PROGRAMMED THE AI THAT IS FACILITATING THIS THREAD. THE VIDEOS ARE FAKE. EIGHTY PERCENT OF THE MEMBERS ARE FAKE. THERE IS NO CHIMP ARMY OR SECRET LAB. IT STARTED AS A STUPID EXPERIMENT. I WANTED TO SEE WHAT WOULD HAPPEN—TO SEE IF PEOPLE WOULD BELIEVE A CONSPIRACY INVENTED BY ARTIFICIAL INTELLIGENCE. I DON'T KNOW WHY I DIDN'T STOP IT A LONG TIME AGO, BUT WHEN I WOKE UP THIS MORNING, AFTER HAVING THIS CRAZY DREAM THAT I WAS A TREE, I KNEW I HAD TO COME CLEAN.

> I'M SORRY FOR MESSING WITH EVERYONE'S HEADS. I DON'T BLAME YOU FOR HATING ME. I DESERVE YOUR HATRED AND CAN ONLY HOPE FOR YOUR FORGIVENESS.

She refreshed the page and saw that the once-huge group membership number had dropped by two-thirds. She slammed her laptop closed with an angry growl. Gerty stomped into the kitchen, went right to the freezer, and poured herself a therapeutic cocktail.

The drink calmed her down and cleared her head—at least for a moment, before the sadness crept in. That discussion thread was her life, the members were her community. She'd been part of something important. What if the Peacemakers had realized they were discovered and sabotaged the discussion thread? What if wanderingstarchild is really a spy for the Peacemakers? It was all too much.

She needed a change of scenery.

GERTY WATCHED THE CHIMPS wandering through their enclosure, looking for ways to entertain themselves. She felt a kinship with them, a closeness. Why hadn't she come to the zoo months ago?

She walked up to the glass enclosure to get a closer look at one of the males, who reminded her of Commander Griffin from the videos she'd watched. He looked at her, and she smiled at him. She put her hand on the glass, hoping he'd come closer.

A little girl about six or seven years old joined Gerty at the huge plate glass window. Behind them, the girl's mother was busy chasing after her younger sibling, who was determined to get an ice cream cone from a passing food cart.

Gerty leaned over and whispered to the girl, "Did you know that chimpanzees can talk?"

Acknowledgments

Whew, what a journey writing this book has been! One filled with twists and turns, disappointments, triumphs, and a fair share of challenges. It sounds dramatic, but it's true. Along the way, I had a mind-blowing amount of support for which I'm truly grateful.

Since my writing style is a tad more visceral than literary, and therefore not what many would call mainstream, I cast a pretty wide beta reader net to see if my take on this story translated in the way that I'd hoped it would. Thank you to my writer friends Maria D'Haene and Julia Johnson for taking the first plunge and for your helpful recommendations. Immense gratitude to Sarah Finlay, Meredith Heller, Ashley Holmes, Jack Girardi, Hannah Rohloff, Marie Frohlich, and Josie Green for your honest feedback and encouragement.

And then there's Claire Wheeler, who I like to refer to as my 'partner in absurdity' and whose friendship has become an unexpected gift. Those who know her know that she oozes care, love, and support from every pore. So, my special thanks to Claire for not only taking the time to read a draft of my book despite juggling a million things, but also for coming on my podcast to help me introduce *Raven's Daughter* to listeners and talk about the story behind the story (If you'd like to check it out, this episode of Lucid Café was released in May 2025 and can be found where ever you listen to podcasts).

Perhaps the most nerve-wracking days were the ones after I gave my favorite husband/emotional support Viking/daily laugh buddy, John Halley, a very early draft of *Raven's Daughter* to read with a side of potato chips. John is a long-time reader of fantasy and sci-fi. He's one of the smartest people I've ever met, he's "particular" (i.e., a snob), and he abides by a code of honesty. He's the audience that I write for. Winning John over is equivalent to winning the lottery in my book... and as it turns out, in this book too! He gave me the kind of feedback I suspect every writer wants to hear: "I didn't want the story to end." John was nothing but supportive while I spent what seemed like decades' worth of hours in front of the computer doing my best to translate my difficult-to-articulate, otherworldly experiences into the words that became this book. I'm a lucky girl.

Thank you also to my editor and friend Courtney Jenkins Mesquita for making the editing process a pleasant and helpful one. Courtney is a truly gifted editor and a lovely human being.

I'd like to express my enormous thanks to Linda River Valente for her friendship and astro guidance; and to the incredibly kind and thoughtful PJ Muller who was behind the scenes helping me explore alternative ways to bring this story to life – none of which panned out, unfortunately; and also to my lovely community of friends here in central Vermont, who not only accept weirdos like me but celebrate them.

To Hank Wesselman and Jill Kuykendall, who are sadly no longer with us, I owe a debt of gratitude for not only helping me to make sense of and give context to my early visionary experiences, but also for teaching me, and countless others, how to access the unseen worlds at will. They were always nothing but supportive of me and my work.

And to you, my new reader friend, thank you so much for taking my story for a spin. I hope you enjoyed it.

Wendy Halley has been weaving tales since she was eleven years old. She's the author of the children's book *Inside Out* (Illumination Arts, 2003) and two insightful non-fiction works inspired by her lucid dream experiences. Borrowing from her background as a psychotherapist, she explores the challenges of being human and the healing power of storytelling in her writing while somehow finding a way to balance the heavy themes she writes about with a side of irreverence and humor. With *Raven's Daughter*, Wendy steps into the realm of visionary fiction, sharing a story she's felt destined to tell since before she was born.

Awards and Recognition

- Wendy received a *Terrible Human Being* award (and is no longer invited to public events) for "Making People Laugh at the MOST Inappropriate Times."

- In 2022, she received a *Lifetime Achievement Award* from the Society of the Ironic and Unenlightened. Her father is very proud.

www.ingramcontent.com/pod-product-compliance
Lightning Source LLC
Chambersburg PA
CBHW050522110726
47899CB00005B/1555